The Unforgiven

Sean Slater is the pseudonym for Vancouver Police Officer Sean Sommerville. As a police officer, Sommerville works in Canada's poorest slum, the Downtown Eastside – an area rife with poverty, mental illness, drug use, prostitution, and gang warfare. He has investigated everything from frauds and extortions to homicides. Sommerville has written numerous columns for editorials for the city newspaper. His work has been nominated for the Rupert Hughes Prose Award, and he was the grand-prize winner of the Sunday Serial Thriller contest. His debut novel, *The Survivor*, was shortlisted for the Arthur Ellis Award.

Also by Sean Slater

The Survivor
Snakes & Ladders
The Guilty

SEAN SLATER
The Unforgiven

**SIMON &
SCHUSTER**

London · New York · Sydney · Toronto · New Delhi

A CBS COMPANY

First published in Great Britain by Simon & Schuster UK Ltd, 2014
A CBS COMPANY

3 5 7 9 10 8 6 4

Simon & Schuster UK Ltd
1st Floor
222 Gray's Inn Road
London WC1X 8HB

www.simonandschuster.co.uk

Simon & Schuster Australia, Sydney
Simon & Schuster India, New Delhi

A CIP catalogue record for this book is available from the British Library

PB ISBN: 978-1-47110-140-3
TPB ISBN: 978-1-47110-139-7
EBOOK ISBN: 978-1-47110-139-7

Typeset by Hewer Text UK Ltd, Edinburgh
Printed and bound in Great Britain by CPI (UK) Ltd, Croydon CR0 4YY

It's true. When my father remarried, I didn't lose a father,
I gained a second family.

This book is dedicated to them.

Most people know them as Adamo, Nick, and Mary, but to me
they will always be Adumbo, Little Nicky, and Granny Mare.

Of course, they hate these nicknames, but what can they do?
I'm family. I'm here to stay.

;o)

ACT ONE
Fuel and Flame

Tuesday

One

There are some acts that are unforgivable, even to God.

Acts so horrendous and evil that, once committed, there is no turning back from them. A breach is made. A finality reached. And there is only one form of restitution that can ever be made.

An *eternal* one.

Monster realized all of this. And he accepted it without question. Absolution did not matter, only the completion of his tasks. And the first step of his new birth was catching the female fleeing across the snow-covered parking lot of the old bus depot.

He could hear her. Just ahead of him. Grunting. Screaming. Whining as she scrambled to get away. She fled across the parking lot and roundabout, under a cover of blackness that only winter nights can bring.

Monster followed her calmly. Unconcerned. Confident. And why not? There was nowhere for her to go. The lot was secure. Three-metre fences with razor wire and iron-spiked gates made sure of that.

This lot was her cage.

The female raced for Bus 17. Across its banner were three words. *Out of Service.* The hydraulic doors were already open wide. Monster knew this because he had left them that way—

As an escape route that beckoned her inside.

Breathing heavily, she did exactly what he had intended. She sprinted across the icy pavement. Slipped once and landed on her belly. Then managed to get inside the bus. The hydraulic doors let out a powerless clacking sound as she manually forced them closed.

It was done.

Seeing this, Monster took in a deep breath. The cold air numbed his nose, and it made the Jelform mask he wore feel unusually hard and inflexible against his damaged skin. When he reached the bus doors, the dirty stink of diesel and kerosene hit him. It was strong in the air – as prevalent as the oxygen itself. And there was a reason for that.

The entire back third of the bus was flooded with fuel.

Softly, absently, Monster began to hum. They were soft words. Old words. His sojourn song.

'Jesus loves me, this I know.'

He reached out. Grabbed hold of the hydraulic doors. And swished them open as if they were nothing more than a pair of weightless curtains.

'For the Bible tells me so.'

He placed one foot on the bus step, and the entire structure groaned from his weight. He stepped up into the cab.

Inside, the female had already made it to the rear of the bus, where she was desperately trying to open one of the windows. After a few good heaves, it gave way, and the window slid open with a grating sound. The female took a second to peer back at him. When she saw how close he had come – and when she focused on the pistol in his hand – her face tightened.

Turned to rock.

'Please . . . God no . . . *please* . . .'

She raised her hands in complete surrender and the tears finally came. They flooded her eyes, much like the diesel fuel had flooded the bus.

Monster stood still and stared back.

'Little ones to Him belong.'

The sobbing woman recoiled – as if soft sung words were themselves harmful.

'Why?' she whispered. 'Why are you doing this to me?'

Monster said nothing, he just looked at the woman's feet. At the pool of diesel and kerosene that filled the back section of the bus. And all at once, the female seemed to understand his intention. It was as if the overpowering smell of fuel had finally reached her senses.

'No!' she screamed. 'NO!'

Monster tightened his fingers.

Raised the pistol.

Took careful aim.

'They are weak but He is strong.'

Two

It was early, just after five o'clock, and the drowsy winter world was dark and cold and terribly still. Few people were up at this ungodly hour, and even fewer were out of their homes, braving the icy chill. Not a single car could be seen on the skating rink that was normally 41st Avenue.

Homicide Detective Jacob Striker was unsurprised. It was only the first of December, and already winter was a bad one.

He and his partner Felicia Santos had begun their day shift early this week. Two hours earlier than normal. They'd popped into the local On The Run at Granville and 41st, and had grabbed a couple of strong coffees – black for Striker; triple-triple for Felicia. Caffeine was going to be required to survive this first Tuesday of the month, because it was going to be one of those days.

Striker could feel it.

On the schedule was a ton of shit that neither of them was in any particular hurry to do: court-ordered follow-ups; a search warrant in need of writing; a vehicle tracker that required execution; and a pile of evidence that still needed to be logged and tagged in the property office downtown. All of these tasks had already taken them hours of report writing, and there would be hours more to follow.

Paperwork – it was the bane of every cop's existence.

Felicia sipped her coffee, muttered, 'Man, that's good,' and gave Striker a sideways look.

'Well?' she asked.

Striker looked back. 'Well what?'

'Paperwork's piling up. You wanna head down to HQ and get started, or what?'

'What,' he said with a grin.

He drank down some brew and grimaced. The coffee was piping hot and burned his tongue, but it was damn good. Rocket fuel. He looked back at Felicia; she was still eyeing him.

'Paperwork,' she said again.

He shrugged. 'I dunno. I kinda had something more fun planned – I was gonna give myself a vasectomy with a fondue fork.'

Felicia laughed softly, and Striker relented. He grabbed the gearshift, put the Crown Vic in drive—

And a piercingly bright flash lit up the entire skyline to the east. The light was followed by an air-ripping percussive force that seemed to reverberate right through the car windows.

Felicia let out a startled sound. 'Oh shit, what the hell was that? An MVA?'

Striker nodded. With the weather and road conditions this poor, a Motor Vehicle Accident was probable.

'Maybe someone hit a transformer,' he said. 'Better call it in.'

Felicia offered no response; she just grabbed the mike and began broadcasting. Striker dumped his coffee out the window, threw the paper cup in the back seat, and turned on the emergency equipment. With the lights flashing and the siren blasting, they sped down the long stretch of 41st Avenue.

Paperwork could wait.

Three

They arrived on scene in less than two minutes, and the first thing Striker noticed was that the explosion had taken place on the grounds of the old bus depot. As they slowed down, the Crown Vic caught a patch of black ice and skidded to a jerky halt in front of the entranceway.

Without delay, Striker hopped out and surveyed the scene.

In the far-off distance, huge masses of black churning smoke unfurled into the night sky, blocking out the stars and moon. At its beginning was the source of the blast.

One of the old buses was engulfed in flame.

Striker stared through the mesh fence at the fiery wreck. The light of the flames illuminated the underbelly of the billowing smoke and highlighted the closed-down office buildings that flanked the parking lot.

Felicia made a concerned sound. 'If that building catches a spark, it'll go up like tinder.'

Striker nodded. 'Better get Fire here too – ASAP.'

Felicia got back on her cell phone with Dispatch. As she called in reinforcements, Striker walked down the fence line and approached the iron-gated entranceway. The caustic stink of burning plastic and insulation filled the air, mingling with the dirty scent of burning fuel. With every crackle and pop of the fire, puffing clouds of ash and debris swelled through the air.

And the southbound winds blew the debris into his face and all over his suit.

Squinting against the ash, Striker placed one hand against the cold bars of the gate. When the entire structure swung inwards, he looked down surprised. There, on the snowy ground, was something square.

A broken padlock.

'Look at this,' he said.

Felicia neared him. Saw the broken lock. 'Great, this is gonna be an arson.'

Striker nodded, almost regrettably. He looked back at the flaming wreck, then at the old office building to the east, and then at the entire lot. As he scanned between the parked rows of buses, a bad feeling spread through his guts.

'We need this place contained now,' he said. 'The suspect might still be on scene.'

Before Felicia could respond, Striker pushed open the gate and began crossing the parking lot. To the east and west, broken-down buses were parked here and there – old rusting shells amidst the slush and snow. In the far northeast, the empty office building sat. The windows were devoid of light and movement. Not even an exterior lamp glimmered.

No power, Striker realized.

He continued scanning his surroundings as he approached the flaming wreck. One hundred metres. Seventy-five. Then fifty. The closer he got, the louder the fire grew, crackling and popping – until it was almost impossible to hear Dispatch chatter on his portable radio.

When he was less than ten metres away, the heat became palpable. Despite the sub-zero temperatures, the fire warded off the winter cold. For a moment, thoughts of the gas tank catching fire and causing a second explosion filtered through Striker's mind. But then he saw the long metal rods – the conductors – and he realized that his fears were groundless.

The bus was an electric model. No fuel tank to worry about.

He began circling the bus, and suddenly, Felicia was there by his side. She raised her voice to be heard above the fire.

'Dispatch is sending Fire and EHS.' She took a quick look around the blaze. 'Anything?'

Striker shook his head. 'No suspect, no victim – at least, not yet.' He pointed in one direction. 'You go west, I'll take east. We'll meet around back.' When she started to turn away, he reached out and grabbed her shoulder.

'What?' she asked.

'Just be ready for anything.'

She smiled, almost sweetly. 'Always am.'

Then she turned and began crossing the slush-filled lot to the west side. Striker watched her go. When she reached a second line of parked buses and disappeared from sight, he turned away himself and headed east. Not ten steps later, he stopped hard.

Swung his hand down near his holster.

Assessed what he was seeing.

To the north, less than fifty metres behind the fiery wreckage of the bus, was a figure. In the flickering light and swelling smoke, any true detail was impossible to make out. But one thing was for certain. The man standing there was *big* – a large, dark, hulking mass.

He was statue still.

Staring back at Striker.

As if he had been watching him all along.

'You there!' Striker called. 'Vancouver Police! Don't move!'

The man did not respond. Did not so much as move.

Striker began moving towards the figure. Because he was out

of uniform and in civilian attire, he drew his badge and held it up for display.

But again, the man did not react. Not in any suggestive way.

And the moment gave Striker a bad feeling.

He stuffed his badge away, kept one hand near his holster, and increased his pace. When he got to less than twenty metres, the south-blowing winds picked up once more and blustered a wave of spark-filled ash and smoke into his face.

He squinted and raised a hand to ward off the burning embers. When his eyes were again able to focus north, Striker still saw smoke and ash and fire.

But not the giant figure.

That man was gone.

Dissipated as quietly and insidiously as the smoke in his eyes.

Four

Striker took a quick step back for a better defensive position and drew his pistol. He then pulled out his radio and pressed the plunger.

'Heads up, Feleesh. We got someone out here with us – and he's a freaking giant.'

He waited for a radio reply to make sure she was alright. When she copied his broadcast, he readied his SIG Sauer and marched towards the area he had last seen the figure. But once near, all he saw was an empty space.

The sight was unnerving. The constant crackling and hissing from the fire muted any sounds the man might have made, and the heat from the flames forced Striker to take a wide arc around the wreckage.

When he reached the other side of the flaming bus, Striker scanned the yard. All he could see was a large rectangular parking lot, most of which appeared vacant, save for snow and slush. To the immediate west sat another line of buses. They were easily a hundred metres away, and Striker doubted the man could have gotten there so fast as to not be seen. Three hundred metres north was the lot fence – another place where the man could not have reached so quickly.

That left only east.

When Striker looked that way, the only thing he saw was the old darkened windows of the office building. He suspected that the place had once been used as a dispatch centre for the bus drivers. But beyond that, he knew little about the site.

He scanned the snow and slush in hopes of finding the man's tracks. But the darkness made it impossible. From his inner suit pocket, he pulled his flashlight – a small Maglite more appropriate for interior searches than exterior – and turned it on. He set the beam to wide and shone it on the ground. At first, he saw nothing discernible in the snow, but then, twenty steps later, he found what he was looking for.

Footsteps. Big ones.

Striker stuck his own foot beside one of them and saw that it dwarfed his own size twelves.

He scanned the flashlight's beam along the trail. Saw that it led in behind the office building. Where not even the light of the fire could reach.

Tightening his grip on his SIG, Striker swept the flashlight beam ahead of him and slowly made his way around the structure to the rear of the building. Here, the roar of the fire was cut off by the building walls and replaced by the soft moan of the wind as it breezed through the manmade channel. The light was no better. Smoke blanketed everything.

All Striker had was groaning wind and brooding darkness.

He adjusted the flashlight beam from wide to narrow, and moved on. When he reached the end of the lot, the footsteps ended abruptly. Striker stared at the old brick wall. It was three metres high, covered in icy snow, and slippery.

A hard climb.

He holstered his gun, took a running jump, and tried to springboard himself to the top. He pulled himself up on top of the icy brick and scanned the area on the other side. What he saw was the triple-lane expanse of Cambie Street. Wide, dark, snow-covered—

And completely devoid of life.

Striker scanned up and down the street, looking for the suspect. Searching for a place of hiding. But he saw nothing.

The man had just disappeared.

Striker scanned the road for tyre tracks. Saw none. And felt a frustration wash over him as cold as the winter air.

For an instant, he considered his options – drop down the wall and begin an aimless search, or broadcast for containment and a canine unit.

He opted for the latter.

He dropped down the wall, back into the lot of the old bus depot, and was just about to broadcast when Felicia came over the radio. Her voice was higher in pitch than usual. *Tight.*

'You okay back there, Jacob?' she broadcasted.

He pressed his own radio mike.

'He got outside the compound – start up a dog.'

Five

By the time Striker finished broadcasting for containment and a dog, he could hear the long undulating wails of the approaching sirens, and he knew it to be the fire crews. He examined the area near the hedge and fence. In the otherwise-untainted snow were footprints. Decent outlines, even some with ridge detail. Not enough for a true casting, but with luck, enough to be used as a comparison tool.

If they ever found their man.

Striker radioed the find for the Ident technicians and had Dispatch log the request into the call data. Time, 05:58 hours. Then he scoured the area once more, the wet snow reflecting back the harsh glare of his flashlight. Search crews would follow, but a cursory examination still needed to be done.

He wouldn't have it any other way.

As always, the goal was to find evidence. Something – anything – the suspect left behind. A wallet would have been perfect. A piece of identification even better. But that almost never happened. Realistically, what Striker hoped to find was a tool the man had used.

Something with a clean enough surface to test for prints.

Twenty minutes later, he ended the search and decided to leave the scene intact for the Ident crew. After the technicians had done their job, search and canvass crews would also be brought in, and they would perform a thorough grid search. Which meant he and Felicia would find themselves in a bit of a waiting game.

Cursing softly, he returned to the primary scene.

Already, firemen were washing down the flaming wreck. The water snapped and fizzled as it hit the hot steel of the bus shell, and the black tunnel of smoke pouring from the vehicle mutated into a billowing charcoal cloud that Hiroshima'd into the blackness above.

Striker covered his mouth to avoid breathing in the toxic fumes and looked around for Felicia. He found her standing in the middle of a large roundabout, probably fifteen metres wide – an area that allowed the long bodies of the buses to make wide turns and exit the yards.

She was staring down and holding a cloth to her mouth. 'Oh Christ,' she called out. 'We got a dead body here.'

Striker frowned; her words confirmed his fears. And so he started her way.

Beside Felicia was a pair of uniformed patrolmen. One of the cops, a young kid with a newbie look, leaned away from the roundabout and threw up in the snow. Were it not for the direness of the circumstances, Striker would have laughed. He'd been there many times before.

Welcome to the Force, kid.

But he did not laugh. He just directed the patrolmen to set up crime scene tape. Once done, Striker turned his stare towards the roundabout, where Felicia was looking over the body.

'What do we have there?' he called out.

Felicia turned back to face him. Even in the red tint of the fire's glow, her face looked tight, her brown eyes hard and darker than usual. 'Judging by the victim's footwear, I'm fairly certain it's a female.'

'*Fairly* certain?' he asked, coming closer.

'It's not pretty, Jacob. Take a look.'

He moved past her and approached the roundabout. As he went, he listened to his radio. More marked cars had arrived in the area, and the Road Boss – Superintendent Laroche – was expanding the containment area. Two dogs were now running the lanes. Plainclothes officers were out on foot. They were doing everything they could.

But time was passing.

Lost in his thoughts, Striker breathed in, then winced. The burnt smell of the burning bus dropped away and was replaced by the strong meaty stench of burned flesh.

Striker looked at the roundabout.

An old tree, felled probably from the heavy snow, blocked the lower half of the partition and the high crests of snow-ploughed banks threw a shadow across the remainder of land.

Striker took out his Maglite and turned it on. One quick flash of the beam displayed the true horror of the incident. Unlike the rest of the depot, the snow here was largely untainted. With the exception of a few trails where people had traversed the roundabout, the snow was powdery and fresh and clean and white. And there, laying within the centre of all that whiteness, was one shrivelled, blackened mass.

Their victim.

Striker closed his eyes for a moment, and once again tried to put himself in the right frame of mind. To see the body as evidence and not a real person. It was easier that way.

He crouched down for a closer look.

The body was lying in a foetal position, arms tightened hard against the chest wall, legs partly drawn up towards the belly. Almost the entire body bad been burned, more than ninety per cent, with the feet still hidden beneath the deepest level of snow.

Striker gloved up with fresh latex and gently brushed some of the snow away from the victim's feet. The skin there was red but appeared otherwise untouched from the ankles down – as if they had been set deep in the snow of the ditch while the rest of the body had been burning.

'Where are her shoes?' Striker asked.

Felicia nodded behind them, towards the bus. 'One of them's over there.'

Striker glanced back at the bus, where fire crews were still hosing down the shell. He could feel the hot spray contrasting with the winter air, but paid it no heed. Instead, he looked at the destroyed back doors. At the blown-out windows. And at the distance between the rear of the bus and the roundabout.

Striker gestured to it and asked Felicia, 'How far do you think that is?'

She looked, assessed. 'From the bus to the roundabout? I dunno. Thirty metres?'

He nodded. 'That's a long way for someone to run while on fire.'

'Maybe she didn't run, maybe the explosion propelled her this way.'

Striker nodded again. 'That's what I'm thinking.' He gestured to the victim's feet, where some uncooked flesh still remained. 'Or at least it propelled her part way. Otherwise she would have been burned all over her entire body.'

Felicia gave him a lost look.

'Think about it,' he said. 'We're talking gas here. Burning up all over her. Dripping down her legs. It would take mere seconds – if that – for her feet to ignite. And yet the lowest parts of her feet took almost no burn at all.'

Felicia walked to a patch of snow and slush ten metres from the roundabout. 'This is where I found the shoe.'

Striker looked at the area. Within the snow, there was a small flattened-out section – indented like someone had rolled through it.

'She must have landed there.' He pointed to the indentation. 'Been thrown in the explosion, hit the ground, and rolled this way from the momentum.' He looked back at the roundabout. 'So either she kept rolling, or she ran and collapsed.'

'Or she was moved here,' Felicia added.

Striker nodded, even though he didn't like the sound of that. Moving the body to a new position was an act of display; a *modus operandi* such as that would take the investigation into other realms – ones that were much more dark and complicated.

He looked in the snow for evidence of this, but with the slush and water and fuel, the scene was quickly turning to fire crew soup.

He grew frustrated.

'Either way, this is where she landed,' he said. 'Her final resting place.'

Felicia offered nothing more, so Striker crouched back down again. He shone the beam of his Maglite at the victim's head. Aside from some obvious skull landmarks – the eye sockets, the mouth, the overall oval shape – the body part was otherwise undistinguishable.

Just one blackened hairless shape.

Like the rest of the body.

And then a glimmer stole Striker's attention. He shone his flashlight in the snow and saw something shiny.

'It's *jewellery*,' Felicia said.

Striker gloved up with latex and fingered through the snow. He found a small silver blob and held it up in the beam of light.

'Looks like a half-melted cross,' Felicia said over his shoulder.

Striker nodded.

Felicia made an uncomfortable sound. 'Was it planted beneath her?'

Striker looked at the item. The heat of the fire had half-melted the thing, to the point where it was almost unidentifiable. 'She might have been wearing it,' he said. 'The flames would have eaten through the thinner chain. And the snow would have cooled the silver before it melted entirely.'

He looked at it for a long moment, then made a worrisome sound.

'What?' Felicia asked

'If it wasn't hers, then why a cross?' He scanned the crime scene. 'And look at how it was positioned – it might just be the way it landed, but the cross was upside-down in relation to the body.'

'You saying this might be *ritualistic*?'

Striker bit his lip. 'I'm not saying anything. Just make note of it.' He bagged the item as evidence, then looked at the rest of the body.

The clothes had also been burned away. Only the leathery strap of a belt remained around the waist, and Striker felt undignified at having to poke and prod at the body.

When he looked at the woman's right ankle, he saw that the skin was swollen and red and had blisters between the separating dermis and epidermis. But when he shone his torch directly on the victim's *left* foot, a sense of disbelief flooded him.

The skin on this foot appeared relatively untouched. It was a deep tan colour – just slightly darker than Felicia's Spanish tone – and it was covered in a curved and swirling design. An ankle tattoo. Blended into the artistic pattern were two numbers – an *eight* and a *one*.

It was eerily familiar.

Felicia covered her mouth. She crouched beside him and pointed at the design. 'What is that?'

'A tattoo,' he said numbly.

'I know it's a tattoo, Jacob. But what kind of tattoo?'

'It's Hindi,' he said softly. 'Sanskrit.'

'You think?'

'I know.' He stood up and wiped his brow. 'The design means *Truth and Justice.*'

Felicia raised an eyebrow and turned to look at him. 'When the hell did you become the Dalai Lama? How you know that?'

'Because I recognize the tattoo.' Striker's face took on a sad look. 'I knew this woman, Feleesh. Her name was Jazz.'

'You knew her—'

'We haven't been close. Not for a long time . . .'

Felicia looked back at the body and the disturbed look on her face grew deeper. 'Are you sure of this, Jacob?'

He nodded. 'The eight and one represent the number of her academy class, Feleesh. The number of my academy class. She's one of us. She's a cop.'

Six

'You lost me,' Felicia said.

Striker said nothing for a moment; he just kept his eyes focused on the small blackened body curled up in the centre of the round-about and struggled to find the words. But the more he tried to think things through, the more distracted he felt – the constant hiss of the water on the hot bus steel; the yells of the firemen hosing it down; the faraway wails of more approaching sirens; the radio chatter of the units searching the area beyond the bus lot; and worst of all, his own anxious thoughts rioting in his head.

Striker prayed to God his thoughts were wrong.

But he knew they weren't.

'*Jazz*,' he finally got out. 'Her name was Jazz. Jasmine Heer. We were the eighty-first academy class – hired during those heavy superannuation years.' He swallowed hard, then looked around the area as if lost. 'I need to draw the scene before the fire crews completely destroy it.'

'Already started,' Felicia said. She pulled out her notebook and continued on with her drawing. As she did so, she looked up at him. 'So you think you know this woman from then?'

Striker gave her an irritated look. 'I don't think, Feleesh, I *know*. Hell, I remember the first time I saw that tattoo. I was in the gym, watching the rookies run the basic training course. Jazz finished. She was gasping hard – had that raspy cough – and she crashed down hard beside me on one of the gym mats. Started bitching about twisting her ankle during the run. When I looked down, I saw it.'

'The tattoo,' Felicia clarified.

'Yeah. She told me it was Hindi. Sanskrit. And she'd even had her graduation class number added at the end of the design to make it unique . . . She was really proud of it.'

Felicia turned her eyes from her notebook back to the body. More specifically at the numbers on the woman's ankle. 'Thus the eighty-one,' she said. '. . . Maybe more than one person got that tattoo.'

Striker shook his head. 'Doubt it. She was damn near protective of it. We'll check that out, but I'd be surprised if two versions of this tattoo existed. The actual Hindu saying is *The Truth and the Life*. But Jazz had it changed from *Life* to *Justice*. Because of her police career . . . Add in the eight and the one, and how could this belong to anyone else?'

Felicia looked back at the body. 'We'll need to confirm the Sanskrit, make sure it actually says *Justice*.'

Striker nodded absently as he thought things over. 'Plus there are other coincidences here, ones I'm not liking.' He turned to face Felicia. 'Jazz is in Major Crimes right now. And her position there fits the bill – she spent five years working Arson before she came to Homicide.'

'Homicide?' Felicia asked. She found that surprising. 'You mean with *Vancouver* Police?'

'Of course Vancouver – why you sound so surprised?'

'Because *we* work in Homicide, Jacob. And have for some time now. I've never once heard of this woman, much less ever seen her.'

Striker nodded as he saw her point. 'That's because the Feds are paying half her wage right now.' When Felicia didn't clue in, he explained in more detail. 'Jazz transferred to an integrated unit a few years back – actually, not long before you came to Major Crimes. But she's still considered VPD property – the brass wouldn't let her go completely, not after all the money they sunk into her training.'

'Into arson?'

'No, into *ritualistic murders*.'

'I'm lost,' Felicia said.

Striker explained: 'Jazz specialized in ritualistic murders these last few years. It's why she was always gone. So much of her time was required at the FBI school in Quantico. And she spent even more time travelling around the province and the country.'

'Inter-jurisdictional files?'

Striker nodded. 'It was what she always wanted.'

Felicia said nothing at first. She was too deep in thought, and suddenly, she looked tired and cold. She finished drawing the crime scene, stuffed her notebook back into her suit pocket, and shivered. She studied the body on the roundabout for a long moment, then looked back at the firemen who were still fighting to extinguish the fuel-fed flames.

'This scene is giving me the creeps,' she finally said. 'I mean, think about it: the woman worked in Arson for five years, and that is exactly what we have here. And then, after that, she specialized in ritualistic murders . . . and well, we have some pretty odd stuff here, don't you think? Being burned in a fire trap – a pool of gasoline?'

'It's a terrible way to go. Though not necessarily ritualistic.'

Felicia studied the scene. 'What about the way the body was curled into a foetal position? Does that not equate to innocence? Destroying innocence?'

'The foetal position does symbolize innocence,' he agreed. 'But it could also be caused by the shrinkage of tendons. From water loss.'

'And the upside-down cross beneath the body?'

'Again, it could have just fallen off her body that way.'

Felicia looked around the scene with a nervous expression. 'Individually, it wouldn't bother me so much, but collectively . . .'

Striker frowned. 'Just keep a separate page for anything ritualistic.'

Felicia started a page, and Striker turned away. He shook his head and muttered the word *nightmare*.

As if to reinforce that opinion, outside the front gates of the lot, a white Crown Victoria pulled up, blipped the siren a few times, then turned into the bus depot. It was the Road Boss. Car Ten. Normally that meant one of the inspectors, but today, Superintendent Laroche had been called out.

It was unusual protocol.

'Captain Kangaroo's on scene,' Striker said.

Felicia looked unhappy. 'Just don't aggravate him.'

'Me aggravate *him*?' Striker said nothing more; he just raised an eyebrow and walked towards Car Ten.

The sedan pulled up close to the scene, skidded on the slushy pavement and came to a jerky stop. A moment later, the door opened and Laroche stepped out. For a moment, he stood, hands on hips, staring out over the scene – as if he was a towering presence and not twenty centimetres below average height.

Even in the darkness, his impeccable appearance was obvious. His slacks were perfectly ironed, and despite the fact he had driven, no crease marred his white superintendent's shirt. He walked stoically across the lot, stepping into the pre-made footprints and tyre tracks, and patting down his thick black hair.

When he reached them, he smiled at Felicia – an honest, genuine grin – and then met Striker's stare and just nodded. 'Well?' he demanded. 'Is this a confirmed arson, or not?'

Striker frowned. 'A lot worse than that.'

'We have a possible homicide,' Felicia clarified.

When Laroche's face tightened, Striker took control of the conversation and explained everything that had happened this morning, from seeing the red light of the fire in the black morning sky to the discovery of the tattoo on the victim's ankle.

When he was done talking, the superintendent said nothing for a long moment. His eyes held a faraway stare and his lips pursed constantly. When he finally spoke, his voice was low and his French accent was soft but discernible – a detail Striker picked up on whenever Laroche got stressed.

'I want this kept *quiet*,' were his first words.

'Of course,' Striker acknowledged. 'But I want Search and Canvass called out immediately. Three teams. One for the office building, one for the major crime scene, and one for the outer perimeter.'

'One's already on their way,' Laroche said.

'I want three.'

'We'll call out two and hold them over if the need is there.'

Striker nodded and let out a held breath. He was happy – grateful – for the compliance. Getting approval for the search and canvass team was always tricky, especially when budgets were at year end and money was tight, tight, tight. Getting Laroche's approval was the first thing that brought him even a modicum of relief. He was about to say more on the subject when he noticed a boxy white van pull up outside the front gate. On the side was a red ribbon-like insignia.

Global News

Striker felt his jaw tighten. 'That sure as hell didn't take long.'

Laroche looked on with a sense of unhappy acceptance. 'We'll need to set up a media point. Cambie and 41st maybe. Mall parking lot.' He got on the phone with Dispatch and let them know of his orders.

South of them, a heads-up patrolman quickly blocked the

entrance to the bus lot and strung up a slash of crime scene tape. The news crew immediately jumped out and cameras began filming through the wire mesh of the fence.

Striker was not surprised. As always, with any tragic occurrence, the media was on scene within minutes – faster than banshees at an Irish wake.

Superintendent Laroche hung up the phone. He looked at the camera crew, saw a second van pull up, and his face darkened. 'A goddam cop?' he muttered. 'I hope to hell you're wrong.'

Striker was about to respond when one of the uniformed patrolmen – the kid who'd tossed his guts in the snow a half hour earlier – came running across the lot, so quickly that he almost bailed in the slush. He reached Striker's side and held out a black leather wallet that was wet and dirty.

Striker took it from him. 'Where did you get this?'

'Found it back there,' he said, breathless. He wheeled about and pointed thirty metres in front of the bus. 'One of the firemen slipped on it.'

Striker brushed the crud and ash off the leather and muttered *good work* to the kid. Once the wallet was clean, he studied it. It was a standard leather number, one that had a secondary pouch on the inside flap. Seeing this, Striker flipped open the facing and looked inside.

The moment he did, a sick feeling overtook him.

The leather pouch contained a police badge: the blue and white waves of the Vancouver City crest; the wreath of golden maple leaves; and the central dogwood flower. Below the badge was an inscription: *Vancouver Police*. And below that, the member's badge number.

1406.

It was the final confirmation needed. Their victim was indeed Jasmine Heer.

Shaken by the find, Striker turned away from the scene. He needed a moment's respite.

He walked away from the roundabout, away from Felicia and Laroche, deeper into the yards. When he found an area that was calm, away from the clutter and chaos, he looked back at the crime scene – and a sense of dread hit him. From this faraway distance, he could see something that had not been visible up close.

Disbelieving his eyes, Striker approached one of the nearby out-of-commission buses. He climbed onto the slippery hood for a better viewing angle. Standing there, he looked down upon the roundabout and reassessed the scene.

The shape of the roundabout was a perfect circle. Within it, dead centre, lay the victim. Stretching horizontally across the circle was the fallen tree, and running vertically on a slightly angular plane – from lateral at the bottom to medial at the top – were two converging trails. Individually, they meant nothing, but *collectively*, they worried Striker greatly.

He drew the scene in his notebook. Then looked down at it in disbelief. The image was not only alarming, but foreboding.

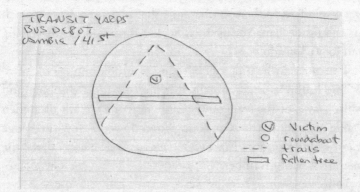

He was staring at a *pentagram*.

Seven

Up high. From the east.

Across the road, on top of the Oakmont Medical Building, Monster stood enveloped by the shadow of the generator enclosure. From his precipice, he watched the scene below continue to unfold:

The police.

The ambulance crew.

The firemen.

And the fire – the beautiful, hungry, *blissful* flames.

Down there was the homicide detective. The big male. Monster had never seen that man before, and yet he felt they would meet again.

It was almost unavoidable.

He watched the cop walk around the scene. Scanning. Assessing. Analysing. First the body, then the roundabout, then the smoking bus shell. After a long moment, the cop stopped moving and looked up. Looked in his direction.

Looked long and hard.

For a brief moment, Monster almost thought the cop could see him. All this way. Up here. Through the churning smoke clouds and billowing ash. Where he was at one with the darkness.

What then, he thought.

What then?

He was risking a lot by still being here. He knew that. This was a bad time – the moment when the odds of getting caught were at their highest. The smart thing would be to leave the scene altogether. To run while he still had the chance.

But run he could not.

It was the flames' fault. They called out to him. Like they always did. The fire, the raging beast – it had a power over him. A dark enveloping magic.

A *life force*.

It was undeniable.

He took in a slow breath, and felt immediate pain in his ribs – sharp, biting, *electric*. It was understandable. When the explosion had gone off in the bus – that wonderful burst of creation – the force had sent him reeling into the darkness. Made him realize, once more, that no matter how strong he was compared to the human traffic of this city, he was nothing when compared to the natural power of the universe.

After the blast, he'd careened backwards through the bus. Slammed into the change box. Tumbled and spun through the hydraulic doors. And had landed face down in the slush and snow of the pavement.

It had been stupid to get so close. Stupid, stupid, *stupid*.

And yet here he was. Close again.

Entranced by the flames.

He closed his eyes. Forced himself to turn away. And moved deeper into the winter darkness where he tried to forget the magic of the flames. The glow. The heat. The hiss. The *burn*.

But forgetting was just not possible. The Jelform mask he wore always made sure of that, as did the burns on his fingers and hands. He stripped off his workman's gloves and then the underlying latex, and stared at the giant blocky flesh extensions that had once been his fingers.

These scars . . . they were physical memories.

Ones he could never forget.

The sight made him sick, and yet it made him complete. The fire was a part of him now – so much beauty, so much violence. They were linked forever.

Fire and Monster, Monster and Fire.

They were one.

Eight

It happened at 06:46 hours, and it was the wagon driver who made the find.

Probationary Constable Mary Morgan, returning from the long trip to the Juvie hall in Burnaby, circled back through the Oakridge area to make her final drop. Just another drunk and surly teenager who was too violent for Saferide and yet not appropriate for the Vancouver jail.

Monitoring the radio, she listened with dark fascination to the ongoing call at the bus depot and drove down the bordering lanes in an effort to help with containment. Halfway down the east lane of Oak Street, she located a dark grey Ford Fusion. One run of the plate told her it was a city-owned car.

Operated by the Vancouver Police.

She radioed the find, and Striker and Felicia came immediately.

Once on scene, Striker gave the vehicle a quick inspection and saw no sign of damage or forced entry. Inside the Fusion was a silver coffee cup, a nylon lunch bag, and on the passenger seat, an old brown leather satchel.

The kind the Department gave to police detectives.

'Think it's Jazz's?' Felicia asked.

'Call the kiosk,' he said. 'Give them the vehicle ID.'

Felicia did. She got on her cell and called the pool lot and gave them the licence plate. Moments later, she hung up and nodded, almost regrettably. 'This is the car Jazz signed out.'

'When?'

'Late yesterday evening. She never returned it.'

Striker tried the handle. Found it locked. Then tried the rest and got the same result. Feeling the seconds tick by, he got one of the kiosk lackeys to bring up a second set of keys. By the time they got the doors open some twenty minutes later, his nerves were on edge.

As he put on fresh latex, the first traces of light began creeping up in the east, turning the smoke-filled shroud of sky a dark purple. He removed the satchel from the seat, then stood by as Felicia performed a cursory search of the interior. When she came up with nothing, he stared at the vehicle for a long moment.

'I want the whole car processed,' Striker finally said.

Felicia agreed; she got Dispatch to start up a tow.

Because the winter wind was strong and blowing their way, bringing with it a parade of snow and ash and other burned debris, Striker opted to return to their vehicle before opening the satchel. Felicia joined him. When they were both inside with the doors closed, he opened the main compartment and found a thick bundle of files inside.

All VPD.

He took them out.

There were three folders in total. The first was simply labelled *Miscellaneous*, and held a collection of statements from victims, property reps, and other assorted emergency personnel.

The second folder was labelled *Forms*, and contained reams of blank police charts and questionnaires – more witness statements, property log sheets, and solemn indemnity papers for court purposes.

The third folder, red in colour, was the one that caught his eye. On the tab was one word, and it gave Striker pause.

Nero.

Felicia looked at the tab. '*Nero*?'

Striker gave her a sideways look. 'He was a Roman emperor.'

'I know that, Jacob, I'm not an idiot.'

'Set Rome on fire.'

'I get that, Jacob.'

'Played his fiddle while it burned.'

Felicia gave him a look like she was going to kill him. 'You think Nero had a hot temper, just throw some more gas on my fire.'

Striker let out a small laugh, and the moment of levity felt good – even if it quickly dissipated.

He opened the folder and pulled out a few separate sections of paperwork, held together by paper clips. Some were old cutouts from the local newspapers and online open sources. Others were printed-up police incidents and fire reports from all over the lower mainland.

Felicia took the bundle of fire reports from Striker and began flipping through it. After a few pages, she made an interested sound. 'Some of these go back more than ten years.'

Striker nodded. 'So do the newspaper cutouts.'

Felicia studied the title on the tab. 'So the word *Nero* really isn't significant in itself – it's just the name she's given her ongoing investigation for all these old arson files.'

'Appears that way,' Striker said. 'Easier to keep them grouped that way – and I doubt the irony of the name was lost on anyone.'

He noted that two sections had been highlighted with bright yellow marker. The first was Holy Cross church – Striker's very own parish. The second was a Jewish synagogue located in the Arbutus corridor. Written next to the highlighted section, in red felt pen, was the name *Kesla*.

Striker had never heard it before.

'Run this surname,' he said. 'Kesla.'

Felicia looked over. 'No first name?'

'No. But there shouldn't be too many hits. Kesla isn't a very common surname.'

Felicia said nothing; she just typed the name into the search box and hit enter. Five possibles came back. Striker pointed to the first on the screen.

'That one,' he said. '*Katarina* Kesla.'

When Felicia clicked on the name, the entity details came up. She read them through and nodded with understanding. 'She's a fire investigator. With the city. We'll have to talk to her.'

Striker flipped through the pages of the reports. 'Her name's on a few of these files.'

'Along with this one,' Felicia pointed out. 'Faust.'

'*Luther* Faust?' Striker asked.

She looked up. 'What, you know the guy?'

'Yeah. Kind of. He's a social worker with the Ministry. Guy's a real odd duck – and that's putting it nicely. He works a lot with troubled teens. Or at least he did when I last saw him.'

'Well, add him to the list,' Felicia said. 'His name is mentioned in more than a dozen files.'

Striker said nothing. He looked away from Felicia and the reports, and stared out the front window at Jazz's car. It was parked on the side of the laneway, underneath the overhang of a barren Japanese plum tree whose branches were now heavy with ash-covered snow. The fact that she had parked out here, a few blocks away from the depot lot, then walked in on foot, rather than simply pulling up to the front gate, told him something.

She had known the meeting was dangerous.

'We need to get her log records,' he said.

Felicia agreed. 'And inform the family.'

The mention of that darkened Striker's mood. Speaking with

Jazz's family was the last thing he wanted to do, but it was also of critical importance. He wanted to see the husband – a man named Torsh Heer – and monitor the man's expression when he informed him of Jazz's death. It was critical to assess Torsh's reaction. His words. His grief. Even if the idea of doing so made Striker feel sick.

He thought about how he would approach the meeting while Felicia continued reading through the various newspaper clippings and case notes Jazz had compiled.

Ten minutes later, when the tow truck finally arrived, Striker was grateful for the distraction. He might not have seen Jazz for damn near a year – not even spoken to her for almost three – but that meant nothing in the end. She had been a cop. She had been an ally. And she had been an old friend.

He had lost someone special today. They all had.

And the feeling left him hollow.

Nine

Striker and Felicia followed the tow truck to the police garage on Alexander Street, just a few blocks up from the Skids. The Ford Fusion Jazz had signed out needed processing. And even though Striker expected nothing from the results, it was one more task that needed to be done. One more box to be ticked.

It was logged for Ident technicians at 08:10 hours.

The day had barely started and yet it already felt long.

With the vehicle secure and tagged, they headed out east. Towards the Heer residence. And as they went, Striker had to force his foot down on the accelerator. It was as if his body was willing the car to slow down. He dreaded death notifications. And today's was especially abysmal.

When they reached the Champlain Heights area of District 3, the sky was no longer a dark bruise. Deeper reds now ruled the east. Striker glanced at this as he drove off of Kerr, down 63rd, and then spotted the house. It was a plain thing. Large, triangular, dirty-white stucco.

Striker hit the brakes hard enough to make the car jerk and let out an angry sound. Upon hearing it, Felicia looked up from her notes to see why. One glimpse at the driveway and she understood his reaction.

Parked out front of the Heer residence were two city vehicles – a white Crown Victoria and green minivan. It was Car Ten, the

Road Boss, Superintendent Laroche. And the Victim Services unit. Which signified one critical thing.

The husband – Torsh Heer – had already been notified.

'That goddam *Laroche*.' Striker slammed his hand on the steering wheel. 'There goes our chance to assess the husband's first reaction and everything he might have said in response . . . *Dammit.*'

Felicia said nothing at first, then cleared her throat. 'He was probably just worried about the story being leaked,' she suggested. 'About the family finding out from some news flash or something. I'm sure he meant well.'

'Yeah, well, the road to hell is built on good intentions.'

'He made a decision—'

'It's not his call to make. Otherwise he can lead this investigation.'

'Well, he *is* a superintendent, Jacob.'

'So what? He should have discussed the situation with us first – *we're* the investigating officers, not him. Laroche has screwed up more investigations than he's solved.'

'Be fair,' Felicia started.

'That is being fair.'

Striker shouldered open the door. Climbed out. Slammed it shut. With the situation already as messed up as it could get, he headed for the front door.

It was time to meet the husband.

Ten

Ten minutes later, Striker and Felicia were inside the Heer residence waiting for the husband to come to grips with the tragedy that was occurring. As expected, Laroche had already informed the man of the horrible news. And the superintendent, upon seeing the anger in Striker's eyes, had quickly made his exit.

In the kitchen, waiting for Striker and Felicia to finish the interview, was the Victim Services worker. Her name was Tamara, and she was young. Mid-twenties. Waiting with her was a rookie constable, some guy Striker had never seen before.

Felicia left the room to speak with them, to see what had been said in their absence. It left Striker solo with Torsh Heer.

The way he liked it.

Striker gestured to the sofa in the living room. 'Please, Mr Heer, have a seat.'

Torsh Heer, pacing back and forth between the living room and den, looked at him with wide, uncomprehending eyes.

'Sofa,' he said. He spoke the word as if it could mean anything.

Striker assessed the man. Torsh was big – almost as tall as Striker and just as thick. The heavy muscle bulk, some of which was hidden behind a thin layer of fat padding, was definitely there.

Easily distinguishable, even under his robe.

Yet no matter how physically intimidating he might have seemed, emotionally Torsh Heer was a wreck. His red-rimmed eyes were wide and disbelieving, his big hands constantly trembled, and his deep baritone voice broke again and again as he continued to tell himself, *this isn't happening*.

Striker walked over to the man. Gently grabbed his arm. Physically guided him down to the couch.

'This *is* happening, sir. And I am so sorry for it.'

The man sat down. Looked up awkwardly at Striker.

'My kids . . .'

No other words came.

The thought of children broke Striker's heart. The kids had already left for school, just ten minutes prior to the police's arrival. And despite their absence, Torsh continuously looked down the hallway, in the direction of the children's bedroom, as if expecting them to come out at any moment.

'How . . . will I ever . . .'

Striker didn't have an answer for the man. Losing their mother was terrible enough for a fourteen-year-old girl and a ten-year-old boy, but when they learnt *how* the woman had died – and that was inevitable; it was on every damn news channel – the truth would be devastating. How could it not? What had happened to Jazz was beyond horrific, it was the stuff of nightmares. And Striker could find no words of comfort for the man, probably because there were none.

He tried to start the conversation on a side note. 'You're a fireman, Mr Heer. I wasn't aware of that.'

The man latched on to the unimportant thought. 'Yes, yes. Hall Eighteen. Shaughnessy.'

Striker took a moment to write this down in his notebook, using it as a delay tactic more than anything else. He looked down at the address and bit his lip. The hall was not all that far from the scene of the crime. Just slightly northeast. And less than a mile.

'Good hall?' he asked.

'Uh yeah . . . yeah. I guess.'

Striker said nothing, gave the man a moment. Then Torsh Heer continued.

'Any . . . any hall would have been good. I just got on with Fire, well, a year ago. December 2nd . . . a year tomorrow.'

'Jazz must have been very happy when you got the position.'

The mention of her name caused Torsh's face to pale. 'Yeah. She was. I guess.'

'You guess?'

His face tightened and he sniffed a few times before looking back down the hall at the children's bedrooms once more. 'You know, I thought . . . when I got on with Fire, that it would be a really big thing for us. You know? Both of us in emergency services and all. I thought it would give us more to talk about.'

'And it didn't?'

Torsh said nothing else. He just swallowed hard and his eyes watered and he looked away, out of the east-facing window, where cold blue sky was slowly appearing.

'The kids,' he said. 'Jesus, I gotta tell the kids . . .'

Striker leaned forward. 'I know this is hard, Mr Heer. Unbearably so. But there are questions I *have* to ask, and I have to ask them now.'

Torsh let out a bemused laugh, almost a sneer, and his head dropped low. His eyes turned down to the ground.

'I had nothing to do with this,' he said softly.

'That's not what I said.'

'It doesn't matter, it's what you're thinking.' Torsh Heer looked up. Met Striker's stare. 'I'm married to a cop, remember? A homicide detective. I know how this works. Am I right?'

Striker ignored the question. 'People investigate in different ways.'

'Check the hall records.'

Striker wrote this down and said that he would. He then changed gears. 'What were your wife's religious beliefs?' he asked.

Torsh Heer looked almost confused by the question. 'A bit of everything, really,' he finally said.

'What about Sanskrit?'

Torsh shrugged. 'She used it. She kept some parts of our culture, but for the most she held a . . . a *general* faith.'

'Did she wear any religious jewellery?'

Torsh shook his head. 'She had lots of stuff.'

'What about a silver cross?'

'Maybe. I'm not sure. I really wouldn't know. She was always wearing *something* new.'

Striker gave Felicia a stymied look, then shifted gears. 'Do you have any idea why Jazz went to the old bus depot this morning?'

'She got a call.'

The words caused Striker's heart to skip a beat. 'This morning?'

'Yeah. Early. Real early.'

'From who?'

Torsh shook his head. 'Didn't say. She just took her cell to the back room, and I could hear her talking. There was tension in her voice. I knew that. A lot of tension.'

'Tension,' Striker said.

'Sure. Like . . . excitement,' he finally said. 'Like maybe she was onto something – I'd seen her like that before. How she got. When she uncovered some new lead or something.'

Striker wrote this down. 'And then?'

'Then . . . she came back into the bedroom. Went into the en-suite. Had a shower. Got dressed and left . . . hurried right out the door.'

'Did she say anything before going?'

Torsh just shook his head slowly.

'Not even goodbye,' he said softly. '. . . She didn't even say goodbye.'

Eleven

The sky was dark blue but clear by the time Monster reached his lair. He exited the van, opened the side door, and carefully removed the cage. In it was the little brown-tailed squirrel. Wherever Monster went, so did Samuel. It had to be so. Anything else was an insult. For Samuel was a gift.

And this was how he had been named.

Cage in hand, Monster trudged slowly across the pristine snow of the field, past the giant pair of snow-covered oaks that fronted the bluff and overlooked the black waters of the bay below.

Normally, on mornings like this, when the sun was slowly rising in the east and the air was crisp and cold and the winds were blowing in hard from the bay, he'd stare out over the strait – much like he had when he was a boy, dreaming of all the places he would go if only he could escape.

But stop and stare he did not.

No, today there was work to do.

He reached the front doors of the facility. The left door was broken, so he pushed through the right one and entered the foyer. As the door shut behind him, he was swallowed by shades of black and grey. By cold faint light and dirty air.

On the north side of the room the glass from the windows had long been broken. Dusty shards littered the floor, amidst the broken patches of old plaster and rotting wood. Covering the pane-less windows were irregular sections of particleboard. The gap between the two boards allowed the winter winds to creep in, and they filled the hall with a soft moaning sound.

A cry without words.

Monster carried Samuel to the other extension of the building. Here the room was long and rectangular and had rows of benches and desks and tables. Here, all the windows were still intact. And on the far ledge was a series of candles, stolen from the old supply hut.

Monster lit all five candles and watched as flames overtook the wicks. It was a beautiful image. It always was. But the most beautiful part of the glimmer was not the candles, or even the flames themselves, but the way the glimmer reflected off his paintings.

His beloved works.

The world he could control and create.

There were many of them placed around the room. Canvases of angry crimson. White-hot gold. And blistering orange. All backdropped by a shadowy black colour – the same blackness that lived inside of him now.

Every one of the paintings was the same. The molten lava. The devouring flames. The human agony.

People burning in the *Lake of Fire*.

Monster stared at his latest work – the most personal one he had ever created. What it stirred in him he could not define. And, as if to make the moment that much more wonderful, Samuel began to chitter.

The sound stole Monster's attention.

'*Sam-u-el*,' he sang.

He placed the cage on the podium – its regular perch – and adjusted the squirrel's water bottle, making sure it was firmly attached to the wire. The cage home also boasted a small plastic running wheel, because Samuel liked that. Monster removed a package of Corn Nuts from his inner jacket pocket. Original flavour.

Samuel's favourite.

He opened the cage door and the little squirrel immediately hopped out and ran up Monster's arm to his shoulder. Samuel perched there, and Monster fed him Corn Nuts. Only when the squirrel's cheeks were so full they looked ready to burst did Samuel scamper off.

Monster watched him go and laughed.

With the squirrel now gone, Monster removed his mask. He peeled the Jelform away from his face and felt a startling damp coolness. The clean fresh air should have felt soothing against his skin. Like freedom.

But it did not. Instead, Monster felt naked. Exposed and vulnerable. The light that warmed most people's skin did not have the same effect on him. Instead, it was cold and unfeeling – highlighting his disfigurements for all to see.

Light was cruel.

Monster sniffed deeply. No matter that the mask always felt gritty, no matter that the rubber made his damaged skin feel sticky, and no matter that the Jelform material always stank of petroleum and other chemicals, he never felt comfortable without it.

Never.

The mask was a part of him now. It was his real face. His new face, covering and replacing the old. And that was a good thing. A necessary thing. Because, after all, he was what they said he was.

A *monster*.

The thought fell heavy on him. As did the actions of this day. Before five o'clock this morning, he had never killed before. Not even an animal.

To his surprise, it didn't feel real.

And to his dismay, he didn't feel any better.

Lost, drowning in a sea of bad thoughts, Monster turned – as he always did during conflicting times – to the east end of the room. Standing there was his easel, and on it was his latest creation: a canvas of blood red, fiery yellow, and hellfire orange. Colours that were so magical, so wondrously alight, that the painting looked like a window to another world. This painting was Monster's masterpiece – the same one he had created over and over again for as long as he could remember.

Pools of lava. Geysers of flame. And the Bad Ones, writhing unto eternity.

It was the Bad Place. The *Lake of Fire.*

And it was everything.

Twelve

Striker and Felicia returned to Homicide headquarters.

Located in the heart of the Skids, the main police building was forever hounded by panhandlers, homeless people, and drug addicts, half of whom were mentally ill and never should have been out in the community in the first place.

But such was the result of the mental health system. Over the years all the treatment centres had been slowly closed down, one by one, and the result was visible to anyone who had eyes. The Downtown Eastside had become Vancouver's largest mental health centre.

As if to make a perfect backdrop to the bedlam out front, the police station was also a shambles. The building was old, having been built back in the fifties, and it showed. Rat- and cockroach-infestations were the norm. And if a day passed by when the building didn't reek of fumigation chemicals, then the janitorial staff weren't doing their job.

Striker was used to it. With Felicia at his side, he bypassed the main entrance, worked his way down Cordova Street, and entered through the annexe. On the fourth floor was Homicide – a unit composed of row after row of thrown-together cubicles. Each one was further adorned by an archaic computer and a monitor that may or may not have been widescreen.

Striker's and Felicia's desks were at the east end of the section.

Striker started that way, but then deviated to the farthest end of the room, and Felicia followed with a curious look on her face.

At the most southeastern corner of the room, almost hidden behind the coffee station, was an empty corner cubicle. Striker pulled out the chair and sat down.

'Who sits here?' Felicia asked.

'Used to be Jazz,' he said softly.

Felicia furrowed her brow. 'I thought you said she was transferred to the Feds.'

'Not transferred – *seconded*.' Striker started going through her drawers as he spoke, looking for something that might lead him in a new direction. 'Seconded so the Department could maintain control of her.'

'What do you mean, "maintain control"?'

Striker shrugged and pulled open another drawer. 'Jazz had a lot of extra training, most of it in the States – FBI, DEA, and God knows who else. All paid for by yours truly.'

'The VPD?'

'Who else?' Striker flipped through a stack of business cards that were bound together with rubber bands. 'From what I heard, her caseload became a bit of a tug-o-war between agencies.'

'Feds versus Munies?'

'Isn't it always?' Striker found nothing in the cards. Put them back. 'In the end, the two managements worked out an agreement, one that allowed Jazz to have an office at each location and work inter-jurisdictional files. But the VPD never lost control of her. They could call her back at a moment's notice.'

Felicia crossed her arms and leaned on the desk. 'Sounds like another pissing contest to me.'

Striker just shrugged. 'She was gone ninety per cent of the time.'

He rooted around the desk a while longer. It was surprisingly sparse, but well organized. A tray filled with pens. A criminal code with colour-coded tags. And a stack of folders in a black wire rack.

Striker leafed through the folders, one by one. All were homicides – domestics gone wrong, gang retaliations, drug-trafficker takeouts, and even a few murders relating back to the sex trade.

But nothing stuck out as glaringly relevant to what had happened.

No pools of gas.

No upside-down crosses.

No pentagrams.

Striker pulled open the last and bottom drawer. In it was a clipboard holding some plain white stationery. On it were some handwritten notes. As he scanned the sheet, with Felicia hanging over his shoulder, Striker began to see some relevance.

A few of the notes Jazz had made were on various fires that had taken place around the city, and once again, the Jewish synagogue in Arbutus and the Holy Cross church in Dunbar were listed. So were a few other religious establishments – an Indian temple on the Burnaby border; a food bank that was sponsored by the Christian Fellowship of Vancouver; and a non-profit that was known for providing food and shelter to the homeless. It was funded by the Lutheran division of the Protestant church.

At the bottom of the list, written in red felt pen, was one word: *Nero?*

Striker pondered that. As he did, Felicia reached out and tapped the page in front of him. 'Look there. Under the *To Do* list. It's those same two names again – Katarina Kesla and Luther Faust.'

Striker saw the names. 'Looks like Jazz was working hard on something. A serial arsonist. Or maybe something worse. Judging by the list of targets she's written down, maybe she was looking for some kind of religious zealot.'

Felicia scanned the list of places. 'Jewish, Catholic, Christian, Hindu – well, at least he doesn't discriminate.'

Striker managed a weak grin. It was the first time since discovering Jazz's body that he'd felt a modest reprieve from the despair. And he tried to channel that focal energy. He thought of Jazz, and how they had found her, and the whole situation still greatly disturbed him.

Disturbed him because it had been predictable and preventable.

'Jazz was a good investigator,' he said softly. 'One of the best, really. But she was horrible operationally.'

'How so?'

Striker shook his head angrily. 'She took chances. A lot of chances.'

'Sounds like you.'

Striker frowned at that. 'She took *unnecessary* chances. Ones she couldn't back up. And she never thought of the ramifications. Of her safety. Or of anyone else's, for that matter . . . Jazz should never have been out there alone like that.'

Felicia finished writing in her notebook and looked up at him. 'You're assuming she went with no backup. Have you actually checked that yet?'

'Just about to.'

He got on the phone and called up the central dispatch line and was relieved to hear Sue Rhaemer's gravelly pitch.

'Shipwreck,' she said. 'How's it hanging, dude?'

Striker felt a weak smile find his lips. He'd known Sue for so long he couldn't remember. Her refusal to leave the eighties behind, her penchant for men in blue – and the backs of their police cars – and her constant need for Coca-Cola had made her notorious. But for her all her quirks and eccentricities, she was ten times the CD of any other he had ever dealt with. Striker got a kick out of her.

'I need you to run Jasmine Heer's unit status,' Striker told her.

'No problem, dude.'

'For the last twenty-four hours.'

'Chill, man, just gimme a second.'

Sue performed the search. When she spoke again, her response was disheartening. Striker listened to it, then said goodbye and hung up the phone.

Felicia was still staring at him. 'Well?'

He swivelled in the chair to face her. 'Not only did she not have any backup, but she didn't even put herself out. She went alone, without cover, and no one even knew she was there. Hell, she wasn't even logged on in the system.' He leaned back in the chair and rubbed a hand through his hair. 'Jesus Christ, Jazz, you're killing me here – what the hell were you thinking?'

Felicia said nothing for a moment. She just rocked back and forth on the edge of the desk and finally made a *hmm* sound.

Striker caught it and looked up at her. 'What?'

'It's unusual,' she said. 'More than just operationally bad. I mean, did she *not* want a record kept? Did she not want anyone to know where she was going, or who she was meeting? And if so, why?'

Striker didn't like the insinuation. 'What are you implying, Feleesh? That she was involved in something crooked? That she was dirty?'

'I never said that.'

'You didn't have to.'

Felicia touched his arm. 'Ease up there, big fella, that's not what I'm getting at.'

'Then what?'

'Maybe she was working U/C. You ever think of that? An undercover op. Or maybe it was never police business in the first place. Maybe this was something personal?'

Personal . . .

The word made Striker think of the husband. 'Torsh Heer—'

'Is clean,' Felicia said.

Striker eyed her. 'You ruled him out?'

'Not five minutes ago. I finally got a hold of his captain. Turns out the man has a rock-solid alibi. He was doing a callout at Hall Seventeen and had just come off shift before we went to his home – like he told you. Man has over a dozen witnesses. He's clean.'

The news didn't surprise Striker. The man had seemed genuinely broken at the news.

'And yes,' Felicia continued. 'I hate to think this way – but maybe Jazz *was* involved in something she didn't want anyone else on the job to know about. You have to consider that, Jacob.'

'I knew this woman, Feleesh.'

'And when was the last time you saw her?'

'I dunno. I saw her round here about a year ago.'

'In the office,' Felicia said. 'But when was the last time you actually talked to her? Socially. Personally. Really had an honest-to-God conversation?'

Striker said nothing and Felicia continued.

'All I'm saying is that you don't know her now as well as you did in the past. And you know what? – Times change. *People* change. Look at the Hodgson affair. Who thought he would have done what he did? A cop caught drug trafficking? My God . . . But he *did* do it. And now he's in jail because of it.'

'What's your point, Feleesh?'

She smiled at him. 'My point is this: you always like to think the best of people, Jacob. I know that. It's one of the qualities I love most about you. But I'd be lying if I said it doesn't sometimes blind you.'

'*Blind* me?'

'There are things about Jazz you're accepting on face value, and we can't do that. We have to investigate her just like anyone else. And with anyone else, you would never, ever leave evidence untested.'

She finished her spiel, and Striker said nothing. He just began collecting the files and the clipboard with Jazz's notes. After a long moment, he spoke again, and failed at keeping the irritation out of his tone.

'I knew her,' he said. 'And I knew her well enough.'

'Jacob—'

'The only thing Jazz ever did wrong was go out there alone . . . and that mistake cost the woman her life.' He stood up. 'We need to contact her bosses with the Feds and we also need to get hold of her police cell records.'

Felicia said nothing for a brief moment, then nodded.

'I'll take care of the records,' she said.

She returned to her desk and got on the phone.

Striker was relieved to see her go. He was glad for the space. He needed it. Sometimes Felicia got to him. She was often blunt to the point of being rude, honest to a fault, and she spoke her mind whenever she felt it was warranted – which was ninety-nine per cent of every waking hour.

Most of the time, Striker found these qualities helpful. But at times like these, it just grated on his nerves. And as much as he hated to admit it, there was a reason for that. One he knew deep down in his core but did not want to admit.

Felicia was *right*.

Jazz had ignored all the standard safety procedures and broken numerous protocols right from the very start. It was an alarming fact. There was probably a reason for that. Maybe even a good one.

But Striker would be damned if he could think of one now.

Thirteen

Fire Hall Eighteen was a modern-looking building, made up of red- and cream-coloured bricks and tall sheets of copper-tinted glass. Surrounding the hall was a crescent of green manicured lawn and perfectly trimmed hedge bushes, all of which were covered in a thick layer of fresh white snow.

As Striker and Felicia pulled up to the hall, Striker assessed the building and its grounds. He raised an eyebrow. 'Nicer than any private residence we'll ever own.'

Felicia just grinned. 'Yeah. Your tax dollars hard at work.'

'There's never enough money to hire more cops, but plenty of dough for manicured lawns.' He shook his head. 'Oh well, this *is* Shaughnessy. What else should I expect?'

'Land of the privileged,' Felicia agreed. 'Why can't I live here?'

'They already did that show – it was called *The Beverly Hillbillies*.'

She smirked at the comment, and Striker rammed the steering column in park, then killed the engine. He looked at the clock, saw it was now 10:25 a.m., and shot Felicia a glance.

'You got those phone records?'

She ruffled through her wad of papers and found the Bell Canada log records. Because Jazz's mobile phone actually belonged to the city of Vancouver, obtaining her mobile phone records had been pretty straightforward. No warrant required, just the usual amount of ass-kissing.

Felicia flipped through the various pages – there were fourteen in all, going back twelve months – and found the information they were looking for: the incoming calls received shortly before Jazz's death.

Striker had seen them already. Some of the information was disconcerting. Torsh Heer had told them Jazz had gotten a phone call early in the morning, and her records backed that up – a call *had* come. From the pay phone station just outside the bus depot lot.

Untraceable.

Forensics was going to swab the phone and dust for prints, but Striker wasn't holding his breath on that one. He couldn't remember the last time they'd gotten a print from a public pay phone.

Maybe never.

Still, the call *had* been made. And that call offered a vague mechanism as to how Jazz had come to be there. But it was not the only phone call on the log sheets that caught Striker's interest. Also on the records was another number – a private cell phone that had been in touch with Jazz six times over the last two days, and fourteen times the entire week. It came back to a man Striker had never heard of, but a man with an interesting connection.

Sherman Ming – another fireman from Hall Eighteen.

'Six calls in two days,' Felicia said. She looked back at the records and frowned. 'Six times *is* excessive. I mean, it's not like he was calling the home, trying to reach Torsh. He was calling Jazz . . . I want to know why.'

Striker pocketed the keys, and the two climbed out of the Crown Vic. Immediately, the smell of bacon and eggs and hash browns hit them. Obviously the fire crew inside was taking care of their first order of the day. It made Striker wish they'd gotten not only a coffee like Felicia had wanted, but some breakfast too.

He was suddenly hungry as hell.

He stepped up onto the sidewalk, got three steps, and then stopped. Felicia was still standing on the roadway, looking down the long stretch of 38th. He waved a hand. 'You coming?'

She shook her head. 'Haven't you noticed? We're not a half mile from the crime scene.' She bit her lip in thought. 'More stores will be open now. Why don't you deal with this Ming guy and I'll do a secondary canvass from here to the bus depot – see if I can dig up some video.'

Striker nodded. Not a bad idea.

He gazed in the general direction of the bus depot. 'How the hell did we ever beat these guys to the scene of the fire?'

'Normally we wouldn't have,' Felicia said. 'But I checked the logs. They were out east dealing with an accident on Renfrew and 1st. That's why they took so long.'

Striker thought it over. Renfrew and 1st had a bad slope in good weather, much less ice and snow. The delay made sense.

'Watch your back,' he said.

'Watch your cholesterol,' she replied.

Striker smiled at that. Then he turned towards the smell of bacon grease and went inside.

Fourteen

Ten minutes later, Striker stood in the mouth of one of the loading bays with the fireman known as Sherman Ming. The man wasn't Chinese as his name would have implied, but clearly a collection of ethnic backgrounds – Asian with a twist of African-American, or maybe Indian. Striker wasn't sure. Of equal notice was the fact that the man was extremely tall. Looked damn near two hundred centimetres. He was one of the few people Striker had interviewed where he actually had to look up to the man.

'That's why everyone calls me Ming,' the fireman said. 'You know. Like the basketball player, Yao Ming.' He spoke the words with a sense of detachment. Ever since Striker had told him the horrible news of Jazz's demise, he had seemed stunned and disconnected.

'You and Torsh close?' Striker asked.

'Not overly,' he admitted. 'Torsh always keeps you at an arm's length.'

'There a reason for that?'

'With me there is.'

That got Striker's attention. 'How so?'

'Well, 'cause of Jazz. I was friends with her long before Torsh transferred in. Knew her from some previous files. And from when we both took the same arson class at the Justice Institute. So we spent some time together. Had some good conversations.'

'Torsh have a problem with that – with Jazz having friendships with other men?'

'The opposite really.'

Striker blinked. 'I don't follow. You mean he *encouraged* her
to have friendships with other men?'

Ming let out an onerous sound and licked his lips. He took an
awkward glance back into the hall, where two of his mates were
loading supplies.

'Outside,' he said, and got up.

They walked out of the loading bay and hiked further down the
snowy drive. High above, moving slowly westward in the eastern sky,
the sun shone down through a thin veil of blue. It warmed Striker's
skin a little, but the moment they passed in behind the crow's nest,
into the shaded area of the garden, the cold returned with force.
Only when they were far out of earshot did Ming speak again.

'The reason Torsh avoids me is pretty simple,' he said. 'And
this is totally off-the-record here, right?'

Striker nodded.

'The guy's a hound.'

'Sleeps around a little, you mean?'

'A little? Fuck, right. *Constantly.* It's common knowledge.
And you know what? I don't think he even cared who knew –
just so long as Jazz didn't know.'

'And did she know?'

He laughed cynically. 'Of course. I mean, how could she not?
It was the reason she was always calling me.'

'She was calling you? Why?'

'She always maintained it was to see how I was doing, but I
knew the real reason. She was calling to see if Torsh was in the
hall or not. I felt like the guy's keeper. To be honest with you, I
was really getting tired of being stuck between the two of them.
Put me in a bad way with the guys.'

'I can see why. Any animosity between them?'

'Jazz and Torsh? Yes. No. I don't know.' Sherman took a deep breath and let it out slowly. 'Hard to tell really. I never saw them together. Hell, no one did. Jazz never came to any of the hall functions.'

Striker could see why. The woman was probably embarrassed. Humiliated. Mortified, even. 'Any problems relevant to what's happened here?'

Ming kept walking along the path as if stopping made him nervous. And Striker needed to take a step and a half for every one the man took. 'I can't see any connection,' he finally said. 'Not that I've been looking for one.'

Striker stepped in front of the man, halting him. He turned to face Ming, and met his stare. 'I want you to answer a question for me right now, straight up. And no covering your buddies, this is serious shit. You know Torsh better than most – could he have had anything to do with what happened to Jazz?'

Ming looked back with an expression of disbelief. 'God, no.'

'You sound surprised I asked the question.'

Ming just shrugged. 'I knew you would. Eventually. But to hear it . . . well . . .'

'So you say no.'

Ming shrugged a second time. 'Torsh messed around and all – everyone knows that. But this . . . this is just too . . .' He just looked towards the west, in the direction of the bus depot, and shook his head sadly. 'No.'

Striker nodded. He watched the man's reaction to the questions, and assessed him. Ming gave all the right indicators to suggest he was genuinely saddened by all that was transpiring. The man looked torn up.

Striker ended the conversation, then handed Ming his business card and promised to be in touch if anything else came up.

He was about to turn away from the hall when Felicia returned from her video canvass. She walked up the drive and met him in the mouth of the bay.

Upon her arrival, one of the firemen – a twenty-something blond Striker hadn't seen – came strutting out from the shadows. He held a tyre iron in one hand, a rag in the other, and he offered Felicia a nice wide smile.

'Well, good morning, Officer,' he said to her.

She smiled back. 'Good morning, yourself.'

'Name's *Paris*,' he said. 'Like the city.'

'I would have thought more like Paris Hilton,' Striker interjected.

The fireman made no reply. He just kept his stare on Felicia for a long while, then jabbed a thumb over his shoulder. 'Got some coffee inside, if you want a cup. Freshly brewed.'

Felicia breathed in. 'It *does* smell good.'

Striker had had more than enough of the scene, and he cut it short. He looked back at the fireman and asked, 'Shouldn't you be posing in a calendar somewhere?'

The fireman grinned. 'Actually, I *was* Mr July in last year's edition . . .'

Striker sighed. 'Why does that not surprise me?'

He gave Felicia a nod that it was definitely time to go. They said their goodbyes, and Fireman Paris remained out on the driveway, watching them leave. When they reached the cruiser, Striker climbed inside and Felicia joined him. Only when the doors were shut did they talk.

'So you get anything?' he asked.

'A nice invitation.'

Striker rolled his eyes. 'Oh come on. From *Paris*? Gimme a break.'

'Do I sense a little jealousy?'

'I don't get jealous.'

Felicia just looked back out the window at the fireman who was still standing in the driveway, cleaning his tool with a rag. She bit her nail.

'Mr July, huh?'

When Striker gave her a dark look, she let out a soft laugh. He started the engine and put the car in gear.

'C'mon,' he said. 'Let's go get that coffee. God knows I could use one.'

Fifteen

They grabbed a coffee at the Starbucks on Granville Street, up in the Marpole area. Felicia opted for a grande eggnog latte while Striker stayed with his usual Americano, though today he put a bit of cream in it. They also grabbed a couple of egg-white wraps and a bagel with cream cheese. They ate in the car while going over the file.

'So nothing on the video canvass,' Striker clarified.

'No. Amazes me how many shops have no exterior video nowadays. Anything good come from the hall?'

Striker explained to her about Torsh and his affairs, and why Jazz had called Ming so many times.

'You sure it didn't go the other way as well?' she asked.

'What way?'

'Jazz and Ming,' she said. 'If Torsh was screwing around on her, maybe Jazz did the same and had some fun with Ming on the side.'

Striker had already considered the idea, and hoped it wasn't true. The fact that Ming had only called Jazz back a few times might have indicated his uneasiness with the whole situation. Then again, he wasn't ruling anything out.

'Hell hath no fury,' he said.

Felicia grinned. 'You got that right. Remember it.'

When Felicia finished the last bite of her wrap, she dug into the bagel. After spreading a thick layer of plain cream cheese on it, she opened the Nero folder they'd pilfered from Jazz's VPD desk.

The first thing Striker saw was the Entities page. The first section was labelled *Institutions*, and under it was the Holy Cross church in Dunbar. He knew the place well. He had grown up there as a boy, had been in attendance with his parents and siblings every week without fail, and had even attended Sunday School classes.

The memories felt so long ago, and yet just like yesterday.

He killed the thought and focused on the investigation.

When he scanned down the page for the Property Reference list and saw the name *Father Shea O'Brien* as the primary contact, Striker was again deluged in a wave of memories. Good ones, bad ones, and a flowing stream of accompanying guilt. He had abandoned the church years ago, and the thought of this made his insides tighten.

Felicia caught him staring at the section, and she nodded. 'We're actually not that far away from this one,' she said. 'Wanna go?'

Striker said nothing, and he made no move to put the car into gear.

'These are all victims of possibly the same arsonist,' she persisted. 'The Holy Cross church was the third one hit – although this was quite some time ago. Still, we should at least drop by. You know Father O'Brien, right? Let's see what he has to say. And the case aside, I'm sure he'll be excited to see you again.'

'Sure,' Striker said. 'Sure.'

He put his hand on the gearshift. Kept it there for a moment. Then put the car in drive and they headed out.

Every kilometre driven felt perpetual to Striker, and he struggled with old memories that were still raw. As they went, Felicia got on the phone and tried to contact the fire investigator they'd seen in many of the old cases in the Nero folder – Katarina Kesla.

But the woman was not in the office and she was not answering her mobile, so Felicia dropped that call and made another. This time, she called up the social worker Jazz had been contacting – Luther Faust. When she hung up five minutes later, Striker gave her a curious look.

'Well?' he asked.

'He doesn't start till noon,' she said. 'Afternoon shift.'

Striker nodded because he understood the shifts. And the work. And also Luther. Seeing the man was an investigative necessity, but Striker wasn't looking forward to it. Luther Faust was a strange man, often closed-off and unhelpful when it came to police matters. He and Striker shared a history together.

And not a good one.

The drive from Marpole to Dunbar was ten minutes in good weather; they got there in twenty.

They parked in front of the church, under the overhang of a barren dogwood tree, and Striker stared at the building. It was old and simple in design. Small, rectangular, and made up entirely of white wooden boards. Had it not been for the arched entrance and the cross on top, people might have thought it an old schoolhouse or a dormitory.

File in hand, they exited the vehicle. Once out, Striker stood on the sidewalk and stared at the dogwood tree. He remembered his mother scolding him for climbing it. Then recalled his dad defending him:

He's a boy, Helen. Boys do that.

Despite the decades, the memory was still fresh. Tender and painful all at once. Striker missed his parents very much. And he realized now that some hurts never end.

Felicia started up the walkway. When she realized he wasn't

moving, she turned about and stared at him. Gave him a soft look. Understood.

She forced a smile.

'Well?' she asked. 'You ready to atone, Bad Boy?'

Striker just blinked out of his reverie and forced himself to smile back.

'Believe me, Feleesh. We don't have that kind of time.'

Sixteen

When Striker walked through the doorway and entered the narthex of the church, many things overtook him – the garish sunlight piercing through the multicoloured windows; the hollow sound of his footsteps echoing off the high sweeping walls; and the smell of candle wax and burning wicks.

It *all* hit him. But none of these experiences were as powerful as the odour of the old place itself. There was a musty smell to the church. Something earthy. The kind that only comes with wood and time.

'I love these places,' Felicia said. 'They always make me feel so warm and cared for . . . so *safe*.'

Striker said nothing. He just looked ahead into the nave and saw a priest he had never seen before. Unlike Father O'Brien, who must have been in his late sixties or even seventies by now, this priest looked to be about forty. And he was like no other priest Striker had ever seen.

The man's chestnut hair was wild in appearance, wavy and loose, and definitely in need of a trim – although the length seemed to be indeterminate at the sides, where the hair from his head fused with a pair of sharply manicured sideburns. Almost touching the sideburns was a large moustache that turned up at the ends like a joker's smile. That, too, blended in with the rest of his face, which held at least a day's growth.

The priest saw them and came walking over.

'Welcome,' he said. 'Welcome.'

As the priest neared, Striker could see lines under his eyes. They gave away his true age. Something closer to fifty, for sure. Yet fifty or not, the man's eyes were deep and acute – lively and warm and welcoming.

'I'm Father Silas,' he said softly.

Striker introduced Felicia, then himself. 'We're looking for Father O'Brien.'

The priest nodded, almost imperceptibly. 'He'll be but a moment; he just finished counselling.' He looked back down the nave at two females – perhaps a mother and a daughter – who were sitting in the front row. Then he added: 'It's been a rather trying time for some.'

Striker looked at the two parishioners at the front of the nave, and as he did, they also glanced back. Definitely a mother and a daughter. The mother had a streak of grey running through the centre of her hair, where the dye had run its course, and the skin around her eyes looked hollow.

She looked very sick.

As much as the sight of her absorbed his attention, it was the girl who really tugged away at him. She was young, maybe sixteen or so, and her strawberry-blonde hair was stuck to the sides of her face where tears had run. Her stare was vacant, lost, devoid of hope.

As palpable as the cold outside.

'She looks like Courtney,' Felicia whispered.

Striker saw it too – though in truth, he saw glimpses of his daughter everywhere, all the time. The moment made Striker want to call Courtney right now, to make sure she was going to her therapy appointment.

She'd missed too many of them lately.

'Maybe we should come back later,' he suggested.

Father Silas cupped his hands and nodded. 'Maybe I can be of assistance. What exactly is it you need, Detective?'

'Information,' Striker said. 'On a fire here that happened a while ago. Behind the church, just out back.'

Father Silas nodded. 'I wasn't here for that.'

'It was last year,' Felicia said. 'You were somewhere else?'

'My own parish is on the other side of Marine Drive,' the priest explained. 'St Jude's.'

'The church just up from the reserve?'

He nodded slowly. 'Yes, there's always much to do there. It is a very . . . *active* community.'

'It sounds like you say that with weariness,' Striker noted.

The priest just scratched at his chin and nodded absently. 'I've been helping Father O'Brien a lot lately with this parish, and maybe neglecting my own in the process.'

'And it's been too much?' Felicia asked.

Father Silas grinned. 'Be careful what you wish for, I guess. My original diocese was at The Heavenly Mother – a small parish just south of Squamish. Sadly, the doors are closing.'

'They're *closing down* the church?' Felicia asked.

The priest forced a grin. 'Yes well, Rome giveth and Rome taketh,' he said. 'Regardless, the responsibilities of the closure have fallen to me. So between assisting Father O'Brien here at the Holy Cross, dealing with my own parish in the Southlands, and closing down The Heavenly Mother, I've been feeling a little . . . spread thin.' He glanced back towards the front of the church, then back at Striker and Felicia. 'Father O'Brien will be but a minute more.'

Striker just nodded.

Felicia spoke next. 'You should take a rest, Father,' she said. 'Have a holiday. Can't Father O'Brien handle his own parish? Or get someone else to run it?'

Father Silas splayed his hands. 'I'm afraid to say it is not as easy as it sounds. There are less and less of us who give our lives to the church nowadays. And Father O'Brien has suffered some rather unfortunate circumstances of late.'

The words made Striker's mouth go dry. 'Is he alright?'

Father Silas only smiled in return. 'It is my duty to help him, and it is a task I welcome. Father O'Brien has always been kind to me, and he has given more to the church than he has ever received. I am truly happy to oblige him.' His smile widened. 'The Lord gives not more than a man can handle.'

Striker thought of all the mental breakdowns he'd seen in the Skids, but held his tongue, and there was a silence in the church.

A breeze filled the nave. When Striker looked up, he could see that the side door in the transept area was open and the woman and her daughter were now leaving. He watched them go, hoping that whatever they were going through, it would soon get better. But somehow he didn't think so.

Then the door closed, and they were gone.

Father Silas extended an arm to guide them forward. 'You will find Father O'Brien just ahead. In the sacristy.'

'I know where it is,' Striker said.

He headed up the walkway with Felicia by his side. They were halfway through the nave when Felicia looked back at the priest and grinned.

'I like the moustache, by the way,' she said. 'Very bold of you.'

Father Silas smiled. 'The world is changing, Detective. We have to modernize with it, or we'll be left behind.' Then he offered them a wink. 'Besides, I ran out of shaving cream.'

Seventeen

Striker approached the door to the sacristy and stopped. Before knocking, he wiped his hands on his slacks. For some reason, his palms were sweaty and a wave of anxiety was sweeping through his core. Felicia caught it and leaned past him.

'Guilty conscience?' she asked, and rapped on the door.

'Enter, please,' came a gentle voice.

Felicia grabbed the doorknob and turned it. She offered Striker a smile.

'Just avoid the holy water,' she said.

Then she opened the door all the way.

Striker stepped inside the room and took it all in. The sacristy was smaller than he remembered – or maybe now he was just that much bigger. The room was maybe six metres by ten, and dimly lit by the peaceful yellowish light from the gold-hued windows.

On the immediate left was a row of old wooden lockers that held numerous gowns and robes. Striker looked at one of them – a white thing that draped down to the ankles – and he tried to recall its name.

An *alb*? A *chasuble*?

He gave up trying.

To the right was a long narrow table, on which sat a golden ciborium, a silver chalice, and some bottles of things he could not define. Holy oils, maybe.

Sitting down at a small desk, straight ahead of him at the other end of the room, was the priest they had come to see. Upon their entry, Father O'Brien stood slowly from his chair, the stiffness of his joints easy to see. He shuffled around to see them.

'Hello, Father,' Striker said.

'Good morning,' the old man started to say, then stopped short. His eyes narrowed, then widened, and his lips broke into a smile.

'Jacob?' he asked.

'It's good to see you, Father.'

'Oh it's good to see you, my boy!'

The elderly priest hurried across the room. When he was close enough, Striker started to extend his hand, but Father O'Brien walked right past his handshake and gave him a wide-armed hug.

'It's been so long, my son. *Too* long.'

Striker took in a slow breath and felt almost trapped by the embrace. Standing one hundred and eighty-eight centimetres, he towered over Father O'Brien – who reached maybe one seventy-six centimetres with shoes on. Still, despite their difference in size, when within the priest's arms, Striker felt extremely small.

After a short moment, the priest stepped back. Took a good long look at Striker. And smiled.

Striker did the same, feeling a strange sense of desperation as he looked back. Father O'Brien was not just older now; he was *old*. His years were apparent in everything he did, from the way he stood partially hunched, to the way he shuffled when he walked, to the way he squinted when he focused on them.

It was life, Striker knew. Time – the one undefeatable enemy of us all. He found the moment disturbing. He did not like it.

'This is my partner, Felicia Santos,' he said.

'I go to the Rosary Cathedral,' she said. 'On Renfrew.'

The priest nodded. 'Father Domicos. A good man. I like him well.'

For a few minutes, the three of them spoke, with Father O'Brien asking Striker most of the questions: How is your brother Tommy? Is he still the wild one? *Yes, Father, he is.* And what about Marcus? I heard he moved to Toronto. *A position with RBC.* And what about Hannah – she always did have the most lovely singing voice – how is she? *Well, Father, well. Living on the North Shore. She still thinks she's going to be a starlet.*

Father O'Brien let out a soft chuckle at the news.

'Well, I hope she does,' he said softly. 'I sincerely hope she does.'

When the priest's expression softened and Striker felt the questions about his own life were about to start, he took control of the discussion and re-routed it back to the reason they had come. The investigation.

'Father . . . last year, you had a fire here.'

Father O'Brien's eyes narrowed as he thought back. 'Yes, I do remember it.'

'Did another detective come to talk to you about it?'

'Yes, a nice young woman. Pretty, I'll say. And sharp too. Her name escapes me now.'

'Jasmine Heer?' Felicia offered.

'That's it. Detective Heer. How is she? Are you helping her with the case?'

Striker held nothing back. 'She died today, Father. She burned to death in a suspicious fire at the bus depot.'

The news clearly shocked the priest. The joyful expression fell from his face and his skin paled. 'Oh dear goodness.' He looked up at Striker with desperation in his eyes. 'Would you like to pray, son?'

'I'd like to *investigate*.'

The words came out rather harsh, more so than Striker had intended, and he realized just how pressurized he was from everything going on – losing Jazz in such a horrible way, having her killer still out there somewhere, and even coming here and seeing Father O'Brien after such a long time.

His blood pressure spiked through the roof.

Felicia saw his need and stepped in. 'We're worried that her murder might be linked to the investigation,' she explained. 'To whoever was going around starting these fires in the first place. Like the one you had at this church.'

Father O'Brien said nothing for a moment. He suddenly looked lost and tired, and old. He shuffled across the room, where he leaned against the table holding the various sacraments.

'I don't . . . don't really see how,' he began slowly. 'The fire out back . . . Gas was used; they knew that. But it happened in the dead of winter. During the homeless crisis. People were freezing to death out there. Maybe someone was just trying to keep warm and it got out of hand.'

'Then why not just come inside?' Striker asked. 'This is a church. Are your doors not always open to those in need?'

'Normally, yes, Jacob. But not that week.'

Striker found this surprising. 'Why not?'

'The cold had caused the pipes to burst – this is an old building, you know – and due to safety precautions, we had to lock the doors while everything was being fixed. It lasted only a few days, but that was exactly when the fire occurred. Let me check my diary.'

He shuffled to the back of the room.

With the priest out of earshot, Striker turned to Felicia. 'I don't like this,' he said.

'Like what?'

'The whole circumstance. The fact remains that Jazz appears to have been *lured* into the bus yard and then murdered. So looking at what happened here, I wonder – could this have been a practice mission? To see if Jazz would actually show up? To see if he could control her by way of her investigations?'

Felicia's face hardened at the words. 'If that's true, then this guy is extremely calculating.'

Striker was about to say more when the priest returned. 'I cannot find it now, Jacob. But I will look more later.'

'That's perfectly alright, Father.' Striker looked intently at the priest. 'You don't happen to recall the fire investigator's name, do you?'

'Oh that's an easy one,' the priest replied. 'Kesla – like the hockey player.'

Kesla, Striker thought. *Same name again.*

Katarina Kesla and Luther Faust; those two names kept coming up.

Striker waited to see if Felicia had any other questions. When she did not, he took a moment to thank Father O'Brien for his time. Then, with the old priest at their side, Striker and Felicia left the small confines of the sacristy and headed back up the nave. When Father O'Brien opened the front door for them, the sun was centred high in the blue sky.

It changed nothing; the world remained cold.

Before leaving, Striker turned to face the old priest.

'It was good to see you again, Father,' he said.

The old man beamed. 'It was good to see *you*, Jacob. I've missed you so very much, my boy. Remember, you are always welcome here. This is your home.'

Eighteen

He was twenty-nine years of age now – a man for the last decade – but to all who knew him, he would forever be known as The Boy With The Violet Eyes. He stood there, in the spacious cold of his secluded warehouse loft, and shivered. The air was cold, freezing in fact, and the winter wind that blew in violently through the south-facing window worsened the chill.

But that was alright.

It was the way he wanted it.

The cold was essential. It made the body retain heat. Made the blood vessels constrict, thereby putting less pressure on the surrounding soft tissues. Less pressure meant less tissue tear. And less tissue tear resulted in healthier, younger skin.

Which was really all that mattered.

He kept the windows open.

He sat there, with nothing more than a tenuous shawl draped over his shoulders, and analysed himself in the mirror as he massaged retinoid cream all over every inch of his body. The man in the reflection was one he had never come to terms with. A man he never wanted to become.

But here he was.

Here he was.

God could be so cruel.

Even through his own eyes, he could see that he was thin.

Terribly thin. *Emaciated*. But it had to be this way. Every rib and hip bone poking through the flesh. Every bony mark visible. Some people liked that look. Longed for it. And it had served him well over the years.

That, and his other features.

His complexion was white as cream, his raven-black hair thick and healthy and long as Cleopatra's. These were benefits to his line of work. But the real lure was his eyes – violet in colour, and *startling*. They were the reason people loved him so; the reason people hated him so. And more than all that, they were the reason people feared him.

The smart ones, at least.

He grabbed the Neoprex brush. Its bristles were coated in neoprene, designed to prevent damage to his silky strands. He gently drew the brush through his raven hair, fussing with it this way and that. Then he tried on a few different berets and pins – a turquoise one, a swirling amber number – in an effort to make himself look young and younger and younger.

More *childlike*.

Like always, it was a futile attempt. And as his eyes caught the mirror, all he saw were the lines at the corners of his mouth and under his eyes.

Daggers in his heart.

He stood up calmly from his chair. Struck out his fist. And broke the mirror apart. The sharp clatter of glass filled the room as the pieces crashed and shattered on the make-up bureau and floor. And then he closed his eyes and shook his head.

Another one . . .

He had broken another one.

He licked the blood from his knuckles and stared at the broken mirror, and was relieved when his cell phone rang. The timing couldn't have been more perfect.

A new customer . . .

It was the best thing that could have happened. Really, just the best thing.

Because right now, he *really* felt like hurting someone.

Nineteen

The moment they left the Holy Cross church and climbed into the car, Striker pulled onto the road and headed south. He wanted to put as much distance as he could between him and the church, and do it as quickly as possible. For some reason, he felt trapped, just being there. Suppressed. *Suffocated.*

'You can breathe now,' Felicia said.

Striker cast her a look of ambivalence, but made no reply.

'So,' Felicia said. She looked at the road ahead. 'We got a destination here, Sinner, or are we just driving away from the Pearly Gates?'

He turned onto 29th and headed east. 'I'm taking us to the Ministry. We need to speak to Luther Faust . . . should be another real treat to add to the day.'

Felicia laughed softly.

For a few miles, they drove in silence, Striker lost in his thoughts and Felicia on the phone checking her emails and voice messages. When traffic backed up at a red light on Burrard and 4th, she brushed her fingers through her hair and smiled. 'I liked Father O'Brien,' she said. 'He seemed nice.'

'He *is* nice,' Striker said. 'The man is a saint. Always has been, ever since I can remember.'

'So why the tension?'

'What tension?'

'Oh come now. You looked like you couldn't wait to get out of there.'

Striker let out a long breath and knew there was no denying it. Felicia could read him better than anyone. 'I dunno. Bad memories, I guess. Anxiety, guilt – take your pick.'

When Felicia said nothing else, but just kept looking at him, he explained in more detail:

'You know my parents died in a car accident.'

She nodded. 'You don't talk about it much.'

He shrugged helplessly. 'I was only eighteen when it happened, Feleesh, and it was a moment that destroyed pretty much everything I held normal in life.'

'Eighteen is young to lose both your parents, Jacob.'

He nodded. 'Yeah, it was. And we had no other family here, so I became the legal guardian of my siblings. Hannah . . . she was okay with my new role. Maybe because she was so much younger. But Marcus and Tommy? They damn well begrudged me for it. It made a bad time even worse.'

'It sounds like it.'

The light changed to green and Striker hit the gas. 'Let's just say the memories aren't great. I'll tell you this: If it weren't for Father O'Brien, I don't know what I would have done. If I even would have made it through. He counselled me. A lot.'

Felicia listened to his words intently, turning slightly in her seat to look at him as they spoke. 'So what exactly did you do? How'd you support them?'

Striker shoulder-checked into the fast lane, then drove onto the Burrard Street Bridge. 'I did the only thing I could do. I got a job at a construction site. Shitty work but decent pay for an eighteen-year-old. And Dad had some life insurance.'

'Enough to get by?'

'Not really. Life was tough. And Father O'Brien knew it.'

Striker cast Felicia a quick glance. 'Every week, a basket of something turned up on the front porch. Things we couldn't afford. Spiced meats, some nice cheeses. A pie sometimes. Maybe even a few colas. Small stuff that made a big difference. Father O'Brien and the church really came through for us. I owe the man more than I could ever repay him.'

Felicia reached over and squeezed his hand. 'Well, I'm sure he's very proud of you. Look how you took care of everyone, and how good everything turned out in the end.'

Striker just let out a sour laugh. 'Yeah, real good. Hannah's never had a real job in her life. Marcus has always begrudged my role and couldn't wait to get away – he transferred to Toronto the first chance he got. And Tommy took off and joined the PDC over ten years ago.'

Felicia raised an eyebrow. 'The Positivist Dominion Church? But they're basically a cult, aren't they?'

'Cult, high-end fraud ring – guess that depends which side of it you're on.' Striker navigated onto Seymour Street and continued north. 'I didn't have the heart to tell Father O'Brien.'

Felicia nodded. 'So that's why you got so edgy back there.'

'Well, that, and other things.'

'*Other* things?'

'Look, I haven't been there in decades, Feleesh. Not to Father O'Brien's parish, not to any of them. I just . . . just couldn't go anymore.' He shook his head as he drove. 'Not after what happened to my parents. And all the problems with the family. And all the things I've seen on this job – not to mention all the problems the Catholic church has had over the last ten years or so: the politics, the abuse, the laundering charges. I just couldn't accept all that. Not anymore. And one day I just stopped going.'

They reached the downtown core in silence, Striker wanting the break from the conversation and Felicia fiddling with the heater controls to make the car warmer. It wasn't until they were almost at Ministry HQ that Felicia spoke again.

'So what did you lose faith in?' she finally asked. 'The church, or God?'

Striker wanted to avoid the question, partly because – now that it had been put to him – he really didn't know the answer. So he put it back on her:

'Frankly, I don't see how you can have such a strong belief in anything – not after all the crap we've seen in this job.'

Felicia took the comment with ease. She pulled down the passenger visor, looked in the mirror, and tried to get an eyelash out of her eye.

'It's not like I don't have questions myself,' she said. 'Ones I'd like to ask the Big Man, if I could.' She got the eyelash out, flipped the visor back up, and looked at him. 'The world's a messed-up place, Jacob. No one ever said it wasn't.'

'And yet you still believe.'

'I *have* to believe.' She gestured to the world around them. 'I see proof of it every day, everywhere I look.'

Striker looked around to where Felicia had gestured: a panhandler on the corner; a broken neon sign for the YMCA; traffic congestion lined up and down Burrard Street. He wished he could see whatever it was that she was seeing.

They were worlds apart.

'It's not a matter of evidence,' Felicia added. 'It's a matter of *faith*.'

'Faith left me a long time ago, Feleesh.'

'Faith doesn't leave you, Jacob. You leave it.'

She spoke the words as if she expected an answer, but Striker had none to give. When they pulled into the Police Only parking spot out front of the Child and Family Services centre, Striker was relieved.

He needed the air; he needed some space.

Oddly enough, it was the first time in his career that he actually wanted to speak to Luther Faust, and that thought alone brought out his cynical side.

It's a messed-up world, he thought, and climbed out of the car.

Twenty

The Ministry office was situated adjacent to the Vancouver court house, in the annexe maze. In many ways, it reminded Striker of Homicide headquarters. The phones were always ringing, the place was always occupied, and the building itself was old, old, *old*. Brown carpet owned the floors, faded and threadbare down the middle, and in the speckled ceiling tiles above, long rows of fluorescent tubing gave the office a dingy, artificial feel, tinting everything below in a smoker's-tooth yellow colour.

In the rear section, far from the front door, was the office of Luther Faust. In the social services world of poverty and squalor, the man was a living legend – though not always for the best of reasons. Luther Faust was known for being a man who did things his own way, on his own terms, and often completely outside of the rules and regulations. His calling cards were being uncoop- erative, inflexible, confrontational, and on some occasions, anti-police. Striker and Luther had met head-on more than a few times in the past.

Striker hoped today would be different.

'So where is Mr Wonderful?' Felicia asked.

As if on cue, the banter of angry words could be heard, and moments later a door slammed. From out of the rear office walked the man they had come to see. Luther Faust was a tall man, standing damn near equal to Striker's height, and just as wide. With his meat-hook hands and barrel chest, he would have made a great beat cop.

Striker eyed Luther up. The man looked no different than he ever had during any of the ten to fifteen times Striker had seen him – old black leather jacket, faded blue jeans, and that same black bowler hat with the red band wrapped around the brim.

His grooming was no less unusual. Barely acceptable by Ministry standards. His greying hair was already shaggy, and way too long to be considered professional, curling down over his collar. His moustache and goatee were equally unkempt, covering his lips and dangling into his mouth like a dead grey crayfish.

'Speak of the devil,' Striker said.

Felicia was holding the file they'd obtained from Jazz's satchel. She shifted it to her other hand and said, '*That's* him?' She pursed her lips in silent appraisal. 'Interesting look. I'll give him that.'

She had barely finished the words when a small Asian woman exited the office behind Luther. She looked small and sturdy and tough. Like iron. The two began arguing, Luther in heated whispers, and her less quietly. The moment Striker saw her, he let out a frustrated sound. 'Oh shit. It just gets better and better.'

'You know her?' Felicia asked.

'Yeah. Her name's Luna.'

'Pretty name. Like *lunar*, like the moon.'

'Like lunatic.'

Felicia laughed softly. 'And does the woman have a last name?'

'Asawa-Tan.'

'Asa— *what*?'

'It's a Thai name. Everyone just calls her the Alphabet Doctor. It's easier that way. She's a psychiatrist.'

'One you don't much like, by the sounds of it.'

Striker offered nothing back. He moved down the walkway, got halfway across the distance, and Luther caught sight of him. The man's expression did not change; it remained one of irritation.

Striker was in no mood for fake pleasantries. He walked up to the bickering pair, stopped a half foot away, and nodded in acknowledgement. 'Luther, Luna – I wasn't aware you two knew each other.'

'Shared file,' was all Luther said.

Luna said nothing. Striker gave her a moment to respond, then continued on. 'I need to talk to you, Luther,' he said.

Before Luther could respond, the psychiatrist stepped forward, placing herself in-between the two men. She put her back to Striker, then looked up at Luther.

'Call me when you're done,' she ordered.

Then she turned back and faced Striker. There was little warmth in her expression and even less in her dark brown eyes. It was a moment of challenge, Striker knew. Of defiance.

And he did nothing to react to it.

When the woman pushed past him, she accidentally bumped her elbow into him and dropped her keys. Oblivious, she stormed off.

Striker bent over and picked them up. The keyring holder had a tab on it that said Lexus, owned a small flash drive, and had a laminated All-Star card for roadside emergencies. There were five keys on the ring.

Striker called out after her. 'Hey, Luna. You want these?'

She marched back down the hall, gave a curt nod, and took them from him.

'You're welcome,' Striker said.

Without so much as a word, Luna turned her eyes from Striker to Felicia. She looked her up and down, then left the office.

Felicia watched her go. When the psychiatrist exited the front door, Felicia let out a bemused laugh, then looked at Striker for a response.

He offered none. He just shook his head, gave her one of his *I'll tell you later* looks, and then introduced her to Luther Faust. Once the formalities were done, they got down to business.

'I wanted to catch you before you went out on the road,' Striker explained.

Luther nodded. 'And you caught me. So?'

'Let's just say it's been an extremely bad day for the police department, and for me personally. One of our officers was killed today.'

'Murdered,' Felicia clarified.

Striker nodded in agreement. 'She was a homicide detective, Luther, and I think you might know her – Jasmine Heer.'

The mention of the woman's name clearly stunned the social worker, and for the first time since they'd seen him, the look of irritation and annoyance washed off his face and was replaced by one of disbelief.

'I . . . I knew who Jazz was . . .' – he rubbed a hand over his face – 'Jesus Christ, I can't believe this.'

'Well, believe it,' Striker said. 'We've been on the file all day. It's why we're here.'

Luther blinked. 'Here? I don't see why—'

'Jazz came to see you.'

Luther took off his bowler hat. Held it in his hands. His fingers dug deep into the felt. 'Came to see me?' he repeated. 'Not that I recall.'

Felicia opened the file folder and read through the notes. 'Jazz documented the meeting right here in the report.'

Luther said nothing. He just moved closer and spied over the edge of the folder and gaped at the page. For a brief moment, he was quiet. Then he made an *ohh* sound and nodded. 'I remember. She *did* come by. But that was two weeks ago. I thought you meant more recently.'

'Sounds recent enough to me,' Striker said.

Luther met his stare. 'It's not like we had an appointment or anything – she just dropped by.'

Striker shrugged. 'I really don't care about the semantics, Luther. I just want to know what she wanted. I mean, why come to you?'

'It was for one of her files, *obviously*.' Luther spoke the word with disdain. Then he seemed to mellow. 'Some arson case, I think . . . She kept asking if I was dealing with any strange youths – ones who were pyros.'

'And were you?' Felicia asked.

Luther scowled. 'Well, what the hell do *you* think? Of course I was. I deal with them all the time. Every damn day. You know what it's like down here. These are Ministry kids. Wards of the court. They're damaged fucking goods.'

'We understand that,' Striker said.

'Then don't ask the question.'

Striker took in a deep breath. 'So some of the youths you deal with had been starting fires?'

Luther waved his hat through the air in an agitated manner. 'What about it? Next to cheap booze and park sex, fire's their best friend. I told Jazz the same thing.'

'Did you give her any names?' Felicia asked.

'A few.'

'I want that list,' Striker said.

'I'll email it to you later.'

Striker shook his head. 'I want it *now*, Luther.'

The social worker said nothing for a long moment, just stood there fiddling with his hat.

'Today is not the day to be difficult,' Striker warned.

Luther swore out loud. 'Busy goddam day,' he said, then returned to his office. Striker and Felicia watched him go, and then waited silently. He returned five minutes later with a piece of paper.

Striker took it from the man and read the list. Eleven names, none of which he recognized.

'Not a lot here, Luther.'

'It's all I got.'

'You sure?'

Luther just splayed his hands in a *what-you-want?* gesture.

Striker nodded. 'Think on it. Let me know if anything else comes to mind.'

'I will.'

The social worker went to leave, and Striker stopped him with a soft hand. When he spoke, his voice was filled with concern. 'Right now it looks like we got a homicidal pyromaniac out there. And Jazz might not have been his only target, Luther. For all we know, the nightmare we experienced at the bus yard might only be the beginning.'

'And you're telling me this because why?'

Striker was tired of the conversation. He gave Felicia the nod to leave and they started down the hallway. After a few steps, he looked back at the social worker with hard eyes.

'Consider yourself warned, Luther. We got a monster on our hands.'

Twenty-One

The apartment was exactly what Monster had expected – a run-down slum. Which made perfect sense since the building had been condemned almost three months ago.

The unit was not only dilapidated structurally, it was a plain mess. Old newspapers covered the floor. Dirty clothes were left randomly about. A sleeping bag was crumpled up beneath the cracked window on the other side of the room. And on the only table the place owned, there were piles and piles of empty fast food wrappers. The place reeked of neglect and germs and filth.

A disease just waiting to happen.

Monster's eyes fell over all of this as he stood in the doorway of the bathroom and looked down at the male who was passed out in the tub. The man was big. Tall. Fat. So wide that his sides touched both edges of the tub. So tall that his feet hung over the edge.

Monster had been waiting for him to wake up. For too long now.

It was beginning to seem useless. The man was really out of it. He didn't so much as flinch when Monster started singing, nor when Monster began filling the tub with kerosene.

Even now, the vapours made Monster feel more off-balance than normal. He wished Samuel was here in the apartment with him instead of being stuck in his cage in the van. He always felt bad about doing that. About not including him.

But this was just too dangerous.

Killing the thought, Monster removed a thin silver cross and gently laid it on the man's chest. He then picked up the nearest jerry can – one of the four he had brought with him – unscrewed the cap, and began singing once more.

'*Jesus loves me, this I know . . .*'

He upturned the can and the diesel fuel rained down upon the man, splashing all over his legs and arms and torso.

'*For the Bible tells me so . . .*'

He adjusted the can. Aimed the fuel over the man's head. Soaked his hair.

'*Little ones to Him belong . . .*'

He emptied the remainder of the fuel on the man's face, splashing it on his lips and around his nose.

'*They are weak but He is strong.*'

When the liquid became too much, the man's air supply was cut off. He jerked in the tub, spasmed, coughed. Hacked and hacked and hacked, like a newbie smoker. Like a man whose lungs wanted to escape his body.

And then his eyes blinked open.

'Waddaya . . . waddaya . . . *whereamI*?'

Monster dropped the jerry can. Sat down heavily on the toilet. Leaned forward and stared.

'You're drunk,' he said. 'Again.'

The man's heavy eyelids fluttered, and then his eyes slowly turned left. They stared at Monster. Focused.

Became aware.

He didn't smile or scowl or frown or show any kind of emotion. He just stared at Monster, as if he was trying to figure where he had seen him before.

'. . . the fuck are you?' he demanded.

Monster said nothing for a long moment. He just felt a pang of sadness that resonated somewhere deep inside.

'You don't even remember me, do you?'

'. . . the fuck should I?' The man winced and looked around lost, as if only now realizing he was in a bathtub. 'Whazzat . . . whazzat *smell*?'

Monster stood up from the toilet and stared down at the man, revealing his massive size. 'It is the smell of retribution. If you remembered me at all, you might understand.'

'Understand what? *Fuck you*. Get the fuck outta my place!'

Monster said nothing back. He just raised his hand. Pulled the trigger. And the flare burst forth.

The entire room flashed a blinding yellowish-white colour as the fire came to life. Burning, crackling, popping, hissing. *Roaring* like the true beast it was.

It almost drowned out the screams of the man in the tub.

Twenty-Two

When Striker and Felicia left the Ministry and returned to their vehicle, they climbed inside and slammed the doors shut. Felicia looked over at him, shook her head, and gave a humourless laugh.

'Well that was enjoyable,' she said. '*Not.*'

Striker started the car. 'I warned you. Luther's an odd guy. Guarded. Defensive. And anti-authority – unless of course it's his own. Guy always has been. We don't get along.'

'Gee. Really? I never would have got that.'

Striker gave her his *whatever* look. 'Luther doesn't share your love for me.'

'Yeah well, it didn't look like there was any love lost between you and that psychiatrist either. What was her name? Luna Asawa . . .'

'Asawa-Tan. And yeah, she hates me too.'

'You're a popular guy, Jacob. Dare I even ask why?'

Striker spotted his coffee cup in the holder. He picked it up, sipped the brew, and found it cold. 'I investigated Luna a while back. Had to ask some pretty hard questions. She took it personally.'

'Investigated her? For what?'

'Abuse of authority.'

Felicia put on her best sarcastic drawl. 'Please, Jacob, don't be so descriptive on the matter. You'll only confuse me.'

Striker just looked back at her, deadpan. 'She was accused of sleeping with her patients – most of whom were troubled teens.'

When Felicia made an interested sound, Striker waved a hand and continued:

'It was completely unfounded. The woman was innocent – I closed the file in the end – but she's always harboured a grudge against me ever since. As if I was personally after her or something. You'd think she'd know better, being a psychiatrist and all, but there you have it. She's nuts.'

'Thus the *Luna equals lunatic* comment.'

'Exactly.'

Felicia said nothing for a long moment, then asked, 'Do you think she was guilty?'

'I just told you, it was unfounded.'

'Unfounded doesn't mean innocent.'

Striker shook his head, put the car in gear, and pulled onto Hornby Street. 'I'll tell you something. That woman's got some serious issues. I'm the first to admit it. And investigation aside, I still didn't like her.'

'There's a "but" coming,' Felicia said.

'A big one. There wasn't one *shred* of evidence to suggest she was having a sexual relationship with any of her patients. Case closed, and happily so. It was a major pain in the ass – for her *and* me.' He scanned the road ahead. 'Look for a Starbucks.'

Felicia did, and found one. 'There. Just before Robson. West side.'

Striker accelerated down the block.

'Well, one thing's for sure,' Felicia said. 'Innocent or guilty, the look that woman gave you was *venomous*. She clearly hates you.'

'Add her to the pile.'

Felicia smiled at that.

They found the Starbucks, pulled over and grabbed a couple of coffees. Felicia also grabbed a slice of raspberry lemon loaf. Then they sat in the car and went over the list of troubled youths Luther had given them.

Youths who had pertinent histories with regards to arson-related calls.

Using PRIME – the Police Records & Information Management Environment database – as well as Corrections' Coronet system, they began checking each name for addresses, street checks, info files, Ministry appointments, and prison times. Within twenty minutes, they had ruled out half the names on the list simply by providing the kid with some form of alibi.

'Just four names left,' Striker said.

He was about to search the next one when his cell rang. He looked down at the LCD display, saw the name *Superintendent Laroche*, and gave Felicia a wry look.

'Speaking of brimstone and hellfire . . .'

He clicked talk and stuffed the phone to his ear.

'Striker,' he said.

Laroche's reply was curt. 'I need you down here in Strathcona,' he said. 'We have a second crime scene.'

Twenty-Three

The Boy With The Violet Eyes used what was left of the broken mirror to inspect himself. He studied the creamy white of his skin. The sharp angle of his jaw. The startling violet colour of his eyes. And all the while, he ignored the soft whimpering sounds of the older man behind him. James was his name.

Jimmy.

'Please,' the man moaned. 'Oh please . . .'

For a brief moment, The Boy With The Violet Eyes stopped studying himself in the mirror and cocked his head – it was as if he had heard an annoying sound. Like an insect buzzing round the room. Then, immediately forgetting the noise, he returned to his daily pattern of monitoring the small lines that were slowly developing under his eyes. The sight cut into him like a blade. Set a panic raging through his mind like wildfire.

From the bureau, he grabbed the syringe. In it was Nasparo – an anti-androgen mixture of hormone-blocking medications. This was yet one more of his daily rituals.

One that unfortunately left needle marks.

To hide the puncture scars, he injected between his toes – always between his toes – and he wished he could afford the proper Hepistad implants. They were the latest technology. The cat's ass, so to speak. Each one of those implants continuously released small secretions of hormone blockers into the blood-stream, ridding the need for needles. And the implant lasted for one entire year.

But implants were expensive. As were his ointments and tinctures and lotions and creams and dietary needs. The thought brought a sigh from his lips.

The realities of life could be so cruel.

'Please,' the man behind him groaned. 'Oh God, *please* . . .'

The Boy With The Violet Eyes heard the man's pleas, and again he ignored them. Instead, he went back to studying himself in the mirror. Nervously, he touched his soft cheeks. His thin upper lip. His delicate chin.

The skin was soft.

So *soft*.

Feeling this, a relief spilled through him, temporarily over-powering the deep underlying anxiety that was always lurking there, somewhere beneath the surface. He was always so worried about change. *Physical* change. Puberty.

He had done everything he could to suppress and delay it, to ward off the ugly side effects of Father Time. But eventually, nature would take its course. It always did. Hair would develop on his face. His jawline might even become square. And more and more wrinkles would inevitably appear.

It terrified him.

So far, all his daily regimens had worked well enough. He was tall no doubt – one hundred and ninety centimetres was tall for any grown man – but there was nothing he could do about that. Height just came. It was unstoppable.

An unsavoury product of his genes.

'Please . . . *Let me go*.'

The Boy With The Violet Eyes finally sighed but did not look back. When he spoke, his voice was soft and curt. Business-like.

'Stop your fucking whining. Might I remind you, you *wanted* this.'

'No . . . not . . . not this.'

Violet dropped the syringe on the bureau. Finally, he turned around in his chair and stared at the older man who was tied up behind him.

Jimmy was in his late fifties for sure. Balding on top; the dreaded horseshoe pattern. And the hair that was left on his head was a blend of greys and whites. A spider-web of light wrinkles owned his old face, and deeper lines were grooved into the front and back of his small ugly head.

The sight of it turned Violet's stomach.

'You *paid* for this,' he said, now getting angry.

'I'll pay more . . . *more* . . . please . . . just let me go.'

'I'm thinking no.'

Violet stood up from his chair and looked at the man. Jimmy was completely naked, his hands tied behind his back with thick bands of strong nylon. He was bent over the apparatus – the *inverter*, as Violet liked to call it – a chair he had personally designed for just such work.

The inverter left the customer in a prone position, head down near the ground and ass end up in the air.

Such a delight.

Positioned perfectly in front of Jimmy's face was a tall standing mirror, one Violet had placed in just the right position so that he could watch the abuse from behind. It always gave him great pleasure.

Even now, as Jimmy raised his head and looked fearfully back at him, gravity was working hard. Blood was pooling in the old man's head, making it look like an overripe tomato, and turning Jimmy's face as red as the welts on his ass.

It really was a thing of beauty.

The Boy With The Violet Eyes wrapped the silk shawl he wore around his shoulders and slowly crossed the room. On the ground next to Jimmy was a long wooden rod. The wood was bowed and bloodied now – just like the tattered flesh of Jimmy's ass.

Violet looked at this and nodded approvingly. He stood back in front of the older man, and snapped on a single latex glove that went all the way up past his elbow to the angle of his shoulder.

'These gloves are special order,' he said. 'You know what they use them for? Elephant insemination.'

The man let out a fearful sound. 'What . . . what are you—'

'Be silent,' Violet ordered.

He grabbed the KY jelly and squeezed it out of the tube, all over the latex glove, so that his fingers, hand, and entire forearm were slathered. Then he moved behind the man once more.

Jimmy gaped into the standing mirror with a sense of horror on his face. 'Stop,' he said. 'Please, God, stop!'

Violet looked back without emotion. 'Now Jimmy, this is what you wanted.'

'Not this—'

'And I never allow my customers to leave without getting what they paid for.' Violet leaned forward so the old man could see him better. 'So now this is what is going to happen: I am going to finish the service you requested, then I am going to untie you, and – when you can walk again – you are going to place the thousand-dollar payment on my dresser and you are going to leave.'

'Stop – I'm the customer. I *order* you to stop!'

'And then, provided you're strong enough, I'll see you next month.'

'No . . . *no* . . .'

Jimmy's upside-down face filled with tears that slid up his forehead.

The Boy With The Violet Eyes found the sight amusing. Smiling, he twirled his fingers around in the air, as if warming them up. He cracked each knuckle, then turned his stare into the mirror and focused on the older man's eyes.

'Why did you contact me?' he demanded. 'I mean, why me *specifically?*'

Jimmy opened his mouth to speak, but floundered, 'I—I—I . . .'

'It was because of my eyes, wasn't it? You liked my eyes.'

'I'll pay anything . . . please—'

But The Boy With The Violet Eyes wasn't listening. He made a fist, raised his arm, and placed the knuckles of his right hand tight up against the older man's anus.

'How do you like them now?' he asked.

'Please— No! *No!*'

'How do you like them now?'

Twenty-Four

The newest crime scene was at Paramount Place, a three-storey dump on Vernon Drive, a stone's throw from the Skids.

Striker knew the place well. During his time as a uniform cop in Patrol, he had investigated so many *Edged Weapon* and *Shots Fired* calls at the hotel that to remember any single one of them was now impossible – they all blended into one giant mass of shit.

A half block down from the site, sitting stationary in his white Crown Vic, was the Road Boss, Superintendent Laroche. As was the norm, he was busy on his cell and had a strict look on his perpetually tense face. A pair of marked patrol cars flanked his vehicle.

Striker and Felicia bypassed the cars and headed for the scene. One look and Striker spotted the pair of fire engines out front. He got Felicia's attention, then gestured towards them.

'Better still your heart. Mr July might be here.'

She just smiled. 'Don't worry, you can be November.'

Striker said nothing back; he just gave her a twisted look as he opened the front door of the hotel and stepped inside. The moment he did, all humour left him. Immediately, the stink of charred wood and old musty carpeting assailed his sense of smell, only to be overpowered by the stench of burnt meat and fat.

Another victim.

There was no doubt.

Leading up from the foyer were two sets of stairs – one to the east, and one to the west. The western stairwell was free of thick churning smoke, but a thin haze lingered atop the eastern stairs. There, several windows had been smashed open to allow for better ventilation.

Striker hoped it would also diminish the stench.

'I'm loading down,' a deep voice yelled from above.

It was coming from somewhere on the next floor. Soon there were more voices, followed by the drum of heavy footsteps. The manager, a man Striker knew as Shin Yee, came ambling down the stairs, his left leg slightly dragging.

Shin had managed the building for as long as Striker had been a cop. Hell, maybe longer. And his thick greying hair was a testament to that. With Shin came the rest of the fire crew – all of their expressions grim and disturbed.

A few nodded at Striker and Felicia, but most kept depressingly silent and just walked down the stairs and out the front door. The last guy, a tall red-headed brute, stopped in front of them. He jabbed a thumb up the stairs and muttered, 'Captain's in the suite.'

Striker nodded. He got the man's crew number, wrote it in his book, then told Shin he'd catch up to him later in the manager's office. He led Felicia upstairs towards the source of the fire.

The moment they reached the top of the stairs, the smoke and darkness thickened. When Striker reached out and flicked the hallway light switch, nothing happened.

'No power,' he said.

It reminded him of the bus depot offices.

The only light that existed was at the far end of the hall, east side. As they made their way towards it, Striker checked every room they passed. All were vacant, not only of people but of furniture too. Of anything.

Not even a single cot occupied any room.

Felicia noted this too. 'Place looks abandoned. No one is living here.'

'*Someone* was here,' he said, and continued down the hall without another word.

They reached the end of the corridor, where two uniformed patrol cops, half hidden by shadow, guarded the scene. Striker flashed them his badge and turned into the room, where a portable light source offered weak illumination.

There, Striker spotted a familiar face, one he had not seen for the better part of six months. Standing at medium height but weighing well over one hundred kilos was Fire Chief Brady Marshall. The man had gained weight since Striker had last seen him, and the rosy hue of his padded cheeks made his harsh blue eyes stick out beneath his bushy grey eyebrows, even in the dimness of the room.

'Hey Chief,' Striker said. His voice sounded oddly loud in the empty room.

Brady looked over, nodded.

'Shipwreck,' he said.

The fire chief was standing in the doorway to the bathroom. Striker approached and looked past the man into the room. He was shocked by what he saw. Visually unidentifiable, twisted up on the white enamel of the tub, were the remains of their latest victim.

The body appeared to be male, but the blackened tissue around the torso made certainty impossible. The feet stuck out over the edge of the tub, skin blackened, and the underlying tissues cooked white. The rest of the body was charred beyond detail, with the exception of the foamy areas that had been doused with fire retardant spray.

Striker closed his eyes for a moment. Struggled to keep his emotions in check. It may have been a new victim in the tub, but to him it was Jazz all over again.

He absently covered his mouth and nose to ward off the stink. It did nothing. Dark grey smoke still simmered off the body, as if there were hidden pockets still burning somewhere deep beneath the skin. The smell of burned fat and diesel gas was still incredibly strong.

'Oh Jesus,' Felicia said behind him. She covered her mouth, and for a moment, looked like she would be ill.

Striker scrutinized the scene, looking for any other signs that might hint of a ritualistic killing. He found no leftover crosses, no vague impressions of pentagrams. But there was the fire trap – two crime scenes with each victim murdered in a nearly identical and horrific manner.

In some ways the scenes matched, in other ways they were conflicting.

Striker moved further into the room. He listened to the floorboards squeak beneath his weight as he studied the scene. Trailing down the outer edges of the tub were streak lines where fuel had spilled. And here and there on the floor were odd blackened patches where the fire had eaten away parts of the linoleum.

'We're lucky the whole place didn't go up,' Striker said. He turned to Brady. 'Good work.'

The fire chief just shrugged. 'Fire was out by the time we got here.'

'It burned itself out?'

'Manager got to it.'

'Shin,' Striker said, and nodded. 'You guys evacuate the place?'

Brady shook his head again. 'No one here to evacuate. Manager says this half of the building was supposed to be empty – problem with the floor structure or something. Our victim here must have been a squatter of some kind. Poor kid.'

'Any idea who he is?'

Brady shook his head for the third time. 'Nothing left behind. No ID. No papers. No wallet. No nothing.'

Striker nodded slowly. While Felicia checked the main room

for evidence, Striker took out his flashlight and squatted down low. He scanned the bathroom floor, looking around the toilet, sink, and under the tub. Aside from the numerous burn marks, there were no other discernible markings to be seen.

In the corner, next to the toilet, a small garbage can had been spilled. Next to it were a few cigarette butts and some empty potato chip bags. *Dill Pickle*. But there was very little else.

Striker gloved up and looked within the tub. It was old, and had missing enamel chips around the faucet, where patches of rust showed through. The bottom of the tub was filled with bits of ash, and there were places where the white enamel had been burned black.

Unfortunately, Striker could find nothing of evidentiary value. The fire had devoured everything in its path.

He placed his gloved hand under the victim's arm. The tissue was still hot. With a slow gentle movement, Striker lifted the body to look beneath it. With much of the tissue burned away, the body was surprisingly light. It lifted slightly, and angled, but again Striker could see nothing but a single grey streak of tub enamel in between the blacker patches.

'Anything?' Felicia asked from the doorway.

Striker turned away from the corpse, the stench playing havoc with his stomach. He stripped off the gloves and took a deep gasp for air, then met Felicia's stare and shook his head.

'No. What about you?'

She shrugged. 'Sleeping bag in there. No pillow. Pair of dirty socks and some cigarette butts. No wallet or ID though. And not much good for fingerprinting.'

Striker said nothing. Scowling, he left the confines of the small washroom and gave Felicia a half-hearted nod to follow.

'Video?' she asked.

'Yeah . . . Right now, it's about the only hope we got.'

Twenty-Five

Like most hotels in the Downtown Eastside, the manager's office desk was located behind a thick row of ground-to-ceiling safety glass. Striker doubted it was bulletproof, but it gave the impression of it. Very little was in the office – a prefab desk, a shelf divider containing the cardboard room cards, and a small coffee machine, which was so clean in appearance, so pristine *white*, that it seemed out of place in the dingy hotel.

Brew was percolating now.

Smelling it, Striker rapped on the window glass to get Shin's attention and the manager climbed off of his stool. He was a small man, thin and wiry. He had an oval face and a gentle demeanour that seemed incongruous with his surroundings.

Shin moved slowly across the office, his back leg dragging with each step – a leftover remnant from an old bullet wound he'd suffered from a botched robbery twelve years ago. The awkward gait made the crucifix he wore around his neck swing and bob with every step until it reached his shoulder and he had to pull it straight again.

Shin opened the door and smiled at Striker and Felicia. 'Detectives. Come in, come in. I put on coffee.'

'Thanks, Shin. That's nice of you.' Striker stepped sideways into the office and Felicia followed. He introduced Felicia to

Shin, then got right down to business. 'We need to see your video security.'

'I was just getting it set up.' The old man lumbered back to his chair and crashed down heavily, as if all the walking up and down the stairs had drained him. Even the action of sitting down clearly pained him, and Striker could see that age was gaining on the man.

On the desk sat a small black-and-white monitor, square not widescreen. The ongoing feed showed four separate boxes, one for each corresponding camera.

Striker was grateful to see a system, even if the digital feed was of poor quality. Video surveillance systems weren't cheap, and because of that many of the hotels and rooming houses in the Downtown Eastside simply put up fake cameras and fake stickers – a technique that might have deterred the dumber criminals but was in no way helpful to the police officers who were eventually called to deal with the aftermaths.

'Where are these cameras?' Felicia asked.

Shin pointed to the different screen sections and spoke with no accent. 'Right-side feeds are for the western building, left-side feeds are for the eastern building.'

Striker noted this. 'Speaking of the building, why is the east side vacated?'

Shin let out a frustrated sound. 'City condemned it. Structural problem, they say. All I know is that it forced out over twenty-five of my residents – people who had no place to go.' He shook his head. 'I know this place isn't the Taj Mahal or anything, but it sure as heck beats freezing to death. One of the women – Caroline from 3B – is tenting it in the park right now. I just hope she doesn't die from exposure.'

Striker nodded, knowing the grimness of the situation and understanding Shin's frustration. Homelessness was an issue in the city of Vancouver and had been for as long as he'd been on the job. It was even more critical during the winter months, when temperatures dropped below zero.

'The poor souls,' Shin continued. 'I found some of them rooms at the Gospel on Cordova, and some at the First United. But not all.'

Felicia asked, 'Is the eastern section shut down for good?'

Shin just shrugged as if he didn't know. 'Only reason the *whole* building wasn't shut down was paperwork – because of the dividing wall and separate business addresses, the building is technically classified as two separate entities. Though the City still might be coming for the west side too. Who knows. Everything's been a nightmare with this new mayor.'

Striker said nothing; he just looked at the black-and-white feeds. 'So these two shots here,' – he pointed – 'they're of the front and back of the hotel?'

Shin nodded.

When Striker analysed the two rear feeds, he noticed that the angle of the camera on the east side of the building was far different than the west – it was pointed on a downward slant, severely so, and showing more sidewalk than lane.

'Something happen here?' he asked.

Shin looked closer at the feed with a scowl on his face, as if he was only seeing this for the first time.

'It wasn't like that this morning,' he said.

Striker read the video timeline. By his own watch, the machine was five minutes delayed, so he made a note of that in his log book. He gave Shin a tap on the shoulder. 'Scroll back till we find something worth watching. Ten times speed.'

Shin did. And it didn't take long to spot what they were looking for. The timeline had been barely scanned back an hour when there was movement on the lower left portion of the monitor. On feed three.

The eastern building. Rear side.

Felicia let out an excited sound. 'There – stop – right *there.*'

Striker saw it too, but what he saw puzzled him. The first movement he saw was that of a smaller figure. Someone moving slowly. Shuffling, more than anything. Because of the awkward camera angle, the feed only caught from the shoulders down, and the graininess of the video made identification impossible.

'Could be our victim,' Striker said.

Felicia turned to Shin. 'Should anyone be using those exit doors?'

Shin shook his head. 'Like I said, entire eastern building's been condemned. No one should be in there.'

Striker and Felicia shared a look, then Shin slowly scrolled back through the timeline some more, though this time at normal speed. Less than a minute later, they discovered more movement.

Striker cursed. 'Keep going. The suspect has to enter the building at some point.'

Shin did. Still at ten times speed.

Within another five minutes they caught sight of the man they were looking for, and a cold stirring sensation flooded Striker's chest. This person on screen was the same man who'd been back at the bus depot – a freaking *goliath*. Tall and thick. A barrel chest. A wide sweeping back.

'Jesus,' Felicia said. 'He's a monster.'

Striker said nothing, he was too busy trying to analyse the video. He watched the figure approach the rear entrance. Over his head, the man wore a dark hoodie that shadowed his face. In each of his hands were two large gas canisters.

Striker pointed to the screen. 'Those look like twenty-five-litre containers.'

Felicia shrugged. 'So?'

'Ever lift one? They must weigh twenty-five kilos each, and yet he's carrying them like they're milk jugs. Two in each hand. This guy's a tank.'

Felicia looked back at the screen. The man on the feed put down the gas canisters, then reached up and grabbed the camera. Immediately, the viewing angle changed. Turned downward. The feed lost sight of the man's face, and instead panned down his body.

As it did so, Felicia caught sight of something.

'Stop it right there, Shin,' she said. When the manager paused the feed, she pointed to the area around the front of his belt. Something was sticking out. Felicia looked to Striker for confirmation. 'Is that the butt end of a gun?'

Striker leaned closer. Nodded. 'Looks like a pistol of some kind.'

'It *is* a gun,' a voice behind them said.

Striker and Felicia both turned around in unison and spotted a woman in the doorway. She had a unique look to her – high prominent cheekbones, doe eyes that were so dark they looked almost black, and puffy lips that might have seemed cosmetically injected to some. Her long brown hair fell around her shoulders in a bob – a remnant style from decades past. Striker would have classified her as hard-looking but pretty.

Very Eastern European.

'It's a *flare* gun,' the woman clarified. 'It's how he's been igniting the fuel.'

Striker nodded. 'I take it you're the fire investigator.'

'Yes,' she said. 'Katarina Kesla. I hear you've been looking for me.'

Twenty-Six

Thirty minutes later, Striker stood back in the target suite, again within the small confines of the washroom. Felicia was still in the manager's office, in the process of obtaining a witness statement from Shin Yee. Then she would be performing a witness canvass in the west building to see if anyone had evidence to give.

Striker hoped she'd come up with something, but had little faith in the matter. Shin Yee may have been a good manager and an even better citizen, but this was the Downtown Eastside. And people here never saw shit.

Striker expected no less from Shin Yee's tenants.

He kept silent as he watched Katarina Kesla investigate. She first sketched out a small diagram of the area, then took a few dozen photographs of the exhibits. Once done, she did as Striker had already done, and proceeded to scan the floor for any trace amounts of evidence.

She was slow, careful, methodical – a good investigator. Striker was watching her to assess her capabilities and approach, and he was pleased with what he saw.

After a long moment, the fire investigator turned her attentions to the body. She took a few more photographs, then scrutinized the victim slowly, beginning with the head and finishing with the feet. When she was done poking and prodding, she stood back. Snapped off her latex gloves. Sighed onerously.

'Well?' Striker asked.

She met his stare with eyes that gave away nothing, and when she spoke, there was a soft accent to her words.

Polish? Austrian?

He could not define it.

'There doesn't appear to be any blunt trauma,' she said. 'At this point it appears as if the fire was the cause of death. Of course, a full post-mortem will have to be done by the ME.'

'That's Kirstin Dunsmuir,' Striker said.

'I know the woman,' she replied, and there was a note of discord in her tone. She looked around the room for a long moment, as if taking a final scan, and then shook her head slowly.

'Incendiaries were used,' she continued. 'Obviously. Diesel for sure, but mixed with something else. Perhaps white gas or even kerosene. Maybe others, I'm not sure yet.'

'It was the same back at the bus depot,' Striker offered. 'You could smell it in the air. A fuel of some kind.'

Kesla manoeuvred to the other side of the tub, being careful not to disturb any evidence. Once there, she used a small crowbar to pry up one of the loose floorboards. She gestured to the area beneath the plank where there was a series of straight burn marks that were positioned every ten centimetres or so.

'There's your evidence right there,' she said. 'Rundown pattern. *Fuel.*'

She grabbed her Nikon and snapped a few shots of the pattern, then dropped the plank back in place. As she did so, some of the leftover foam from the fire retardant spray splattered into the air, and Striker took a step back from it, covering his mouth. The fuel, the chemical retardants, the filth – everything was a health risk.

Kesla spoke unemotionally. 'A trapped victim. A pool of gas. Both ignited by some kind of heat source that would allow the suspect to remain at a safe distance. As I said earlier, I'm thinking a flare gun.'

Striker looked at the position of the victim in the tub. He saw no leftover evidence to suggest bindings.

'Would he not have been able to leap out?'

'You would think,' Kesla replied. 'Pain or not, it's an automatic reaction. Obviously, if he was set on fire, holding him down would not be possible, so why would he have stayed in the tub?'

'Intoxication,' Striker wondered aloud.

'Or drugs,' she replied. 'Anything is possible.'

Striker turned his mind away from the body and the scene before them. He faced the fire investigator. 'Jazz came to you,' he said.

Kesla nodded and her eyes took on a faraway look. 'She thought some of the arsons around the area might have been set by a Satanist,' she explained.

'A *Satanist*?'

'Because of the number of churches and other religious affiliations involved.'

'What *exactly* did Jazz ask of you?'

Kesla dragged her forearm across her brow to wipe away the perspiration. 'She had a list of pyromaniacs – youths she was looking into.'

'The same list she got from Luther Faust?'

Kesla shook her head. 'I wouldn't know.'

'Do you still have that list?'

Kesla nodded. 'In my briefcase.'

She exited the washroom without a word and walked into the hall. Striker followed. There, she bent down and opened her briefcase. From it she withdrew a folder, and from that, the paper list.

She handed it to Striker.

He gave it a quick read over and saw that it was the exact same list as the one Luther had given him. But when he looked in the left column of the page, where the times and dates were recorded, something was wrong.

He looked back at Kesla. 'When did Jazz give you this?'

'Oh, over a month ago now.'

'You sure about that? About the time?'

She thought back and nodded. 'Yes, completely. The date is right there. November 7th. I know it's correct because she gave it to me the day before I left on my annual – for Maui. And that was on the 8th.'

Striker said nothing back. He just wrote down the date in his notebook, underlined it several times, and then snapped the book shut.

'Does it help at all?' Kesla asked.

Striker nodded at her.

'More than you could know,' he said.

He turned to leave the room and regroup with Felicia. He got less than halfway down the hall when Kesla called out to him. Curious, he U-balled and headed back. When he re-entered the washroom, he found the FI bent over the tub, closely examining the convex area of the victim's chest.

Possibly over the sternum.

There, buried deep within the blackened tissue, was something globular and hard. When Kesla used a soft brush to clear away the flaking debris, the colour of the item showed through.

Dirty silver.

'Might have been jewellery,' Kesla said. 'Melted by the heat, then trapped in bone. But what kind of jewellery it was, I have no idea.'

Striker closed his eyes and let out a deep breath. For him the investigation had just become darker.

'It was a cross,' he said softly. '. . . It was a silver cross.'

Twenty-Seven

The driveway leading into the cellar was long and steep and icy.

Monster backed the white van in until it was flush with the building. Once he had both the cellar and van doors open, he began loading up the plastic jerry cans. They were all pre-filled with his special blend of fuel, and all the same in appearance.

These jerry cans were the most suitable ones he could find for the job. Suitable because of three simple reasons: they were a fairly standard make that could be found at any local hardware store; they each held thirty litres of fuel; and they each had a handle that was deep enough to allow his thickened blockish fingers to fit through the opening.

There was always so much to consider.

Monster continued loading until he was hit by an odd sensation. A memory? A feeling?

He was not sure.

Feeling suppressed by the darkness of the cellar, he turned slowly and gaped at his surroundings. A lost expression found his face, like a blank screen on a crashed computer.

The memories were colliding.

He rarely came down here. To the cellar. Almost never, in fact. Too many horrific times gone by. Too much pain and anguish. And the coldness of that thought owned him every bit as much as the damp darkness owned the corners of the room. Everywhere he looked, there was a constant reminder of the bad things that had happened. Here in the cellar. In the boiler room.

Just the thought of it caused his heart to race, and suddenly it was difficult to swallow. A few drops of sweat rolled down his brow, reached the outer edge of his mask, and ran around the rim. Exhausted not by the physical work but by the memories, Monster moved through the garage doors and sat down heavily on the bumper of the van.

He peeled off his second face. The cold air did not feel good. But he needed the release from suffocation.

Still seated, he reached down and grabbed one of the gas canisters from the floor. He threw it into the van like it weighed nothing. As if it was empty and not filled to the rim with fuel. It knocked something over inside the van and made a metallic clang.

Monster grimaced at the sound.

His head was bad today.

Real bad.

And it was getting more difficult to stay focused on the tasks at hand. Regretfully, almost unwillingly, he pulled the small pill bottle from his shirt pocket and thumbed out the last of his medication. The pills were small. Oval. Pale blue in colour. And he found it amazing how such a tiny thing could have such an enormous impact on his life.

Then again, *she* had done the same. And she was small.

So maybe it wasn't so surprising after all.

He popped the pill into his mouth and swallowed it dry. Then he sat there and waited for the medication to take effect. He hated it, the Priazoral. It was supposed to help with his symptoms – give him the focus, the impulse control, the mood stabilization.

And to some degree, it did. But it also gave him a wicked case of restless legs at night and made sleeping even more of a battle than it already was.

He sang softly:

'Little ones to Him belong.'

And suddenly, Samuel was there. The little squirrel sprang up onto the van bumper, then onto Monster's leg, and finally up to his shoulder. A sense of lightness filled Monster, and he smiled at the little creature. Samuel was one of the few things in this world that could make the darkness go away and mute the pain of this world that always screamed in his head like an angry beast.

'Sam-u-el.'

Monster reached into his shirt pocket and pulled out the collection of crosses. They were silver, on thin silver chains. Now there were only six of them left, whereas once there had been eight. Eight crosses for nine deaths. He was one short on purpose, because one of the bad people did not deserve a cross.

That person would forever be *The Unforgiven*.

Samuel pawed at the dangling silver crosses, like he always did, and this amused Monster greatly. After a long moment, he put the crosses away and instead pulled out the last of the Corn Nuts. He held them out and the little squirrel took the treats, nibbled them for a bit, then bounded away into the darkness.

As Samuel vanished, so did the smile on Monster's deformed face.

He stood up and threw the last container of gas into the van and slammed the doors. The fuel was needed. For the next sinner on the list.

The man he called *The Deliverer*.

This man would not be as easy as the last. For The Deliverer was strong. Capable. Smart.

There could be no mistakes with this one.

Monster took out a pen. On the back of his hand he wrote *Corn Nuts.* Then he slammed the van doors closed and set off for Langara Street – the place where he would finally punish The Deliverer.

The transmission clanked loudly as Monster backed up the cellar driveway, and the engine let out a rumbling growl as he stepped down on the gas pedal and drove through the fir- and hemlock-covered path, moving farther and farther away from that horrible, haunted place that he now called home.

'. . . *They are weak but He is strong.*'

Twenty-Eight

The police building located at 312 Main was less than a mile from the crime scene at Paramount Place. Striker and Felicia wanted somewhere to go over things in private, have a good cup of strong coffee, and – more than all of that – shower and change their clothes. The smell of the burned body had been a bad one. It had invaded everything from their clothes to their skin and hair.

So they headed for headquarters.

Along the way, Striker informed Felicia of his suspicions regarding the last homicide, of what Kesla had found melted into the burned tissue and calcified bone of the victim's body – the possible melted remains of a silver cross.

Possible, but not for certain.

'A comparison of samples will need to be done,' she said.

Striker nodded. 'Already requested.'

But like all forensics, analysis took time. With any luck, three days.

Following the discussion, they drove on in silence. The cross detail was one that excited them both – and yet the implications it brought with it darkened the mood of the car. When they reached HQ, both of them couldn't wait to get out of the vehicle and back inside the unit.

They took the stairs up.

In the men's locker room, Striker took a long shower, extra hot, then returned to his desk. After attending the last two crime scenes, feeling clean was impossible, but at least he no longer felt contaminated.

It was an unsettling thought. Dead body calls were always bad with regards to the stink, but a regular sudden death was nothing compared to what they'd seen today. The stench. The residue. The traces of ash in the air. Both scenes had been viscerally overpowering.

Striker tried not to think about it.

Instead, he looked down the hall. Felicia was still showering and would be for some time. No matter how much time he required, she always needed more. Even at home, her morning process took her damn near an hour.

Today, she got a pass on it.

He used the time to catch up on some of the miscellaneous details of the file – ones that were still nagging at him like a whispering voice in the back of his mind.

He contacted Ident technician, Jim Banner – better known around the Vancouver Police Department as *Noodles*, ever since he'd almost choked to death on a creamy linguine at the Noodle Shack. Striker asked the man whether he'd found anything pertinent at the bus depot or at Paramount Place.

The answer was a quick, 'Still processing.'

Striker frowned. 'How much longer?'

'Depends on how much more of my time you waste keeping me on the phone.'

Striker sighed. 'Just keep me informed, Noodles.'

He hung up and called the patrol sergeant in charge of the bus depot crime scene to see if anything else had arisen. Soon, he got the same answer from her. The search and canvass team had found no critical evidence.

Nor had Kirstin Dunsmuir, the medical examiner, when he called her regarding the autopsies.

And nor had their newfound colleague, Fire Investigator Katarina Kesla.

Everything was one big negative.

Frustrated, Striker let his associates do their work and instead focused his attention elsewhere. He tried to call up Jazz's last sergeant. The woman's name was Melinda Belle, and she was an Inspector for IHIT – the Integrated Homicide Investigation Team. That team was run by the Feds, the Royal Canadian Mounted Police, and so it took Striker some directory searching to find the right local.

'Inspector Belle,' the woman said, her voice so gruff she sounded like a man on the line.

Striker spent twenty minutes questioning her and getting nowhere. By the time he hung up it was five o'clock and felt even later. He considered getting up to make a pot of coffee – it was gonna be a late night again; he could feel it – but then Felicia appeared in the entrance to Major Crimes.

She strode confidently down the walkway towards their desks. She was wearing a new cut of dress suit – charcoal in colour, with an underlying cream dress shirt that was unbuttoned at the top, revealing the soft flesh of her throat. Because her hair was still damp, it looked darker than usual, and that in turn made her eyes appear even deeper. Almost *black*.

It was alluring.

Striker watched her come. Whether it was from what they'd been through today or just his mood in general, he wasn't sure, but Felicia looked beautiful. He always thought so. Was always aware of it. But sometimes, at times like these, it would hit him for no real reason.

And he would catch himself just watching her.

She saw his look and smiled back at him.

'What?' she asked.

'Nothing,' he said.

And suddenly he felt tired. He rubbed his hands over his face, felt his brain thud, and squinted against the fluorescent lights.

Felicia touched his shoulder. 'Another headache?'

'It's okay.'

She leaned closer, where no one in the office could hear, and smiled. 'I'll give you a massage tonight . . . and maybe something else. Depends how much of a good boy you are.'

'I wish we could go home now.'

She straightened up and smiled. 'Much to do, I'm afraid.'

Striker heard her words and nodded. She couldn't have been more right. And so he got back down to business. He told her of all the people he'd called, including Jazz's Federal boss, and how they were still no closer to any real discovery than they had been before he had started making the calls.

'However—' he pulled out his notebook and flipped to the last page. 'Listen to this: after talking to the fire investigator, I found something . . . *interesting*. The dates don't match.'

'What dates?'

'The dates on the list Luther gave us.' He tried to explain. 'When Jazz went to speak to Luther, she wasn't there talking generalities like he insinuated. Not only did she not go to him for a list, but in fact, she *already had* a list of kids in mind.'

'And you know this how?' Felicia asked.

'From Kesla. Jazz had already shown her the list. But Luther made it sound like Jazz had come *to him* for those names. And it's simply not true. *She* gave Luther the list, not the other way around.'

Felicia brushed some of the drying strands of hair out of her eyes and nodded. 'But why? Why would Luther lie about something as trivial as that? It's not like he would get anything by taking credit for the list of names.'

'First off, it makes me think it's *not* trivial. And secondly, it makes me wonder if the reason he lied has nothing to do with the list – maybe that was just misdirection.'

Felicia sat down beside him and thought this over. 'In what way?' she finally said.

Striker turned to face her better. 'I think Jazz went to him for something else – something he doesn't want us to know about.'

For a moment, Felicia said nothing. She just crossed one leg over the other and rocked slowly in the chair – a habit she often did when thinking things through. After a brief moment, she shook her head.

'The problem here is we're just guessing,' she said. 'For all we know, Jazz might have gone to Luther to get addresses – you know how those Ministry kids move around nonstop. Especially if they're wards of the court. Maybe Jazz was just amassing as much of their personal histories as she could. And who other than Luther would know all that?'

Striker allowed that. 'Fine. Then why not just tell us that in the first place?'

Felicia had no response for that.

'And why, for that matter, lead us to believe it was something else?' Striker continued. 'It's not the lie that concerns me, Feleesh, it's the reason behind it.'

It took Felicia a moment but she finally nodded her agreement. 'Looks like we got some digging to do.'

Striker couldn't have agreed more.

They got to work and began separating the different forms they'd acquired from the last two crime scenes – witness statements from neighbours, evidence log sheets Patrol had taken, reference statements from property owners, canvass lists from the search teams, and all the rest of the miscellaneous forms. When Felicia handed Striker the written statement she'd obtained from the manager at Paramount Place, Striker gave it a quick peruse, then stopped a third of the way down.

He looked over at her.

'The fire was already out?' he asked.

Felicia stopped rifling through her papers and turned to look at him. 'What?'

'The fire was already out?' He scanned the page again. 'It says here that Shin smelled smoke and called 911. Then he went upstairs and found that the fire was already out.'

She nodded. 'That's right.'

'Then who put it out?'

'Well, the Fire Department, I assumed.'

Striker shook his head. 'Brady says no. Says it was already out when they got there. And according to Kesla, that blaze would never have gone out on its own. So someone else had to put it out for them. Maybe a potential witness.'

Felicia grabbed her cell.

'We'll get Patrol to re-canvass,' she said.

Striker nodded. He thought about it for a long moment, then got up. He crossed the office towards the coffee station, then stopped two-thirds of the way there when he saw Jazz's desk.

The phone's red light was flashing.

A message.

Striker grabbed the receiver and hit the voicemail button. There was only one message on the machine. From a guy named Moses. And he found the message odd and intriguing at the same time:

I don't know who told you I was an expert on this kind of thing, but it's a lie, Detective. I'm not – and I sure as hell don't appreciate people going around spreading rumours like that about me. It can be very damaging. Now please, no more phone calls . . . I can't help you.

The message ended with the hard click of a phone being slammed.

Striker read the last incoming number on the call display. He then blocked his cell phone and dialled the number.

'You've reached the Recovery House,' a woman said. 'How can I help you?'

'I'm sorry,' he said. 'I must have the wrong number.'

He hung up the cell, then wrote *Recovery House?* in his notebook, followed by the name, phone number, and time the call had come in. He then returned to his desk.

Felicia had just finished organizing all the paperwork they'd acquired, and she gave him a fake sad look. 'What, no coffee?'

'Just get your coat,' he told her. 'We're gonna go check out a guy named Moses.'

Felicia stood up and smirked. 'Think he'll part the Red Sea for us?'

'Probably not,' Striker said with a wink. 'But at this point I'd be happy if he even helped us make some waves.'

Twenty-Nine

The Boy With The Violet Eyes perched on the stool like a bird, with his shawl wrapped lightly around his bare shoulders. On the ground, crumpled and bloodied, was the elephant insemination glove he had been wearing. He stared at it emotionlessly now as he nibbled on celery and slowly sipped a herbal tea made from Black Cohosh, Chasteberry, and Saw Palmetta. The flavour was terribly bitter. Foul really. But it was yet another necessary regimen of his day.

Black Cohosh, Chasteberry, and Saw Palmetta suppressed testosterone.

In behind him, Jimmy moaned softly. The Boy With The Violet Eyes was happy to hear this – a moan was so much better than that godawful whimpering he'd been spouting for over a half hour.

Please, I'm bleeding.

Please, there's so much blood.

Something's ruptured.

God, it was so utterly and completely classless. Really, was the man without shame? What was the world coming to?

'You know,' The Boy With The Violet Eyes said. 'Celery is a *negative* food.'

In behind him, the man said nothing.

'It's true. I promise you that. It's one of only a few foods that actually costs your body more calories to digest it than it takes in. Zucchini and carrots are negative foods too, but I'm all out of them.'

'. . . *Please* . . .'

The Boy With The Violet Eyes took another bite of celery. Crunch, crunch, crunch. 'Some people say that oranges are also a negative food, but that can be misleading. Oranges contain high levels of sugar – and sugar causes a build-up of inflammatory processes and, therefore, unnecessary ageing.'

'Pl— Pl— Please . . . I could die.'

The Boy With The Violet Eyes let out a cruel laugh and clapped his hands together as he sang out: '*Melodrama* – I call *Melodrama!*'

The humour that spilled through him was dark and cruel. When he finally turned his eyes back to the man who was bloodied and hogtied upside-down in the chair, when he saw the oldness of the man's face, that anger overflowed. Hatred spouted out of every pore he had, erupted like a bottle of Diet Coke when a Mentos mint is added.

The Boy With The Violet Eyes wished he could just kill the man. Just pick up that wooden rod and bash and bash away until nothing remained of his wrinkled old scalp and his disgustingly old flabby body.

But he could not, of course. There were rules after all. Ones he had to abide by. Because you never knew . . .

That day might still yet come.

The phone rang. Not the elegant tones of his cell phone – not 'Bohemian Rhapsody'. No, this was just the plain, ordinary ring-ring-ring of the landline. So it was not a customer.

Cautiously, he grasped the receiver. He put the phone to his ear and heard a sweet, succulent, wonderful voice. The most beautiful voice in the world. The most beautiful voice that had ever existed. It was heavenly.

'I may have need of you, Violet.'

'I will do whatever I can,' he replied. '*Whatever I can!*'

His voice broke as he spoke, and he cupped his hand over his mouth. He shuddered with nervousness. This was the call – the one he had been dreaming of for so long. For *years*. Waiting, hoping, praying that it might come.

It was a reprieve. A chance at salvation.

At *bliss*.

The Boy With The Violet Eyes felt so good that he laughed out loud and cried and clapped his hands in joy. His emotions were overflowing – jubilation, transcendence, joy. Even the unusual light of benevolence was there, just peeking through the cracks of his pain. It gave him hope that something more was still possible.

And so he untied the old man.

'Go home, Jimmy,' he said. 'God has smiled on you this day.'

Thirty

Felicia googled the Recovery House's phone number the moment they got in the car. As it turned out, the place was a treatment facility for numerous problems – alcohol and drugs primarily – but there were also sub-groups that dealt with everything from sexual abuse to homelessness.

It was a multi-assistance centre.

As they drove, Striker filled Felicia in on the odd phone call Jazz had received from a guy named Moses.

It piqued her interest.

The facility was located, surprisingly, in the expensive area of Oakridge. When they circumnavigated around Langara Station for the Millennium Line branch of the subway system, and pulled up the listed address for the centre, Striker thought they must have made a mistake.

'This can't be it,' he said.

They were parked in the residential area, directly behind the Langara Station, and the building they were staring at was not a medical building but a regular house – three levels, with tinted windows, solid-looking doors, and a camera and intercom system in the front alcove.

The place looked like an enormous quadplex.

'I thought this place was a *facility*,' he said.

Felicia nodded. 'This is the right address.'

'But it's a *house*.'

She shrugged. 'More and more charities and non-profits are doing this nowadays. With all the budget deficits and red ink, getting government to spring for a new facility is all but impossible. Lots of these buildings are actually *donated* by private citizens – it's a hundred times cheaper to remodel the inside than to build new.'

Striker just nodded and took her word as true. A few years back, Felicia had been seconded to assist on one of the Department's social projects: *Mental Illness, Addiction, and How It Relates to Modern Day Policing*. The paper had won numerous awards, and was the résumé credit that spring-boarded her into Homicide at such a young age.

'Well, let's get to it,' he said.

They walked across the road. Striker was about to knock on the front door when it opened and a tired-looking woman barged through. Her eyes were red and underlined heavily from lack of sleep.

'Outta my way!' she snapped.

From inside the house, someone yelled out, 'Savanna! Savanna – you're not supposed to be here if you're drinking. You know the conditions!'

'Lemme alone,' the woman screamed back. She stormed down the walkway.

Striker watched her go, then stepped through the front door.

Inside, the house no longer looked like a house, but a treatment facility. A small waiting area sat to the immediate right. A staff kitchen area lay just ahead. And the staircase had a large black sign:

The Only Place Where Recovery Comes Before Trust Is In The Dictionary.

Striker read the sign and smiled.

A short, red-haired woman, mid-thirties and more plump than a Christmas pudding, sat at a receptionist desk to their left. She listened to Felicia's story, then guided them down the main hallway to an office just around the bend.

Inside the office stood a man Striker had never seen before. He was a black man, with exceptionally dark skin. He was slightly shorter than average height, with hard eyes and a receding hairline. Despite the fact he was probably in his mid- to late fifties, he looked like a bad choice for an enemy. His shoulders and arms easily foretold his years of weight training experience, and the scars that trailed down the side of his face hinted that he'd suffered some violent times in his past and had prevailed.

'Moses?' Striker asked.

The man looked up from the folder he was flipping through and eyed them. His stare was neither fiendish nor friendly. He just nodded.

Striker flashed the badge.

'VPD,' he said, and then introduced himself and Felicia. 'We're here because—'

'I know why you're here,' Moses said. The look on his face hardened as he snapped closed the folder. He nodded to the red-headed woman who was still standing in the doorway.

'That will be all, Ginny.'

'Yes, Mr Sabba.'

The moment she left, Moses walked over and closed the door, blocking off the outside world. For a moment, he stood with his back to them, silently, and still. Then he turned around and spoke in a low tone. 'You're here for the same reason Jazz came here – do you share the same file?'

Striker said nothing for a moment. He just studied the man, then nodded. 'Something like that.'

Felicia stepped forward. 'Why was Jazz trying to contact you, Mr . . . ?'

'Sabba,' he replied. 'Moses Sabba.' He looked at both of them. 'Detective Heer wanted my opinion on some particular matters.'

'What kind of matters?' Striker asked.

He paused. 'Religious beliefs.'

'What *kind* of religious stuff?'

'Non-traditional.'

Striker felt the irritation growing. 'Look, you can cut the dog and pony show here, we don't have the time. This is an important matter.'

'*Everything's* important, Detective.' Moses gestured to a stack of files on his desk. 'Aside from being the case manager of eighty-three patients here, I'm also the programme manager. And I've had a million people calling me today with problems of their own.' He gestured to the paper pad of names on his desk. 'Every one of these people is one injection or one depressive episode away from an early grave, and I can't find a damn room for them. So as important as your time is, Detectives, so is mine.'

Striker went to speak, but Felicia beat him to it. 'We understand that, sir. God knows there's not enough funding for dual diagnoses patients nowadays. We know how busy you must be. And we wouldn't be here if it wasn't absolutely essential to the file.'

'Dual diagnoses,' Moses said. A faint grin found his lips and he laughed softly. 'Wow. Now that is impressive. You actually know something.'

Felicia offered her best smile. 'I'll take that as a compliment.'

'It was meant as one – if worded poorly.'

'I wrote some papers for the Department,' she said. 'A few years back now, but I know how hard this type of work is.'

The near-defiant look on the manager's face slowly faded, and he took in a deep breath. For a moment, he looked like he was ready to talk to them, but then a hard rapping came on the door.

'One second, please.'

He opened up the door.

In the hallway stood the red-headed woman. Her chubby cheeks were rosy and her breathing was blustery. 'Savanna's out front again,' she said. 'And she's really freaking out, sir.'

Moses sighed, then looked back at the detectives. 'Please. Allow me one minute,' he said. Then he left the room.

The second he was gone, Striker walked to the doorway and stared down the hall. When he saw no sign of the man and heard the loud chatter of an unhappy woman out front, he closed the office door and approached the man's desk.

'What are you doing?' Felicia asked.

'Playing Snoopy.'

She made an uncomfortable sound.

Striker ignored it. He looked at the computer screen. It was dark, so he moved the mouse and a password request appeared. Not bothering to even hazard a guess, Striker instead focused on the papers on the manager's desk. He saw a list of names, suffered addictions, associated treatment facilities the patient was housed in, and how long their stay had been.

He didn't recognize any of the names.

'I think he's coming back,' Felicia said.

Striker didn't respond. He grabbed the phone receiver and started scrolling through the contact list. Within five presses of the button, he found a name he recognized.

L. Asawa-Tan

'Luna's listed here,' he said.

He continued scrolling through the list of names.

'And Luther Faust too.'

'I can hear footsteps,' Felicia said.

She'd barely spoken the words when the office door opened and Moses returned to the room. He walked two steps into the office, saw Striker looking through his phone contacts, and a look of indignation spread across his already-hard features.

'What the hell are you doing?' he demanded.

Striker looked up. 'Scrolling through your phone contacts – I thought that was rather obvious.'

'Well, stop it.'

Striker put down the phone. 'We spoke with Luther Faust and Dr Asawa-Tan this morning. I wasn't aware that you knew them.'

'I know of them. Many people down here know Luther and Luna.' Moses walked past Striker, up to his desk, and placed the portable receiver back on the cradle. 'That's the way it is in the mental health sciences.'

Striker found the comment interesting. 'I always thought addiction and mental health was a much *larger* field . . . yet everyone down here seems to know everyone.'

'Well, it's large now, yes.'

'But it wasn't always?' Felicia asked.

The beefy manager looked at her for a moment, then shook his head and sat down on the edge of the desk. 'It sure as hell wasn't when I started two decades ago,' he said. 'Fifteen, twenty years back, there weren't that many people who committed their lives to helping the mentally ill and addicted. So back then, everyone in the field knew everyone.'

'And nowadays?' Striker asked.

Moses shrugged. 'It's not so much like that anymore. Like I said, I know Luther and Luna from a long time ago. From older times.'

Striker wrote this down in his notebook. 'I didn't know you were friends.'

'We're *not*.'

He stopped writing, looked up.

'There were problems?' Felicia asked.

Moses stared back, deadpan. 'Ones better left forgotten.' He forced a smile. 'Bad thoughts can be more poisonous than the drugs and alcohol.'

Striker steered the conversation back to the investigation. 'So why did Jazz come here exactly?'

'I would really rather not get into this,' Moses replied.

For a brief moment, an uncomfortable silence filled the room. Then Felicia and Striker shared a look, and Felicia continued the conversation. 'Mr Sabba . . . are you aware of what happened this morning? To Detective Jasmine Heer?'

The man's face took on a less guarded look. 'Well, no. Is . . . is she alright?'

'She's dead,' Felicia said.

'Dead?' The word left the man's lips like a breath.

'Murdered,' Striker said. 'Possibly by one of the people she was investigating. Which is why we came here to see you . . . I heard the message you left on Jazz's machine. You weren't too happy. So I need to know, Moses. Why was she in contact with you?'

For a brief moment, the man said nothing. He just looked at the ground, unmoving. His fingers curled into fists.

'Moses?' Striker pressed.

The manager shook his head and swore, but in the end relented. 'She wanted to talk to me,' he admitted. 'About Satanism.'

'Satanism?' Striker let the word hang there for a moment. 'Why you?'

Moses still did not look up. 'Look, it's . . . it's *complicated*, okay?' He closed his eyes and took in a deep breath. 'I got a good job here now. A pension. A life. If people—'

Before he could finish the sentence, the red-headed reception-ist appeared back in the doorway. 'I'm sorry, sir,' she blurted. 'But she's back again. And she's been drinking real bad. She's going to wreck it for the other patients.'

Moses Sabba sighed. 'I'll be right there, Ginny.'

He looked back at Striker and Felicia and met their stares. There was a weariness in his eyes. A kind of numb acceptance.

'Come back in an hour,' he said.

Striker looked at his watch. 'It's almost six now.'

'A half hour then,' the man said, and there was a pleading look in his eyes. 'A half hour – give me that.'

'And if I do?'

Moses Sabba frowned and his entire posture sagged.

'I'll tell you everything.'

Thirty-One

Monster sat in the driver's seat of the white van and monitored the situation. He was parked across from the Recovery House treatment centre, just down the lane, under the overhang of a barren maple tree. He stared at the house, and recalled the times he had used this place as temporary shelter in between his sojourns.

It now seemed like someone else's life.

On the seat next to him, chittering away in his cage, was Samuel. The little squirrel wanted Monster's attention, but that would have to wait.

Monster was too focused on other matters.

Two detectives were just leaving the Recovery House. Monster watched them trudge slowly across the snowy roadway. The female cop was talking about something, flipping through a folder and making gestures. The male cop said nothing. He just listened and walked alongside her, a distant look on his face. Monster recognized the man immediately – he was the same cop from the bus depot this morning. And his being here was no coincidence.

The man was tracking him. And getting dangerously close. So Monster watched him and assessed.

He *always* assessed.

It was impressive. The big cop had a sense of determination

about him. Supreme focus. And mental will aside, he looked *strong*. A force to be reckoned with.

Monster would be careful with this one.

The two detectives reached their undercover police vehicle and hopped inside. Monster watched the cruiser drive down the street, with slush and snow spraying out from under the tyres. Moments later, the car turned south towards the main drag of 41st Avenue and was gone from sight.

Their exit did not lessen the bad feeling.

So Monster waited. He gave the two cops another ten minutes. To see if they would return. When they did not, he said goodbye to Samuel, then exited the vehicle. He walked to the rear of the van and opened the doors. From the back, he grabbed the required supplies.

First was the hammer and some nails. Then a piece of felt and some twine, followed by a tube of silicone. He tucked the flare gun behind his back. Hung the small fire extinguisher off his belt. And last of all, grabbed six jerry cans of fuel.

Gear acquired, he marched down the narrow laneway, with the hard-packed snow crunching beneath his size seventeen boots. His destination was the south side of the house. Basement door. And there was no time to dawdle.

After all, killing a man was hard work.

It took time.

Ten minutes later, Monster had gained entry.

He stood in the basement level of the Recovery House and looked around the area. The layout was exactly as he remembered it – a furnace and boiler room to the east; a storage and laundry room to the north.

To the immediate south was the staircase, next to which were two small rooms. Thick doors with thick locks. And bars on the windows. These were the *Level 1s*, as they called it. Where the facility housed the most problematic patients – which were usually the ones trying to kick the crack cocaine habit. Monster had heard them so many times before, screaming and pounding and pacing and crying.

It was drug-fuelled insanity.

The rooms were empty now, containing nothing but plastic mattresses on the floor and empty puke buckets. The rooms still smelled of sweat and urine and bleach. They always did, no matter how many times they were cleaned.

And they probably always would.

Monster closed his mind to the rooms and instead looked to the west. To the one section he was really interested in.

The shower.

Where vindication would take place.

Monster started that way, then hesitated and looked up.

Directly above him on the next floor was the office of Moses Sabba. Through the vent, the man's voice could be heard in a one-sided conversation. Clearly he was on the phone, and not happy about it.

Monster eavesdropped for a moment:

'. . . Two cops in my office!' the manager was yelling. 'Asking me questions about Jazz Heer and Satanism!' There was a brief pause before Moses exploded again. 'Don't tell me to calm down – you're not the one at risk of being exposed here. I won't have my life ripped apart by this. Nor the centre. I won't go through all that again!'

'You won't have to go through it, Moses,' Monster said softly, as if he was a part of the conversation.

He moved away from the vent. Ignoring the angry tones that were resonating down from the floor above, he marched down the hallway to the community shower and assessed the room. It was exactly what he needed – one small communal cubicle.

A perfect place for the firetrap.

He got to work.

First things first. And that was fresh latex, triple XL. Once the gloves were stretched over his blocky hands, he took out the silicone. It was Palmer's, a fast-drying epoxy.

Seals in less than 90 seconds! was the promise on the tube.

Monster squeezed the silicone all over the drain. Once done, he placed the fire extinguisher just outside the shower room and turned to face the fuel. He unscrewed the caps to all the gas cans, then upturned them all, one by one, and let the fluids gurgle out. Soon the entire stall floor was flowing with diesel and kerosene.

The air was heavy with vapours.

Monster took out the hammer and three nails. He dropped to one knee, placed the felt pad over the nail head, and drove the nail into the wall at ankle level. He then repeated the process on the opposite wall, and strung a piece of twine between them. He gave it a firm tug, felt it was strong, and then stood up.

Last of all, he drove one nail into the ceiling, just an arm's reach into the shower room, then hung more twine from it. At eye level, he attached one of his remaining silver crosses, then stood back and studied it. It gleamed in the dim light of the basement.

A human fishing lure.

Satisfied, Monster moved into the shadows of the hallway. He stripped off his gloves and took out his cell phone. Using Call-Block, he hid his number, then dialled the main desk and asked to speak to the manager. It took less than thirty seconds to get him on the line:

'Moses Sabba speaking.'

'I need help downstairs. I got a guy here.'

'Downstairs? In the centre? Who is this?'

'In the shower room. I think he's OD'd. He's convulsing.'

'I'm coming.'

The line went dead. Seconds later, the sounds of footsteps could be heard from above – fast, heavy, thumping sounds, first in the hallway, then on the stairs. Monster listened to the frantic rambling coming from down the hallway, and knew it was time.

The Deliverer had arrived.

Moses Sabba hurried towards the shower area. Once close enough, he spotted the hanging cross and his face took on a confused look. He walked forward and reached out for it – and his foot caught the twine.

The momentum sent him sprawling forward into the stall. He hit the ground hard and a loud splash sound echoed off the walls. For a brief moment, he just laid there, stunned, flat on his back, his clothes soaking up the fuel.

'What . . . what the hell?' he finally asked, and started to sit up.

'Hello, Moses,' Monster said.

He took a half step towards the shower room, reached up and grabbed the hanging cross. With a gentle twist of his huge hand, he broke the twine and dropped the silver cross on top of the fallen man's chest. Then he raised his arm and aimed the flare gun.

Moses Sabba brought his arms up to cover his chest. 'Please – no – take anything you want! Take anything!'

Monster looked at the man in disbelief. 'You don't even remember me, do you?' He felt his muscles tighten up with rage. 'I came to you, Moses . . . *I came to you.*'

He stepped forward, into the better light, displaying his true size.

Moses blinked, then his face filled with dread.

'Dear God,' he whispered.

Monster shook his head.

'God is not here for you, Moses. Only his wrath.' Monster raised the flare gun and took aim. 'Your time for atonement has finally come.'

Thirty-Two

'I don't like this Moses guy,' Felicia said.

It was the third time she had told Striker this in ten minutes.

'He's stalling,' she added. 'Buying time to make up a story.'

Striker didn't disagree.

They sat in the car with a couple of sandwich wraps they'd grabbed from the local Subway – a meatball with mayo for Striker and a seafood club for Felicia. Like always, they ate in the cruiser. It was their preference. And good police practice. Quite often when calls came in, things happened quickly. The extra minute gained by already being in the car sometimes made the difference between catching the suspect or losing him.

Coming up Hero or Zero, as Felicia liked to put it.

Striker took a bite of his wrap and felt like his mouth was on fire. Too many jalapeños, too much hot sauce. He guzzled some Coke to wash it down.

Parked just ahead of him was an old pickup truck with a ton of bumper stickers. He read one of them. *Jesus Saves, My Kids Spend.* Striker smiled at the saying, and thought of his own daughter. Courtney would be going to college soon, and thoughts of her possibly leaving home bothered him – especially when they worked on files like this one.

There were bad people out there.

'I thought stuff like this was only for the movies,' he said.

Felicia grabbed his Coke and took a sip from it. 'What are you talking about?'

'The satanic reference in the file,' he continued. 'I thought that was all outdated by now. You know, Hollywood stuff. *Rosemary's Baby. The Exorcist* . . . I mean, you hear about the odd wing-nut like Dahmer or Gacy, but really, are there that many of them out there?'

Felicia swallowed another bite of sandwich. 'Don't kid yourself, they're around. I remember just before I came to Homicide. We got this call about mutilated animals up in Everett Park. Went there thinking some coyote had gotten hold of a cat or something. But it ended up being some pretty nasty stuff.'

Striker put his wrap down. Left it untouched.

'What was it?' he asked.

'Went way beyond what we expected. Found the mutilated animals alright – and a friggin' *altar* in the woods. Thing was all covered in dried blood and candles, and there was this long curved ceremonial knife sitting there. Someone had even chalked out a big star on the ground. Whole thing gave me the creeps.'

'You ever catch the guy?'

'No.' She guzzled some more Coke, then sat back in the seat. 'But the SPCA was all over it like a fat kid on a Smartie. It never led to nothing in the end, but it was proof enough to me.'

'On what?'

'That the world is full of sickos.'

Striker said nothing back. He just sat there, not eating his sandwich wrap, not drinking his Coke. He wondered what the hell they were dealing with here. With Jazz's death and the arson file she'd been working on. And the suspect. And Luther. And now this Moses guy.

So much seemed connected and yet disconnected.

He looked at the radio clock and saw it was going on for 7
p.m. They had given Moses more leeway than he had asked for.

'Time for some answers,' he said.

Before he could turn the key, the warble went off – one loud
strident tone blasting across the radio, indicating a Priority One
call. Immediately, the dispatcher came over the air: 'We've got
three calls of a fire,' she broadcasted. 'Coming from the Oak and
49th area.'

'Oak and 49th?' Felicia asked.

Striker felt his pulse race. 'That's the Recovery House.'

He started the engine and hammered on the gas. Being less
than a mile out, they were on scene in minutes. As they entered
the block, Striker scanned the entire area. From the front, the
building looked no different than before, except now there was
a heavy mist of blackish smoke flowing out the north side
windows. The front door was closed. A few people had gathered
in the yard. And the air was beeping with the sound of smoke
detectors.

Before Striker had even brought the car to a full stop, Felicia
jumped out. 'I'll get the front door open and make sure everyone's accounted for,' she said. 'You check the back.'

Striker nodded in agreement and jumped out of the cruiser.
Before Felicia could run off, he circled the car and grabbed her
by the shoulder.

'Be ready for anything,' he said.

She only nodded, then raced towards the front of the facility.

Striker hurried across the road, onto the neighbouring lot,
where a bunch of looky-loos were already forming a small pack
and chittering:

Must be a fire.

. . . So much smoke.

Hope everyone got out . . .

Striker yelled for everyone to get back, then cut between the houses towards the rear of the facility. When he reached the corner, he swung west and was suddenly suffused in smoke. Squinting against the hot blast, he made out a cement stairwell, leading down to a back entrance.

The door was already cracked open an inch.

Striker took two steps towards it, then stopped hard.

Through the screen of smoke, down at the far end of the lot, he saw something. Almost cut off by the row of hedge bushes and a tall retaining wall stood a solitary hulking figure. A man. Dressed in dark pants and a black hoodie. He was tall. Wide. Barrel-chested. The same man from the bus depot.

And he was looking right back at him.

'Vancouver Police!' Striker called out. 'Don't move!'

But the man didn't listen. He took one step backwards, faded in the churning blackness, and was suddenly gone from sight – as if he had never been there in the first place. Like an apparition or a phantom.

A creature of the smoke and fire.

Thirty-Three

Striker drew his pistol and initiated pursuit.

Behind the Recovery House was a row of hedge bushes, which were further reinforced by a cement retaining wall, designed to block off traffic noise from 49th Avenue.

Striker raced through the blustering smoke towards it. When he reached the corner, where the row of hedge bushes met the retaining wall, he found a set of massive footprints.

The man had jumped the wall.

Striker did the same. He climbed over, hit the other side, and got on his radio, demanding air priority. 'This is Detective Striker,' he announced as he raced around the building and headed for 49th. 'We got a runner. Forty-ninth and Cambie. How close is the nearest unit?'

Sue Rhaemer, the central dispatcher, took a moment to study the GPS grid. 'Twenty-ninth and Cambie,' she said. 'I'll log them to your call.'

Striker cursed at the distance but kept running. He reached the intersection of 49th and Cambie, and scanned the area. Across the road to the south was a gated community of luxury townhomes, and on the other three corners were old private residences. Lots of houses – but no sign of the suspect.

It was as if he had dissipated with the smoke.

Striker turned left and peered down 49th Avenue. Far down

the road was the Langara College campus, but that was over two blocks away. Almost three. There was no way the suspect could have gotten there that fast. So where—

And then it dawned on him.

Striker spun slowly about and looked back the way he had come. The first thing he spotted was the Millennium Line transit sign and the stairway leading down to the subway system.

The man had gone underground.

Striker grabbed his radio again.

'He's in the subway tunnels. Langara and 49th. Call the SkyTrain Police and see if anyone's at this station.'

Before Dispatch responded, Striker raced down the steps, taking them three at a time. The moment he hit the concrete platform, he was already scanning for threats. Fortunately, the boarding areas were relatively slow for seven o'clock. Only a handful of passengers cluttered the area.

Passengers, but no Transit Police.

And no suspect.

Striker searched the area for an escape route, and located none. All he saw was a pair of men's and women's washrooms. He checked both out. Cleared them. Then scanned the area once more.

He found a possibility.

In the middle of the onramp section to the southbound train, a lady was stooped over. On the ground at her feet was a pile of groceries – some oranges, a carton of milk, some batteries.

Striker ran up to her.

'Detective Striker – Vancouver Police,' he said. 'Did a big man just race through here?'

The woman looked up at him from her crouched position, almost fearfully, and then nodded. 'The bastard almost knocked me onto the tracks,' she said, and pointed. 'He ran down there.'

Striker looked to where she was pointing.

South.

For a moment, he thought she was talking about the wash-rooms again. But then he reassessed the direction of her finger and knew without a doubt the area of indication. Not the wash-rooms, but down into the tunnels.

'Jesus, he ran onto the *tracks*?' he asked.

She shook her head. 'No. Onto that cement thing.'

Striker looked on the other side of the rails and spotted a narrow median with a thick yellow stripe running down the middle – one possibly used by the Transit personnel for safety and maintenance procedures.

He hurried to the edge of the platform, then paused for a moment. He looked at the pure blackness of the tunnel ahead. There was no light down there. Just more darkness and the high-pitched hiss of hydraulics.

Striker didn't like the feeling. He could sense a strange static charge near the tracks. And he felt a cold wind being funnelled out from the mouth of the entranceway. His eyes caught sight of the black-and-yellow steel rails below, and he couldn't help but wonder: just how much power was running through those lines?

One hundred amps?

One-fifty?

Not that it really mattered. Anything over *one-tenth* of a single amp could stop a person's heart. Which made things pretty straightforward here. If he got zapped by those lines, it would be all over for him.

He'd be one bad barbecue.

He brought the radio to his lips. Hit the plunger. 'Cover all the transit exits – he's running the tunnels.'

When Dispatch copied the call, Striker took in a quick deep

breath, and – against his better judgement – jumped out across the tracks.

He landed on the other side. On the cement median. And his momentum almost took him into the northbound line. He got himself balanced, turned south, and pressed forward into the darkness beyond.

The moment he breached the mouth of the tunnel, the light from the station dimmed and the high-pressured rumble of the coming trains echoed off the walls. They sounded like they were all around him. Grabbing on to the median railing for support, he took out his flashlight and pressed on.

He made it only another ten metres before the median widened and became a small swelling of land. Like a long cement patio, maybe fifteen metres long and four metres wide. It appeared to curve slowly, following the bend of tunnel.

Striker followed it with his eyes. All along the walkway was an array of thick cement support pillars.

He stopped hard. Scanned.

In the darkness of the tunnel, it was difficult to see. So he adjusted the flashlight in an attempt to widen the beam. Before he was finished, a large fist swung out from behind the nearest pillar.

A haymaker punch. Head level.

Striker saw it just in time. He ducked low, spun around in a defensive position, and swung out his right arm – slamming the butt of his pistol against the side of the suspect's head.

The steel connected with a solid crunching sound.

The blow was harsh – a direct hit – and it sent a shock tremor running all the way up Striker's arm, right into his shoulder. Feeling that force, he'd expected the fight to be over. Expected to see his opponent crumble to the ground.

But he was wrong.

The suspect did not so much as move. Instead, he remained standing and drove his fist forward.

Before Striker could react, the punch hit him. Hard and direct. His jaw let out a harsh cracking sound and his head snapped backward. In less than a second, the world around him went from calm and stable to warped and spinning.

He faltered backwards. Out of control. And the gun left his fingers, disappeared somewhere in the darkness. An instant later, he felt the unforgiving hardness of the concrete as his back slammed flat against it. All the wind left his lungs and the back of his skull snapped hard against the floor.

Stunned. Off his feet. On the ground.

A bad place to be.

He tried to get up. Felt the world spin. Saw a distorted image of the man above him.

Striker tried to get up. Got halfway to his feet. But another punch came. Directed downward. Heavy. Slow.

He raised an arm to block it, then felt his hand being swatted away like a mosquito. The punch caught him in the temple. And suddenly he was reeling back down to the cement median. He landed in an awkward position – his back twisted on the concrete, his head dangling in the air.

The tracks . . . I'm on the goddam tracks!

From somewhere around the bend, he could hear the growing scream of the next train coming, its rubber catchers grinding against the steel rail. Its hydraulic hiss resonating throughout the tunnel.

A large hand enclosed his neck. Fingers locking down.

Closing off his windpipe.

With both hands, Striker grabbed the man's wrist and tried to hyper-extend the joint. But it was useless. The man was just too strong. His hand didn't budge and his grip remained iron-tight.

Desperate, unable to breathe, Striker tilted his eyes back and scanned the ground for his pistol.

Couldn't find it.

Lightheaded, going under, he did the only thing he could do. He let go of the suspect's wrist. Reached out with both hands. And clawed his fingernails down the suspect's face – aiming for the eyes.

And what happened shocked him.

A part of the suspect's face just . . . *tore away*. And the man let out a strange howling sound. The suspect let go. Arched away. Grabbed at his mask and pulled it back into place.

With his lungs burning, Striker rolled right. He splayed his fingers out across the cement median. Searched blindly for the SIG. Seconds later, his hand touched the cold comfort of gun steel, and he rejoiced. He snatched it up, wheeled around, and took quick aim.

But he did not see the suspect.

Instead he spotted two Transit cops. Both in uniform. Flashlights out, guns drawn.

They had him lined up.

'SkyTrain Police!' one of them said. 'Don't move!'

'I'm a cop,' Striker told them.

'Raise that gun one more inch and I'll take your fuckin' head off,' one of them said. 'Drop it. *Now!*'

There was nervousness in the man's tone. Striker could hear it. If he wasn't careful, these guys were gonna turn him into Swiss cheese. Cursing, but seeing no other option, he did as he was told.

'I'm putting it down,' he said.

He laid the SIG on the concrete floor, then slowly raised his hands in the air – all the while looking around the tunnel for the man he'd been chasing.

But there was no one there now. Just darkness and stillness and a narrow median with giant cement pillars. Somewhere down the tracks, a train was nearing. Its loud rumbling echoed off the tunnel walls.

Striker turned his eyes right. Saw a door on the other side of the tracks.

Emergency exit.

It was slightly ajar.

The sight of it took more out of Striker than the fight had done.

It was too late now. He had failed.

The monster was gone.

Thirty-Four

By the time Striker got the mess in the subway tunnels under control and had a pair of female paramedics checking out his injuries, Vancouver Police patrol units had set up a ten-block perimeter around the Langara Station. Units from Districts 3 and 2 had been pulled in, with only the remaining cars from District 1 available for the rest of the city.

Dogman Harry Hooch was out tracking with Sable. The dog had hit on the scent immediately, right where Striker had gotten into the fight. And sure enough, she had beelined for the emergency exit doors.

For Striker, the sight of it was frustrating beyond measure.

'Jesus almighty,' he now muttered to himself.

'Don't talk,' the paramedic told him. She was a young blonde thing who had looked easy-going and spunky, but was proving to be anything but. 'Open and close your jaw one more time.'

Striker did as told, but kept looking at the emergency exit and thinking of all that had happened. It was maddening. And the repercussions of their failure could be seen everywhere.

As a result of the debacle, all trains had been stopped on both sides of the Langara Station and commuters were lined up along the platform and up the stairs. Traffic was backed up all along both 49th Avenue and Cambie Street, where patrol cars were now stationed as containment points, their red-and-blue emergency lights reflecting off the snow and slush and flashing across the dark winter skies.

Striker had little faith in the track. It was all window dressing now. Boxes to check off so that no blame could be laid in the suspect's escape.

'You should get the jaw X-rayed,' the paramedic told him. 'It might be broken.'

'It's fine,' Striker said, but his throat was sore from being choked, and the words came out raspy.

'It's definitely *not* fine.'

'I'll make do.'

Before the woman could say more, Striker stood up and thanked her for her time. Then he returned to the Recovery House.

Being well after seven now, the sky was black, and the darkness made it difficult to tell if any smoke was flooding the sky. The emergency lights of the fire trucks lit up the lingering haze like rock concert strobe lights. Firemen, having now extinguished the flames, were milling about the area.

Striker scanned the roadside. Parked a half block down was a white fire investigator truck with an extended cab.

Katarina Kesla was here.

'. . . another body in there,' one of the firemen was saying to a counterpart.

The words grabbed Striker like a pair of physical hands. He looked over and recognized the man. It was the guy he and Felicia had met earlier in the day. Paris.

Mr July.

'Burned to a fuckin' crisp,' the fireman added.

Striker said nothing to the comment; he just realized that this crime scene had turned even uglier.

He headed up the walk.

Inside the Recovery House, smoke hung about the first-floor foyer like an unwanted guest, despite the fact that all the doors had been opened and all the windows had been shattered by the fire crews. The smoke thickened as Striker descended the stairs to the lower level. With every step he took, that same unmistakable stench grew – burnt fuel, burnt fat, burnt meat.

Another victim.

The stink was making Striker's stomach do cartwheels.

He marched down the basement hallway, passed an unused fire extinguisher that was mounted into the glass wall case, and found his partner. Felicia was wearing a flimsy paper mask over her mouth. Upon seeing him, she came over and touched his arm. Looked at his face. *Examined* him.

'Your jaw—' she started.

'It's fine.'

She frowned like she wanted to say more, but then kept silent when he gave her a look. She handed him a mask, and he put it on and turned to face the crime scene.

'It's Moses,' she said.

Striker made no reply. He had already guessed as much. And it was terribly disappointing – not just because another life had been lost, but because anything the man had been prepared to divulge had been burned up with him.

'How'd you make confirmation?' he asked.

'Process of elimination and witnesses.'

They moved closer to the scene.

In the corner of the shower, someone had set up a portable battery-operated light source, and the illumination highlighted the blackened smoke that still flooded the room in hazy, uneven patches. Katarina Kesla was standing in the forefront, all gloved-up and suited, with a respirator covering her face. Like before, she was drawing the scene.

Striker nodded to her.

She returned it but said nothing and kept sketching.

Striker wasted no time. He gloved up with new latex and began assessing the scene himself. Sprawled out on the floor, in a three-quarter prone position, was the body of the victim. Moses Sabba looked as if he'd been trying to crawl out of the inferno but hadn't made it very far – just to the lip of the shower room. There, he'd been completely overcome.

Striker took his eyes off the scene as a whole and focused on the victim. The physical evidence of the body was the same as before. Burned thoroughly, to the point of being completely deformed and unrecognizable. The skin crisp and black, with the underlying muscle and fascia tissues now an odd whitish colour.

Clutched in the victim's blackened claw-like fingers was what appeared to be a silver blob of metal.

'The remains of another silver cross?' Felicia asked.

'I have no doubt.' Striker looked back at her grimly. 'We'll need to add this as another comparison sample.'

Lying not too far from the body was a fire extinguisher. Striker moved closer and took a look at it. Unlike the extinguisher in the hallway, the tank on this one was easily twice the size. The label on the side was covered with smoky grime, so Striker wiped away as much as he could in order to read it.

Felicia stood behind him, looking at the extinguisher as well.

'It looks like an industrial unit,' she noted.

Striker read the label aloud. 'Class B. There's a big red square on the label.'

He placed the fire extinguisher back down, then left the shower room. He wandered down the hall, located the fire extinguisher on the wall, and read the label. It had a green triangle on it.

The difference was odd to him.

He noted that, then took the stairs up to the first floor where he searched for more fire extinguishers. He found two more – one in the hallway of the main floor and one near the bedrooms on the upper floor. He read the labels on both of these and saw that they both had green triangles on them. He wrote this information down into his notebook.

When he returned to the crime scene, Kesla was just finishing her sketch. He got her attention. 'What kind of extinguisher would you keep down here?' he asked her. 'What *class*?'

The fire investigator lowered her pad. 'Probably a Class A. It's fairly standard.'

'A is it's for normal stuff, right? – paper, wood, cardboard, plastics.'

'That's correct.'

Striker thought it over. 'The one in the hallway is a Class A,' he said. 'And so are the ones upstairs. They're *all* Class A's. But this one,' – he pointed to the extinguisher lying on the floor of the shower stall – 'this one is a Class *B*. What is B for?'

'For grease and fuels.'

'Like diesel and kerosene?' he asked.

Kesla nodded.

'Kind of an odd coincidence, don't you think?'

Kesla said nothing, but Felicia spoke up. 'Maybe they stocked both down here,' she suggested.

Striker shook his head. 'Why would they? Nothing down here runs on diesel anymore – it's all electric. And this extinguisher isn't an old one – it's brand new; check the label. It doesn't even expire for two years. Plus this is an entirely different make than the others. A Fire King. Like you said, Feleesh, it's industrial.'

'So what are you saying?' Felicia asked. 'That our arsonist brought it himself?'

'That's exactly what I'm saying – and that he put out the fire for us. Not just this one, but the last one as well. At Paramount Place.'

Felicia's face tightened behind the paper mask. 'Why would an arsonist want to stop his own burn?'

Kesla, who had been silently thinking things through herself, finally spoke up. 'To put out his victims?' she asked. 'To make them survive longer? To suffer more?'

Striker thought about that for a long time. It was an abysmal thought. Horrific. But in the end, he shook his head. 'If torture was the plan, he could have done this somewhere else. Even at the bus depot with Jazz, the only reason we knew what had happened was because of the flash in the sky. I don't think torture is his game. And I don't think the fire is either, for that matter.'

Felicia gave a half-hearted nod. 'Well, if he's putting out his own fires, he's not a typical pyro, that's for sure.' She looked down at the industrial fire extinguisher and wondered aloud. 'It's almost like he doesn't want anyone else to get injured.'

Striker stripped off his gloves. 'I think you're right about that. His purpose here is murder. There's no doubt about that. And the fire is a means to an end for him – but a *specific* one. It must be symbolic in some way. To him or to his victims.'

'Like the crosses.'

'Yes. Like the crosses.'

A look of irritation spread through Felicia's face. 'The victims have to be connected in some way. Maybe through the files Jazz was working on. But either way, we're onto something here. I mean, what are the odds? The moment we come to talk to Moses about Jazz, he ends up getting murdered.'

'What led us here in the first place?' Striker asked.

'The phone message Moses left for Jazz.'

'Regarding what?'

'Satanism.'

Striker rubbed his brow and thought. 'This Moses guy – he listed in PRIME?'

Felicia shook her head. 'Not much. From what I've found so far, he was a ward of the court as a kid. So no parents, no brothers, no sisters. And he never married. The guy's got no connections.'

Striker looked back into the shower stall, where Kesla was again inspecting the body.

'He's got *one*,' he said. 'We just need to find out who.'

Thirty-Five

A half hour later, with Felicia finishing up at the crime scene – logging notes with the fire investigator, obtaining witness statements, and speaking with the city's structural engineer on condemning the site – Striker returned to Langara Station.

He found one of the SkyTrain police constables and got the man to lead him to the security station. Soon, he sat in a large command room. Without asking, one of the on-scene first aid workers brought him an ice pack for his swelling jaw, and Striker muttered a thanks and plastered it against his cheek.

The bone felt broken, the joint out of line.

He wished he could stuff another ice pack down his throat. His windpipe felt hot and swollen and sore as hell too.

Forcing the thought from his mind, he stood next to a pencil-thin clerk who reminded him an awful lot of the Department's own tech specialist, Percy Wadsworth – same thin build, same giant Adam's apple, and also pounding back a sugar-free Red Bull. The clerk's last name was Melville. Striker didn't ask for a first.

Together, they watched feed after feed of the security footage.

Striker found the process frustrating, and couldn't hide his irritation. He was even further dismayed to find that the quality of the digital feed was as poor as most gas stations'. He pulled the ice pack away from his jaw. 'Jesus, doesn't the tunnel have any cameras?' His jaw was clicking whenever he moved it and his head was pounding. 'I mean, what do you guys do when a train breaks down in the tunnel?'

Melville's already-large eyes widened at the comment, as if he was stunned by the insinuation that their system was in any way lacking.

'Digital video is expensive,' he said. 'And we have two hundred miles of track to cover. There *are* internal cameras down there – just none at that bend. Had your altercation happened another ten metres down the line, we would have had everything on feed. But unfortunately, not here.'

'Great. Next time I'll ask him to clobber me a half mile down.'

'It would help,' the tech said dryly.

Striker listened to the words with bemusement. *Your altercation*. That was what the man was calling it. The suspect had damn near killed him down there on the tracks. Almost choked him out and pinned his skull to the high-voltage rails of the track. But it was just an altercation.

Silently, Striker watched a few more feeds.

'There!' he said suddenly. 'There! Stop the feed!'

Melville did.

On the monitor was the best image of their suspect Striker had seen so far. It was a shot of the southbound platform. Where the suspect had raced around the corner of the stairwell entrance and slammed into the woman with the groceries.

'Run it in slow motion,' he said. 'Quarter speed.'

Melville did. Striker watched as the suspect appeared, then clipped the woman. She snapped forward like she'd been hit by an NFL tight end. Crashed to the ground. Her groceries went everywhere. A few oranges rolled onto the guide rails.

'Stop it there and pan down.'

Melville did. As the zoom increased, any illusions Striker had harboured over his embellishment of the man's size vanished completely. The suspect was a *beast*. Easily five centimetres taller than Striker, and wider by two. He must have been damn near a hundred and sixty kilos, and then some.

'Zoom in on the face,' Striker said.

The man made an unhappy sound. 'Angle is bad.'

'Just do it. As good as it gets.'

As the camera panned in, the image became more pixellated and less clear. The downward angle of the feed cut off the bottom half of the suspect's mouth and jawline, but it was obvious for anyone to see that something was wrong with his appearance.

'His face is . . . *wrong*,' Melville said.

Striker just nodded.

'It's a mask. I almost pulled it off him when he was choking me out.' He thought back to raking his fingernails down the man's face, and how the rubbery disguise had just peeled away like a second skin. 'The mask looks like flesh, but it's not. It's some kind of rubber or neoprene.'

'So why the disguise?' a voice said behind him.

Striker knew it was Felicia before even looking. How long she had been there, he did not know. He left the question unanswered and told Melville to burn the feed. Then he and Felicia found an empty spot in the room, where they could have maximum privacy.

'*Why* is exactly the right question,' he said. 'Is he wearing this thing simply to disguise himself? Or because there's something wrong with his face?'

'Could be he's just extremely cautious about being identified on video,' Felicia said. 'Maybe he's someone we already know – could be he's listed in one of our systems. A jail photo. A youth offender hit. Some gang surveillance tags. And maybe he knows that. Maybe he's concerned that we might actually recognize him.' She took a quick look across the room, back at the monitor and the pixellated image. 'Did you see any part of his face?'

Striker shook his head. 'Sorry. I was too busy watching my life flash before my eyes.'

Felicia said nothing for a moment. Then her eyes focused back on his injuries. On the ice pack he was holding. On his swollen jaw. And his scratched-up face. She reached out and touched his arm. 'Are you okay, Jacob?' she asked. 'I mean, really okay?'

'I'm fine.'

'You don't look it.'

He let the ice pack fall from his jaw. Frowned. Came clean.

'I been in a lot of fights, Feleesh. With a lot of big guys. But there's something different about this one. He's strong – he's *freakishly* strong. Overpowered me like I was nothing. Like I was a fucking child.'

'We'll catch him again.'

Striker let out a bemused laugh. 'We better be damn well ready for him when we do.' He looked back at the image on the screen for a long moment and felt concern wash over him. 'Next time we grapple, I won't get a second chance with him.' He spoke the words with finality, and when he noticed Felicia's concerned stare lingering on him too long, he changed the subject.

'You get anything back there at the scene?'

She blinked, coming out of her thoughts. But then nodded and took out her notebook. 'You could say that.'

He gave her a curious look. 'Do tell.'

She flipped through the pages. 'It's about Moses. Get this. I checked his office line. He made a call not five minutes after we left his office – guess where?'

'Should've been a last confession hotline.'

'You're close,' she said. 'To the Holy Cross church in Dunbar.'

Striker thought she was joking. When he realized she wasn't, he frowned. 'What number?'

She showed him.

'That's Father O'Brien's office.'

They both sat there silently and let the information sink in. Jazz had been investigating an arson at the Holy Cross, Striker and Felicia had attended there in response to her death, and now Moses Sabba had called Father O'Brien just moments before being murdered in his own trial by fire. It seemed that everywhere they looked, there were invisible threads in this giant web of an investigation.

One more thing to look into.

'And that's not the weird thing,' Felicia continued. 'I went through Moses' coat. At first there was not much in there to go on – just some credit cards and a social insurance number. Some business cards too.'

Striker nodded. 'But . . .'

She grinned. 'But then I took a good look through his desk once more.'

'I miss something?'

Felicia nodded. 'In the very back of the upper drawer is a locked compartment. I got it open and found a small envelope inside. Look what I found.'

She pulled three photographs from the back of her notebook and showed them to him. The images were shocking. Not just because they were pornographic, with Moses Sabba laying on top of a woman, but because of the identity of the woman on the bottom.

Striker looked at one photo for several seconds. In the image, the woman was younger and her hair was longer, but there was no doubting her identity.

The woman was their social services psychiatrist.

Dr Luna Asawa-Tan.

Thirty-Six

Once back in the undercover cruiser, Striker took a good long look at all three of the photographs of Moses and Luna, in which the two were naked and having sex. In all three images, Moses was always on top, the only difference being in the first one, Luna was on her back, in the second she was on her stomach, and in the third, she was on her side.

In each of the photos, Moses had his arm extended out of sight, suggesting he was the one holding the camera and taking the shot. And in each of them, Luna was looking back with a playful grin.

'What do you think?' Felicia asked.

'I think I'd like to take up photography,' Striker said. He looked over at her. 'What d'ya think, Santos? Wanna go home and snap some shots? Maybe make a movie or two?'

'I mean about *Luna*,' Felicia replied dryly. 'She doesn't look exactly forced into the situation, does she?'

Striker just nodded and looked back at the photos. On the bottom of the image, the date taken had been imprinted. 'These are five years old,' he said. 'Taken in December. The twenty-first. Not too far from Christmas.'

Felicia grinned. 'I bet he's a great stocking stuffer.'

Striker grinned back. 'Yes, I'm sure he's good at roasting the chestnuts.'

For a moment, they shared a laugh, then Striker got serious. Something about the date bothered him, but he didn't know what. He took out his iPhone, googled the date, and saw a bunch of events that had transpired on the same day as the photo – a monstrous wave had crushed people at Black's Beach; baseball great Elrod Hendricks had died at the age of sixty-four; and the Supreme Court of Canada had made the act of having group sex in a public place legal – a precedent of great importance to every swingers' club.

Felicia watched him fiddle with the phone browser. 'What are you searching for?' she asked.

'The date on the photos,' Striker said. 'Maybe it's important.'

Felicia smiled. 'You just leave the internet searches to me,' she said 'You're – how shall I put it? – *technologically challenged*.' She punched the date into her phone and started searching.

Striker didn't disagree with her comment. He hated that kind of stuff. He clicked off the internet search and pocketed his phone.

'Which addresses you got for Moses?' he asked.

'He's got *four* addresses,' she said. 'A PO box at MBR – that's Mail Box Rentals; very creative business name, by the way – and three other addresses in his file. 93 East 61st, 2351 Somerville Street, and 5351 Kerr Street.'

'We'll check them all,' Striker said.

He put the car in gear and pulled out onto the main drag.

A half hour later, they stopped outside a small white house on East 61st Street. It was old, covered with dirty crumbling stucco. Striker killed the engine and looked at Felicia, who was still going through the few pieces of mail Moses Sabba had stored in his PO box. Most of it was junk mail, and the rest were credit card and bank statements.

If numbers didn't lie, the man was broke.

Striker looked at the house before them. The address was listed as 95, not 93. In fact, 93 East 61st did not even exist – just like 2351 Somerville Street hadn't existed.

Felicia put the mail down, saw the address and swore.

'Here, too?' she asked.

'Another dead end.'

She shook her head, then gave a shrug. 'Well, let's give it a knock and see who lives here anyway. Then we can check out the last one on Kerr.'

Striker nodded, but then, as he thought it over, he realized that the Kerr address would be a waste of time. 'That's a fake address too,' he said. 'There is no 5300 block of Kerr – after the Kingsway divide, Kerr becomes Staunton. It's another bullshit address.'

Felicia sighed. 'I guess it's not too surprising. All his important mail – driver's licence papers, insurance documents, banking and credit card statements – they all go to the PO box at MBR. Maybe he doesn't actually have a place of residence.'

'Or maybe he's trying hard to hide it,' Striker replied.

Felicia thought it over. 'He'd have a good reason for that.'

That got Striker's attention. 'Such as?'

'Well, look at his job. Look at what he works with – mental illness, drug abuse, alcohol addiction, youth offenders. A lot of clients who go to that Recovery House have some pretty troubled paths. Some pretty dangerous diagnoses – paranoid schizophrenia, antisocial personality disorder, borderline personality disorder . . . some of these people can be extremely dangerous, Jacob. And they often blame the very people who are trying to help them. Moses hiding his address might be nothing more than a precautionary decision.'

Striker saw her point and admitted it was valid. 'We still need to find it though.'

'Agreed.'

Striker took a moment to sort things through in his mind. 'Moses and Jazz are connected. We assume it's through the file, but I don't like assuming things. Could there be another way?'

Felicia nodded. 'Well, Jazz worked on dozens of homicides that either involved ritualistic murders or the appearance of it. Most of her suspects probably fit one of those personality disorders we were just talking about. For all we know they might have had several crossings.'

'It's a definite link,' Striker said. 'But I want some solid tangible proof. I mean, there's got to be more here than we're seeing. The fact is, Jazz was calling Moses for a *specific* reason. She wanted to talk to him about Satanism. And now he's dead, just like Jazz – burned to death in a pool of fire.'

Felicia let out a weary sound and rubbed her temples. 'It feels like we're going in circles here.' She went back to searching the web for anything related to the date on the photograph of Moses and Luna having sex.

Striker continued talking things out. 'We need more information. We need to talk to someone who actually *knew* Moses on a personal level. And there's only two people I can think of that apply here.'

Felicia didn't look up from her cell. 'Luther and Luna.'

'Exactly.' Striker looked at his watch, saw that it was going on for nine o'clock. 'They're working the night car right now. Call their dispatch and see if they've logged themselves out anywhere.'

But Felicia didn't answer. She was too intent on her phone. She scrolled down the page, then let out a sound somewhere between excitement and concern. She looked over at Striker and met his stare.

'What you find?' he asked.

'The date on the photographs,' she said. 'You were right. It *is* important. December 21st was the darkest day of that year. Meaning it was the New Moon . . .'

Striker shrugged. 'What's relevant about that?'

She held up the phone so he could read the screen.

'It was a *satanic* holiday.'

Thirty-Seven

For the next twenty minutes, Striker and Felicia tried to get hold of Luther and Luna. Neither one of them were answering their work cells, office numbers, or home telephones. Furthermore, they had not bothered to put themselves out on scene at any address.

It was odd.

Were they purposely trying to hide their location?

When Striker called up Ministry headquarters, all he got was the standard recording. And when Felicia called the after-hours line, she was directed to a woman named Nora who told her that this was 'typical practice' for Luther. No one ever knew where he was or what he was doing.

It had been that way for twenty years.

Finally, Striker called up their own central dispatcher, Sue Rhaemer, and asked if she could use the GPS system to locate the pair.

'It's not one of our cars,' she replied. 'I got no access to it.'

Striker cursed.

'I can tell you this though,' Rhaemer said. 'Luther went 10-7 an hour ago.'

10-7: Done for the shift.

Striker thanked her and said goodbye. Frustrated, he got Felicia to look up Luna's address. They found that Luna was listed as living in Deep Cove, which was an outcropping of steep land flanked by the sprawling woodlands of Mount Seymour Provincial Park and the cold straits of the Burrard Inlet.

It was damn near in the wilderness.

Striker had been to Deep Cove before. On a summer day, the drive there was beautiful, filled with dark blue waters and deep forest greens. But in the middle of the winter, it was an icy, slippery, treacherous trek. And with the snow falling and winds pounding like they'd been for the last two days, there was a good chance the roads in would be closed.

'She won't be going back there in this weather,' Striker said. 'She's *got* to have a second place down here somewhere. When I was dealing with her before during her investigation, she was staying at the clinic a lot . . . but that place is no longer there. It got closed down during the initial investigation, and even after the charges were dropped, it never reopened.'

'Is that a surprise?'

Striker ignored the remark. 'We need to find Luther. Where does he live?'

Felicia ran his name. Saw the address.

'Way out in Ladner.'

'That's twenty minutes,' Striker said.

She laughed. 'Be real. It's closer to three-quarters of an hour in this weather – and that's if there's no problem in the Richmond tunnel. You know how that thing gets.'

Striker looked back at her and could tell she was tired. Had hit the wall. He felt the same way. More than anything, he felt like calling it a night, but every time he thought of doing so, the image of Jazz returned to him.

She deserved better.

'I'm going there,' he finally said. 'I'll drop you off first.'

Felicia let out an onerous sound. 'Fine. Just go.'

'You sure?'

'Drive, before I change my mind.'

Striker did. They took Oak Street all the way down to Richmond where it turned into Highway 99. Despite the nonstop efforts of the snow ploughs and salt droppers, ice and slush covered the highway like a slippery skin. Combined with the deep blackness of the winter night, it was a recipe for tragedy.

Every mile there seemed to be a new accident.

Still, they pressed on. They kept in the bus lane and drove straight through the tunnel before taking Exit 17. Soon, they found the city of Ladner, and eventually the expansive rural lands of Deltaport Way.

Felicia looked at the barren patches of land that seemed imbued with darkness. She shivered. 'I always find it so creepy out here – one minute you're in the middle of the city, the next you're in miles and miles of *nothing*.'

'It's not nothing, it's farmland,' Striker said. 'We're a ten-minute drive from the highway.'

'Sure. In a place where no one can hear you scream.'

Striker said nothing, just gave her a look.

He took the corner of 36th, felt the wheels crunch and slide on the icy surface, and slowed down. They were on an old country road now, single lane and flanked by deep irrigation ditches. If the car went into one of them, they could be seriously hurt. And even if they weren't injured, it was a helluva long hike down to the nearest farmhouse.

He slowed down a little more.

Soon, they spotted a small break of bush, and Striker knew it was the farmhouse driveway. He turned the corner and entered Luther's land. The lot was huge, multi-acre, and the driveway was longer than most people's property. They passed a broken-down barn and two silos before coming flush with an old farmhouse.

Striker stopped the car and looked at it. In the pressing darkness, it was difficult to see any real detail. Just a big sprawling farmhouse with shuttered windows and a wraparound porch.

No cars were visible.

'He's not even home,' Felicia said dejectedly.

Striker made no reply. He just got out and walked up the drive. By the time he had made it to the front porch and was taking the rickety steps two at a time, Felicia caught up. They reached the door together, and Striker went to knock. But before his knuckles rapped the door, he noticed something alarming and stopped.

The lock was broken.

The door was already ajar.

Thirty-Eight

'Get your gun out,' Striker said.

Felicia drew her pistol, then nodded she was ready.

Slowly, Striker pushed open the door. Inside, everything was still and quiet and dim. Most of the lights were out, except for a single lamp in the corner of the living room and a kitchen light which was nothing more than an exposed fluorescent tube.

Striker kept himself behind the door frame. 'Luther?' he called out. 'It's Jacob Striker. Luther, are you here?'

No answer.

'Luther?' he called again, then added, 'Luna?'

When no response came, Striker gave Felicia a nod and they stepped inside. He moved slowly, scanning the way ahead. The floors were hardwood, except for the kitchen, which was made of black and white laminate squares. On it, he could see no footprints, no signs of melted snow.

'Cover right,' he said.

'Copy. Cover right.'

Together, they worked their way around the main floor of the house, clearing the living room, kitchen, a small den with an old wood-burning fireplace, and then the main bedroom and a guest bedroom.

'Everything looks normal,' Felicia said.

Striker agreed. No drawers had been dumped. No cupboards

had been rifled through. Nothing had been broken. For all intents and purposes, the place looked in relatively good condition. Clean, orderly, well cared for.

Then they reached the stairwell going down to the basement level.

'Hold back,' Striker said.

'I'll take right,' she said.

He shook his head. 'Forget that – it's a fatal funnel here. If someone's down there, all they got to do is start blasting. We'll both be screwed.'

'Call for a dog then.'

'Way out here? No way. Not unless we find something.'

'Jacob—'

'Just cover me from above, Feleesh. I'm going down.'

Before she could argue the point, Striker stepped onto the first stair leading down. The moment he placed his full weight on it, the wood groaned and the sound echoed all the way down the stairs. '*Fuck*,' he muttered. He reached out through the darkness for a light switch but couldn't find one. So he took out his flashlight and aimed it down at the darkness below.

All he saw was a steep stairway leading down to a grey-brown floor.

'You down there, Luther?' he called out.

But again, nothing.

'Vancouver Police!' he warned, then slowly made his way down. Gun aimed. Finger indexed along the guard.

When his feet touched the bottom, the beam of his flashlight caught a line of cord hanging down from the ceiling. He reached up, grabbed the cord, and gave it a soft tug. A barely audible *click* filled the room, and the overhead light turned on.

What Striker saw took his breath away. There on the ground

before him was a ring of rope, maybe three metres wide, laid out in a circle. Surrounding it were numerous candles.

On the other side of the circle was a large steel block of some kind. At first glance, it looked like an anvil, but when taken in context with its surroundings, there was only one name for what he was looking at. And the realization turned his blood cold.

He was looking at an *altar*.

Thirty-Nine

'You okay down there?' Felicia called softly.

'*Don't* come down,' Striker called back. 'Just watch your back up there.'

Still in disbelief, he scanned the basement. Took in as much as he could from the surroundings. And he tried not to get distracted by the imagery in the centre of the room. Striker swept his eyes beyond the circle of rope and the altar, and examined the rest of the room.

Essentially it was one giant rectangle. In the far right corner was a hot water tank and a furnace. In the far left corner was a row of shelves containing old leathery books, candles, and a variety of different golden cups.

Chalices and goblets.

'Jacob?' Felicia called.

'In a minute,' he called back.

'Someone's coming – there's headlights coming up the drive.'

Striker cursed. He looked at everything on the shelves once more, then back at the altar in the centre of the room. He felt creeped out just by being there, but something else in the room was bothering him. Like it didn't fit.

'It's a car,' Felicia said. 'It's parking right now.'

Striker moved back towards the altar, looked down, and saw a long doubled-edged knife with a black leather handle. It was pristine. And it told Striker what was bothering him down here. It was the *smell*. Not the old earthy smell of the leather books, not the paraffin scent of the candles, not the metallic grit of the altar. No, none of that was what he smelled.

What he smelled was *bleach*.

The entire place looked like it had been cleaned – thoroughly and recently. Everything was immaculate.

'Jacob, someone's getting out of the car – he's coming up the walk!'

Striker turned and made his way back up the stairs. The moment he stepped into the hall, he closed the door behind him, then turned to face the foyer.

The front door swung open and Luther Faust stepped inside. He spotted them immediately, took a half step backward in surprise, and then scowled.

'What the hell—' he started.

Striker cut him off. 'You've had a break-in, Luther.'

The social worker's eyes flitted around the room. 'What? When?'

'We're not sure,' Felicia said. 'But your front door lock was broken when we got here.'

Luther's eyes narrowed and his jaw tightened. 'That lock's been broken forever.'

'Well the door swung open the moment we touched it,' Striker said. 'And you weren't answering your cell, so we thought we'd better check.' When Luther's eyes turned to the stairwell door, Striker added, 'We've already cleared the main floor, but not downstairs yet. I don't mind—'

'That'll be quite alright,' Luther said.

Striker met the man's stare. 'We really should clear the place.'

'This is Ladner,' Luther said. '*Farmland*. No one comes out here, Detective. Not ever.' He walked into the hallway, and got between them and the doorway leading downstairs. He gave it a solid push to be sure it was closed.

'Up to you,' Striker said.

Luther turned around slowly. 'So. What *are* you doing out here?'

Striker got down to business. 'You hear about the Recovery House in Langara? Where Moses Sabba works?'

'Yes, I know of it. Almost everyone in my field does.' Luther gave them a wary look. 'A fact I'm sure you're already well aware of.'

Felicia said, 'We verify our facts, Luther – always.'

Luther did not respond. He just stood there looking back at them.

Striker spoke next.

'Moses Sabba is dead,' he said.

For a split second, the defiant look on Luther's face remained. Then, the hardness of his eyes drained away and his face took on a stunned – almost worried – look.

'Moses,' he said. 'But . . . *how?*'

Felicia explained. 'Same way Jazz was killed this morning.'

'In a pool of gas and fire,' Striker said.

Luther opened his mouth, but no words came out. He just stood there looking lost, bewildered, and his eyes took on a distant look. Like they were staring at something very far away.

'Odd thing is,' Striker continued. 'Jazz had just called him the day before. You know why?'

Luther shook his head.

'To speak to him about *Satanism*.' Striker stopped talking for a moment to see if Luther would respond, but the man never did. He just stood there, the lost expression slowly leaving his face and being replaced by a look of wariness. 'Any ideas why she would call Moses about that?'

Luther licked his lips before speaking. 'Why would I know?' he asked.

'We just thought—'

'Moses was known to take an interest in *all* world religions. He was a very smart man. Very . . . out there, I guess. But I don't know much beyond that. We haven't really spoken in years.'

For a moment, silence filled the room, and Striker purposely let it. He gave Felicia a look to not say anything, to let Luther continue, but the man never did.

'Anything else?' Striker finally asked.

Luther stared back, unblinking. 'What else is there?'

Striker shrugged. 'You knew this man for twenty years, Luther. Twenty years. And you don't know anything else beyond the fact that Moses was *out there*?'

'I wasn't his keeper.'

Striker laughed bemusedly. 'Interesting. Everyone seems to know everyone in the mental health fields, especially people of your generation. And yet, strangely, no one knows anything when you ask them questions.'

The hard look returned to Luther's eyes and his face darkened to a purplish-red colour. 'What is it you really want, Detective?'

'I want answers, Luther. On why I have some psycho out there burning people in pools of fire.'

'And how the hell would I know the answer to that?'

Striker shrugged. 'You tell me.'

For a brief moment the two men locked eyes, then Luther let out a long slow breath before speaking. 'I've had enough of the game,' he said. 'I got court first thing tomorrow morning, so I'll ask you to take your leave.'

'Your house, your rules,' Striker said.

When they reached the door, Felicia spoke up in almost a

plea. 'Luther, we really need to talk to Luna as well. Do you know where we can find her?'

'Yes, I do.'

He did not offer the address.

Felicia frowned. 'Would you mind—'

'I'll be sure to tell her you were looking for her, Detective.'

The door closed with a slam, one hard enough to rattle the porch. A moment later, the outside light clicked off, and Striker and Felicia were left standing in darkness. Striker didn't care about the rudeness. For the first time since this investigation had begun, he knew they had found their path.

'We're onto something,' he said.

Forty

It was late by the time they got home – after eleven – and Striker felt beaten down in every way. He was weary from the long day, hurting from the beating he had taken, mentally drained from trying to uncover all the lies everyone had been telling them, and exhausted from the spiritual tug-of-war he'd been having with his faith for the better part of the day. On top of all this, lurking in the back of his mind, was the understanding that this investigation would become a media nightmare the moment the true details of the story got out.

And that was only a matter of time.

He headed up the front steps onto the porch. The planks groaned like he felt. Exhaustion was setting in now. Surprisingly, the hardest part had been seeing Father O'Brien again.

It had seemed to knock the wind right out of him.

The moment he and Felicia walked through the door, he spotted Courtney. She was sitting by the gas fireplace in her flannel pyjamas, with the phone tucked to her ear. Upon seeing them, she said, 'Goodnight, Nate – miss ya,' and hung up. She took one look at Striker and spotted the bruise alongside his face.

'Get too fresh with Felicia again?' she joked, but failed to hide the concern from her voice.

He forced a smile. 'You know Spanish women – they're hot-blooded.'

Courtney maintained her concerned look, and Striker faked ignorance. At times, she was so much like Felicia. He felt bombarded by both sides.

He hung his coat on the rack. When it fell off and landed on the floor, he left it there.

Felicia picked it up behind him. As she did, Courtney crossed the room for a better look at her father.

'What happened?' she demanded.

'Rodeo clown accident,' he said. 'You should see the bull.' Striker gave her a quick hug and a kiss on the head, then walked into the kitchen.

From the living room, he could hear Courtney and Felicia talking about him. He tried to ignore it and grabbed a couple of cold ones from the fridge – Miller Genuine Draft. He uncapped both of them, dropped the caps in the recycling box, and took out his cell.

He dialled a contact of his in the Information Services of CFSEU – the Combined Forces Special Enforcement Unit. Primarily, they dealt with a lot of high-end gang stuff, and they were damn good at it. His contact's name was Stone, and all Striker wanted of him was one thing.

'An address,' he said. 'Of a guy named Moses Sabba.'

Stone's voice was quiet but deep. 'Where you been already?'

'To four of them.' Striker gave the man a rundown of all the places they had checked so far. Then Stone cleared his throat.

'If another one exists, I'll find it for you – can I call late?'

'The moment you get one.'

Stone laughed. 'You haven't changed a bit, Shipwreck.'

'Why mess with perfection?'

'I been telling my wife that for years.'

The two men shared a laugh, then Stone hung up.

The moment Striker returned to the living room, he spotted

Courtney standing by the hallway entrance. Her arms were crossed and her face looked guarded. She again scrutinized his bruised and battered face, and all at once she reminded him of her mother. She was just like Amanda at times. So much that it scared him.

'How's Nate?' he asked.

She didn't uncross her arms. 'Fine.'

Striker grinned; she had stolen his own line. 'Still Justin Bieber gorgeous?'

A small smirk found her lips. 'Bieber's out, Dad. Live in the now.'

He nodded. 'Mel Gibson gorgeous? Ricky Martin gorgeous? *Donny Osmond gorgeous?*'

Courtney looked imploringly at Felicia. 'How you work with him all day is beyond me.'

'I drink a lot,' Felicia said.

Courtney walked up to Striker, gave him a quick kiss on his uninjured cheek, muttered *Luv ya, Dad*, then headed off to bed. As she walked down the hall, Striker watched her go – watched her gait – with concerned and analytical eyes. He tried not to. Struggled not to. But always had to.

Ever since the accident, he had to.

It was not a choice.

'She's walking better,' Felicia said.

Striker said nothing, but agreed. She was doing much better. Around the house, she didn't even bother with the crutches anymore – not unless her back was really aching. Striker hoped that soon she'd stop using them altogether.

One day.

The second Courtney's bedroom door closed, Felicia pilfered one of the beers from him and dropped down on the couch.

Striker joined her.

She opened up her briefcase, pulled out a thick file folder, and started separating the paperwork into different piles – witness statements, police statements, doctors' reports, fire crew and EHS forms, and so on.

Striker watched her for a while. Her long dark hair kept spilling forward into her eyes, and she kept brushing it back. She looked as tired as he felt, and yet still, God she was beautiful. She caught his gaze as she put the papers back into a pile and stuffed them inside the folder.

'Your jaw looks sore,' she said.

'I'm an autumn. Purple's my colour.'

She frowned. 'Do you always have to have a response for everything?'

'It's my sparkling wit.'

'It's a defence mechanism.'

Striker said nothing back, and then Felicia wrapped her arms around his neck. She pulled him close and kissed him softly on the lips. It was a long kiss, a soft kiss, and her lips lingered on his.

He breathed her in, and she raised an eyebrow mischievously.

'What's on your mind?' she asked.

'We got three victims now – Jazz, Moses, and our John Doe – this guy isn't going to stop killing, Feleesh.'

She gave him a wry look. 'That wasn't the response I was hoping for.'

Striker knew that, but he couldn't help it. 'There's a pattern here, Feleesh. Somewhere in this mess. We just can't see it yet.'

'Rest your mind, Jacob. If only for the night.'

'I *can't* rest my mind – not when he's still out there somewhere.'

'There's nothing you can do about that right now. If you don't get some rest you'll be useless tomorrow. And unsafe. You need some downtime. Everyone does. Otherwise you'll burn yourself up.'

'Appropriate choice of words.'

Felicia pressed her finger against his forehead. 'Rest in there. *Rest!*'

Striker listened to her words, but they were easier said than done. He felt wired. On edge. And there was a reason for that. Everyone had been dishonest with them all day long: lies. Half-truths. Deflections. Avoidance.

Just what the hell was going on?

Felicia stood up, grabbed him by the hands. 'Come with me.'

Knowing she wouldn't let up, Striker finally got himself moving. He followed her down to the bedroom, then stripped down to his briefs and laid back on the bed. Once Felicia had changed into a long t-shirt, she joined him. She nestled up to him with her head on his shoulder and patted his chest.

'Rest your mind,' she said softly.

Striker made no reply. He just laid there and felt her warmth. Felt her softness. Felt her breathe. For the first time since finding Jazz's body at the bus yards, the world felt good again. And Striker sucked up as much of those feelings as he could.

He needed it. To heal his body. To repair his mind. To not only recuperate but *rejuvenate* himself. And that was essential. Because tomorrow he was going to need all his strength. If Striker had learnt anything in his career, it was this: monsters didn't stop unless you stopped them.

It was part of what made them monsters.

ACT TWO
Beast and Burden

Wednesday

Forty-One

It was dark when Monster got up, and that was normal. Sleep was never restful, and slumber never peaceful. It was almost a blessing that he only managed three to four hours a night. Sometimes a little less, sometimes a little more. The length and depth depended almost entirely on the medications.

It had been like that ever since the accident.

He got up from the mattress he slept on, his long legs half-draped across the old floorboards. As always, his joints felt tight and his skin inflexible.

The chamber was cold. Terribly cold. The temperature had dropped once more. He looked out the dirty pane of the north-facing window, and saw that the inlet was a mass of murky blackness. Thin sheets of icy rain slashed down from clouds that were so dark they blended perfectly with the night sky above.

So dark.

Everything was so dark.

Monster lit one of the candles that sat on the floor beside the mattress, and the room took on a warm golden feel.

'Samuel,' Monster called. *'Sam-u-el!'*

Moments later, a scuffling sound could be heard and the little squirrel appeared. It skittered across the room as if the floor was not old wooden boards but a rink of ice. Once close enough, it sprang up on the windowsill, then hopped onto Monster's shoulder in one giant bound.

Despite the dreariness and pain Monster felt, a smile cracked his disfigured lips. He reached into his pocket and pulled out one of the Corn Nuts he had purchased at a 7-Eleven last night – before the incident in the subway tunnels. The store had been out of original flavour, so Monster had bought ranch, then washed and air-dried them overnight.

It was more than worth the work. Just watching Samuel roll the dried corn in his paw and nibble it into his cheeks brought Monster a sense of joy that he never felt when alone.

That he never felt with anyone.

Once full, Samuel leaped onto the window ledge. The orange light from the candle flame reflected off the window pane and made the squirrel look like he was backlit by a ring of fire.

The vision brought Monster back to old times. Memories of when he was a child. Of a time when The Boy With The Violet Eyes was there, looking down at him in that cold detached way of his.

'*You love that squirrel, don't you?*' he had asked.

Monster had been too afraid to answer.

Even now, a lump developed in his throat, and he tried to force out the bad thoughts. But they lingered. Swirled. Stormed through his head.

The pain he'd been in – the absolute *agony*.

The peeling of his flesh.

The vomiting induced by the medications.

And that horrible smell of the skin disinfectants.

So many memories, colliding and bumping into one another. It had been a horrific time back then. One giant cluster of pain and medications and surgeries. And the only thing that had brought him any happiness had been the little squirrel who had often perched outside his recovery room on the window's ledge.

The *first* Samuel.

As if jealous of the memory, this Samuel chattered at Monster, breaking him from the sad thoughts of the past. He tried to smile at the little creature, but no matter how he tried, he just could not do it.

Today, the world was too dark a place.

And when Samuel finally finished the Corn Nut and bounded off into the next room, Monster was swallowed by the darkness. Any sense of happiness was consumed as well.

Monster crossed the room. Located his mask on the podium. Began fixing the rubbery mould to his face. The time for peace was gone. A woman was next on the list.

She was going to be very, very hard to kill.

Forty-Two

Striker sat alone in the small den of his home and struggled with himself. As bad as his neck and jaw felt from his fight in the subway tunnel – the joint still throbbed and his head still ached – his conscience felt even worse. His mood was as dark as the world outside his window.

And it was little better inside his home.

The room was dim. The only source of light was the artificial brightness of the standing lamp in the corner. Still, it was better than nothing, chasing away the worst of shadows.

He sat in the old recliner, under that lamp, and flipped through the yellowing crinkly pages of his King James Bible. Doing so brought him back to older times – happy, wonderful times that now left him so terribly sad: days when the family had gone to the Holy Cross church. When he'd walked up the sidewalk with Mom and Dad. Listened to the service. And had taken the gospel as gospel – as if it were pure uncontested fact.

How he missed those days. And he wondered exactly when and where those beliefs had shattered.

One of the best memories was *after* church, going out for breakfast following the sermon. It had been a family tradition, one done every Sunday.

But those times had died along with his parents.

Died along with his faith.

He flipped through the pages, remembering as much as reading. He got to the passage *Footprints*, and read it through. This one had always been his father's favourite.

Soon, the memories became too painful.

Striker closed the book. Sat in the darkness. Felt lost and bothered and worried about everything that was going on. Images haunted him – the blackened bodies of the victims, flashes of Luther and Luna and Moses, subway tunnels and altars, the underlying sense of smoke and fire, and within it all there was the monster with the rubbery face.

He was always there.

Striker dropped the Bible on the side table.

'It's a fucked-up world,' he said to no one.

From somewhere down the hall, a door creaked open. It sounded like Felicia was getting up. Striker was amazed she managed to sleep at all, much less so well. She always did, no matter what file they were investigating. The woman could be so damn calm. So cool. Like *ice*.

It bothered him and amazed him all at once.

Just as he was deep in thought on the matter, his cell phone rang, startling him and tearing him from his thoughts. He leaned forward and snatched it from the coffee table. Hit talk. Pressed the cell to his ear.

'Striker,' he said.

'Wakey-wakey, Shipwreck.'

'Stone?' His contact from CFSEU – the Combined Forces Special Enforcement Unit. 'You get something? – tell me you got something.'

'I do. On this Moses guy.'

'An address?'

'You got it, baby. Windsor and 16th – the Kensington area.'

'You're an information God.'

Striker grabbed the pen and paper from the table and took down the information. According to Stone, the address came back to a single residence. Unrented. Owned by an M.J. Sabba. There was no previous IHL – or Incident History Location – so no previous police files for Striker to read.

All in all, it was a relatively unknown locale.

'I owe you one,' Striker said.

Stone made a sad sound. 'I knew Jazz, Shipwreck. Just find this prick. And when you do, take him down hard – show him as much mercy as he showed her.'

The words troubled and inspired Striker all at once. By the time he heard a dial tone, he was already moving down the hall to get Felicia. A newfound energy surged through him. A newfound hope.

He wanted to hold on to it for as long as he could.

Forty-Three

It was just after six o'clock by the time Striker and Felicia pulled onto the street where Moses supposedly had lived. High above, the sky was still a lightless vacuum, and the street before them seemed no better. Not a single street lamp dotted the road, and all the houses on the west side were so completely dark that it looked as if the power had gone out.

'Cheery neighbourhood,' Felicia said. 'I think I'll move here in two-thousand-never.'

Striker said nothing back. He just drove down the road until he found the correct address and stopped the car. The headlights offered some illumination, bleaching the road in a white halogen glare.

Striker studied the house. It was like nothing he had expected. What he had been looking for was an ordinary house on a middle lot. But what he found was a small shack of sorts that had one large bay window that was fronted by iron bars and backed by a dark blue bed sheet.

'It's the new take on sheers and curtains,' Felicia said.

'Yeah, sure. Very Ikea.'

Above the front window was a large square piece of wood that had some kind of faded writing on it. Felicia pointed to it. 'Looks like this used to be a store of some kind. Strange.'

'Of course it's strange,' Striker said. 'Everything about this file's been strange from the beginning – why stop now?'

He killed the engine and climbed out. Felicia followed. As they made their way up the sidewalk, under the snowy branches of a nearby tree, the darkness felt impenetrable. When Felicia took out her flashlight to offer them some light, Striker did the same.

They reached the front door, and Striker inspected the lock. It was intact. And when he gave the door a slight pull, he saw that it was sturdy and secure. He took a quick look down the side of the house and spotted two more windows at the back end.

'Looks like it was a shop of some kind, with a rental unit in the back,' he said. 'Moses is listed as the tenant here, but who knows for sure.'

He knocked on the door, waited, and no one came. While Felicia called Info to dig up any extra information they could find on the address, Striker rounded the building. Once out back, he found a rear door. He knocked on this one too, and got the same result. No one was home. When he tried the handle, he found that it was locked and secure as well.

His frustration was growing.

He looked at the rear windows. Like the ones out front, they were fortified with iron bars and backed by what appeared to be bed sheets. The bluish fabric hung down, blocking off any inside view.

Striker returned to the front just as Felicia hung up.

'Any luck?' he asked.

She shook her head. 'No contact list whatsoever.'

Striker frowned at that. He looked at the lock on the front door. It was steel and appeared to be strong. So did the door. But the frame? Not so much. The wood looked old and weathered, bowing out a little in the middle.

A weak point.

Striker took out his police knife and unfolded it.

'What are you doing?' Felicia asked.

'Getting in.'

'We should probably get a warrant.'

Striker shook his head. Getting a warrant would take too much time – over five hours to write it, another two hours just to get it handed in to a judge, then another three hours waiting for approval. That was a total of ten hours – and that was *if* the judge approved it on the first write. Or at all.

The process was maddening to Striker. What should have been objective was completely subjective most of the time, and it often came down to which judge you got on any given day. In the city of Vancouver, getting a warrant approved was like playing craps – you never knew if you'd be lucky.

And on most days the dice were loaded.

Striker wasn't prepared to waste the day going through all that. Not with a homicidal pyromaniac on the loose. He jammed the blade of his knife deeper into the space between the door and frame, and kept prying.

Felicia didn't hide her concerns. 'This is going to be a problem in court.'

Striker kept prying. 'It'll be a problem in court no matter what we do. If we don't get a warrant, they'll fight it on the grounds that we should have. If we do get a warrant, they'll fight it on the grounds that the warrant was faulty. Either way, we're going to end up defending something. Besides, this is *exigent*.'

Felicia looked ready to say more, but the wood let out a low groan and buckled; the front door popped open with a soft rattle. Striker looked back at her with a wink.

'Warrant approved,' he said.

With the door now open, Striker took a long look inside.

Everything was dark and silent and still. He waved the beam of his flashlight around the interior and saw that it was basically one giant common room.

At the far end was a small kitchen area with a table big enough for two people, and at the nearer end were a pair of old loveseats that flanked a coffee table. In the corner of the room sat an old television set – big, deep, one of those old projection units that looked like it weighed eighty kilos.

'Vancouver Police!' Striker called. 'Anyone home?'

There was no reply.

He took another long look, then focused on the back wall, just beside the kitchen. Two doors were there. A bedroom and a bathroom, he guessed. He gave Felicia a nod to cover them, and they stepped inside.

The first thing Striker did was drag his free hand along the wall. When he found a switch, he flicked it on and the entire room lit up from a row of long fluorescent tubing that ran down the centre of the ceiling.

Striker turned off his flashlight. 'This was definitely a convenience store at some point.'

Felicia nodded. 'Look at the kitchen nook – it looks like an old checkout area.'

Striker moved past the two loveseats into the kitchen area. On the small section of counter was a scattering of papers. He scanned them, then picked one up. Saw the words *Recovery House Schedule* at the top, followed by the name *Moses Sabba*, and his signature at the bottom.

'Well, we're in the right place,' he said.

He put down the paper, then moved on. He approached the two doors at the far end of the room and indicated for Felicia to cover the south one. When she did, he opened the east-facing door and looked inside.

The room was small and vacant. A single bed. A dresser. A small en-suite that consisted of a toilet, sink and a shower. No bathtub though.

Scattered on the floor beside the bed were a few more papers. At first glance, Striker thought they were more therapy forms from the Recovery House, but when he looked at them more closely, he saw a bunch of swirling patterns and strange symbols, next to which was a list of corresponding dates.

February 2nd.

March 1st.

December 21st.

Striker recognized the last one – it was the same exact date that Moses had taken the photo of him and Luna having sex.

It was odd.

He seized the paper. Folded it. Stuffed it into his pocket. As he turned around, his eyes caught sight of a safe in the far corner of the room. It was small, compact, and not bolted into the wall.

It looked like a fire safe.

He went over to it, tugged on the handle, and the door wouldn't budge. He picked up the safe. It was relatively heavy, probably weighed more than thirty kilos. When he shook it, he felt something move around inside.

Noodles would have to open it later.

Curious, Striker returned to Felicia, who was still in the common room, covering the last door. She had her hand on the butt of her pistol, and a tense look on her face.

'Last room,' he said.

''Bout time – this place is giving me the creeps.'

Striker gave her a nod to be sure she was ready, then opened the door.

What they found inside was disturbing. All the windows had been blocked with dark blue sheets, and standing in each corner of the room were four candelabras, each one complete with dark red candles. In between the closest two candelabras, against the east-facing wall, was a replica of the same altar Striker had seen back at Luther's house – a steel and wood platform, upon which rested a long double-edged sword.

The handle wrapped in blood-red leather.

'*Jesus*,' Felicia said. 'What the hell is this place? Some kind of dark church?'

'It ain't Disneyland,' Striker said. He scanned the room one more time, then added, 'It's almost the exact same layout as what I saw at Luther's house.'

He stepped into the room, felt for a switch and found one. When he clicked it on, nothing happened, so he took out his flashlight once more and scanned the walls. Just like the windows, they were covered with a thick blue-black material, but were otherwise empty.

He moved further into the room and approached the altar. Beside the sword were two more candles. Then some odd-smelling incense in a silver bowl, and a grey goblet filled with what appeared to be wine.

Felicia stepped forward for a closer look herself. As she did, her foot struck something. She tripped and almost collided with the altar, but Striker steadied her with a quick hand.

'What the hell?' she asked.

Striker shone his flashlight on the floor. They both looked down and saw a long braid of red rope.

'Lucky it wasn't a tripwire of some kind,' he remarked.

The rope ran all the way around the room in a full circle, similar to what Striker had seen back at Luther's place. But within the circle here were other braids of rope. Five points in all. And when Striker looked down upon it, in all directions, he realized exactly what he was seeing.

'We're standing in the middle of a giant symbol,' Felicia said.
Striker nodded.
'A pentagram.'

Forty-Four

A half hour later, at quarter to seven, Striker stood in the centre of Moses Sabba's bedroom and felt a swarm of frustration envelop him. The Ident tech had arrived to process the scene, but so far he and Striker had found nothing of any true value.

Striker found the situation odd. There was little doubt Moses had lived here. But the man must have been a minimalist, because – aside from a few pieces of identification and some miscellaneous bills – there was nothing else here linking him to the residence. No videos or photos or letters or emails or anything.

Moses Sabba was an enigma.

From the other room, Striker could hear Felicia directing some of the patrolmen, telling them what needed to be logged as evidence and what was to be left alone. Her voice sounded jittery and on edge. It made Striker wonder if the whole religious aspect of the file was getting to her too, only in a different way; for all Felicia's lightheartedness, she was a Catholic. And a pretty devout one, for the most.

'Can I break the lock, or what?' a surly voice asked.

Striker left his thoughts and looked over at the Ident tech. Noodles was analysing the small safe, his bushy eyebrows scrunched into a frown.

Striker nodded. 'Do what you have to do. Just get in.'

Noodles kept looking at the safe, as if pondering something. After a long moment, he shook his head. 'You know, there's some pretty weird shit going on here with this file. I think I'll have it X-rayed first.'

Striker agreed. It wasn't a bad idea.

'Call me the moment you get it open,' he said.

When Noodles took the safe to his van, Striker helped Felicia finish processing the exhibits they needed from the other room. Once done, he took out his notebook and made a list of the different items they had found, where they'd found them, and then he drew the pattern of rope Felicia had tripped over. Following this, the two of them left the scene under Ident's authority and returned to the car.

The moment Felicia closed the door, she shivered.

'Place gives me the willies,' she said.

Striker started the engine. 'If that creeps you out, wait till you see what I found in his bedroom.'

'What?'

Striker took out the paper he'd seized with the strange pattern of circles and signs, and the corresponding dates. 'Look at this one,' – he pointed to December 21st – 'This is the same date that Moses took the photo of him and Luna having sex. Well, I googled it, and guess what? You were right. It's a satanic holiday. Feast Day – in honour of the Beast. And there's a corresponding sex ritual involved. I haven't figured the others out yet.'

Felicia said nothing, she just looked at the dates and her eyes were dark. 'This is getting really twisted.'

Striker agreed. 'So we have a murdered homicide detective who specialized in arsons and ritualistic murders, and two of the people we've talked to about it – names that were specifically listed in Jazz's notes – have altars and pentagrams in their houses.'

Felicia nodded. 'One of whom – Moses Sabba – is now dead.'

'Burned to death in a pool of fire.' Striker let it all sink in. 'Seems eerily fitting, doesn't it?' When Felicia just let out a heavy breath and turned silent, Striker returned to assessing the MO. 'This is what we know: people are being targeted and burned to death, possibly by someone they all know. And much of what we're finding at the scenes – the burning of the victims and the left-behind crosses – hints at ritualism.'

Felicia nodded. 'Add in the type of files Jazz was investigating, the fact she had been in contact with Moses and Luther, and what we've now found in Luther and Moses' homes, and you have to wonder – are we dealing with the occult here?'

Striker thought it over.

Felicia snapped the folder she was reading closed. 'All I know is Moses and Jazz are both dead. But Luther's not. So I say we just drag his ass down to the station now and get him on video.'

Striker shook his head. 'Bad idea.'

'Why? You saw what he had in his basement.'

'So? Nothing illegal about having an altar and some rope.'

'We'll go on circumstantial evidence,' she pressed. 'We got the same creepy crap in Luther's place that Moses had in his place, they're both connected to Jazz's file, and now Moses is dead.'

'Correlations do not equate to conspiracy,' Striker replied. 'It's pretty thin, Feleesh. We'll burn our only chance for a custodial interview.'

'I'm not saying we have to arrest him, Jacob. We can just take him in for questioning. Say it's for his own safety.'

Striker looked out the window, where the day was finally growing lighter, albeit a bit grey. He thought their legal grounds through for a long moment before speaking.

'The problem isn't taking Luther down for an interview,' he finally said. 'We can do that easily enough. But the moment we do, Luther will know we're investigating him. Hell, he's already anti-police – you saw how he acted towards me back at the Ministry and again at his house. The moment he knows what I saw in his basement, he'll clam up completely. He'll avoid us. And he'll look for logical explanations.'

'Like what?'

Striker shrugged. 'I dunno. He could say the altar and rope were just a bunch of props for Halloween. There's no judge on the planet who'd allow them to be entered as evidence against him. Not without some solid proof that they were connected to the crime. And right now, we have nothing on the man. Everything is circumstantial.'

'He's involved in this somehow. He's *lying* to us.'

'I know he is,' Striker said. 'I can feel it. But we need more information before we act. Otherwise we're going into a gunfight with blanks.'

He put the car into gear and drove up to Kingsway. Turned west.

Frustrated, Felicia rested her head against the window. 'Where we going now?' she asked plainly.

'To see a specialist,' Striker replied. 'I know a guy who can help us with this satanic stuff, legal and otherwise. Name's Solomon. He's a real weird guy – an asshole, really – so he should fit in well with the file.'

'He a professor?'

'No.'

'Cop?'

'Nope.'

'Lawyer?'

'Closer,' Striker said, and a smile broke his lips. When Felicia gave him a confused look, he 'fessed up:

'Solomon is a *convict*.'

They headed for the Vancouver jail.

Forty-Five

Monster approached the complex more fearful of the painful memories than the brutal task ahead.

The building had no name, but those who lived here called it the Green Box because it was square and covered in a flaking green paint that was at least twenty years old. As Monster neared the lot, a strange feeling flooded his chest like a cold wave. It was something he couldn't define. A mixture of being cold. Tight. Hollow.

It was from the memories, he rationalized. Had to be.

They always seemed to clash with the present.

The stairs of the fire escape were at the rear of the building, and they were as rickety as ever. The entire structure shook beneath the weight of his body, making it difficult to balance the supplies he was carrying. They were the same as always: four jerry cans of fuel. A fire extinguisher. His flare gun. His hoodie, top up. And his gloves. Triple XL's.

He opened the fire exit door that led to the third floor. Once opened, he stood there for a moment, as if a force field of some kind blocked him from entering. Going here was turning out to be more difficult than he'd thought.

It took something out of him.

He closed his mind to the bad thoughts. He stared down the hallway. And he assessed.

The building was small. Each floor had only four units, two per side. The unit he headed for was the closest one. Immediate right. He knew this because he'd already been here twice, scouting out the place.

Nothing had changed – not with the building and not with Jolene. The bitch had been in the hallway the last time he'd come, drunk and yelling at the other tenants, like she always did.

Monster could still hear her calls:

Ya shit-fuck nobody!

Ya cocksucker fuck!

Ya dick-mouth faggot!

Her taunts were always the same. Angry, hostile, full of filth.

Monster stood in the doorway and listened for the sounds of anyone that might be approaching. When he heard none, he moved forward into the hall until he reached the right room.

The door was labelled 3B. And when he grabbed the doorknob and turned it, he found that the lock wasn't even engaged. It swung open and he walked inside. Closed the door behind him.

And he prepared.

He placed his supplies down on the floor and scanned the room. From the doorway, he could see the small living area, kitchenette, and bathroom. Newspapers and cigarette butts and empty beer cans covered the living-room floor, as did old pizza boxes and food-crusted Styrofoam takeout containers. In the kitchen, the countertops were covered with old food – half-eaten noodles and stale bread and an expired jar of mayonnaise that left the air sour. The kitchen floor was littered with empty bottles of rice wine and empty containers of mouthwash.

Foul smells owned the air. Of food gone bad. Of toilets backed up. Of stale cigarette smoke.

Of so many dirty things.

Monster lumbered into the centre of the living area. As he did, his boot stepped on a crack pipe and the glass broke on the floor. When he looked down at it, he also saw other drug paraphernalia – blue water packets, burnt spoons, used rigs, and a dozen or so push-rods.

The sight of it all awoke something inside of him – the beast he fought to keep subdued. His fists tightened, as did his jaw. He could feel it coming back out again. Raging against control.

His eyes found the only other door in the room, the one that led to the bedroom. The bitch would be in there, no doubt. Zoned out. Drunk. High. Whatever the daily poison.

He grabbed the door handle. Turned the knob. Opened the door.

And saw her.

Jolene was sprawled out on the bed. Face up. With only her top on. Her legs were spread wide open, revealing a big patch of greying pubic hair. One smell of the room told Monster that she had shit the bed.

Anger overtook him.

'Wake up,' he ordered.

But she was too zoned out to even respond.

'I said, wake—'

He stopped mid-sentence.

Something was wrong here.

The arched angle of her back. The stiffness of her limbs. The bluish pallor of her skin . . . And all at once, it hit him.

She was already gone.

Overdosed from whatever drug she was on.

The moment hit him like a physical blow. And it turned his legs surprisingly weak – as rubbery as his mask.

Monster dropped to his knees. Hunched forward against the bed. Felt his head droop low. And suddenly, without warning, deep and heavy sobs came from his throat. He shook and heaved and felt the tremors inside his body fighting to get out like some beast refusing to be caged.

It wasn't fair.

It was *never* fair.

He wanted to be the one responsible for killing her.

Life had robbed him once again.

Forty-Six

'His full name is Solomon Slowitzski,' Striker said. 'And he's the only person I've ever arrested who proclaims himself to be a Satanist.'

They drove down the one-way stretch of Powell Street towards the Vancouver jail. As usual, Oppenheimer Park was filled with drug dealers selling their poison to the addicted and mentally ill. Striker saw more than a half-dozen transactions taking place. Normally, he would have busted their asses.

But there was no time for that today.

Felicia was still looking through the file, but her face showed the uncertainty she felt in meeting this man. 'What kind of rapport you got with this guy anyway?' she asked. 'You think he might actually help us?'

Striker smiled. 'Not willingly.'

He rounded Main Street and came back on Cordova, before parking outside the south door of the Vancouver jail.

'What you arrest him for?' Felicia asked.

'This time? Aggravated assault. Last time? Child pornography.'

Felicia made a face and Striker nodded. 'He's a real piece of work.'

'He's a piece of *something*,' she said. 'What's he doing down here anyway? Shouldn't he be out at Matsqui for something like that?'

'He was. But as luck would have it, he's down here for a bail hearing today. He even got past the teleconference stage, so the judge might actually be considering a conditional discharge.' He smiled at Felicia. 'We're gonna use that to our advantage.'

He climbed out of the car, slammed the door and approached the jail. After badging the camera and announcing his name, rank and number, the steel door clicked loudly and popped ajar.

Striker pulled the heavy door open and they went inside.

Ten minutes later, they were standing outside a jailhouse interview room, looking at Solomon through the wire mesh window.

Solomon Slowitzski was exactly what Felicia would have expected had she closed her eyes and thought of a Hollywood-style Satanist. His head was shaved. His eyebrows had been plucked in such a way that they angled upwards in the middle. And the moustache and beard he had grown were not only a goatee, but trimmed down pencil-thin.

'Is this guy for real?' she asked.

'He wants to be,' Striker said.

'All he needs is a helmet with horns and a red cape.'

Striker smiled at that. 'Solomon tried to start up his own church – Church of the Underworld – but then he found out that Church of the Underworld was already the name of a night-club, and he got sued.'

Felicia laughed.

'He's a total wannabe,' Striker said. 'Everything from the shaved head and goatee, to the story he'll probably tell you about having had his two extra vertebrae – the ones which made up a tail – surgically removed when he was a kid.'

Felicia kept peering through the window. 'Guy looks like a metrosexual Satanist to me.'

Striker grinned. 'Maybe so. But don't take him lightly, Feleesh. This guy knows his stuff. And he's dangerous. Don't forget that – and don't *ever* turn your back on him. He's had a sling of assault PO charges. And you don't even want to know what he did to some of the children. He's a real sicko.'

The mention of child victims killed any humour Felicia might have felt. Her face showed that.

Striker looked at his watch and saw that it was already 7:50 a.m. Solomon's lawyer – Alfred Weismann – was pencilled into the log book for 8:15 a.m. It gave them very little time, and Striker just hoped that Weismann wouldn't be early, like he normally was. If that happened, his entire plan would be trashed.

Striker opened up the door and they went inside.

The moment Solomon saw him, his eyes narrowed with recognition, and a scowl crept over his face. '*Striker*,' he spat. 'What the hell do you want – I thought my lawyer was coming in.'

'He will be. In time.'

Solomon stood up. 'I'll wait in my cell.'

Striker moved between him and the door. 'Sit down.'

'It's my right—'

'You got a choice to make here, Solomon. A real easy one. You wanna leave and not talk to me, that's fine – but I came down here specifically for your parole hearing. Had it scheduled on my calendar with a big yellow happy face for weeks now. Know why? I'm gonna screw it up.'

Solomon said nothing, he just stood there and his eyes narrowed.

Striker offered the man a smile. 'I can hardly wait to tell the judge what a threat I feel you still are to society.'

'That's bullshit.'

Striker looked over at Felicia. 'I can't remember. Did I say I was gonna tell the judge he was a threat? Or a *serious* threat?'

'Just a threat,' she said.

'I should probably say serious.'

Felicia made an uncertain sound. 'I dunno. *Grave* has a stronger connotation than serious.'

Striker snapped his fingers. 'Oh you're right. Let me try it. "A *grave* threat, Your Honour." Oh, I like that. It sounds dire – *blameworthy* on the judge if he lets him out and something bad happens to another kid.'

Solomon's face turned red and he slammed his fist on the table. 'This is bullshit and you fuckin' know it, Striker.'

'Oh my, there's that anger again . . . You see that, Feleesh?'

She nodded and crossed her arms. 'Yup, a *grave* threat to society.'

Striker looked back at Solomon and waited for a moment. Gave the man a few seconds to reconsider. Already, the man's white face was turning redder by the second, and the muscles at the sides of his temples were pulsating.

'This is fucking *illegal*,' he finally said. 'You're threatening me, and I'm telling my lawyer about it.'

Striker splayed his hands. 'I'm doing no such thing, Solomon. Just telling you why I came down here. But if you sit back down and give me what I want – information that has no bearing on your charges at all – then I might just fail to show for the hearing. The choice is yours. Help me out, and we walk our separate ways. Screw me, and I'll give it ten times back to you in court.'

Striker stepped out of the man's way and opened the door so that he could leave the room and return to his cell.

'Well?' he asked. 'What's it gonna be?'

The angry look on Solomon's face remained. But in the end

he sat back down in his chair, crossed his arms, and muttered, 'What the fuck you want already?'

'Information,' Striker said. He closed the door. 'Some that's right up your alley. It's why we're here. I need your *expertise*.'

The words seemed to pique the man's interest, or at least feed his ego. A smug look slowly spread across his face. 'Do tell,' he said dryly.

Striker sat down on the other side of the table and took out his notebook. Felicia remained standing behind him, in the corner of the room, before the doorway. Striker flipped forward through the pages until he found the list he'd made and the pentagram he'd drawn back at the strange residence belonging to Moses Sabba.

'I've already done some research on this stuff myself,' Striker continued. 'And I've reached some conclusions on some of the matters. But I don't have answers for everything yet.'

Solomon grinned. 'Which is where yours truly comes in.'

Striker made eye contact with the convict. There was an amused look in the man's eyes. Solomon was enjoying this. 'Listen up,' Striker said. 'February 2nd, March 1st, and December 21st – do those dates mean anything to you?'

Solomon let out a dark laugh and he cupped his hands together in his lap. '*Of course* they mean something to me. They're all satanic ritual days.'

'Ritual days?'

'Great Rites.'

'And what *great rites* are these?'

Solomon leaned forward in his chair, as if the discussion was exciting him. 'February 2nd is Candlemass. March 1st is St Eichatadt Day, and December 21st is—'

'Feast Day,' Striker finished. 'It's on the solstice.'

'Exactly.'

Striker wrote all this down in his notebook, then met Solomon's stare once more. 'So what exactly happens on these days? How do you celebrate them?'

Solomon splayed his hands and spoke in a tone of condescension. 'During Candlemass, we honour our Lord through initiation. During St Eichatadt Day, we honour our Lord through sacrifice. And during the winter solstice, we honour our Lord through carnality.'

The second one stuck out to Striker, and he and Felicia shared a quick look.

'What do you mean by *sacrifice*?' he demanded.

'It's rather self-explanatory, I think.' Another flicker of amusement crossed Solomon's features, a perverse darkness – a look that clearly told Striker the man was in his glory. 'Some texts suggest the slaughtering of a goat. Others the drinking of its blood.'

'And what of human blood?' Striker asked. 'Human sacrifice.'

Solomon just looked back at them and a crooked smile turned the corners of his mouth. 'You're dating yourself, Detective.'

'What's that supposed to mean?'

Solomon sighed as if explaining the matter was onerous. '*Older* texts suggest human sacrifice. The drinking of human blood. Wedding a sixteen-year-old virgin to our Lord. All of that. But if you're going to believe that, you may as well believe that Christians are still out there murdering people in the Crusades.'

Striker said nothing in response, and Solomon spoke again with a sneer on his lips. 'Of course, there's *always* a radical somewhere. And if you've lowered yourself enough to come to me for help, then I wonder just what you're up against. Sounds like you're in for a lot of bad times.'

Striker still said nothing. He just looked down at his watch and monitored the time. Solomon's lawyer would be here soon enough, and then their time would end. He pulled out a piece of paper and drew the image of the five-pointed star he had seen back at the place Moses had lived.

'What is the significance of this?'

Solomon looked down at the drawing and shrugged. 'There is no significance. It's just a star.'

Striker looked back at the page, then remembered the thick red rope that had encircled the star. He drew that in as well and turned the page back around.

'And now?' he asked.

'*Ahh*,' Solomon said, and he laughed darkly. 'Well now, *that* makes a difference. Now, it's a pentagram – a source of much power.'

'Why the circle?'

Solomon used his fingers to draw a circle on the desk as he spoke. 'The circle surrounding the star is the part of the symbol that contains the power within.' He reached out and pulled Striker's drawing back across the desk. Looked at it. Then he gestured to the pen in Striker's hand and raised an eyebrow. 'May I?'

Striker nodded. 'Raise it against us and you'll leave this place in a body bag.'

Solomon gave him a long uncertain look, but said nothing. He took the pen and began drawing in certain parts of the star. The top two points of the star he changed to horns. The middle two he turned to ears. And the bottommost point, he made into the long tuft of a goat's beard.

When he was done, Striker turned the drawing around and looked at it. The star was now a goat of some kind.

'I've seen this before,' he said.

Solomon sneered. 'Most people have – often without ever knowing what it is.'

'And what is it then?'

'The *Sigil of Baphomet*,' – Solomon smiled wickedly – 'It is my Lord.'

Solomon spoke the words with a disturbing veneration, and Striker found the moment unsettling. He was about to end the interview, when Solomon spoke again, his tone filled with a dark sense of excitement. 'You have a very bad man out there, Detective Striker. Very, very bad . . . I wish him well.'

Before Striker could respond, the door to the interview room was yanked open and a short bald man in a dark green suit peered in. It was Solomon's lawyer – Defence Counsel Alfred Weismann. And he and Striker had no love lost between them.

'This interview is ended,' the lawyer said.

Striker just smiled at the man and stood up.

'No problem,' he said. 'We already got what we came for.'

Forty-Seven

Fifteen minutes later, Striker and Felicia sat in the undercover police cruiser and drank bad coffee in Styrofoam cups – brew they'd pilfered from the jail staff's kitchen. Striker was deep in thought, rehashing everything he'd heard during the interview and trying to wrap his head around it.

Satanic holidays. Pentagrams. The Sigil of Baphomet.

It all seemed so very dark.

Felicia, meanwhile, was using her cell phone browser to scan the internet for more information on what Solomon had told them. At half past nine, she let out a long breath and began speaking. 'Okay, I've done some research here, so listen up.'

Striker turned in his seat to face her.

'Baphomet is essentially an old pagan deity,' she said. 'Though over the years, it's become more synonymous with the image of something called the *Sabbatic Goat.*'

'Sabbatic *what?*'

'Goat,' she replied. 'Though it's more a creature than anything else. It's a winged figure with the body of a man, the breasts of a woman, and the head of a goat.'

'Sounds like Laroche's wife.'

Felicia laughed softly, and then continued: 'It's a very convoluted idea. The sigil itself goes all the way back to the 1800s. To a French occultist named Elaphis Levi. Looks like he started the whole Sabbatic Goat thing, maybe even drew the first image. And then, throughout the years, others slowly transformed and altered the drawing – a French poet named de Guiata; a Swiss occultist named Wirth; and some French woman called Maurice Bessy. They all contributed to make the sigil what it is today.'

Striker rubbed his temples. 'It sounds overly complicated.'

Felicia shrugged. 'It is and it isn't. The general *idea* has always been the same – the Sigil of Baphomet is about as synonymous with Satanism as the crucifix is with Christianity. And get this – colour holds an importance as well.' She turned in her seat to face him better. 'Back at Luther's house, and at Moses' place, what colour were the ropes of that circle?'

'Red.'

She scrolled through the site in search of symbolism. 'Red is reflective of blood,' she finally said, 'and physical life and gaining energy.'

Striker thought this through and a bad feeling wormed through his guts. Blood, life, energy – it sounded very much in line with sacrificing someone.

Felicia looked up from her cell and shivered. 'Man, this stuff is interesting, but it's giving me the creeps.'

Striker felt the same way. He was about to ask Felicia to look up more on the strange list of supplies they had found – the oils and incense, the silver bowls and goblets – when his cell phone rang. He looked at the screen, saw the name *Jim Banner*, and picked up.

'Gimme some good news, Noodles.'

'Sure. Your whole life is a crisis, so midlife won't matter.'

Striker grinned. 'You have no idea how appropriate that is right now.'

'Got the safe open.'

Striker sat up a little. 'And?'

'Hate to burst your bubble, but there's nothing satanic inside of it. Just a bunch of papers and other legal junk – though some of the documents are interesting in their own right.'

'How so?'

Noodles cleared his throat. 'Most of the paperwork comes back to a place called the Faint Hope Foundation – lawsuit documents, with Moses Sabba listed as the client.' There was a shuffling sound as Banner sorted through what he had. 'The lawsuit claims that there was an illegal takeover. Looks pretty nasty.'

'How old are those papers?'

'Hmm. Not very. Eighteen months.'

Striker nodded. Eighteen months was nothing when it came to court battles, where cases moved with the breakneck speed of tectonic plates. Chances were the two parties hadn't even talked settlement yet, much less appeared for any court deliberations.

'Who's the defendant?' he asked.

'There's two of them,' Banner replied. 'Luna Asawa . . . Asawa . . .'

'*Asawa-Tan*,' Striker finished.

'You know her?'

'Unfortunately, a little too well. And the other?'

Striker knew the answer before Noodles even spoke it.

'Luther Faust.'

Forty-Eight

Monster's tears had long gone dry by the time he managed to fight back from that cold and hateful place inside of him. It was always a battle to reach the surface once more. Like swimming through tar.

How long he'd been fading in and out, he had no idea. The fog – the *pressure* – was constantly flooding and ebbing in his brain. One moment his head was pressurized and throbbing; then, seconds later, the dark pull of unconsciousness beckoned him.

It all signified one thing.

He needed his medications.

Monster removed his workman gloves. With his thick blocky fingers, he reached up and wiped the leftover tear residue from the inner edges of the eyeholes of his mask. The rubber felt grainy now, the Jelform material rough.

As he retreated from that inner darkness, the image of the room slowly filled his eyes once more – the empty beer cans and rice wine bottles; the used rigs and crack pipes; and the old woman, naked from the waist down and dead on the mattress in front of him.

The sight sickened him.

He climbed to his feet. Reached down and picked up the woman. She came easily – she was light, so unbelievably light. Just skin and bones. Her limbs were rigid, and even the muscles of her face were stiff now, pulling back her eyes and lips into a maniacal smile.

Like a joker in a deck of cards.

As he carried her, he tried to sing his song.

But it would not come.

Not today.

He laid the woman down in the tub, slowly, gently, with her head and back on the flat surface, and her stiff legs sticking out the far edge, almost straight into the air. Then he returned for his supplies.

Within seconds, he had uncapped all the jerry cans and was pouring the fuel all over her body. Soaking her waist and chest and especially her face – that awful face – with the diesel and kerosene. Last of all, he laid the silver cross on her chest.

Done . . . it was done.

He drew the flare gun. Took aim. Right at the centre of her hateful face.

'Lake of Fire,' he said softly.

Lake of Fire.

Forty-Nine

The lawsuit from Moses against Luther and Luna was over a place known as the Faint Hope Foundation. And if it required a lawsuit, it was obviously of great importance – at least to them.

'We should rule out any connection between what's going on here and that lawsuit,' Felicia said.

Striker agreed. It wasn't a bad idea.

He called up the city records office to see what listings they had for the Faint Hope Foundation. To his surprise and dismay, there were none. Not a single listing. Felicia assisted the search by googling for a website. She didn't find one.

But within other web links, there were mentions of the foundation.

'Look through them,' Striker said.

He leaned over Felicia's shoulder and read through the electronic pages. The first hit was a direct link to a non-profit called the Salvation Society. In brackets were the words *Faint Hope Foundation.*

'Maybe they're one and the same,' Felicia suggested.

She clicked on the address and went to the site. On the screen were four separate links, each one with the image of one person being helped by another. Each image had a caption beneath it:

Addiction. Mental Health. Poverty. Family.

Felicia clicked on the 'About Us' tab, and read the introduction. After a long moment, she got the gist of it. 'They're a support centre,' she said. 'A non-profit society designed to help the needy. Everything from acting as a placement provider for children in need, to finding recovery houses for drug addicts, to getting women out of the sex trade. They even have safe houses for battered women and shelters for the homeless. It's all Ministry-related.'

With Luther being a social worker, the connection was immediately apparent.

'Ministry-*related*?' Striker asked.

'Supported by, but not run by.' Felicia read through the rest of the page, then made an *ahh* sound. 'Okay here we go, now it makes sense. The Salvation Society was originally called the Faint Hope Foundation, right up to a couple of years ago – so it's the same damn place, just restructured. And look here. There's a list of the founders.'

Striker looked over the names, then pointed.

'Moses Sabba and Luther Faust and Dr Luna Asawa-Tan,' he said. He leaned back and closed his eyes. Pinched the bridge of his nose. 'Everywhere we turn, we find Luther's name.'

Felicia nodded. 'Let's go talk to the man.'

Striker looked at his watch. 'It's only quarter to ten. His shift doesn't start until noon.'

Felicia smiled. 'No. He has court this morning, remember?' She pointed west, in the general direction of Robson Square and the downtown court house, then put on her best elderly voice. 'Ready, Mr Colburn, sir?'

Striker returned the smile and laughed.

'Yes, Miss Daisy.'

They headed for the downtown core.

A half hour later, Striker and Felicia stood under the long glass ceiling of Vancouver's family court house and scanned the area for Luther Faust.

Striker hated the downtown court house. The building was a mishmash of dark passageways and long corridors which were labyrinthine in nature. One corridor led to Youth Court, another to Traffic, and another to a variety of courts that Striker had never attended. Despite having been here a hundred times in his career, testifying on everything from youth assaults to traffic offences, he had never gotten used to the layout.

It was a maze.

Felicia found the court listing board and located the corresponding room for the trial in which Luther was testifying. It was on the bottom floor. North side.

Once there, Striker went to peer through the inset window into the court room, but the door opened before he could get a proper look.

Out from the court room walked Luther Faust. His face was red, his eyes narrow. An angry, frustrated expression owned his face, and the look darkened even further when he spotted them.

'Oh Jesus Christ,' he muttered.

Striker smiled. 'We get that reaction a lot.'

'What is it now, Striker?'

'Wanna go for coffee?'

Luther slid some papers into his folder. 'The day's already shit, why make it worse?'

Striker gave Felicia a quick glance and shrugged like he didn't much care, and Felicia stepped forward. 'We've been directed to a place called the Salvation Society,' she said. 'Have you heard of it?'

Luther looked back at her, unblinking. 'Obviously you know I have, or you wouldn't be here asking questions. What about it?'

'It started out as the Faint Hope Foundation.'

Luther took off his old-school bowler hat, scratched at his greying black hair. 'Why don't you tell me something I don't know, Santos – I was on the goddam board, for Christ's sake.'

'I only bring this up because of the impending lawsuit,' she pointed out.

'Not that you have to worry about it now,' Striker interjected. 'Looks like the complainant won't be making it to court.'

The words came out harsher than he had intended, and they hit Luther like a smack in the face. His expression turned blank for a moment, and his mouth dropped open. Then the anger returned and his fingernails dug into the red rim of his hat. 'Are you actually suggesting that I had something to do with what happened to Moses? – with his *murder*?'

Striker did not look away; the tense conversation had been unplanned, but now that it was here, he tried to use it to rattle the man. 'All I'm saying is it's awfully convenient for you that Moses is gone . . . Hope his lawyer got a good retainer up front.'

The red on Luther's face deepened. 'You're a real fuckin' prick, Striker.'

'You don't like what I'm saying, then prove me wrong – talk to us a little.'

When Luther said nothing, Striker laid all their cards on the table.

'It's pretty straightforward, Luther. Moses Sabba was suing you – alleging an illegal takeover of the Faint Hope Foundation. The lawsuit states that he was forced out by you and Luna. Whether or not this is true, I have no idea – but I do know this: once Moses was gone from the Faint Hope Foundation, the name was legally changed to the Salvation Society. Why is that?'

'For legal reasons.'

'Such as?'

'Such as it's none of your business.'

Striker nodded slowly. 'You don't think it's any of my business? Fine by me. Maybe Luna will.'

Luther's jaw set hard at the words. 'Haven't you done the woman enough harm already?'

'*Harm?*' Striker asked. 'And how is that?'

'Through your previous investigation.'

Striker looked back at the man, deadpan. 'You might want to check your facts on that one, Luther – I was the one who *cleared* the woman of sleeping with her patients.'

Luther let out a bemused laugh. 'Sure, yeah. Good job, Striker. You cleared her alright – right after you fucked up her career with all the stupid shit you were asking everyone. Everyone avoided her after that – you might as well have turned her into a fucking leper.' He tapped a finger against the side of his head. '*Think.* Sometimes what you say is far more damaging than what you do – regardless of the truth.'

Striker saw the man's point, but it was irrelevant. The investigation had been mandatory. Allegations had been made.

Serious ones at that.

'That may well be true, Luther. But you're overlooking two critical facts here. One, I had no choice in the matter – the investigation was my *duty*. And two – your opinion is clouded.'

Luther furrowed his brow. 'Clouded?'

'Damn right it is. You're dating her.'

Luther offered no response, he just stood there with a look of dark amusement on his face. 'There you go again, Striker. Always digging.'

'It's my job,' he responded. 'So? Am I right? You two an item?'

Luther just shook his head and turned to leave.

Striker stopped him with a few words. 'Two people who were connected to you have been burned alive: Jazz through her investigations, and Moses – not only through those same investigations, but through your shared history with these non-profits. And that's to say nothing about our third victim – we don't even know who he is yet.'

Luther said nothing; Striker continued.

'Also, your name keeps coming up in all the related files . . . If it was me, I'd be pretty eager to talk to somebody – to anybody – who could help me.'

'I don't need your help.'

'Apparently not. It's just surprising, is all. You do the exact opposite of what I would do, if it were me in your position – you act like a man with something to hide.'

'I act like a man who has learnt never to trust anyone with a badge,' Luther replied. He glanced from Striker to Felicia, then back again. 'Am I under arrest here?'

Felicia spoke first. 'Of course not.'

'Then this conversation is over.'

Luther turned away from them and slowly made his way down the long corridor, adjusting his red-rimmed bowler hat as he went. When he reached the corner, he didn't pause, he didn't look back. He just turned the bend and was gone.

Felicia sat down on one of the hall benches. She shook her head. 'Smooth, Jacob, real smooth. We came here to coax the man out a little, not piss him off.'

Striker kept his eyes trained on the hallway, to the area where Luther had disappeared from sight. 'That how you took it?' he asked.

She looked up at him. 'What do you mean, *how I took it*?'

'Anger,' he replied. 'You took Luther's reaction as anger.'

'Tight face. Red expression. Aggressive and hostile. Yeah, I saw some anger there. What the hell did you see?'

Striker turned his eyes towards her and spoke with concern.

'Fear,' he said. 'What I saw was a lot of *fear*.'

Fifty

The night had been long. Excruciatingly long. But despite the weariness of his mind and the fatigue of his muscles, The Boy With The Violet Eyes could not stop pacing his room. He kept the shawl wrapped tightly around his shoulders, as he moved back and forth from the inverted sex chair to the small night stand that was covered in containers of special oils, herbs, skin creams, and hormone blockers.

His so-called Youth Station.

Several times he stepped on the small pieces of broken mirror, for he had yet to clean up the mess. The shards cracked and splintered beneath the rubber soles of his moccasins, and he barely heard them.

Besides, he was *glad* the mirror had shattered – it prevented him from seeing himself this morning. God, he could only imagine what he must have looked like. On any normal night, he would have slumbered fourteen hours, minimum. But with all the stress and uncertainty the phone call had brought, he had barely gotten nine.

It was a tragedy, his lack of sleep. But one that made unfortunate sense. After all, how on earth could he sleep now? When knowing that he might be summoned again. When knowing he might be of use once more. When knowing that his one chance of redemption might finally be at hand.

There was so much good happening right now. He could have cried.

And yet . . . so much bad.

His nerves were getting the better of him, and though he knew it, he could not calm them down. Like static charge, just building up and up and up. He forced himself to sit down. To close his eyes and take in slow, deep breaths.

Mantra, mantra, mantra.

He grabbed a piece of celery – more zero calorie food – and took but a single bite before dropping it in the garbage and slathering on more and more of his oestrogen creams.

Then a soft blipping sound caught his attention.

He turned and stared at the computer. On the monitor, the chat-room window was open to his favourite site. *The Dungeon.* On the screen was his code name. *Lazarus.* It was only appropriate, since he had felt like the walking dead for so many years now.

Ever since Monster had taken away everything he loved.

The screen blipped again, and this time, words scrolled out across the screen. It was a new friend. *Pinhead 21*. Asking if he was there.

The Boy With The Violet Eyes leaned over and typed:

Lazarus: Y
Pinhead21: Weeee. Happee Daze R here again.
Lazarus: BFFL?
Pinhead21: Haha! . . . R U n2 piercing?
Lazarus: Yes . . . *below*.
Pinhead21: I like!!!!
Lazarus: Slicing & Dicing?
Pinhead21: No knives 4 me . . . :o(

Violet made no reply, and the screen flashed once more:

Pinhead21: Nips and scrotes?

The Boy With The Violet Eyes did not type in a goodbye, he just logged off. For some reason, the conversation had grown tiresome. He went to power off the computer and his hand trembled over the keys. The tremor made him feel weak and fragile and, suddenly, *old*.

He grabbed his celery from the Youth Station, took another bite, caught sight of the phone sitting there and jumped up and threw the vegetable at the receiver.

'Ring, you *fuck* – RING!' he screamed.

He wanted to rip someone's fucking head right off. Ram an ice pick through the front of their fucking skull. Through their face. Gouge their fuckin' eyes out and feed it to them. Kill them all, kill *the world*.

The emotions came out of him like carbon dioxide, and they exhausted him. Hot tears fell. His eyes twitched to the phone and a desperate, longing, pathetic feeling owned every inch of his soul.

'Please,' he said softly.

'Please,' but a whisper.

Please . . .

But the phone remained silent.

Fifty-One

They sat in the car, together but separate.

Striker was on the phone with some of Jazz's colleagues – Federal cops with the RCMP – and then with the morgue, requesting if any further forensic evidence had been recovered from Jazz's body.

Felicia was on her own cell, trying to dig up more information on Moses, Luther, Luna, and the Faint Hope Foundation, which had now been restructured into something called the Salvation Society.

By the time the clock struck 11:15 a.m., both of them were weary of it.

Felicia was already off her cell when Striker said goodbye to Jazz's IHIT inspector, and hung up. His ear was hot from the phone battery, and he wondered how much radiation his brain had absorbed.

It felt like an egg cooked white.

Felicia rubbed her neck and stretched. 'If you managed to dig up even one single piece of information, you beat me.'

'Nothing on Jazz.'

'Great,' Felicia said. 'What next?'

Striker didn't respond right away. His thoughts were still on Luther Faust and his combative reaction back at the court house. The man was always anti-police, and not usually very helpful.

But in this instance, he had been more than that – completely unhelpful, antagonistic, even defensive.

It told Striker they were close to something.

Finally, he turned his eyes towards Felicia. 'Last night, when we were at Luther's house, you tripped over the recycling bins in the driveway.'

An embarrassed grin found her lips. 'Okay. I'll admit I'm a little out of sorts with surveillance, but it's been a while. Thanks for bringing it up though. Not my smoothest moment.'

Striker shook his head. 'That's not what I mean. When you bumped into it, the bin didn't exactly knock over. It hardly moved. Was it frozen to the ground, or was it *full*?'

She thought back. 'Full. With papers.'

'When do the recycling trucks come?'

Felicia used her cell to look up the pickup dates. 'Today,' she said.

Striker looked at the time. Saw it was still before noon. He made the decision. He started the engine, put the car in gear, and pulled out onto Cordova Street.

They headed south. Back for the frozen fields of Ladner.

It was exactly 12:20 hours when they first caught glimpse of the fields surrounding Luther's old farmhouse. It looked like a plain of greyness beneath a stone sky. From this distance, and in the dreary light of the overcast day, the house looked much smaller than it had at night.

The driveway was empty.

Striker pulled slowly around the bend of 36th Avenue, feeling the car skid on the frozen rain that now iced the road. He slowed their speed for fear of skidding into one of the storm ditches.

The moment they were close enough, he scanned the road for

any sign of the blue recycling bins and found them. Trailing away from the base of the nearest bin, grooved in the snow, was a pair of wide tyre impressions.

Felicia saw them and swore.

'Recycle trucks,' she said. 'We're too late.'

Striker shook his head. 'Recycle trucks have *two* tyre tracks per side.'

He pulled over to the side of the road and climbed out. The two recycling bins were nestled just outside the wooden fence, directly beside the storm sewer. He could see that the contents hadn't been picked up yet. Relieved, he grabbed the first bin and dragged it to one side; Felicia grabbed the other.

Although the bin wasn't full, it held mostly tin cans, beer cans, and a few wine bottles. Also nestled inside the bin was a yellow recycle bag for any paper product that was not newsprint. Striker dumped the entire contents out on the snow and started going through it.

It didn't take long.

Within seconds, he came across credit card statements and bank records. He looked at them, then up at Felicia. 'Luther needs a shredder,' he said with a smile. 'If he's not careful, some-one's going to find something damaging in his garbage.'

Felicia didn't respond. She was too busy frowning at a piece of paper she had found in four ripped-up sections. She was piecing them back together on the hood of the car.

'What you got?' Striker asked.

'Something . . . I dunno . . . *creepy*.'

He moved closer for a better look. The piece of paper was standard loose-leaf. Lined. Double-sided. Three-hole punch stuff. On it was a bunch of barely legible handwriting. In black ink.

Morningstar,

Here's the leather wrap you needed. Red, just like the last one. I pulled it from an old athame. So enough of this fighting already. It's time to move on. The 21st is fast approaching.

–Firesong

Felicia made a curious sound just as Striker finished reading it. 'Who the hell are Firesong and Morningstar?' she wondered aloud.

Striker didn't take his eyes off the page. 'I have no idea. But whoever they are, it sounds like there's some bad blood between them.'

'Firesong seems like an odd name – with all the arsons going on.'

Striker agreed. 'Seize it.'

Felicia documented the find in her notebook and placed the paper in an evidence bag. She marked down the date, time and location, along with the incident number.

Striker, meanwhile, started digging through the yellow bag again, looking for any more loose-leaf. When he discovered more, he pulled the papers out and found more of the same writing. Real messy stuff. This time the writing was a list of standard groceries. He also found another paper with handwriting on it. When he read it over, he saw that it was a cover letter for a new position within the Ministry of Child and Family Services.

A rough draft maybe.

'This is Luther's handwriting,' he said.

Felicia neared him. 'Let me see.'

They compared the writing of the résumé papers with the letter Felicia had found.

It was exactly the same.

'Luther is using Firesong as an alias,' Striker said.

The word caused a dark look to form in Felicia's eyes. 'Why would he do that?'

'I can't think of anything good.'

Striker recalled the image of the altar he'd seen in the man's basement, and then the similar one he'd located in Moses' place. Both had held strange religious tools on them.

Striker looked at Felicia. 'When we get back to the car, do a search on the name Morningstar. See if it links back to anything pertinent. And do a cross-reference for Moses. With the same strange sacrificial props and the imminent lawsuit, I got a feeling that Morningstar might be him.'

Felicia nodded. 'It would make sense.'

She collected all the papers and stuffed them into her folder. When they finished going through the yellow bags and were cleaning up, the loud heavy grind of a city recycling truck filled the air.

Striker looked east and saw the big truck turn the corner. As it did, he spotted another car in behind it. The vehicle was parked at the mouth of the road. With its lights off and the engine running.

It was too far to get a plate or see inside the cab.

'You recognize that car?' he asked.

Felicia looked up. Before she could respond, the vehicle backed up, did a one-eighty, and drove down the road. It disappeared behind the tall sweeping roof of the neighbouring barn.

Felicia scowled. 'Is it just me, or are you starting to feel paranoid too?'

'It's not you,' Striker replied.

They headed for the car.

Fifty-Two

The midday sky was heavily overcast and looking like a sheet of slate as Striker and Felicia drove under it, heading back towards the city core.

Striker wanted to get back to the Recovery House in Langara, where Moses had been killed. Noodles was still processing parts of the scene, and Striker wanted to talk to the man – see what the forensics was bringing them.

He wasn't holding his hopes too high.

They turned the corner of 41st Avenue, and upon Felicia's urging – 'I'm famished, Jacob. *Famished*' – stopped in at a mom and pop coffee shop that was known for its sandwiches and cookies. Striker didn't mind the delay; he needed to get out of the car for a moment.

He ordered two Italian subs, two biscottis – traditional almond; nothing too fancy – and a pair of whole milk cappuccinos. Felicia got some vanilla in hers.

They sat in a small booth by a tinted front window, where the air smelled strongly of peaches and cinnamon from the baking crostatas.

'Thanks,' Felicia said. She took a giant bite of her sub, made a surprised face, then sipped her latte. 'Wow, is that ever *spicy*.'

'Capicola and bell peppers,' Striker said.

Felicia looked hesitantly back at the sandwich, then braved another bite.

As they ate, Felicia used her cell browser to scan through the numerous websites. After a long moment of reading and crunching, she looked up with a curious expression.

'You find something?' Striker asked.

'Names and meanings,' she said. 'It's kind of weird, really. I don't know what to make of it.' Felicia turned the phone so he could see it. 'Look at this. *Morningstar* is the name given to the planet Venus.'

'So?'

'To many of the pagan religions, Venus is of great significance. And it's synonymous with being called the *Light-Bearer*.'

'Because it reflects the sun.'

Felicia nodded. 'Exactly. Now look at the Bible. Whose name in scripture actually *means* Light-Bearer?'

'Lucifer,' Striker said.

'So could calling yourself Morningstar be a twisted way of paying homage to the devil?'

Striker thought it over. He wasn't sure.

'Maybe I'm reaching too far here . . .' Felicia said.

Striker shook his head. 'If you don't reach, you'll never grasp anything.'

Felicia turned the phone back around and used her finger to swipe through the electronic pages. 'I was also looking at the initials. *MS* – Morning Star. *MS* – Moses Sabba.'

'They're the same.'

She nodded. 'Now it might just be coincidental, I know that. But there sure seems to be a lot of strange coincidences with this file – too many for my liking.'

'Mine too.'

Striker wrote those names and initials down in his notebook, and stared at them as he sipped his cappuccino. Again, he looked at the letter they'd found in Luther's recycling:

Enough of this fighting already. Time to move on.

He wondered: Could that really be in reference to the legal papers Noodles had found? The ongoing court battle between the two? He wasn't sure. Everything felt a stretch – connected and yet disconnected, together but separate, relevant yet irrelevant. It all came down to how you interpreted the facts. And Striker hated that. His head was swimming with possibilities.

He crunched his biscotti and stared out the window at the busy traffic of Hastings Street, and thought about it some more. Ten minutes later, when he was no closer to a decision, Striker pulled out his phone. 'I'm calling Ich,' he said. 'I want all the emails scanned.'

Felicia nodded.

Ich was short for Ichabod. Also known as Percy Wadsworth – their technological guru for all things electronic. He was a Vancouver Police Department icon, as far as Striker was concerned. Had saved his bacon a few times over the years.

'Ich already seized Moses' computers,' Felicia said. 'The work one and the home one. He's probably going through them right now.'

'Not Moses' computers,' Striker clarified. '*Luther's.*'

Felicia put down her phone and shook her head adamantly. 'You'll never get a warrant for that.'

'Don't need one. This search is *off the record.*'

Felicia made an uncomfortable sound. 'Just a *light* breach of the Charter of Rights and Freedoms Act. I'm sure the courts will understand.'

'The courts will never know.'

'And if they do find out?'

'We're just bending the rules a little.'

Felicia's frown deepened. 'One day, these *bending the rules* ploys are going to come back and bite us in the ass. I don't like it.'

Striker let out a heavy breath. 'We did things your way when we opened up to Luther, Feleesh – before I wanted to. And look where that got us. We got nothing from it, and now he knows we're looking into him – he's going to do everything he can to cover up and avoid us.'

'It wasn't a full interview. Be fair.'

'It was close enough. And I *am* being fair. We tried your way, now let's try mine. And I say the best way to figure out what was going on between Luther and Moses is for Ich to do a little trolling. Off the record.'

Felicia said nothing and Striker continued.

'We have grounds here: they both have altars in their place. Luther has been nothing but uncooperative and hostile with us from the beginning. And so was Moses until he got killed . . . There's something going on between them, and my bet is that Moses is Morningstar and Luther is Firesong. I want that *proved*.'

Felicia still wasn't happy about it. 'So what if they are? Even if we can confirm that, it still doesn't tell us *why* they're using fake names. Especially ones connected to fire and Satanism.'

'Maybe not. But we've got to start somewhere.'

Striker picked up his cell and made the call. He told Ich what he wanted, and the time frame he was looking for, then hung up. When done, Felicia gave him a look filled with irritation.

'Satisfied?' she asked.

'No.'

Striker paid the bill and they returned to the car.

Still wanting to speak with Noodles about the scene and its processing, Striker drove them back to the Recovery House. They pulled in behind a black Lincoln sedan that was parked out front.

Striker rammed the gearshift into park, and stared at the vehicle in front of them. It was partly blocking access for the emergency vehicles and he wondered whose car it was. Then he saw the bumper sticker:

Headed the wrong way? God allows U-Turns.

He blinked. 'That's one of the church vehicles,' he said. 'Run it.'

Felicia did. 'The registered owner is Shea O'Brien.'

'*Father* O'Brien?'

Striker had no sooner spoken the words when he spotted the priest's gentle face through the front office window. Father O'Brien was standing there, speaking to a red-headed woman who was in tears.

'What the hell is he doing here?' Striker asked aloud.

Felicia shrugged. 'Counselling, I would guess. He helps with all the non-profits. You know. The needy.'

'That's not what I meant. What's he doing here *specifically*?'

He was about to say more on the issue when his cell phone went off. He looked down at the screen and saw that it was the Road Boss calling. Superintendent Laroche. Striker cursed, but he picked up.

'Detective Striker speaking,' he said.

Laroche's reply was hard and curt.

'We got another one.'

Fifty-Three

His desperation had peaked twenty minutes ago. Now the sharp thrust of anxiety was all but ebbing and a calmer sense of exhaustion was flooding him.

The Boy With The Violet Eyes sat on the edge of his stool, slathering his palms with oestrogen cream and massaging it into his hands and face in gentle circular motions. The creams had a strange smell to them. Almost citrus-like. Like oranges and lemons turning bad.

He had become resigned again to the phone not ringing. He had found a way to survive the godawful silence. Just another up and down on his rollercoaster of life. And then, just when he thought he was nearing a sense of acceptance, the phone rang.

It actually fucking *rang*.

Violet let out a series of shuddering laughs – sounds of relief and rejoicing all at once – and put the receiver to his ear.

'I'm here,' he said.

The caller let out a pleased sound. 'Listen to me very carefully, Violet. I have never had greater need of you.'

And The Boy With The Violet Eyes gushed at those words. When he heard what he was needed for – and more importantly, when he heard the names of the victims involved – his heart leaped in bounds. His spirit soared. And he felt a euphoria he could barely contain. The reason for it was as simple as it was wonderful. He saw something no one else saw.

A connection of Monster's kills, a definitive pattern evolving.

When the phone call ended, Violet clapped his hands together, felt the tears stream down his cheeks, and he let out a strange high-pitched hyena laugh.

He was excited now. So very, very excited.

Revenge on Monster would soon be his. And more important than that . . .

Salvation was coming.

Fifty-Four

The latest crime scene was at an old rooming house, which was not only ugly with its faded green paint, but in overwhelming need of repair. The entire structure slanted to the north, so badly that the yellow police tape cordoning off the lot looked more stable. On every one of the four floors, a window or two had been broken and replaced with particleboard.

'Not exactly *Lifestyles of the Rich and Famous*,' Striker said.

Felicia raised an eyebrow. 'Why this place hasn't been condemned yet is beyond me.'

Striker agreed with her. He stared at the third-floor windows, where a thin, barely noticeable waft of smoke trailed out. Unlike the other scenes, the air here looked relatively clear. Were it not for all the fire trucks out front, people might have thought someone had burned something on the stove.

Striker counted the five engines, and frowned. It was a perfect example of overkill and it would bring even more unwanted media attention. As if to highlight that thought, a female newsperson, standing in front of a Global News van, called out his name.

'Detective Striker – Detective Striker!'

'No comment,' he said.

As he moved closer to the scene, he saw two more reporters, one from CTV, the other he wasn't sure. A man holding a microphone yelled, 'Is this in any way related to the bus yards?'

Striker eyed the man. 'Gather at the media point,' was all he said. Then he moved on past the yellow police tape.

Parked in front of the fire trucks were a pair of marked police cruisers and an Ident van. In behind them was the Road Boss car, a white Crown Vic. In it sat Superintendent Laroche, cell pressed hard against his ear. As always, his hair was perfectly combed back into place and his shirt appeared to be without crease.

The guy was an image machine.

Striker pretended not to notice Laroche and walked ahead into the building. While Felicia went in search of a manager, Striker took the stairs to the third level and found the correct suite. Standing outside was a uniformed patrol cop who requested his name and badge number.

Striker gave it and walked inside.

The smoke was still thin in the air, but not as bad as he had expected. Noodles and Katarina Kesla were already processing the scene, both of them wearing respirators. Even still, they had opened all the windows to air the place out.

Kesla was busy sketching the scene and making notes while Noodles was on his knees, taking low-end shots of the room with a digital Nikon. They worked in the same space but completely independent of one another – as if they were unaware of the other's existence.

Then they both looked over at Striker.

'Anything?' he asked them.

'Nothing yet,' Kesla said in a muffled tone.

Noodles stripped off his mask. 'It's a carbon copy evidence-wise, which means he left us jack shit. But check out the body. There's another silver gift he left you.'

Kesla raised an eyebrow behind her mask, as if to agree. Then she went back to drawing the scene.

Striker moved across the room towards the bathroom. The slum was like any other of the thousand he had seen in his career in the Downtown Eastside. A ramshackle den, filthy, the floor filled with streams of garbage and the counters covered with piles of old rotting food, most of which was cheap takeout.

He reached the bathroom where the remains of the smoke was thicker.

On the floor were empty bottles of rice wine, red wine, and mouthwash. There were also numerous beer cans, most of which were the cheap stuff. With the windows open, he could feel the draught coming in from outside. It was helping clear the air of smoke, but the stench was still strong.

Striker approached the tub, and saw something different with this scene than the last. Unlike the bodies of Jazz and Moses and the John Doe whose identity they still had not uncovered, this victim's body had not contracted into a foetal position from the water and fat loss. Instead, the body was in a supine position, legs rigidly draped over the edge of the tub.

It told Striker one important thing.

'She was already dead.'

Noodles nodded from his knees. 'That's full rigor, baby.'

'And yet he still burned her.'

'Guess he doesn't like to discriminate,' Noodles said, and laughed.

Striker pondered the situation. It seemed such an odd thing to do. And it pointed out one important fact: this was not about torture. Otherwise, the moment the suspect had discovered that the woman was already dead, he would have turned and left. Because what would have been the point?

But he *hadn't* left. He had still gone ahead with his plan. Despite the chance of finally being caught. Whatever the man's motivation was, it was on a much deeper level than violence.

Symbolic maybe.

As he thought this over, his eyes trailed up the body to the centre of the chest. There, covered by thick flakes of skin, was a grimy silver glint. Striker gloved up, used his thumb to gently wipe away the ash and charred flesh, and saw what he had expected – the leftover remains of what he believed to be another silver cross.

'Want me to remove that for you?' Noodles asked.

Striker shook his head. 'Leave it for the ME.' He finally turned his eyes away from the victim's body and found Noodles and Kesla. 'We get a name yet?'

Both shook their heads in a side-to-side fashion, but then Felicia suddenly appeared in the doorway. She had brought the laptop with her, and the look in her eyes told Striker she had found something.

'Her name is Jolene Whitebear,' she said. 'And she's got one hell of a history.'

Striker unstrapped his gloves and moved over to where Felicia was standing. He stared at the laptop screen. One look at the history listed and it was easy to see that Jolene Whitebear was a down-and-outer. Under her contact lists were a dozen names, all of which came back to Ministry workers, probation officers, and drug-and-alcohol counsellors.

A carbon copy of every Skid Row lifer.

'My God, what a life,' Felicia said, as she skimmed the entries. 'This woman's been in and out of recovery houses her whole life. She's been assaulted too many times to count, had her kids taken away, been raped a dozen times, and God knows what else. She's also gone missing more times than I can count.'

Striker said nothing. Sadly it was all par for the course down here. In the Downtown Eastside, it was more difficult to find someone who *hadn't* been through the same ordeals.

He looked at her entity page. Linked to it was a list of files. In many of them, Jolene was listed as the suspect, subject of complaint, or the charged accused. There were robberies, assaults, disturbances, and a string of shoplifting calls. But in just as many other files, she was listed as the victim – and those files were serious crimes as well. Assaults, sexual assaults, robberies, and criminal harassments which most likely extended from domestic situations.

One file grabbed his attention. 'Bring up that one – the crim. harass.'

Felicia did.

As they read through the narrative, a sense of nervous excitement began to fill Striker. There were over a dozen documented incidents of a man named Roy Baker. He went by the moniker *Big Roy*. And his physical attributes were uncannily familiar: one hundred and ninety-two centimetres tall and a hundred and thirty-five kilos heavy.

There was no mugshot attached.

Felicia pointed out the man's size. 'My God, he's a giant,' she said. 'And look here – the victim had to call 911 on this guy a half-dozen times over the last two months alone. He's a violent prick.'

Striker heard the words, but didn't react. He was too busy staring at the bottom of the screen at an arson call in which Roy Baker – AKA Big Roy – was listed as the primary suspect. He got Felicia to open the link and read the details. A few stuck out to him. He turned to Felicia and summarized those parts of the report aloud.

'So a man named Billy George had a fight with this Big Roy guy. And Roy threatened to burn down the man's house.' He skimmed down the page. 'Later that night, George's house goes up in flames.'

Felicia pointed to the outside agency statement page. 'And the fire investigator says that an accelerant was used.'

'*Diesel*,' Striker clarified.

Felicia looked up with excitement on her face. 'We've got to find this guy.'

Striker looked at the listed address and saw that it was on Salish Drive. 'That's Musqueam land.'

He put the car into gear and headed south.

They were going to the reserve.

Fifty-Five

The time spent at the Green Box – the old slum – had been a surreal and overwhelming experience for Monster, so it took him over an hour to feel right again in his head – as right as he ever felt, that is. He stood at the gas pump and refilled the jerry cans and relived all that had happened.

The numbers on the pump kept spinning, making a soft click sound every time they passed a new dollar mark, and the fumes were heavy in the air. Oddly, the smell was calming to him – a little bit of celestial vapour drifting down from heaven.

It told him he was one step closer to completion.

Only four crosses left.

Somehow, thoughts of Samuel forced out the bad memories and found their way into the forefront of his mind. As always they brought Monster a certain level of serenity. He loved the little brown squirrel, and he knew he'd have to grab a few more packets of Corn Nuts from the gas station.

Maybe even a new flavour.

It would be a treat.

As he stood there, pumping the fuel and comparing Corn Nut flavours in his mind, a small black sedan drove slowly by on the main drag. It was heading back in the direction of the fire. Through the window, Monster caught a glimpse of the driver—

And an ice-cold hollow feeling burst through his chest like lead buck from a shotgun blast.

That face . . .

Dark lifeless hair. Skin as white as a corpse. And pale purple eyes that looked right through you with an inhuman coldness. Like something that should never have been born.

Something *unnatural.*

Unconsciously, Monster took a step back. The pump nozzle slipped from the jerry can and diesel poured all over the cement, soaking his boots and pant legs. He barely noticed. It had been years now. *Years.* And yet the terror was still here. With him always. Like a second heart, pumping ice water through his core.

The sedan faded in the distance, and Monster stood there, wavering. Face tight beneath the mask. Hands trembling. His heart hammered inside his chest. So hard it felt like it would escape the rib cage.

He reached up. Touched his face. And stared out across the road at the empty spot of pavement.

You're not a little boy anymore, he told himself.

You're a man now, he told himself.

You're big and strong – a power to be reckoned with!

But the words did nothing. Because they were only words.

He was absolutely terrified.

Fifty-Six

The sky had been a sheet of dark grey the entire day, and now that the clock was ticking closer to 3 p.m., the darkening sky made the cloudbanks appear angry and turbulent. Defiant enough to block the light from coming through.

Felicia glanced at them as they drove west on Marine Drive.

'Gonna snow soon,' she said.

Striker agreed with her prediction. It had been an unusually harsh winter, following a fall that had also been bad. Dreary and damp, wet and bitterly cold. There were no signs of the bad weather letting up, and the coming darkness only helped deepen the chill.

The Musqueam Indian Reserve was located in South Vancouver, on a swelling of land that was mostly hidden from sight to anyone above the Marine Drive divide. From Marine, the land just dropped away and extended out towards the river's inlet, where the reserve ended in the brown muddy waters of the Fraser.

Many people didn't even know it was there.

Striker steered down the decline of Dunbar into the lowland sections. Here, large acre lots with horses and stables appeared. Striker always marvelled at the area – it was a hidden gem in the city. Made for multi-millionaires of course. Not regular folk.

They passed through the Southlands towards the Musqueam land and soon spotted St Jude's church.

Felicia pointed at it. 'Isn't that the church where Father Silas presides?'

Striker nodded and looked at it. The church was one of the first built in South Vancouver, done long before he could even remember. It was quite different than the Holy Cross where Father O'Brien presided. Whereas the Holy Cross in Dunbar was small and white, St Jude's church was made of old brick that had turned such a dark red over the years it was almost black. It was also twice the size of the Holy Cross, and even had a bell tower on the east side, though the structure was currently under repair and surrounded by beams and planks of scaffolding.

The building had been deemed to have heritage status by the City. It was a truly beautiful church.

'I wonder if Father Silas is there now?' Felicia said.

'No time for stopping,' was all Striker said.

He drove on, far down the road until they were almost at the banks of the Fraser River, until he found the dead end turn of 51st Avenue. Here a sign with an arrow pointed west towards the Musqueam Indian Reserve. They crossed over a small wooden bridge and found themselves driving through an area rife with pickup trucks and Vancouver Specials – houses built cheaply, with plain square designs but maximum square footage.

Despite the snow and slush that blanketed the roads, a group of teenagers had set up a pair of nets and were playing hockey in one of the cul-de-sacs. Upon seeing the undercover police cruiser, they all stopped and looked, waiting to see what, if anything, was up.

'They know we're cops?' Felicia asked.

Striker just laughed. 'They're street-smart around here. But most of them are actually pretty good kids. Chief Charlie really fought against the alcoholism within the community, sought out help.'

'Sounds like a good man.'

'One of the best. This band has always had good leadership. It's a tight community for the most.' He turned down Salish Drive. 'They got a few shit rats here; don't kid yourself about that. But what neighbourhood doesn't? Most of the people living here are good, honest folk. I know a few of them.'

Striker had barely finished the words when he came to a slow stop out front of a small brown rancher. One look and it was easy to tell that additions had been made to it over the years – a garage on the north side, a shed on the south.

Snow-shovelling the front walkway was a man in his fifties. He was small, but thick with muscle – not the singular defined type gained from lifting weights, but the overall symmetry earned from years of hard manual labour. Upon seeing them, the man stopped what he was doing and leaned on the shovel. He gave them a big toothy grin.

Striker killed the engine and climbed out. Felicia did the same.

'Hey Charlie,' Striker said.

'Detective Striker,' the man replied. 'What brings you out this way?'

Striker didn't answer the question right away. Instead, he took a moment to introduce Felicia to the Chief. Then, for a few minutes, Striker and the older man caught up. When the small talk was done, Striker got down to the meat of the business.

'Big Roy,' he finally said.

The two words caused the Chief's toothy grin to fade a little. 'Oh boy.'

Striker laughed. 'I take it you know the man well.'

The Chief just shook his head. 'I spend more time dealing with Roy Baker's problems than I do the rest of the band. He likes to drink. He likes to fight. And he's got an explosive temper. There's not much he won't do – you heard about the deal with Billy George last year?'

'The house that burned down?' Striker asked.

The Chief nodded. 'Yeah, that's the one.' He shrugged in frustration. 'No proof it was Roy. But everyone knows. We were just damn lucky no one got killed.'

'Well, I need to speak to him.'

The Chief let out a cynical sound. 'Lots of luck,' he said. 'He's not exactly a talkative guy to the rest of us, much less the police. And to be honest, I haven't seen him around lately. Ever since the fire at Billy's, he's kind of made himself scarce. Word is he's been hanging round the Downtown Eastside. Getting into trouble there for a change.'

Felicia spoke up next. 'His ex-wife,' she said. 'A woman named Jolene. Did you know her?'

'Jolene? Not personally. She's actually not from this band. Came back with Roy from Saskatchewan a few years back. Lives off-site mostly. And from what I hear – and from I know about Roy – it can't have been the best of situations.'

'Kids got taken away,' Striker said.

'Kids? Which ones? Roy's got a *dozen* of them with a half-dozen women. Funny, everyone always thinks of the alcoholism, but unwed pregnancies are one of the biggest problems we face on the reserve today. The two seem to go hand-in-hand.'

'Can you dig up a phone number for me?' Striker asked.

'Sure,' the Chief said. He pulled out his cell and started scrolling through the contacts. When he made it to the Bs, he found what he was looking for. 'It might be out-of-service by now. Never know with Roy. But it's all I got for him.'

Striker wrote down the number and called it immediately. It was answered on the fourth ring – a loud, uneven, baritone. *'Yuh?'*

'Roy?' Striker asked.

'Yuh.'

'Detective Striker. Vancouver Police Department.'

'Fuck you, pig.'

'We need to talk, Roy. Now.'

Click.

Striker hit redial. This time the phone rang several times, but was never answered. It went straight to voicemail. He tried again, and again. On the fourth attempt, he gave up.

It was time for step two.

He looked over at Felicia and gave her the nod.

'Call up your guy,' he said. 'We need a trace.'

Fifty-Seven

The Boy With The Violet Eyes stood beside the pay phone outside the 7-Eleven convenience store and stared across the main drag of Hastings Street. Two blocks north was an array of media vans, fire trucks, marked police cars, and a white-yellow van that said *Fire Investigator* on the side. The vehicles were all parked directly out front of the green building.

And that made The Boy With The Violet Eyes smile.

He knew that building. From many years past. It had always been a deplorable place – the walls filled with so much rot that the air forever held notes of mildew and dampness. A musty stink. The walls also had asbestos and the floors had been fumigated so many times there were giant patches of bleached colourlessness on all the rugs.

In short, a shithole.

Violet waited and watched. Until a short tubby technician came out for a smoke. Until a hard-looking woman exited the building and returned to the fire investigator van. Until two tall men in jeans and sweatshirts stretchered out the victim from the building.

The body was wrapped in a stiff case of white plastic, but Violet did not need to see the victim to know her identity. She had been removed from suite 3B.

Jolene Whitebear.

The visual did something. It excited him. Because once again, he could see the pattern emerging. And that pattern brought forth a flourish of emotions he hadn't experienced in . . . well, perhaps never: excitement, nervousness, nausea – and *rage*. He stood there and watched the body removal team load the victim into the back of the van, climb inside, and drive away on Lakewood.

When they were gone, he went over the names he knew of.

Jasmine Heer.

Moses Sabba.

And now Jolene Whitebear.

The Boy With The Violet Eyes let out a high-pitched laugh and felt his breath flutter. Was it happening? Was it really, truly happening?

Had Monster finally come home?

It was the only possible connection. The only thing that made any sense. And as Violet stood there thinking of all this, a grin found the corners of his thin lips. Monster thought he was coming home for vengeance, but what he was really doing was opening himself up. Becoming vulnerable. And allowing Violet to extract his own revenge.

The thought of all that made him laugh out loud.

It was the *names* that brought such promise and delight. Those names were everything to him. They were lighthouses on the shore. Beacons in the night.

They showed Violet the way.

They showed him how to find Monster.

Fifty-Eight

The coordinates from Big Roy's cell phone came back to the fourteen hundred block of West 70th. That location was less than a five-minute drive from the reserve, and when they finally got there, Striker took one look at the block and nodded in understanding.

On the south side of the street was a small dilapidated two-level house. The pale blue paint was flaking and the windows were dirty and dark. The snow-covered lawn was further blanketed by a collection of old broken-down vehicles and a couple of overturned garbage cans some animals had gotten into.

'This is the place,' Striker said.

Felicia looked farther down the block at a ramshackle apartment. 'You sure? Could also have come from down there – the signal's good to two hundred metres.'

Striker shook his head. 'Signal nothing. I know this place from years past. Trust me. He'll be inside.'

They trudged up the walkway to the front door. From somewhere inside, the sounds of a TV could be heard. Canned laughter.

Striker banged on the door, waited, and no one answered.

He tried again. On the third time, a young native girl with dyed platinum hair answered the door. She was rake thin and her skin had an off colour to it. Her pupils were too small for the darkness and the outer edges of her red-rimmed eyes were caked with grime.

Looked like she had a nasty infection.

'What already?' she bitched.

Striker just flashed the badge and she muttered, '*Shit.*'

'I'm looking for Roy,' he said.

'Uhhhh. Not here.'

'Really? Know where he is?'

She just shrugged. ''Round, I guess.'

Striker said nothing else. He just took out his cell, dialled the number Chief Charlie had given him, and waited. A half second later, a soft ringing sound could be heard. It was coming from somewhere ahead of them. Up the stairs.

'Out of my way,' Striker ordered.

'You can't—'

Striker pushed the girl away and she leaned against the wall like she was suddenly half asleep. He stepped inside. The first thing he noticed was that the foyer was dim – only a few lights were turned on. The second thing he noticed was the foul smell that hit him: sweat, staleness, body odour – your typical flop-house stink.

Felicia joined him in the foyer.

'Upstairs,' he told her.

He took the stairs two at a time, and Felicia followed, watching their backs as they went. When Striker reached the top level, he saw that it was relatively small. A bathroom to the right, a closet straight ahead, and just around the stairway's bend, a bedroom.

The door was closed.

Striker didn't bother knocking. He grabbed the handle, turned it, and opened the door. It collided with something – a dresser or a chair blocking the path.

He peered through the crack and spotted a huge thick native man sitting on the bed with his back against the wall. Staring at nothing. In his hand was a crack pipe and a lighter.

'Vancouver Police, Roy!'

The words jarred the man awake. His eyes turned from the wall to the doorway. When he spotted Striker and Felicia there, he rolled off the bed, ran across the room, and started opening the window.

Striker wasted no time. He used all his might to shoulder open the door, and it collided with the dresser, upending it. By the time Striker rushed into the room, Roy was already halfway out the window, his leg dangling.

Striker grabbed the man by the collar of his sweatshirt and dragged him inside. 'Show me your hands!' Striker ordered.

'Let da fuck go! Da fuck go! Lemme go!' the man bellowed.

Striker made no reply. He just slammed the man down on the ground, onto his stomach. Dropped his knee into the centre of his back. Locked the arm and cuffed him. Once the man was no longer a threat, Striker eased his weight off the man's back and stood up.

'Watch the door,' he told Felicia. 'Who knows who else is downstairs.'

She nodded and took up a position.

Roy, hands cuffed behind his back, spat on the floor – a mixture of blood and saliva. 'Ya split my fuckin' lip,' he said. 'Whadda fuck, man? Whadda *fuck!*'

Striker said nothing. He just gloved up with latex and searched the man. In Roy's pockets he found an old nylon wallet, a cell phone, three quarters, and a wad of silver Bristol pads used as filters.

Phone in hand, Striker called the number Chief Charlie had given him, and the cell rang. Nodding, he handed the phone to Felicia, then opened up the wallet. Inside, there was no ID of any kind. Only some bus passes, some rolling papers, and a condom.

Striker dropped it all on the floor. He then squatted down low, grabbed Roy and sat him up. He met the man's stare. As Striker looked at him – as his eyes finally adapted to the dimness of the room – a sense of disappointment flooded him. This man was big and thick and native . . . but he was maybe twenty years old. At best.

Not Big Roy.

'Tell me your name.'

'Fuck you.'

'What a horrible name. You really should be pissed at your parents.'

The man on the ground said nothing, and Striker just shrugged. 'Doesn't really matter to me. You can either tell me your name, or I'll charge you with obstruction and have you fingerprinted. You can rot in the jail all week long till the prints come back. Either way, I *will* find out.'

The big man said nothing, he just looked away and swore again.

'So?' Striker asked.

'Roy,' he finally said. 'Roy Baker.'

'Nice try.'

The guy looked stunned. 'Huh?'

'Roy Baker is forty-two years old,' Striker explained.

'He's my fuckin' dad.'

Dad?

The word hit home like a sucker punch, opened Striker's eyes. And he cursed. 'You're Roy *Junior*?'

The guy just nodded.

Striker stood up and gave Felicia a frustrated look, one which she returned.

'Where's your dad then?' Striker demanded.

Roy Jr, sitting there in cuffs, fell over sideways. He struggled to roll onto his side, then looked up at them sideways with a look of indignation. 'How da fuck should I know? I ain't seen the guy in fuckin' weeks.'

Felicia stepped forward from the doorway. 'You got his phone.'

'So? I needed one.'

Striker helped the guy sit up. 'How long have you had his cell for?'

'I dunno. Few weeks. Maybe more.'

'And your dad doesn't mind?'

'Who cares whadda fuck he wants?'

Striker turned away, looked out the window, and thought of all the time they had wasted. Felicia spoke up next. 'Where is your father, Roy? We really need to find him. It's important.'

The big youth looked back at Felicia for a long moment. Licked the blood off his split lip. Nodded slowly. 'Look. I dunno. Check Detox. Guy spends half his life there. I ain't seen him in weeks. No shit.'

Striker nudged him with his foot. 'Why you try to run on us?'

He said nothing.

'You got a warrant? Or are you breaching? What is it? Parole? Bail?'

Roy Jr looked away. He rolled onto his back and just lay there, looking at the dirty window he had tried to escape from. He let out a tired sound. 'Recog,' he finally said. 'No drugs or alcohol.'

Striker said nothing back. A broken recognizance meant a return to jail. Do Not Pass Go. Which suited Striker just fine. One less high asshole on the streets of Vancouver to deal with.

He called up the central dispatcher and got a wagon started

up immediately. The quicker Roy Jr got lodged, the quicker they could go back to finding his father.

Hopefully before any more murders took place.

Fifty-Nine

The detox centre was located just off Scotia.

Striker and Felicia arrived there at four-thirty exactly. They drove in through the back alley and heard the loud intermittent beeping of the police wagon reverse indicator as the VPD brought over its latest batch of drunks not suitable for the jail.

Striker buzzed the back door and they waited.

When the nurse inside the centre spotted them through the wire-mesh window, he held up his badge and the lock disengaged.

One step inside the centre, and Striker smelled that all-too-familiar stink of urine and bleach. Detox was in so many ways just like the jail – lots of bad smells, lots of yelling, and lots of paperwork that needed to be filled out in triplicate due to the ever-increasing liability insurances. The only difference between the jail and detox was the lack of violence.

And even that was unpredictable.

The nurse who let them in was small, and she didn't look sturdy. If anything she was diminutive. Striker wondered how she managed to lift the drunks back onto their mattresses when they fell off.

Maybe she just never bothered.

The lines under her big blue eyes suggested she was overly tired, and maybe near the end of a long shift. Loose hairs had broken free of her ponytail, and her voice had an edge to it.

'Can I help you?' she asked, a clearly perfunctory offer.

'We're looking for a man named Roy Baker,' Striker said.

She harrumphed. '*Roy.* What's he done this time?'

'You know him?' Felicia asked.

'Everyone knows Roy,' she said. 'And not for good reasons. He's been blacklisted from Detox a dozen times. I don't know why they keep letting him come back.'

'Blacklisted because he's violent?' Felicia asked.

'Well, not to the staff. But to the other patients, yeah. He likes to fight, that one. And management keeps forgiving him – I have no idea why.'

'When was he last here?' Striker asked.

'Last Monday,' she said.

That gave Striker pause. 'So that would have been . . . November 30th. You sure about that?'

She nodded. 'I booked him in. He likes to call me *woman.*'

Striker opened his notebook. 'What time was he booked in and what time did he leave?'

The nurse moved in behind the booking station and pulled out the log book. 'Let's see here. I booked him in at 3:55 p.m. And I know that's the right time because he walked in five minutes before the start of my shift, and I remember thinking, *Great, it's gonna be one of those nights.'* She paged through the log book and tapped her finger on the next page. 'There it is. He was released clean and sober at twelve noon on the 1st.'

Striker and Felicia shared a quick look.

'And he was here the whole time?' Striker asked.

The nurse nodded. 'Yeah. Had to be. For all the shortcomings this place has with availability, it's pretty sound on security. No one gets in or out without being logged. Roy was here alright. And the log book aside, I can attest to that myself. At three in the morning, he pissed himself at the front desk, and I had the pleasure of cleaning up the area.'

Striker said nothing. He just clicked his jaw and felt a sense of frustration wash over him.

Felicia let out a curious sound. 'Well that pretty much clears him from Jazz's murder.' She looked disappointed with the news. 'We still need to find this guy. See what he knows about Jolene.'

Striker agreed. He looked back at the nurse. 'Any idea where we can find him?'

She shook her head. 'He always gives us his address on the reserve, but everyone knows he's not staying there. He crashes in the Downtown Eastside somewhere. Last we knew, he had a place somewhere on Hastings. Near Vernon Street.'

'*Vernon* Street?' Striker said. He looked over at Felicia and saw that she had made the connection too.

'Roy Baker isn't our suspect,' she said.

'No. But he might just be our John Doe.'

Sixty

Armed with a possible identification of their second victim, Striker and Felicia beelined up to Vancouver General Hospital. Southside.

That was where the morgue was located.

They took the cargo elevator to the basement level and walked down the long grey corridor to the autopsy rooms. Standing beside a dull steel examination table was the medical examiner.

Kirstin Dunsmuir was wearing a blue smock and a matching blue hairnet. The combination of the two made the cobalt blue contacts she wore stick out against her salon-tanned skin. She fixed Striker and Felicia with a brief look when they entered the room, then continued writing in her log book without pause.

Striker was used to the cool approach. Kirstin Dunsmuir was like that – exceptional at her job, and warm as an ice bath. No one had ever been accused of calling the woman personal, and on most days, one was lucky to get a simple hello.

Striker didn't mince words. 'We might have an ID for you.'

'Name?' she asked without looking up.

'Roy Baker – ex-husband of the fourth victim, Jolene Whitebear.'

'I'll do a records search.' She finished writing down her notes, placed the pen on the blotter, and finally looked up at him. 'You were right about the female, by the way. Jolene Whitebear was dead long before he set her on fire.'

'Any idea how long?'

'Preliminary, I'd estimate five or six hours. Maybe less. Long enough for the rigor to start though.' Without another word, Kirstin Dunsmuir turned away and walked back into her office. Moments later, she was on the phone – presumably searching for medical and dental records.

'She's a cyborg, right?' Felicia asked.

Striker just smiled. 'I think robot would be more appropriate – cyborgs still have some emotions.'

Felicia turned her eyes away from the medical examiner and went back to reading through the various PRIME entries listed for Roy Gerard Baker. There were many. 'This guy's got a ton of hits – all alcohol-related. Look at this: Disturbance. Disturbance. Disturbance. Disturbance. The list just goes on and on. There's a ton of fights and assaults too. Domestics and criminal harassments. This idiot's spent half his life in the drunk tank.' She tabbed through the pages, stopped, tapped the screen. 'And look at this.'

Striker looked over her shoulder. Under Roy's contact list was the title, Social Worker, followed by an all-too-familiar name:

Luther Faust

Felicia sat back from the laptop and shook her head. 'He's *always* there. Everything and everyone connects right back to Luther – Jazz, Roy, Jolene, and even Moses. He's the one connection we have in all of this. And all that sacrificial stuff you saw in his basement . . . I mean, as much as I hate to say it, he's a possible suspect, Jacob.'

'Or a potential victim,' Striker replied.

'He's hiding something from us,' Felicia said. 'I can feel it.'

'Regardless, the cat-and-mouse game ends here and now. Let's pull him in.'

Felicia looked relieved by the words.

'If Luther *is* involved in this,' Striker said, 'we can put the heat on him. And if he's not – if he is a possible next victim – then he'll need our protection anyway. Besides, we need to find the next-of-kin for Roy and Jolene. Luther might know where their kids are located.'

'Let's just hope he'll be more cooperative this time. God forbid he lawyers up on us.'

'Let him try,' Striker said. 'I've had enough of the charade. We got enough circumstantial evidence now to detain him, and we'll do just that.'

'*Detain*,' Felicia clarified. 'Not charge. We can only hold him a reasonable amount of time. Then what? What if he doesn't talk? He'll just walk on us again.'

'No, he won't,' Striker replied. 'Not this time. This time, I think Luther will be *extremely* cooperative – after we threaten to release the pictures we took of his basement when we cleared the house.'

Felicia turned in her chair to face him. 'Nice plan. There's only one problem with it – we never took any pictures.'

Striker just smiled at her.

'Luther doesn't know that.'

Sixty-One

Ten minutes later, Striker and Felicia sat in the undercover cruiser, parked on the south side of Broadway. At six-thirty, the traffic rush hour was still going strong and showing no signs of ebbing, and the slush and black ice that covered the pavement made for a horrendously slow go.

Striker watched the parade of cars inch by, their taillights a never-ending line of red in the growing darkness. He took out his cell and dialled Luther. If the man didn't pick up, then Striker would call Ministry HQ, Luther's home number, and then all of Luna's contact numbers. But on the third ring, Luther answered.

'What do you want, Striker?' he demanded.

'We need to talk.'

'Not now.'

'It's not a request.'

Luther responded with something garbled that Striker couldn't quite make out, then began talking to someone else who was obviously with him. Striker thought he heard a female voice in the background. Maybe Luna. He couldn't be sure.

'Luther,' Striker said again. 'Where are you?'

'HQ. Look, I can't talk right now. I'm dealing with some-thing . . . *delicate* here.'

'Stay where you are, I'm coming down.'

Luther said nothing back. The line just clicked off.

Striker put the car into gear and pulled out onto Broadway. They headed for the downtown core.

Due to the lingering traffic congestion and the bad roadways, it took them a half hour to reach the headquarters of Child and Family Services. Striker parked out front in a loading zone and approached the building. Felicia followed and brought the laptop with her.

It was always needed.

Since it was now after hours, the building doors were locked. A security guard had to let them inside. When they marched down the hall to the main office, the first thing Striker saw upon entering was that Luther's door was wide open.

No one was inside.

Striker stepped into the office and looked around. A few women in the far corner of the room were typing on their computers. A heavy-set woman with a headset looked up, a cigarette dangling from pink glossy lips.

'Can I help you?' she asked.

Striker held up the badge. 'We're here to see Luther.'

'He's gone,' she replied. 'Left here, oh, probably twenty minutes ago now.'

Striker swore and looked at Felicia. 'The prick left the moment he hung up.'

Striker looked back at the clerk. 'Listen, we're extremely concerned about his and some other people's welfare right now regarding this file. Do you have any idea where he went?'

The woman with the dangling cigarette grimaced. 'No. But he was more than upset about something when he left. Running round the office in a panic. Is . . . is everything alright?'

'No.' Striker looked back at her, and could see the eagerness for a new rumour in her eyes. 'He say anything unusual? Anything odd?'

She shrugged. 'Just talked to himself. Said "I can reason with him," but he didn't sound overly confident. Like I said, he looked real nervous. I just guessed it was a custody thing or something.'

Striker took out his phone and called the man's cell again. Suddenly, a phone rang in Luther's office. Striker walked to the doorway, looked inside, and spotted the cell on the desk blotter. He hung up. Also on the desk were the keys to the city car. Which meant no GPS to follow.

'He left the cell *and* car here,' Felicia said.

'So we can't trace him.'

Felicia swore under her breath. 'I'm really tired of this guy. He's *disrespectful*. I mean, I expect that from the toads on the street, but not a government employee. I say we haul his ass down to the station and make a scene – make an example of him.'

Striker listened to her words, then looked left and realized that all the clerks were watching them. He could just hear the rumours starting. Needing some privacy, he pulled Felicia into Luther's office, then closed the door.

'One small problem,' he said. 'We don't know where Luther is – we can't haul his ass downtown if we can't find him.'

Felicia said nothing for a moment, then she shrugged. 'We could always stake out his farmhouse again. He's got to come home sometime.'

Striker made a face. The idea wasn't a bad one, but definitely a last resort. Stakeouts could last days, and that was time they didn't have. Besides, the way Luther was acting, Striker wouldn't have been surprised if he stayed somewhere else for the night.

Maybe even with Luna.

'*Luna,*' he said. 'Luther was with Luna earlier in the day.' He took out his phone and dialled her cell.

It didn't even ring, but went straight to voicemail.

'She's powered it off,' he said.

'So it's untraceable too.'

Striker searched for another way. Then recalled Luna dropping her keys the previous day in the office. 'Her car – she's got All-Star on it, remember?'

Felicia nodded. She knew the emergency road service. She had it herself. 'Unfortunately, they're sticklers for information. They won't give us her location without a warrant.'

'They sure as hell will – or I'll charge them with obstruction.'

Felicia shook her head. 'My God, Jacob, anyone ever tell you about flies and honey?' When he didn't answer and just looked back at her, she added, 'Let me handle this.'

'You gonna cast one of your spells on the man?'

She smiled sweetly. 'It worked on you.'

Striker said nothing else, he just let Felicia get to work. She placed the laptop down on the desk and opened it. The moment the screen lit up, she entered the British Columbia Driver's Licence database.

'What's her last name again?'

'Asawa-Tan,' he said. '*Normal spelling.*'

'That joke is older than you.'

Striker laughed anyway.

Felicia brought up the psychiatrist's driver licence information and also her insurance history. Then she got on her cell, spoofed the call to read *L Asawa-Tan,* and called up All-Star Road Service.

'All-Star,' a man said.

She put on her best helpless voice. 'Oh thank God you

answered. I need a tow, bad. My car's, like, totally broken down. I think the battery's dead.'

'Your name, Ma'am?'

'Luna Asawa-Tan.'

She spelled the name for him, and when he asked her questions to confirm her ID, Felicia used the BC driver's licence profile and the insurance cooperation database to answer them. Keywords and all.

'And where exactly are you, Ma'am?'

She made a desperate sound. 'Oh jeez, I don't know this area . . . uhm, let me see if I can find a street sign somewhere . . .'

'That's okay, Ma'am,' the All-Star assistant said. 'I can use the GPS to locate you . . . it just takes a second or two . . . There we go, I got you. Two hundred block of Clark Drive.'

'That's right,' she said. 'I just found the street sign.'

'I'll send a tow right away. Be less than fifteen minutes.'

'You're a dream,' she said.

'Anything else, Ma'am?'

Felicia gave her best embarrassed sound. 'Oh my god, I can't believe this . . .'

'Ma'am?'

'I left the car in *drive* – no wonder it wouldn't start.'

The man on the phone laughed softly. 'You still need the tow?'

'No, cancel it please – oh God, I'm *so embarrassed.*'

'Don't be. Happens to the best of us, Ma'am. Call anytime. And thank you for using All-Star.'

Felicia hung up the phone, looked over at Striker, and rested her arm on the window ledge. 'How's that for magic?'

Striker smiled at her.

'You've just been upgraded to apprentice.'

Sixty-Two

The Boy With The Violet Eyes understood what was going on.
It was easy for him. Simple, really. Because he knew the history.

It was, after all, a part of his own.

He'd been following Luther Faust, ever since the social worker
had left the office of Child and Family Services. This was a necessity. Not that Violet cared for Luther, because he didn't, but
because Luther would undoubtedly lead him right into Monster's
arms – whether Luther intended to or not. It was out of his
control. If he did not find Monster, Monster would find him.

The avalanche was coming.

Patiently, diligently, Violet trailed the man down East Hastings
Street, until he turned north on Clark Drive.

Towards the Vancouver ports.

Violet's patience was worn thin. Every mile traversed caused
the pent-up energy inside his body to rampage against his bones.
Like millions of oscillations beating him from the inside out.
The excitement was almost too much to bear.

Finally, it was going to happen.

Finally, after all these years, he would see him again – that
giant hulking figure. That brute.

That ungodly *monster*.

When Luther parked the small sedan in the north lane of
Powell Street, Violet parked in the south lane. And when Luther

got out and began making his way across the overpass, towards the loading docks, The Boy With The Violet Eyes followed.

The winter winds were strong, and the heavy darkness of the pressing night seemed to make them all the colder. They blustered against him, so harshly they tore the hoodie from his head and made his eyes water. He pulled it back on, held it down, and continued across the overpass. Keeping his distance. Being patient. Playing it safe.

And then, at long last, it came – confirmation.

From the southeast, there was a soft sound, like that of a door closing.

Violet glanced back towards the boundary of the lot and spotted a generic white van parked in the alleyway. Between the north lane of Powell and the chain link fence of the yards. Leaving the van was a giant of a man in a dark kangaroo jacket. Hood up.

Violet's heart almost stopped.

It was Monster.

The image was fleeting. There one moment, gone the next. Like a patch of darkness being sucked away by the light.

He had been right. He had been right all along! Monster had returned home. And the very thought of this caused The Boy With The Violet Eyes to shiver. A wormlike sensation burrowed throughout his body – a feeling of shock and resentment and revulsion and all-consuming *hatred*.

Monster – the one who had taken everything away from him.

Monster – the Chosen One.

And Monster – the one who destroyed it all in the end.

Violet watched Luther wander out towards the docks, where the large steel shipment containers sat in blue and red rows. From the overpass above, the storage yards looked like a maze. And Luther was definitely the tiny mouse running through it.

The man's expression was one of fear and his posture was tense as he passed row after row of shipment container. He was calling out for Monster, looking around for the man, but receiving nothing in response.

Just silence.

Violet could see the scene unfolding, and it intrigued him, from a dark and twisted perspective. Hell, it was even entertaining – the utmost form of reality TV *sans* the television set.

'I'm coming for you, Monster,' he said. 'I am coming.'

He let out a soft hyena laugh.

Shivered with excitement.

And headed down into the ports.

Sixty-Three

When Striker and Felicia reached the two hundred block of Clark Street, Luna's car was nowhere to be found. They circled the block twice, performed a four-block radius search, and still found nothing.

Striker scanned all down Powell Street, where there were a half-dozen low-income shelters for people who were mentally ill and drug addicted – perfect clients for Luna. But there was still no sign of her or her vehicle.

'It's an Arctic Pearl Prius,' Felicia said. 'For God's sake – it should stick out down here.'

Striker cast her a glance. 'Arctic Pearl?'

'Silver-white. It's an unusual colour. Metallic. *Bright.*'

They did another search – twice the size of the first – and still found nothing. Striker was about to suggest that maybe they'd missed Luther and Luna once more, that maybe the pair had already left the scene, when Felicia pointed upwards and said, 'What about up there?'

Striker averted his eyes to the overpass and nodded.

The overpass was a side branch of Clark Street that looped over the railroad tracks and ended on the federal land of the ports.

'Worth a check,' he said.

He turned the wheel and started across.

Sixty-Four

'This isn't solving anything,' Luther said.

'You need my help,' Luther said.

'I can fix this,' Luther said.

But Monster ignored the man's pleas.

They were mere words. Empty and untrue. He had heard those spiels too many times before, from too many people. The words were as hollow as the souls of their promisers.

He stood up high on a transport shipping crate. It was the standard size – 2.4 metres tall, 2.4 metres wide, and 3 metres long, and made of strong thick corrugated steel that was painted the same red colour as the patches of rust showing through. These were the defective containers. The ones in need of repair – warped steel, dented doors, broken hinges.

Monster had chosen the second container specifically, for two reasons: it loaded from the top, as opposed to the front. And because the broken latch allowed the lid to swing *inside* as opposed to out.

That was essential.

The container Monster stood on was the third in a row of five.

The middle one.

Luther stood on the cement pad of the loading dock, looking up. 'I can take care of you,' he said. 'I can repair everything.'

Monster said nothing still, he just looked down at the man and assessed.

Luther was on ground level. Standing shin-deep in snow and slush. Staring up at him with those lying eyes of his. He was wearing his standard leather jacket, and that stupid bowler hat that Monster had always hated.

With the heavy darkness of the night pressing down, and only the weak illumination of the safety lights offsetting the blackness, Luther Faust looked more like a silhouette than a real person. And that was fitting because Monster felt about as much sympathy for the man.

'Some things are irreparable,' he finally said. 'Some things can never be undone.'

Luther Faust struggled for some words. Found none.

And Monster knew that the time had come.

He turned around, put his back to Luther, and stared northward. Out there, the shipping docks extended all the way to the waterfront of Burrard Inlet. Just before them, rising out of the earth like prehistoric beasts, stood a series of giant gantry cranes. Each one was over sixty metres high and dominated the skyline. Here and there, below the cranes, the red and white lights of the forklift drivers could be seen removing and delivering cargo.

But they were few. The docks were relatively quiet tonight. The snow and winter winds had slowed down everything in this city.

The world felt dead.

Monster stood there, looking at all of this, and purposely ignoring Luther. When it became clear that Monster would not answer Luther anymore, the social worker tried a new approach. He climbed up onto the first shipping container. Then he slowly and cautiously made his approach.

Monster waited . . .

Waited . . .

Waited . . .

And then he heard it – the loud metallic *shrenk* of the shipment container lid giving way, followed by the thunderous clang as it slammed against the inside wall. There was a sound of surprise coming from Luther – a short abrupt cry – and then a flat splashing.

Monster turned around.

The lid to the container had buckled inwards as planned, and the only sign left of Luther was the red-rimmed bowler hat that had fallen just outside the container's edge. It now sat upturned in the snow and slush.

Monster moved up to the edge of the container. Looked down.

On his knees, stunned and looking lost, was Luther Faust. He wiped his eyes, spat out a mouthful of fuel. Screamed, 'Jesus Christ! What the hell?'

Monster was unmoved by the words. 'Where is she?' he demanded.

'Let me out of here!'

'Where is she, Luther?'

Luther stopped spluttering. Met his stare. 'She's done nothing—'

'*Nothing?*' The words fell from Monster's lips with disbelief. 'She may as well have labelled me with the mark of the beast.'

'She's not here,' Luther said. 'She's far, far away from here. And she will never be coming.'

Monster was disappointed by what he heard, but not surprised. 'You always were clever.'

'Listen to me—'

Monster raised the flare gun and took aim, and all at once, Luther let out a horrified sound – as if he was only now fully aware of what was about to happen to him.

'Please!' he screamed out. 'Please! For the love of God – show some *mercy!*'

The word hit Monster like a sucker punch, and the gun momentarily dipped in his hand. He reached into his inner pocket and pulled out a silver cross. With a flick of his wrist, he cast it into the fuel-filled container, and Luther caught it reflexively. The social worker looked at the cross as if confused, but then his eyes filled with recognition and his expression crumbled into despair.

'There is your mercy,' Monster said.

He raised the gun, and this time, he fired.

Sixty-Five

Striker and Felicia looped onto the overpass, reached the halfway point, and still found nothing. For a brief moment, Striker scanned his eyes out across the bay beyond.

The night sky was winter black and further backed by a wall of cloud that blocked out any trace of moon- or starlight. Here and there in the dreariness, small red and white and yellow lights could be seen flashing around the ports – the forklifts, trucks and cranes of the trade. Their lights were but pinholes in a giant black tapestry that looked otherwise deep and cold and empty.

Then there was a giant flash of brilliant orange-white light.

Felicia raised her hand instinctively. 'Jesus,' she said.

Striker did the same.

The flash was *blinding*. Terribly bright and white hot.

For a moment, Striker thought that there had either been an explosion on the port somewhere, or that an electrical arc had occurred. Then he focused straight ahead to the storage yard and spotted a row of steel shipment containers. One of them was open from the top with flames leaping out of it. And standing just back from the edge, on the next shipment container, was a giant hulking figure staring down.

'Jesus – it's him,' Felicia said.

Striker didn't hear her words. He had already jumped from the car and was racing across the snow-covered tarmac.

Racing towards Monster.

Sixty-Six

Striker ran across the ten-lane driveway, where semi-truck trailers transported freight from the trains to the loading cranes of the dock. He already had his pistol out, finger itching alongside the trigger guard.

When he reached the beginning of the storage yards, where all the transport containers were kept, the hulking figure standing atop the burning container turned slowly about. Spotted him. And jumped down to the snowy pavement below.

'Don't move!' Striker yelled.

But the man was still far away. 200 metres, maybe more. And the sounds of the wind and the flames drowned out the warning.

On his portable radio, Striker heard Felicia calling in the incident. Requesting more units. A dog. The marine boat. A chopper too.

And it was almost as if the suspect had heard this as well, for he paused awkwardly, then looked up into the cloud-covered sky as if searching for the bird. Then he bolted north. Towards the cranes.

'Stop!' Striker bellowed once more.

He initiated pursuit.

Far ahead, the suspect ran and got ten steps, maybe fifteen. And then he came to a hard stop – as if he had run into some giant invisible barrier. There, not twenty steps ahead, another figure emerged. A man – tall, lean, gangly.

And for a moment, neither one of the two men moved.

Then there was a clash.

Striker wasn't sure who had moved first. But the battle was as instantaneous as it was short-lived. The suspect grabbed the thinner man by the throat. Slammed him to the ground. Clawed at his face.

Even from a hundred metres away, Striker could hear the man screaming.

Monster was ripping him apart.

Killing him.

Striker took out his pistol. Took aim. Opened fire.

The first shot rang out into the night, and the suspect craned his neck backwards. The second shot ricocheted and sparked off the steel container, not ten centimetres from the man's head. The metallic sound echoed through the ports.

This time, the suspect turned and fled.

Striker raced after him, his feet slipping and skidding on the intermittent patches of snow and black ice. When he reached the burning bin, where the fire was still going strong, lighting up the immediate area with a flickering yellow-red and sending a plume of oily smoke billowing into the night, Striker spotted something else.

Something that turned his blood cold.

Resting upside-down in the snow, was a bowler hat with a red brim.

Luther.

For a brief moment, Striker was torn between going to the storage container or continuing pursuit. But then he got his legs moving again and raced after the suspect. God forbid, if Luther was inside that burning bin, it wouldn't matter anyways. No one could survive that. No one. And more important than anything was the suspect. He had to be stopped.

He was a killing machine.

Striker raced on. Past the injured man on the ground, who was still clutching his cheeks and letting out a strange high-pitched whine. 'My face – MY FACE!' he wailed.

'Get to cover!' Striker yelled at the man. 'Get to goddam cover!'

He reached the next row of containers, and spotted the suspect. The man was running even faster now. But not towards the cranes, like Striker had previously thought. No, he was heading for the end of the ports. Towards the inlet. And for the first time, Striker wondered if perhaps he'd anchored a boat there.

He grabbed the radio from his side and broadcast. 'He's running for the inlet – how far's the marine unit?'

'Not even boarded,' came the reply.

Striker swore. As he monitored the suspect's speed, he could see that he wasn't slowing down. Not a bit, despite the fact he was now but five metres from the edge of the docks. He was going to jump. Into the icy waters of the inlet.

He was going to escape.

Striker stopped running. Took aim. Opened fire.

As the gunfire erupted in the night, the monster ahead of him dove straight out into the inlet. He reached mid-air, jerked hard, and then disappeared from sight below the grade of the dock.

Striker raced across the pavement, up to the edge of the dock, and stared down into the murky waters below. He saw no boat. No sign of the suspect. Only black cold waters.

He waited there for a long moment, more than five minutes, scanning the water and the entire length of dock. Looking for any sign of movement. But none came. And it worried him greatly. The inlet was huge, the waters deep and dark.

Drowning would be possible.

But so would escaping.

As he continued scanning the waters, Felicia finally found him. Out of breath, she came rounding in from the east. From the direction of the loading cranes.

'You okay?' she asked between breaths. 'You okay?'

Striker nodded absently.

'Call for the boat, call for SCUBA,' he said. '*He's in the water.*'

Sixty-Seven

The Boy With The Violet Eyes shambled out of the storage area of the ports, dragged himself over the chain link fence, and fled down the long narrow alleyway that paralleled the yards. His face felt ravaged. Torn. *Desecrated.* And the moment had completely shocked him.

So strong.

Monster was so undeniably strong. So *powerful.*

Violet had not expected it.

With his heart hammering in his chest and the flesh of his face feeling hot with blood, he ran away from the blazing fire of the ports. Away from the incoming lights of the police emergency vehicles. Away from Monster.

It was all he could do.

He reached the cross-street of Clark, considered running south and then circling back to his vehicle—

And then he paused.

Parked down the lane, maybe fifty metres away, was the white van. *Monster's* van.

Thoughts of lying in wait flooded his mind, but he quickly quashed them for fear of the police finding him inside. Next his thoughts turned to the notion of possible ID or registration papers in the glove box – anything that might give him a permanent address for the man who had done this to him.

In the nearby distance, the wail of police sirens was growing louder.

There was little time.

The Boy With The Violet Eyes seized the moment. He hurried down to the van, found it unlocked, and opened the door. Inside, he did not find any registration papers, nor any identification, but he found something infinitely more pleasing.

Sitting in a cage on the passenger side of the van was a tiny squirrel. On the wire mesh of the cage hung a little name tag.

Samuel

Violet brought a hand to his mouth in surprise.

It was perfect. It was just too perfect.

He even named it the same.

The squirrel looked up at him with interest, then turned away and bolted under the shredded papers in his cage.

Violet laughed.

It was almost as if the squirrel knew what he was thinking.

Sixty-Eight

It was hours later by the time Striker finally turned away from the water.

Out in the inlet were the only two boats the Vancouver Police Department owned. The bigger of the two, an aluminium thirty-footer named the *McBeath*, was acting as a loading station for the divers, while the secondary craft was patrolling the shorelines to the west.

To the far east, Air One, the Vancouver Police Department chopper, was hovering, using its high-powered beam to scan the beaches of Cambridge Park and the neighbouring area of Wall Street, where row after row of low-income apartments were lined up. Both dogs on duty – Sable and Bullet – were out there tracking now, but so far all they'd come up with was a big fat zero.

The suspect had escaped. Striker knew it. Somehow in the darkness, he'd swum his way to freedom.

It just didn't seem possible.

And as if that wasn't bad enough, the mysterious stranger who had fought with their suspect had also disappeared. Striker had gotten a decent look at the man – long black hair, pale skin, high cheekbones . . . and there had been something else about him. Something odd.

In the darkness, it had been difficult to tell.

Regardless, he was a witness, and now he was gone.

Striker broadcasted the man's description and got patrol units to do a sweep of the area, mainly out of fear that their witness might also be the next victim – that he may have been hurt somewhere where no one could find him.

But nothing so far.

The entire situation was a nightmare.

And the coagulating news crews weren't helping any. Striker looked at the media chopper flying on the north side of the ports, under which Superintendent Laroche had amassed a large media conference. The news stations were all there now – Global, CTV, and the minors. Newspapers too. It was becoming even more of a media fiasco than before.

Which at one point had seemed impossible.

Striker headed back up the tarmac. As he did, he spotted Felicia crossing the other way, having come back from assisting at the press conference. Striker reached the shipment container and stopped. Fire crews had long since put out the flames, but the bin was still smouldering. Patrolmen had taped off the area, and Noodles was busy taking night shots with his Nikon.

Inside the bin was the burnt-up body of Luther Faust. Burnt so badly that recognition would not even be possible.

Striker said nothing to Noodles as he approached. His eyes trailed to the small red cone set beside the bowler hat with the red brim. *Evidence sample 3.* That was what Luther Faust's life had come down to – an evidence tag.

Striker stared at the hat and felt an overwhelming sense of culpability. He should have seen this coming. The evidence had been there. He should have gotten there sooner. Done something. Done . . . *anything.*

But it was too late now.

'Press is going nuts up there,' Felicia said.

Striker just nodded. 'Laroche too, I'll bet.'

'He's none too happy.'

Noodles spoke for the first time. 'Yeah, well, add me to that list. I was supposed to be at the Canuck game tonight. Box-fucking-seats. Instead I'm out here with this shit again.' He gave them a hard look. 'Hurry up and catch this asshole already, will ya?' He took a few more shots, then began fiddling with the camera settings.

The tech's callousness got to Striker, and an anger arose within him. He struggled to hold his tongue, moved away from the scene, and stared back at the burnt-up shipping container. He thought of going up there and searching the bin.

But in the end, he did not. The fire had simply been too hot. Any thoughts of finding silver cross remains or other trace evidence was a fool's dream now. It was lost for good.

Striker looked at Felicia and tried to keep the desperation from his voice. 'Any luck on Luna?'

She shook her head. 'They found her car though. Just off Powell. No damage. No signs of a struggle.'

'But nothing on her?'

Felicia shook her head. 'No idea where she is or who she's with. And she's not answering her calls either – not on any line. I sent a North Van unit to her home – she's not there. Sent a car to Luther's house – she's not there either. And we have no idea which, if any, clinic she works at. We got nothing.'

'What about associates?' he asked.

'I tried, Jacob. No.'

Striker looked up at the frenzy of reporters crawling all over one another like bees at a hive. Camera flashes were going off, feeds were recording. A big drama for the viewers.

Striker looked away.

'List Luna as a missing person,' he finally said.

'Already done – with us to be called twenty-four-seven if she's found. Both our cells are listed.'

Striker nodded his understanding.

He thought everything through one more time, came up with nothing else, then motioned for them to leave. They headed back towards the undercover cruiser, passing clusters of patrol cops as they went – most of them from District 2, but a few who had been called in from 1 and 3.

When they were back inside their own cruiser with the doors closed, Striker sat back in the seat, sighed, and rubbed his eyes. They felt heavy. Grainy. *Dry.*

'What time is it?' he asked.

'After eleven now.'

'Jesus – we've been going at this sixteen hours straight. No wonder my brain's not working.'

Felicia nodded. 'Unless we get a call from someone running Luna's name, or unless Noodles finds some forensics at the scene, there's not a lot more we can do tonight. We should head in and get some sleep. Because tomorrow's going to be another early start and a long hard day.'

Striker said nothing. Logically, he knew that she was right. But emotionally, he felt torn. Before he could respond, his cell went off. He looked down at the screen, expecting it to be Laroche intent on berating him. Instead, he saw the name *Percy Wadsworth.*

'It's Ich,' he said.

Striker hit answer. Stuck the phone to his ear. Didn't bother with the niceties. 'What you got?'

'Something you'll find interesting, I'm sure,' the tech replied. 'I've been reading through some of Luther's emails and chat-room stuff here, and well . . . just how well did you know this guy?'

'Why you asking, Ich?'

'Because he's into some pretty twisted shit.'

Striker recalled the altar in the basement of Luther's home. 'So I gather.'

The sound of keyboard typing filled the receiver, and Ich spoke again. 'I'm not sure what Luther was getting at in this particular text conversation I'm reading here – he's talking about specific dates and how each one holds a different kind of power – but it's definitely creeping me out. And get this . . . guess what his login name is?'

Striker closed his eyes. 'Firesong.'

'Exactly.'

'Which would make Moses Sabba Morningstar, right?'

Ich made an annoying buzzer sound. '*Wrong.*'

That got Striker's attention and he sat forward a little. 'Wrong?'

'Dead wrong. This Moses Sabba guy is part of the same online group alright, but he's not Morningstar. Moses goes by the name *Starchild.* Which I didn't think that was too big a deal until I found a quote in one of the chat-rooms that refers to Satan as *The Star* – fallen from heaven and given the key to the underworld.'

'Let me guess,' Striker said. 'Revelations?'

'What else? Revelations 9:1. You can look it up yourself.' Ich took a sip of something, then cleared his throat before continuing. 'Anyway, you connect the two words, *Star* and *Child,* and, well, it doesn't take a religious scholar to figure out the inferences – it's *Child of Satan.*'

Striker said nothing for a moment. He just thought of the fires people were dying in, and the altars and pentagrams he had found in both Luther's farmhouse and Moses Sabba's strange abode. And lastly he thought of the weird pseudonyms they were all using. All in all, it was leading them to a very bad place.

'That still leaves out Morningstar,' he said.

'Actually, no, it doesn't. She's there too.'

That word made Striker pause. *'She?'*

Ich let out a sour laugh. 'You've been on top of her all along, man . . . Morningstar is *Luna*.'

Thursday

Sixty-Nine

Thursday morning.

When Striker woke up, the pain in his jaw was still excruciating and he was beginning to wonder if he had broken something. Talking was tender, but eating was downright painful. Waking up brought him a focal stiffness in the jaw joint. Like it had locked on him.

He looked at the clock. It read 5 a.m., and boy did it ever feel like it. It felt like they'd been working this file for weeks, not days.

He found it difficult to relax, and even more so to sleep. Dreams of the hulking figure in the rubber mask flooded him, as did night terrors of people on fire and screaming. He got up after yet another nightmare-filled jolt. Made some coffee. Nursed it in the living room.

He read over the file notes, starting with the passage Ich had quoted from Revelations, the one that referred to Satan as the Star:

And the fifth angel sounded, and I saw a star fall from heaven unto the earth: And to him was given the key of the bottomless pit.
– Revelations 9.1

Striker read that passage a half-dozen times before flipping back through the pages of his King James. The book was old, the black leather spine cracked all the way down and faded.

The Bible had been given to him by his father, who had received it from his father. Now, as Striker held the book and smelled the old leather, he felt a growing sense of guilt – as if he'd not only turned his back on the church, but on the memory of his father and all the man had sacrificed for him. All the man had believed in.

Everything this morning felt bleak and cold.

When his cell phone rang, startling him from the pages and sad memories, he was all too happy for the disturbance. He looked at the display, saw a number he did not recognize, and brought the cell to his ear.

'Striker,' he said.

'Hello, Detective, it's PC Gonzales, from Echo 13,' came the reply. 'We've found someone I think you're looking for. A woman named Luna Asawa—'

'*Asawa-Tan*,' Striker finished. He sat forward in his seat. 'Where are you?'

'Vancouver General.'

The hospital. 'Is she injured?'

'In the head maybe. Woman's had a total breakdown.'

Striker frowned. 'She seen a doctor yet?'

'We got her here on a mental health apprehension – *Hold Psych.*'

'It's that bad?'

The man cleared his throat. 'You got no idea, Detective. The woman has totally *lost it.* She just keeps saying the same thing over and over again.'

'And what is that?'

'*Burned him alive.*'

Seventy

The Boy With The Violet Eyes was a complete wreck.

He'd spent the entire night trying to repair the damage that Monster had caused to his beautiful, boyish, celestial face. He'd washed and rinsed the deep gouges with purified water. Applied a poultice of silica, zinc and vitamin E cream. Then covered the wounds with a homemade salve of coconut butter and some aloe vera gel he'd squeezed right out of the plant leaves – anything to stop the scar formation process.

He had prayed – *prayed* – it would work.

But now, as he awoke from what should have been some unholy dream, he swept his trembling fingers across the floor and found one of the broken pieces of mirror. He held it up. Stared.

Gaped.

Damaged. His beautiful, wonderful face – damaged. It was an ungodly sight. The skin so red and swollen, so distended that not even the beautiful violet colour of his eyes could save him.

'This wasn't supposed to happen,' he found himself saying. 'THIS ISN'T HOW IT WAS MEANT TO BE!'

Not only had Monster destroyed his life and stolen from him everything he loved, but he also taken from him his one chance at redemption. For without his face – his *boyish*, beautiful face – what hope did he have of regaining that love once more?

Tears flooded his eyes and trailed down his cheeks, stinging the wounds when they hit. Violet knew they would only aggravate his skin even more, but he could not stop them from coming. The sobs he had held deep inside were released, and his entire body shuddered with every breath. The despair was overwhelming.

Not even thoughts of what he had done to Monster's little squirrel could bring him any peace now.

He collapsed on the floor and lay within the greyness of the room.

How long he stayed like that, he was unsure. The despair was all-encompassing. But soon it mutated. Turned into fury. Turned into rage. And he knew without a doubt that he and Monster would meet again.

It was their destiny now.

Perhaps it always had been.

Violet couldn't wait to kill the man.

Seventy-One

Striker and Felicia got down to the hospital by 7 a.m.

It wasn't a second too soon. As they walked through the emergency doors of Vancouver General, Striker spotted the woman they were seeking. Luna Asawa-Tan was uncuffed – because it was an apprehension assessment, not an arrest – and by the looks of things she had already spoken to a psych nurse.

Striker assessed the woman's demeanour.

Luna was standing in the admitting area, fingers balled into fists, face red, posture tight. Even though just one hundred and fifty centimetres tall, she had managed to back the rookie cop detaining her into the corner of the room, and her angry demands could be heard all the way through the front door.

'Luna,' Striker said. *'Luna.'*

The psychiatrist craned her neck to an odd angle and stared at him with heat in her eyes. 'You have no right to hold me,' she said. 'No right!'

Striker and Felicia crossed the room. When they were near enough, Striker approached Luna while Felicia took the young constable aside for a quick debriefing.

'*No right!*' she yelled again.

Her words were not only loud, but spoken unevenly. Not slurred, but unclear. Striker took a closer look at her eyes. Aside from the smudges of mascara-filled tears that had trailed down her face, he could see that her pupils were overly large.

'Did the doctor already see you?'

'I'm cleared.'

Striker looked at the young constable standing next to Felicia; he nodded to Striker that this was true.

Striker looked back at Luna. At her large pupils. 'What sedatives did they give you?' he asked.

'Oza . . . Ozapam . . . it's none of your business.'

'How much did you take?'

Her eyes watered, and the tightness of her face broke. The anger dissipated into nothing and she began crying.

'Luther . . .' she said. *'Oh, Luther.'*

She pulled some tissues from her purse and began blowing her nose and wiping her eyes. Striker said nothing. It was clear that she had likely witnessed the horrific murder, maybe from somewhere hidden close by, maybe from afar. Either way, she was understandably wrecked. He wanted to give her the time she needed to regain some composure.

In behind him, a pair of paramedics brought in an old drunk who had fallen and hit his head. He was holding a bandage against his temple and bitching about something that was impossible to make out. Between his maudlin whines and the constant ringing of the admitting phones, the foyer was in constant clatter.

Striker looked back at Luna, who was now brushing some of the hair out of her eyes. Trying to fix herself up a little.

Striker spoke gently. 'We're going to catch the man who did this,' he said. 'I can promise you that. But in the meantime, I have to ask you some questions here. Some personal ones that might make you uneasy. Where were you last night?'

She sniffed hard. Fought for emotional control. Ran a finger beneath her eye to wipe away the tears and crud.

'I was with a patient,' she finally said.

'Who?'

'That's confidential.'

'Where did you see this patient? At your clinic?'

Luna crossed her arms, turned slightly away from him. Looked down the hall at nothing. When she spoke again, there was building anger in her tone. 'I haven't had a real clinic since your last investigation, Detective. All my appointments are walk-in clinics or home visits now. Not that it concerns you.'

'At this stage, everything concerns me – your whereabouts included.'

The words seemed to strike a chord with Luna, and she turned to face him. 'Am I under arrest here?' She spoke the word a little too loudly, and the other patients in the waiting room looked over.

Striker looked across the foyer and spotted Felicia. She just shrugged at him, and he continued. He looked back at Luna. 'Maybe this would be easier for you in a private setting. We could take you down to HQ, then get you a ride home after—'

'Am I under arrest or not, Detective?'

'No, Luna. You're not under arrest.'

'Then leave me be.'

Striker found her response extremely odd. 'Given the circumstances of what's going on here, I'd have thought you'd be eager to help us out a little. This isn't a game, Luna. This guy's a homicidal maniac. A serial killer. And for all we know, he might have been one of Luther's apprehensions. Or one of the clients Moses worked with. Or maybe even one of your own patients for all we know.' He gave her a pleading look. 'Can you think of anyone who might do this?'

She didn't even look at him. 'Anything between me and my patients is confidential.'

Striker splayed his hands in frustration. 'I'm trying to help you here, in case you haven't noticed.'

For the first time, a small grin found Luna's lips. One that did not touch her dark eyes. 'You're good at that, aren't you, Detective?'

'Good at what?'

'At playing the martyr.' She fixed him with a cold stare. 'I remember the last time you were trying to help me.'

'If you're referring to the investigation, you might also want to remember that I cleared you.'

'Sure. After my name had been dragged through the mud. After you cost me my clinic. I lost everything.'

Striker was getting tired of this story. 'The choice wasn't mine, Luna. You know that. An investigation had to be done, and I did everything I could to be as private as possible.' He looked back at Felicia. 'If you'd prefer, you can speak with my partner over there. Detective Santos.'

'Your partner? – or your lover?' Luna asked.

When Striker made no response she laughed angrily. 'You see, Detective, I'm not the only one with secrets.'

'Luna—'

'I'm leaving,' she said.

When she turned to go, Striker played his best card.

'I know about the altars,' he said. 'Moses and Luther both had one in their basements. And I've seen the pentagrams too.'

The words stopped Luna in her tracks, but she did not turn around.

'I also know about *Morningstar*,' he continued. 'And *Starchild*. And *Firesong*. I know about your relationship with Luther, who is now dead, and I know about your previous relationship with Moses, who is also dead. I even know about December 21st. About the sex rites and Feast Day. I know it *all*.'

Luna finally turned to face him, and when she did her eyes were as dark as he had ever seen them. But cold. Hollow. Detached.

'Then if I were you, Detective Striker, I would be extremely careful what I say. You destroyed my career once. I won't let that happen again.'

'Is that a threat?'

'Yes it is. Of a civil lawsuit.'

Striker laughed softly, more out of frustration than any sense of humour. 'If I were you, Luna, I'd be more concerned about criminal charges right now – and about my own personal safety.'

'And if I were you, I'd be more concerned about losing my house and my pension plan over false allegations and slander.'

Striker listened to her words but made no reply. There had been enough bickering between them, and it was getting him nowhere.

'You need police protection,' he said.

'I need nothing,' she replied. 'From you.'

'Luna,' he tried one last time.

But she wasn't listening. She turned and walked out the emergency doors, and Striker was left with nothing but the sounds of the phones ringing and the drunk old man crying in the corner.

Seventy-Two

Monster shuddered.

The nightmare was always the same – the fear of being left alone in the cellar; the wood stove blazing with fire, its black iron grille like a twisted smile; and The Boy With The Violet Eyes, standing in front of the room's only exit.

He was always there, Violet. A smile on his face and hatred in his eyes. Even now, in Monster's head, he could still hear the other children chanting out their heartless cries – *Monster! Monster! Monster!*

It was always the same.

Feeling the chill of the room against his overheated flesh, Monster opened his eyes. With his brain full of the bad memories of the distant past and the more recent ones of the previous night, he half-expected to see himself back at the school, he half-expected to find himself back at the ports.

Sore from the collision with the docks, tired from the eight-kilometre swim across the harbour, he lay there and felt his anger brood as he stared into the darkness of the ceiling above.

Only the weak glow of the candles provided any light, and it was just enough for him to see. To get his bearings. Up high, he saw thick wooden beams arching across the ceiling, and the realization that he was once again back in his lair fluttered through his mind.

He turned his head, looked around.

'Samuel,' he called out. '*Samuel!*'

But the squirrel never came.

He smacked his lips. Felt his inner cheeks stick to his teeth and gums. Felt his tongue swell in his mouth like it was two sizes too large.

Thirsty . . .

So thirsty . . .

He rolled left to reach for the water bottle, and a sharp, tearing sensation hit him. Grinding his teeth, he fell back against the mattress and touched his side. The wound was sore as hell. Hot to the touch. And wet.

Still bleeding.

He was lucky that this wound was all he had to contend with. The bullet had torn open the side of his ribs. Stripped off an entire piece of flesh, like a giant hangnail. Maybe it had even taken some of the bone with it.

Had he not been diving when the shot came, and twisting down towards the water, the bullet might have done far worse. After all, being in pain was one thing; not being able to breathe was quite another. He was fortunate the bullet hadn't punched *through* the lung. If that had happened, he wouldn't have survived the night.

He touched his side once more. Felt more wetness through the gauze and pads. The wound required medical attention. Stitches at the very least. Which was something he could have done himself had the angle been on the front of his torso. But this was closer to the rear.

A difficult spot to reach.

Sleep beckoned him. He was so tired. He closed his eyes and took in a slow deep breath. And then realized: the room had a *bad* smell, thick and putrid. And the stink was him. If he wasn't

careful, infection would set in. And that was always the killer –
the infection.

The one thing that couldn't be fixed with fuel and fire.

He looked at the first aid kit, and realized the wound was
beyond its abilities. He needed to get his old battle box, the one
his foreman had given him when logging the Crow's Nest Pass.
It was a Level 5, and had all the supplies every lumberjack needed
in case of emergency – the Ioplast to stop infections, the
Quickclot to stop the bleeding, and the Sentinel Seals to hold
the wound closed.

It was damn near the same list given to the army.

And it worked like a charm.

He placed one hand against his injured ribs, applied pressure
and forced himself to sit up. As he did, sweat trickled down his
brow and cheek, causing the Jelform mask to slip.

He tore it from his face. Immediately, the coolness of the air
against his cheek made him feel weak and vulnerable – exposed.
And when he glanced left and spotted himself in the dirty reflection of the window, he realized, once again, that it was like
looking in a funhouse mirror.

The Gargoyle.

The Beast.

The *Monster*.

He turned his eyes away from his reflection and narrowed his
focus. He needed to get healthy fast. There were still more people
to kill. And there was little doubt that The Boy With The Violet
Eyes would be out there looking for him.

Their collision was unavoidable now.

Perhaps it always had been.

Clutching his wound, Monster headed for the cellar. That
was where the battle box was located.

Seventy-Three

'Luna may not want police protection,' Striker said to Felicia. 'But she's getting it anyway.'

He got hold of the Alpha and Bravo sergeants, and got them to put their plainclothes cars on surveillance duty. Mobile work, on the fly. If the psychiatrist laid low, so much the better. One car at the front, one out back; one man mobile, the other on foot.

Striker was unflinching on the matter. It was needed.

A Priority 1 response was also placed on her residence in Deep Cove, and her name was flagged on the Canadian Police Information Center database, requesting all intelligence be logged as proper calls. Luna Asawa-Tan needed to be monitored. Striker believed that without question, because yes, she needed protection . . .

But also, she was hiding something.

They left Vancouver General and took an immediate right on Broadway. When they were out front of the local Future Shop electronics store, Striker parked the cruiser by a meter and stuffed the Police On Duty sign on the dashboard.

'Why we here?' Felicia asked.

Striker pointed across the road at the four-storey business centre that was a wall of tinted glass and purple-brown stucco. 'College of Psychiatry's in there,' he said. 'Let's see if Luna has any clinic listings. I don't believe her when she says she only does walk-in clinics and home appointments. Besides, who knows what else we'll drudge up.'

Felicia smiled. 'Time to poke the bear a little?'

'Yeah. With a cattle prod.'

Broadway was bumper-to-bumper with the morning grind, and the black ice was making the roads and sidewalks treacherous. Striker and Felicia hurried across the crosswalk to safety. They entered the building and took the elevator to the fourth floor.

The moment they entered the office they were greeted by a cheery woman with plump cheeks and a yellowish bob hairdo that looked like the remnants of a seventies home perm gone wrong.

She looked up at them and smiled. 'I just unlocked that door ten seconds ago,' she said. 'Good morning.'

Striker looked at the wall clock. It was exactly 8 a.m. 'Lucky us,' he said.

He introduced himself and Felicia, and showed his credentials.

The receptionist gave Striker a long look. 'Do I know you from somewhere? You look familiar?'

Striker immediately thought of all the press coverage they'd been receiving these last two days. 'I guess I have that kind of face,' he said, then changed the subject. 'We're here to speak to you about one of your doctors – a psychiatrist named Luna Asawa-Tan.'

At the mention of the doctor's name, the receptionist's expression changed.

'You know her?' Felicia asked.

'Yes, we all do. Dr Asawa-Tan is rather . . . how shall I say this? – *unique*.'

'How so?' Felicia asked.

'She believes very much in a hands-on approach. Spends a lot of time out there on the streets, doing home visits – that kind of thing.'

'Well, we're trying to locate a clinic address for her,' Striker said. 'We haven't had much luck so far.'

'To the best of my knowledge, she doesn't have one.' The receptionist typed her name into the computer and nodded. 'None listed. I direct all her mail to her home address. Do you have that?'

'Deep Cove,' Striker said. 'Yes, I do.'

Suddenly, the receptionist's eyes widened and she snapped her fingers. 'That's where I know you from – you were the officer here a few years ago, during the previous investigation.' She leaned forward and whispered. 'The sexual misconduct.'

'Which was proven to be unfounded,' Striker said immediately. He leaned with his forearm on the desk and met the receptionist's stare. 'But I do need to look at her complaint file. To see if there's been any more unforeseen submissions since then – it's standard follow-up procedure.'

The receptionist nodded, but her eyes took on a distant look. 'You normally have to apply through the Freedom of Information Act for that kind of thing. How did you obtain copies the last time?'

'The warrant,' he explained. 'A copy of which should be in your records.'

'And this is related to the *same* investigation?'

'Of course,' he lied.

She nodded, then asked them to wait a moment. She left her desk and disappeared into the records room down the hall. As they waited for her return, the smell of the percolating coffee hit Striker's senses. It smelled good. Damn good. And he suddenly realized he was hungry as hell too.

Felicia echoed his feelings. 'Coffee next.'

'Agreed.'

A few moments later, the sound of a photocopier filled the room, and Striker knew the receptionist was copying the file. It was done in ten minutes, and fifteen minutes after that, Striker and Felicia were back in the car, each with a hot cup of Starbucks in their hand, going through the file review on Luna's previous sexual misconduct allegations.

Striker flipped the pages, one by one.

'There sure seems to be a lot there,' Felicia noted.

'Actually, there's not really all that much. Everything is done in triplicate – initial form, review process summary, inquiry committee report, explanation of findings. It's rehash and rehash of the same stuff. It just goes on and on.'

'Sounds like a bunch of CYA to me.'

'Everything is Cover Your Ass.' He smiled. 'Not much different from the police department.'

Striker paged past the older complaints – the ones he had long since deemed unfounded. When he reached the end of them, he found only one other complaint. An allegation had been filed: *Unprofessional Behaviour.* Under which a subheading was written: *Disgraceful, Dishonourable and Unprofessional Behaviour.*

Striker scanned the page for further explanation, but found none. Only the registrar's words: *Interview granted. Allegation Summarily Dismissed.*

'Odd summary,' Striker said.

Felicia agreed. 'It really doesn't tell us much.'

Striker flipped through the report. 'It looks like we're missing a page.' He got on the phone, called the college back up, and got the receptionist to look through the file one more time. When he hung up, his tone was one of disappointment.

'That's all she's got,' he said.

Felicia said nothing back. She was too intent on the bottom of the page.

'Look at the complainant,' she said.

Striker did, and the name shocked him, for it was a man they both knew.

Father Shea O'Brien.

Seventy-Four

'I want to talk to him,' Striker said. 'There's something weird going on here between Luna and Father O'Brien, and we need to know what.'

Felicia agreed. 'Everything connected to these non-profit groups has been twisted and convoluted from the start. We need to know what happened there. Why the politics?'

Striker tapped his knuckles on the steering wheel and thought aloud. 'Luther. Moses. Jolene. Big Roy. They all make sense in one way.'

'How so?'

'They're all interconnected through the Ministry. Luther and Moses through their work there, and Jolene and Roy through their domestic squabbles.'

'But why Jazz?'

Striker frowned as he thought it over, and when the idea came to him, it was like the hub of a wheel connecting all the spokes. He put the car into gear, U-balled, and took a hard right on Burrard.

'Where we going?' Felicia asked.

'Ministry HQ,' Striker said. 'I got a hunch Jazz might have worked in one of our integrated units.'

'It would explain her connection to the others,' Felicia said. 'But it would have been a long time ago – she's been in Major Crimes for ten years now.'

Striker eyed her. 'I'm thinking even farther back than that.'

Despite the snow and traffic, they reached the front of the court house in ten minutes. Striker parked the cruiser under the Smithe Street overpass and climbed out. Felicia followed him.

The moment they returned to the office where Luther worked, everyone looked up at them and an uncomfortable silence filled the air. Word had travelled fast. Everyone knew of Luther's demise, and everyone knew that Striker and Felicia were on the case.

The woman from the previous night was nowhere to be seen, so Striker grabbed a young clerk with unruly Harry Potter hair and hawkish nose that was so large it dominated his other features.

'What's your name?' he asked.

'Darren.'

'Listen up, Darren. I need a list of logs for the Family Car. Attendance sheets and pairings. And I need it as far back as twenty years.'

'Twenty *years*?' he said. 'It will all be archived.'

'Have you heard what happened to Luther?'

The young clerk just nodded and got the point. He got up from his desk. 'I'll be a few minutes,' he said. Then he walked down the hallway and disappeared around the corner.

They waited.

The silence of the room lingered. Uncomfortable, almost overbearing. And when the office phone began to ring, it was a welcome distraction. After a moment, one of the other ladies wearing a headset offered them coffee. Striker was about to accept the offer when he spotted Darren returning down the hallway. In the young man's arms was a pile of old black leather books.

Ten, or more.

Striker bypassed the woman offering them coffee and took the old log books from the young clerk. With Felicia's help, he laid them down on the counter and started arranging them in order of date, starting with the oldest and ending with the newest.

Felicia opened the first ledger. 'What exactly are we looking for here?'

'Anything with Jazz's name or badge number.'

She just nodded, and they got to work.

It didn't take long. When Felicia was a third of the way through the second binder, she let out an excited sound and stabbed her finger on the page. 'Right here. Badge 1406 – that's Jazz.'

Striker dropped his book on the counter and looked over. There it was. In fading red ink. And right beside her name were the initials L.F., followed by the number 86.

'LF?' Felicia asked. 'Luther Faust?'

'You got it.'

'And the eighty-six?'

'The eighty-six is for Car 86 – what they now call the Family Car. Back then, they were a little less PC about things – they just called it the Apprehension Car. It was responsible for taking kids away from abusive or neglectful parents.' He frowned. 'Look at the date.'

Felicia did. 'That was almost twenty years ago now.'

'It tells us something,' Striker said.

'Yeah. That Jazz and Luther were the city's apprehension team.'

'It tells us something more specific than that,' Striker added. 'Jazz and Luther were the ones who took away Jolene and Roy's kids.'

Seventy-Five

How much time had passed, Monster had no idea. Time, like always, was a strange thing to him. A quantity that could not be measured. And he didn't try to. He simply stood in the darkness of his living quarters and assessed the wound to his ribs.

Already he had removed the splinters of bone, flushed the injury with sterilized water, sanitized it with the Ioplast, and then applied the Quickclot. The binding took a good ten minutes to form, but once it gelled, it held well. Monster overlaid the wound with the mesh covering of Sentinel Seal and taped up the ribs. The whole process was not only painful but exhausting, and he was slick with sweat.

A fire was raging in the wood-burning stove. Despite its heat, the room owned a chill, one that invaded every fibre of Monster's body. Maybe it was the fever, maybe it was shock. But there was little doubt his body was taxed. It needed rest.

Unfortunately, he would get none today. Today, there was work to do.

Not only did he now have the police to deal with, but The Boy With The Violet Eyes as well – and Violet was more dangerous than any of them. Even now, the moment back at the ports felt surreal. Monster had been shocked – so completely and utterly stunned to see him standing there. This horrible, hateful presence that had forever altered his life so many years ago. Fear and terror had overwhelmed him.

But how things had changed. He had fought back. Overpowered the man. Taken him down and had him at his mercy. All in all, it showed Monster one very important thing.

He was no longer that little boy anymore; he was a man.

The Boy With The Violet Eyes.

Violet.

Simon.

He had many names, and Monster knew them all. But that was all they were – names. In reality, Violet was nothing more than a shell. An outer layer filled with nothing but hatred and jealousy and an overwhelming sense of desperation.

Violet was the reason Monster had become the monster.

And retribution would be coming.

With that thought refusing to leave him, Monster lumbered into the other room – into the special area he had created.

For the performance.

There, lined up against the far wall, was a row of sandbags. He grabbed the first one, feeling his rib bones ache and muscles tear. He dropped it in the centre of the room. This would be the beginning of the circle.

It was fitting. For everything had come full circle, hadn't it? From Alpha to Omega. Beginning to End.

He went to grab another sandbag, and as he leaned forward, Corn Nuts spilled from his shirt pocket. The sight of them reminded him of his little friend, and he called out to the squirrel.

'Samuel . . . *Sam-u-el!*'

But again, the squirrel did not come. Just as he had not come the last time Monster had called him. And then, to his horror, he remembered – *the van*. Samuel was still back in his cage. On the passenger seat of the van.

He was still back by the ports.

Seventy-Six

It was after ten in the morning by the time Striker and Felicia found what they were looking for. The old storage box was located in Ministry archives, way up high on the top shelf. It was covered in a fine layer of dust that puffed into the air when Striker moved it.

'I'm surprised they still have the file here,' Felicia said. 'I thought anything older than seven years was scanned to disc and shipped to IronLock.'

'If this was a Ministry-only file, you'd be right,' Striker said. 'But it was Car 86 who attended. The Apprehension Car. So it was a shared file between them and us. They *have* to keep a copy here. In case we need it.'

He dropped the box on a nearby counter, pulled off the lid, and found the syllabus inside. He scanned his finger down the page until he found the name *Whitebear*. The corresponding report number was 10771, and it was seventeen years old. He quickly fingered through the folder tabs until he found it.

Once in hand, he passed the folder to Felicia, then pushed the box aside. She opened the folder and laid everything out on the counter.

There wasn't much. Just a four-page report. One page for the synopsis, one for the occurrence report, one for the concluding remarks, and one that held no information at all, save for the entities of the parties involved – Jolene Whitebear (mother), Roy Baker (father), and their two children, Jordan Whitebear (age thirteen), and Terrance Whitebear (age twelve).

'Well, at least we finally got all the kids' names,' Felicia said.

Striker nodded. 'Note that the children got the mother's surname. Probably because Roy was never around.'

He read through the apprehension report. The facts were as simple and sad as they were terribly common for District 2:

Police Constable Jasmine Heer, in company of social worker Luther Faust, had come by to check on the children. When they arrived on scene, Jolene Whitebear was unconscious on the floor and surrounded by empty rice wine bottles and used crack pipes. The children showed not only signs of neglect, but of physical abuse. They were apprehended under the Child Services Act by the Ministry and taken to the Faint Hope Foundation for temporary lodging.

'There it is – the Faint Hope Foundation,' Felicia pointed out.

Striker skimmed ahead to the concluding remarks page. The conditions were clear and concise: Jolene was to attend treatment for her alcohol and drug dependencies, and anger counselling in order to deal with the matters of physical abuse.

The last line in the follow-up section said it all:

To date, Jolene Whitebear has done neither. The children remain in protective custody and will continue to do so for the foreseeable future.

That was where the report ended.

'So they took away the kids for good,' Striker said.

Felicia nodded. 'I wonder if they took away her *Mother of the Year* cup too.'

Striker didn't respond. His thoughts were focused on other details. After a long moment, he turned to face her and his mood was bleak. 'So, essentially, what we have here is two kids who were taken away from an abusive mother by the Ministry.'

'And put into the hands of some social workers who were involved in Satanism.'

Striker let out a long breath. 'Now some of those very people are being burned alive.'

'Revenge?' Felicia asked.

'I don't like where this is going.'

Striker scanned through the report for a listing of the children. They would be grown up now, but he needed addresses. After a quick search through the file and a longer search through the Ministry database, they were S.O.L. The only address in existence for the children was the very first one they had – and that was the Faint Hope Foundation.

Now known as the Salvation Society.

Striker leaned against the counter and pinched the bridge of his nose. A headache was developing behind his eyes – one that matched the throbbing of his jaw. His entire face felt pressurized.

'Let's go back to the car and check PRIME,' Felicia said.

'The PRIME system has only been around nine years. The file's too old for that. Any reports that haven't been purged over the years will be paper-based only. We'll have to hit the archives again – only this time, *police* archives.'

Felicia's face filled with doubt. 'That won't be as easy as you think,' she said.

'Why not?'

'Last time I was down there, the Department had transferred all files older than fifteen years to the new building out east – in preparation for The Big Move.'

Striker cringed at the words. The Big Move was the name people were using regarding the impending transfer of all the investigative sections from 312 Main Street to the new building out east. It was supposed to have happened months ago, ever since the VPD had received the hand-me-down building from the Winter Olympics, but like any big project, the planning had all gone to hell. Entire sections were divided here and there. Chaos reigned supreme. People had even been demoted over the ordeal.

The thought of locating a seventeen-year-old file in all that mess was the proverbial needle in the haystack.

'This is going to be a nightmare,' he said.

Felicia looked at it from a different angle. 'Why not try the Salvation Society instead? They're still technically the ones who placed the children. They'll have records on it. They have to. It's the law.'

Striker liked her way of thinking.

'Congratulations,' he said, and smiled. 'You've just been upgraded from apprentice to journeyman.'

Felicia offered him a weak grin but took the compliment.

They made a copy of the Ministry file, then shelved the box and headed for the undercover cruiser.

It was time to pay the Salvation Society a visit.

Seventy-Seven

Kingsway was the old two-lane highway, built long before the creation of the four-lane freeway to the north. As a result, the Kingsway connection had built up steadily over the years and, despite the new freeway, it was still a central hub in many connected neighbourhoods.

Flanking Kingsway on both sides now were strings of small businesses – computer shops, dry-cleaners, numerous Vietnamese noodle shops and tons of Chinese bakeries. Most signs were in a foreign language – line and circle characters occupied every street banner.

Striker liked the area. It had not only character, but one of his all-time favourite cafés – Pigs Thai, a small speakeasy that made the best pork wraps in the city.

The main office of the Salvation Society was nestled just off of the Kingsway connection, in the Sunset Plaza Mall. Striker and Felicia parked out front of the centre. The moment they went inside, a strange smell hit them. Some chemical air freshener, or something.

'Lemony,' Felicia said.

Striker looked around the front desk area. The place offered mixed messages as to its function. A business licence hung over the front desk, along with numerous pamphlets, not only on substance abuse and alcoholism, but on Catholicism as well. On the wall behind the counter was a large crucifix, and on all waiting-room tables were several copies of the Bible.

Felicia noted the incongruence too. 'Looks like a tornado picked up a medical facility and slammed it into a church.'

Striker smiled at that.

He approached the front desk, flashed his badge, and explained their predicament. The young girl behind the counter was surprisingly helpful. Five minutes later, at 11:35 a.m., she led them down the hall to the director's office.

Striker and Felicia had just taken a seat when an average-looking man of average height and average weight walked in. His hair was brown and parted on the side like a 1950s salesman, his teeth were neither straight nor really crooked, and his face was entirely forgettable. He wore a sweater that was cream in colour and had no design.

'Gabriel Sullivan.' He extended his hand. 'I'm the director here.'

'Mr Sullivan,' Striker started.

But the director held up a hand. 'Please. Gabe will do.'

'Fine. Gabe it is.'

The director smiled. 'We make an effort to keep things relaxed around here. Keeps a little less tension in the air for the patients. A lot of them are rather . . . well, *highly strung.*'

Striker nodded. 'I can understand why.'

The director closed the office door for extra privacy. 'I heard about Luther,' he said softly. 'And Moses too. I'm terribly sorry.'

Striker offered no reaction. 'Then you can understand why we're here?'

For a brief moment, a look of concern flooded the man's face. 'You don't think whoever did that is coming *here*, do you?'

Striker raised a hand to relax the man. 'We have no reason to believe that.'

The director let out a heavy breath and seemed to shrink a little. 'Well, that's a relief. Who is this man? Do you have any idea?'

Striker ignored the question. 'We came here for a couple of reasons,' he explained. 'The first of which is to understand the situation here a little better.'

'The situation *here?*'

Felicia nodded. 'Gabe, what exactly happened here ten years ago?'

He looked back, confused.

'With Moses and Luther and Luna.'

'*Ohhh,*' he said, as if he should have known all along. 'That mess was before my time, really. But I do know a bit of it.'

'Even a bit would be helpful,' Felicia said.

The director cleared his throat. 'Moses was the one who started it all. He came from a pretty rough background, you know. Had a lot of his own problems with addiction and alcohol abuse. And he had a heck of a time getting over it – back then there wasn't a whole lot of help for that kind of thing.'

Striker nodded. 'So I hear.'

'It was a long time ago. There were certainly no treatment centres for dual diagnosis patients back then, that's for sure. So you really have to tip your hat to the man. When Moses cleaned up, he cleaned up for good. And when he did, he then looked for other people who were having the same problems. Many of them were youths who needed help. So he and Luther started a non-profit organization.'

'The Faint Hope Foundation,' Striker said.

'That was what they called it, because that was what it offered their clients – a faint hope.'

'Sounds like a good idea to me,' Felicia said.

'It was a *great* idea,' the director said, 'especially for its time.

Moses Sabba's project spurred on a dozen others. It's the reason why there's so much help in the city nowadays – in Strathcona, and Burnaby, and the downtown core. He did a really amazing thing.'

'And yet he was forced out of here,' Felicia said.

'Yes, that he was.' The words sounded flat. 'That was when I came on. It was pretty tense around here for a while, let me tell you that. Real hush-hush. And no one talked about it.'

'About what?'

The director raised his hands as if in futility. 'About what was going on. Somehow Moses had pissed off a large group of the donating shareholders, and there was something of an uprising. He left the president little choice but to have him removed.'

'The president being Luther Faust?' Striker confirmed.

'That's correct,' the director said. 'At least, on paper.'

Striker eyed the man. 'On paper?'

'Luther was the one in charge of removing Moses. And they kept everything that happened between the three of them.'

'The three of them?' Felicia said. 'You mean Luther and Moses and *Luna*?'

'No. I mean Luther and Moses and Father O'Brien.'

That caught Striker off guard.

'Father O'Brien?' he asked.

'Yes, Father O'Brien. He was the one urging to have Moses removed in the first place . . . Was real adamant about it. Luther didn't want it that way, and there was some in-fighting. It was a very stressful time for the rest of the staff.'

Striker felt lost in the process. 'I don't understand. How is Father O'Brien involved here in any way?'

The director leaned forward as he explained: 'The Faint Hope Foundation was a non-profit. Father O'Brien helped out with a lot of these over the years. Here, especially. He acted as . . .

well . . . a *conduit*, I guess is the best word for it. He was the connection between the non-profit and the church. And most of the sponsors were parishioners of the church. So, indirectly, Father O'Brien brought in a large bulk of the money.'

'Most of it, by the sound of things.'

'I don't have the numbers.'

Striker took out his notebook and wrote down this information. Once done, he looked up and changed the subject. 'What about Jolene Whitebear?' he asked. 'Did you ever deal with her yourself?'

'Oh God yes, many times. Terribly addicted woman, terribly addicted. Willing to use almost anything – alcohol, crack cocaine, inhalants. I once caught her breathing *oven cleaner*. Whatever she could take into her body, that woman did. And no matter what we did to help her fight the addiction, it only got worse with time. It was a sad thing, really. A very sad thing.'

Felicia asked, 'You ever deal with her husband?'

For the first time, the director frowned. 'Big Roy? Yes. Too many times for my liking. He's a dangerous man, that one. Unpredictable. You could always feel the stress around him, like you were just one wrong word away from violence.'

'And what about their kids?' Striker asked. 'You ever deal with them?'

The man got quiet for a moment. 'No, never myself. Would've been Luther or Moses who dealt with them, I think. We're talking a *long* time ago now. Near a couple of decades maybe. But I do know this – it was no temporary measure. Those kids were taken away by the Ministry for good, and they were later adopted by the Calvert family.'

'Calvert?' Striker asked. He wrote down the name immediately.

'Yes, the Calverts. Good people. Honest folk. Don't get much better in this world.'

'And how did that go?' Felicia asked tentatively.

'Well good, I would think. God knows, I never heard from them again. Those boys must be all grown up by now. In their twenties, for sure.'

'Got an address?' Striker said.

The director nodded at them and his words were the first good news Striker had heard all day.

'Of course,' the man said. 'I'll get it for you.'

Seventy-Eight

Monster drove the stolen Camry back towards the ports. It wasn't easy. His head was bad and growing worse by the minute. He needed his medications. But medications would have to wait.

Samuel came first.

Monster broke all the rules in returning. He didn't watch his speed. He didn't circle the block. He didn't scout the area for police. He just drove right down Clark Street, parked behind the barren patches of blackberry brambles, underneath the port overpass, and made his way down the lane on foot.

The moment he reached the van, the smell hit him – faint, familiar, and terrifying. He yanked open the driver's side door and felt his breath catch in his throat. On the driver's seat was the cage.

Or what was left of it.

It had been burned, along with everything inside. No paper remained. No wood shavings. No water bottle. The thin wire mesh was now a grimy black colour, and the plastic playhouse and running wheel had melted along with the water bottle into an unrecognizable lump.

In the middle of the cage, curled up and blackened, was his little squirrel.

'*Samuel,*' Monster said softly.

He could barely breathe. Barely think. Barely focus.

And suddenly he wasn't there in the laneway by the ports anymore, but back in the cellar again so many years ago. And Violet was there. Playing with his emotions. Taunting him. Tormenting him:

You like this squirrel? he was saying. *He's a fucking rodent. A rat!*

Please, Monster said.

Violet held the squirrel in the air. Let it dangle like a rag doll, and Samuel was making strange screeching noises.

He's vermin, Violet continued. *Filth.*

Violet kicked open the front grate to the wood stove. Inside, the fire burned a deep glowing red. And suddenly Monster realized what was happening. Realized – and froze.

Violet threw the animal inside and slammed the grate closed, and for a brief moment, loud horrific screeches could be heard. Ones that vibrated through every one of Monster's bones.

Ones that would stay with him for the rest of his years.

When Violet turned back around, the look on his face was one of cruel amusement. He met Monster's stare, and nodded slowly.

Next time that will be you . . .

The memory ended as abruptly as it had begun. And Monster found himself standing there with tears running over the ripples of his deformed eyelids.

'Samuel,' he said softly. '*Samuel . . .*'

He began to tremble, then his entire body shook. *Hard.*

He stood back. Fists clenched. And fought to control his thoughts. Fought to kill the emotions. But it was impossible. The memories were too thick; the medications in his blood too thin.

He turned away from the cage. Reared back across the snow. And once again, ran away from what he could not accept. He fled to the only place he knew where he could still find any sense of love or peace or understanding or solace.

He ran to *her*.

Seventy-Nine

It was eleven-thirty now, not long before noon, and the winds were picking up.

Striker and Felicia left the dingier area of Kingsway and headed back west towards Dunbar. The address that Gabriel Sullivan had given them for the Calvert family was near 34th and Highbury Street, which was not all that far from Striker's own house – though in the much more expensive section of the Dunbar community.

They came into the area from the north, and had to deviate from the main drive due to a three-car fender-bender that was blocking most of the road. By the time they'd gotten back on track, they found themselves driving down Alma Street, right in front of the Holy Cross church.

Standing in the doorway, speaking to Father Silas, was Father O'Brien. A large smile owned his face, and his cheeks looked slightly ruddy in the cold weather. After a brief discussion, the old man patted the younger priest on the shoulder, then returned inside. Father Silas remained where he was, smoking a cigarette and staring at the snowy barren branches of the dogwood tree.

'I've never seen a priest smoke before,' Felicia said.

'Beats chew,' Striker said.

Felicia laughed, then gestured for him to pull over. 'We're here now anyway,' she said. 'Why don't we see what Father

O'Brien knows about these kids – and everything else for that matter? God knows his name has come up enough times with all this talk about non-profits and charities.'

Striker said nothing, but he nodded. He pulled over in front of the dogwood tree and climbed out. The moment he did, Father Silas waved a hand, the smoke from his cigarette wafting through the air. By the time Striker and Felicia were at the end of the walkway, he was blowing smoke rings through his over-grown moustache.

'Smoke rings?' Felicia asked. 'Seriously.'

Father Silas smiled back at her. 'It's okay – they're actually little halos.'

She laughed softly.

'I thought you were heading back to Squamish,' Striker said. 'To close down one of your churches.'

He sighed onerously. 'I am. In time. Once Father O'Brien can spare me. But he's been pretty busy as of late – communions, funerals, weddings, and of course regular old mass. We're already understaffed, and have been for a long time. So it's been trying times for the both of us.'

'What about your own church – St Jude's?' Felicia asked.

Father Silas let out a long breath of smoke. He looked tired. 'Yeah, my own parish has been busy too, but not as busy as the Holy Cross. Dunbar's always been the hub of this area.'

Striker smiled. 'Maybe the nicotine will help.'

Father Silas pulled out a silver cigarette holder and stubbed out the cigarette against the case. 'The Lord doesn't give a man more than he can handle – or at least that's what they keep telling me.'

The three of them spoke for a while longer, then the priest excused himself – caffeine was also needed, he said – and Striker and Felicia walked through the front doors.

Once inside the narthex, Striker spotted Father O'Brien. The old man was on the other side of the nave, wiping down the podium. Striker stared at him, then at the entire crossing, where his mother had stood in the choir so many years ago. No matter how he tried to wrap his mind around the fact that years had passed and this was a different time, he still felt stuck between the two.

Being here felt bad.

He got his feet moving and approached the priest.

'Father O'Brien,' he said.

The old man turned around from the podium and, upon seeing them, beamed. 'Jacob,' he said. 'Have you returned to the flock?'

'Still looking for my wings, Father.' Striker forced a smile, one that didn't come easily, then reintroduced Felicia. He got right down to business. 'We've been dealing with a lot of issues during the course of this investigation, and oddly, your name has come up an awful lot.'

'*My* name? How so?'

'With a place called the Faint Hope Foundation, for one – now called the Salvation Society.' When Father O'Brien made an *ahh* sound, Striker continued. 'How are you involved with this place? And how exactly did you know Moses Sabba? And Luther Faust?'

The old priest smiled, then gestured for them all to take a seat in the nave. Once they did, Father O'Brien began to talk.

'Initially, the connection was Moses,' he said. 'He came to me, seeking help for his addictions. He had many demons, the poor soul – the alcohol, the drugs, even pornography. He had come from a hard life, and he had suffered much. Moses was a very empty man.'

'And you helped him past all that?'

'Well, yes. Me, and others from the church. It took time, of course. And there were failures. Many of them. But we always overcame them. And in the end, not only was Moses clean, but grateful. He wanted to give something back to the community that had helped him.'

'Thus the non-profit,' Felicia said.

Father O'Brien nodded. 'The idea belonged to Moses. He wanted to create some kind of an organization that could help people of all sorts. We started out focusing on addiction and alcohol issues, but before we knew it, we had people wandering in from all walks of life – the poor, the homeless, the youth.'

'Sounds like it really boomed,' Felicia said.

'Boomed is right.' Father O'Brien splayed his hands as he spoke. 'You have to understand, at that time, there was nothing else like this. It wasn't like today, where you can find help in every area of the city. The centre Moses created was it.'

Striker finally spoke up. 'You keep saying the centre belonged to Moses – and yet you had him removed from it. Why?'

The smile fell from the old priest's face. 'There were complications.'

'That tells me nothing, Father.'

'Conflicts of interest,' he continued. 'Primarily, the relation-ship between Moses and Luna. It was . . . how should I word this? – openly *intimate*.'

Striker recalled the photographs he had found of the two having sex.

'And then there was the problem with Luna herself,' Father O'Brien added.

'I know you made a complaint against her. With the college.'

The old man raised a finger, and for the first time, his face was tense. 'That woman is a magnet for trouble. Look her up and you'll see. She has quite a history.'

'The investigations,' Striker said. 'I know much of them,

Father. I was the one in charge of them.' When the priest made no reply, Striker continued. 'You know, I'm not a fan of Luna's either, but to be fair, she was never found culpable on any of those grounds. They were merely allegations made against her, and every one of them was proven unfounded.'

Father O'Brien shook his head. 'The allegations against her were not what concerned me.'

'Then what did?' Felicia asked.

'Her *labels*.'

Striker shrugged. 'What labels?'

'That woman never saw the forest for the trees. She made life *very* difficult for us at the foundation, for everyone involved in the process. Her constant interference and reports made it almost impossible to place some of these children. She was careless with her labels. Reckless. And with no concern of the consequences.'

'You mean her *diagnoses*,' Felicia clarified.

Father O'Brien waved a hand dismissively. 'The terminology is not important to me, Detective. Call it what you will. The fact remains the same – Luna Asawa-Tan is highly arrogant and highly irresponsible. She does more damage than good to some of these kids – and quite often she is wrong.'

'Wrong morally?' Striker asked.

'Wrong *professionally*. Have you ever checked into how many of her diagnoses have been overturned by other mental health professionals? *Ten per cent*. That's one out of every ten kids who has to live the rest of his life with an unfair label attached to him. It's unjust, it's irresponsible, and it's unprofessional. It's the reason why I filed a complaint against her with the college.'

'I've seen it,' Striker said.

The old priest remained incensed on the matter. 'She's an incorrigible woman – just look at how she treated poor Moses after we had to have him removed.'

'And how was that?'

'She left him.'

'Right then?'

'The very day it happened. The poor man was already angry with everyone involved in the process, but he felt absolutely *betrayed* by Luna. And he never got over it.' Father O'Brien shook his head and suddenly looked tired. 'It was a terrible situation. You can imagine my reaction when I later found out she was having a relationship with Luther. Terrible, terrible, *terrible*.'

Striker let it all digest and was satisfied with the answers. He allowed a moment for Father O'Brien to calm down on the subject – the old man had gotten visibly upset – and then looked at Felicia to see if there was anything else she cared to add. She did not.

'We're headed for the Calvert place,' he finally said.

Father O'Brien's expression was one of surprise. 'I wasn't aware you knew the family.'

'We don't. We just need to talk to the two boys about some past issues. For all we know, they don't even live there anymore.'

Father O'Brien's face paled slightly. 'The two boys? . . . You mean Terry and Jordie.'

'Yes. We're going to interview them now.'

'You can't do that, son.'

'We can and will,' Striker said. 'They're a part of our investigation, Father.'

The old priest looked back at Striker, and a sad look took over his face. 'You misunderstand me, son. I'm not talking about legalities here. I'm speaking of things far greater.'

'Which is?'

'Life,' he said softly. 'Terry and Jordie Calvert are both deceased.'

Eighty

The Boy With The Violet Eyes walked slowly down Highbury Street, his eyes scanning out beneath the black lip of the baseball cap he wore. Down at the end of the street, on the corner lot, sat the Calvert home. It was easy to spot. Big lot. Old house. Red wood and white wood. Very country.

Violet had business in that home. In the basement.

Things he needed back.

Across the road on a duplex lot, a trio of children were playing in the yard. A young girl with pigtails ducked in behind a snowman as her two brothers pelted her with snowballs.

Violet watched them out of the corner of his eye – held hostage by the beauty of their youth. Their pink cheeks, their lineless eyes. Did they ever consider their mortality? Did they realize they were ageing even now? Every goddam second of every day? One day soon, there would be no more innocence for them to be had. Just an empty tank, like him.

Just year after year of knowing that all you had is forever lost.

When one of the boys stopped playing the game and instead focused in on him, The Boy With The Violet Eyes broke free of the thoughts that plagued him. He pulled his baseball cap down to hide the wounds of his damaged face, slipped between the houses, and hopped the fence into the Calverts' backyard.

He studied the house. The rear door on the lowest level led to the suite he was targeting. The lock was buggered and had been for some time now. It always popped open with relative ease – just a single twist of a blade.

And this time was no different. The moment the door swung a few centimetres open, Violet slipped inside. He melded into the darkness of the basement and gently closed the door behind him.

He stood there, listening to the footsteps of Mother Calvert above. Or maybe it was the girl. Not that it mattered one way or the other; anything above was irrelevant – so long as they didn't come downstairs into the suite. And he was pretty sure that they wouldn't. There were too many memories down here for them to face.

Happy ones that he had turned bad.

As his eyes adjusted to the lower level of light, Violet saw the photograph on the shelf of the hutch. It was one of Terry with his family. Mother Calvert. Father Calvert. Jordie. And of course little Sarah with her naïve blue eyes and angelic creamy skin.

Terry stood centremost in the picture. Smiling that nervous smile of his. The lack of confidence was always there with him, the snivelling little fuck. The disgusting weakling. He had been pathetic as a child, and was even more so as a grown man.

The meek shall inherit the earth? This made Violet laugh.

Not if he had anything to do with it.

He got moving. The basement suite was half-below ground level, and as such, the windows were small. Placed there for light more than décor. As Violet looked at them, movement on the street caught his eye. He crouched. Approached the dusty pane. And looked outside to the front yard.

A tightness formed in his belly.

An undercover police cruiser was there. And inside it was the big cop – the one he had seen out on the ports.

Here already.

Another hyena whine escaped Violet's lips because everything had changed. He had to get to work, and fast.

Removing surveillance devices took time.

Eighty-One

Striker stared at the Calvert family home from the driver's seat of the undercover police cruiser. He did not want to get out of the car.

The story Father O'Brien had told them about the Calvert family was one of great sadness. Gregory Calvert, the adoptive father of Terry and Jordie, had died suddenly and unexpectedly from a massive heart attack just over a month ago. He had been an outstanding man, an even better father, and the core stability of the family. The loss had impacted on everyone in the Calvert home, but perhaps it had taken the greatest toll on the boys, for not long after Gregory's passing they had followed their father.

By taking their own lives.

It was a horrific family tragedy, one of the worst Striker had seen in his long police career. And he sure as hell didn't feel like going to the Calvert home to talk to anyone. Not now. Not after all they had been through. But there was no choice in the matter.

Policing could be an ugly business.

'Well?' Felicia asked after a long moment of stillness.

Striker just climbed out of the cruiser in silence.

The Calvert family home was on Highbury Street, a narrow stretch of old road that was flanked with barren snow-covered maple trees. The house itself was Victorian in design, made of mostly red-painted wood with white trim. Like most of the old homes in this area, it was quite large – easily five thousand square feet, Striker deemed – and was further expanded by two single-car garages that backed out onto the rear lane. The lot was a double wide.

Worth a pretty penny.

Striker made his way up the sidewalk, feeling like his boots were weighed down with lead. Up high in the far left window, a young blonde girl stared down. He could feel her eyes on him the whole way. He glanced up. She was maybe sixteen. And her eyes and face were filled with concern.

The curtains swished and she was gone.

Striker climbed the front steps, knocked, and the door opened almost hesitantly. In the crack between the door and frame stood the young blonde girl. Her face was blank and tight, as if she was expecting more bad news. Striker took a good look at her and was filled with sudden recognition—

She was the same girl he had seen in the church that first day. *Sarah*, Father O'Brien had said. The adopted sister of the two boys.

She reminded Striker a little of his own daughter, Courtney. Same age. Same height. Same build. And same hard times.

'Yes?' she said politely. 'Can I help you?'

'Detectives Striker and Santos,' he explained. 'Vancouver Police Department.'

The girl nodded, a confused look on her face.

Felicia added, 'We came to talk to you about your brothers, Jordan and Terrance.'

'*Jordie* and *Terry*,' the girl corrected. Her voice had a note of resentment in it, and sounded ready to break. 'They've both . . . passed on.'

Striker nodded. 'Father O'Brien explained the situation to us.'

'The situation?'

'Can we come in, please?'

The girl said nothing, but her chest heaved deeply, as if she were about to break down right there in front of them. Seeing this, Felicia reached out and touched the girl on the shoulder.

'We're very sorry, dear,' she said.

Felicia had barely finished the words when the door suddenly opened all the way. In the opening stood the other woman of the house, the lady Striker had seen in the church that first day. Leaning on a cane, she kept her back straight and fixed them with a hard expression. Striker couldn't help but notice that the whites of her eyes were slightly yellow and her skin held a subdued greyish hue that made it look like she was standing in shadow.

'You must be Mrs Calvert,' he said.

The woman said nothing for a moment, just stared back at them with those lingering eyes of hers. She scanned the houses behind them, then finally nodded.

'Come inside, Detectives,' she said. 'This is a private matter.'

Eighty-Two

Ten minutes later, Striker and Felicia sat on the leather sofa in the den, across from Mrs Calvert and her daughter. Striker studied the woman intently. She kept her posture straight, her head held high, her stare strong. Her obvious attempt was to appear resolute, but what she looked like was worn and depleted – a once-strong structure that was bowing in from the building stress.

She was a fading matriarch.

Politely, she insisted on all of them having tea, and because of that, the four of them were now waiting for the kettle to boil. Striker found the moment awkward, and he occupied himself with studying the room. It was a nice setting. The walls were freshly painted white, the floors a dark hardwood.

A good contrast.

The fireplace, still an old wood number, hinted at the house's true age, as did the plaster walls. Striker's eyes trailed those walls until he found a family photograph on the mantel. It had been taken right here in the den, though done professionally.

Mrs Calvert caught his gaze. 'Last Christmas,' she explained and her eyes took on a distant look. 'If I had known . . .'

From the other room, the kettle began to boil.

'Help me gather the tea, Sarah,' the woman ordered, and the young blonde girl jumped up from the sofa. She hurried into the kitchen, and Mrs Calvert followed her. The moment they were gone, Felicia let out a heavy breath.

'The air is kinda thick in here,' she said. She tilted her head towards the woman in the kitchen and whispered. 'What you think – cancer?'

Striker believed so.

'She's in a lot of pain,' Felicia added.

Striker frowned. That much was clear to see. And with only her daughter there for support, he felt for the woman. Hell, he felt for both of them. How much could one family take?

It was a waking nightmare.

Antsy, he stood up, if only to move his restless legs, and approached the picture. For a long moment, he stared at it and listened to the mother and daughter rummaging around in the kitchen. When he turned to come back, he looked down at the side table and spotted a rectangular white pamphlet with white lace bordering. On it were seven words:

In Loving Memory of Gregory Charles Calvert

Striker picked it up, looked it over. On the inside flap was an inset photograph of Greg Calvert. He looked healthy and happy and middle-aged. Beneath his photo was the inscription: *Loving Husband and Father*. On the opposite page was the schedule of the wake reading, with the presiding Father being Shea O'Brien.

It felt heavy in Striker's hands, and he put it down.

He looked around the room. Saw more photographs of Gregory and Terry and Jordie. And he realized how much this family had lost. And how fast it had happened. Now, with the mother clearly ill, the entire family had almost been wiped out, and the thought of the young girl being all alone left Striker with an empty feeling.

It was a cold world sometimes.

'Tea is ready,' Mother Calvert announced. She limped into

the room, leaning heavily on her cane as Sarah followed behind her, carrying a silver tray with four cups, a silver bowl of sugar, a small decanter of cream, and a platter of sugar cookies.

'Really, you didn't have to,' Felicia said.

But Mother Calvert made no reply; she just nodded for Sarah to dole out the cups, and the girl did.

For the next ten minutes, the parties talked. Striker learnt more of the family's recent tragedies, and also of Mrs Calvert's illness. As they had suspected, it was cancer. Breast. Stage 3.

The thought was hollowing. To go through what Mrs Calvert was going through was terrible enough, but especially after losing her husband to a heart attack, and then her two adopted sons to suicide. It was unthinkable.

She tried to explain:

'Losing Greg was hard on all of us,' she said. 'Only faith got Sarah and I through the ordeal. But losing him was something that Jordie and Terry just couldn't handle.' She paused in her words, to gather more breath, and a palpable sense of grief and despair cloaked her like a barely visible shadow. 'Greg was always the one who got them through the memories. Of their mother. And their father. Of the *abuse*.' She looked sad in the memory. 'After the funeral, the boys were lost. Worse off than any of us understood . . . and things went badly.'

Striker wasn't sure how to respond. 'I lost my wife too,' he said. 'Grief can be a debilitating thing.'

'Terry was the first to start breaking down . . . I found a needle in his room.' She looked over at his photograph and winced as if it pained her. 'He always was the soft one . . . and in the end it cost him. He broke down. Gave in. He took his own life.'

'I'm so sorry,' Felicia offered.

Mother Calvert looked out the bay window at nothing that was there. 'I will never forget that day. The ninth of November.

A Tuesday. It rained like I've never seen it before.' She looked away from the photograph on the mantel and found Striker's eyes. 'Jordie followed not a day later.'

Beside Mother Calvert, Sarah let out a soft sound and she hunched over with her palms pressed hard against her eyes. Mother Calvert placed a hand on the girl's back and allowed her a moment, then ordered her to regain her composure. The young girl did as instructed. She sat back up, wiped away the tears, and her face took on a blank look.

Striker did not pry into the details. They would be in the police report. He would read it later.

Without warning, Mother Calvert slowly stood up. Her face was hard as porcelain and just as white. 'I'm sorry, Detectives,' she explained. 'But I'm quite unwell at the moment. Treatment begins at four; I need some rest before then.'

'We understand completely,' Felicia said.

'Finish your tea,' she urged. 'Sarah will show you out after.'

Striker thanked the woman for her time, and watched her struggle out of the living room. She turned the foyer corner and headed up the stairs, the soft shuffling sounds of her weak legs fading.

Felicia put down her cup. She stood up and looked at the girl. 'Use the church for support,' she said. 'From what my partner tells me, Father O'Brien is a good man.'

'He *is* a good man,' Striker said. 'Father O'Brien got me through some very bad times when I was your age. I lost both my parents too.'

The moment he said it, he regretted it. Not *too*. Mother Calvert was still alive. He looked back at the girl with embarrassment.

She said nothing. Her face remained blank, her eyes vacant. When she finally spoke, there was a sense of disorientation in her voice. 'Faith is . . . kind of hard right now . . .' She got up and walked them towards the front door.

Once there, Striker looked back at her. 'Where exactly did your brothers live, Sarah? I'll need their addresses.'

The girl edged into the foyer and spoke softly. 'Jordie had his own place. Just up in Marpole there – Mom and Dad helped him out with the rent. But Terry never left home.'

'Never left?'

'No. He had a little suite downstairs. No one's . . . no one's been in there since.'

Striker met the girl's stare. 'I need to see it.'

Eighty-Three

Terry's downstairs suite was small and dim, despite the white walls and pine-coloured laminate flooring. It looked well cared for. Clean. No dishes sat in the sink, no food or wrappers cluttered the counters. In the small den, everything was immaculate. The local newspapers were stacked squarely and the remote controls were lined up parallel on the coffee table.

Striker turned to face the young girl. Sarah was standing just outside the suite, as if fearful of coming inside.

'Did someone clean up this place?' he asked.

She nodded. 'Mom did. After they took Terry's body away . . . when the police were done . . . I think she just wanted it all washed away.'

Felicia nodded. 'I don't blame her.'

For a moment, Felicia began chatting with the girl. Striker took the moment to walk around and survey the rest of the suite. It was moderate in size, consisting of a cosy living room, a small office, a small bedroom, and a bathroom complete with tub and shower. All in all, a very nice place. It had obviously been remodelled, and not all that long ago.

Striker searched through the den, found nothing, then carried on to the office, where he found more of the same. When he reached the bathroom, he couldn't help but notice how the tub gleamed.

Freshly cleaned, he thought again.

The bedroom was the one room that looked like someone still lived there. The bed had been made. Family photographs still adorned the walls. And the Bible sitting on the nightstand had a plain white bookmark in it. Striker opened it up and saw the passage.

Footsteps.

He closed the book.

On the bureau was a notepad and a red pen. When he opened it up, he saw that several pages of writing had been torn from the spine.

He closed the book, put it down, and looked in the trash. It had been emptied during the clean, so he moved on. He walked to the closet and began searching through the pockets of every pair of pants and jacket he could find. When he was near done – searching the last of the jackets – he found a folded-up piece of yellow paper. A Post-it note. Covered in red felt ink.

On it were only three names:

Jeremy Stol. Frances LaFleur. Vincent Calbrese.

Striker had never heard of any of them. He stood there for a long moment, looking around the room, repeating the names in his mind, and thinking. As he did this, he noticed that there was a small bracket on the ceiling – circular, white, plastic. It looked like the mounting bracket for a smoke detector, but it was empty.

Inside the ring, drilled into the ceiling, were two more screw slots.

He took note of that and left the room. He returned to the living room, and spotted Felicia and Sarah. They were seated on the couch now, talking softly, the girl's eyes still more lost than a child adrift at sea.

Striker showed her the names on the sheet of paper he had found in the closet. 'You recognize any of these?'

Sarah took a long look, then shook her head. 'No.'

It was disappointing. Striker walked over to the corner of the room, found the phone, hit redial. Numbers appeared on the display screen, along with the name *Vincent*. The line rang, clicked, and a recorded message played.

Striker hung up.

Thought.

Scanned the room.

Above Felicia's head was another empty bracket. And when Striker searched the office, he found a third one. Three smoke alarm mounting brackets, and yet no smoke detectors in place. Not a one. And in the centre of the bracket were two more holes drilled into the ceiling.

'Did you remove those?' he asked the girl, and pointed.

She looked lost.

'The smoke detectors,' he clarified.

'No,' she finally said. 'Of course not. Mother would kill me if I did – she's always worried we'll have a fire. That's why she put up so many of them. She's even got smoke alarms installed upstairs with the security system. She's paranoid.'

Striker said nothing. He just moved down the hall in search of more.

At the far end, he found one spot where a smoke detector remained. It was right overtop a table with a second phone. The location bothered him. He took a lighter from his jacket pocket, raised it under the detector, and flicked the flint.

The flame came to life, but the detector did not.

Striker repeated the process four times, and still no alarm. Finally, he put away the lighter, grabbed a chair, climbed on top of it, and removed the device. The second he opened it up, he saw the removable internal USB drive, and he knew.

Not a smoke detector, a listening device.

The place was bugged.

Eighty-Four

The Boy With The Violet Eyes waited just outside the rear lane of the Calvert house, in the soft shadows of the neighbour's garage. He did not move, just as he hadn't moved when the two homicide detectives had entered the suite. He stood there and thought things through and felt a curious concern wash over him.

The actions of the male cop were disconcerting. The big detective had gone around the entire suite, looking at all the locations where the smoke detectors had been removed.

The plan, of course, had been to *replace* the false detectors with their originals, but time had not permitted that. Now, as he monitored the situation, he wondered what repercussions it might hold. Before leaving, the big cop had also scrolled through the phone messages.

Searching the call history, no doubt.

It was one more link that should have been deleted.

Seeing no other option, The Boy With The Violet Eyes waited for the cops to leave, then headed back for the suite. When he reached the midway point of the backyard, an eerie feeling flooded him, and he stopped. He looked up at the windows. The drapes moved slightly, and suddenly, there was Mother Calvert. He looked back up at her, at the hard edge to her sickly pale face, and wondered if she could see him.

A second later, the drapes swished shut, and he was alone again.

He moved on.

When he reached the suite, he broke back inside once more, and immediately went to the phone. He picked up the receiver and scrolled through the call history. There were only three names listed. The first two were Mother Calvert. But the last name was like a blast of energy.

The name was Vincent Calbrese. And it told The Boy With The Violet Eyes the only thing he needed to know.

The cops *knew*. They would be coming.

The idea of them closing in sent a strange shiver through his body – a strange kind of perverse joy he could not quite define. The closer the cops got, the more exciting the moment. Nervous, over-stimulated, and filled with energy, he let out a soft laugh and got his legs moving again.

It was time to pay Vincent a visit.

Eighty-Five

The clock struck exactly two-thirty when Striker and Felicia reached Jordie's place. It was located in the heart of the Marpole area. The apartment complex was small and ordinary – grey stucco, soft blue trim, lots of crumbling patches.

The building looked old.

The name of the landlord listed in PRIME was forty-eight-year-old Ralph Assaez. Striker called him on the cell and the landlord met them in front of the suite. He wore red track pants, a bright Hawaiian shirt, and had a Playstation controller in one hand and a gaming headset on his skull.

Striker looked at the controller first, and the headset second, and furrowed his brow.

'Sorry,' the manager said. 'LAN party.' He fiddled with the keys, almost nervously. 'I haven't been in there since . . . well, since he did it. I just didn't have the heart.'

'You knew Jordan well?' Felicia asked.

'Jordie? Oh yeah. Better than most of my tenants. He was a good kid, Jordie. Liked gaming, was a part of the online community. Real good kid. Saddest thing, just the saddest thing . . .'

He found the right key, slid it into the lock.

'Any friends ever come around?' Felicia asked.

Before turning the key, the manager looked back. 'Friends? God, no. Jordie didn't really have any friends, just me and the online guys. He was a loner, for the most. Only ones who ever came round here were his brother and sister. Other than that there was no one . . .' He paused. 'Well, maybe one.'

'*One?*' Striker asked.

The manager nodded and unlocked the door. 'Never met him, really. At least not to say hi. Didn't even know his name. I just saw him leaving a few times, coming and going. To be honest with you, he looked a bit *off.*'

'Off?' Felicia asked.

'Hey – not that I'm one to judge.'

'What did this guy look like?' Striker asked.

The manager absently fiddled with his headset and thought it over. 'Young, but not really young – if that makes any sense to you. Like a giant boy. Or a man that had never grown up. He was tall and skinny. Had real white skin. And there was something about his eyes. I don't know what.'

'The man from the docks,' Striker said to Felicia. He looked back at the manager. 'You never talked to him?'

'I try to mind my business.' He looked at the door to Unit 404 and a sad expression took over his features. 'I dunno. Maybe this time, I shouldn't have.'

Striker added nothing else to the conversation. He just gave Felicia the nod, and they all made entry into the suite.

The moment they stepped inside, Striker found himself at odds. The place was a mess – completely the opposite of Terry's immaculate suite – and yet the smell of cleaners and disinfectant ruled the air.

Striker stepped through the foyer and proceeded down the short hallway. He bypassed a small sliver of kitchen where the sink was overflowing with dishes and the limited counter space was cluttered with cereal boxes and Tupperware containers.

In the small living room, the only decorations were the empty bottles of beer that littered the floor, alongside a few bottles of hard stuff. Silent Sam vodka. Jack Daniels whiskey.

'Looks like he had a problem,' Felicia said.

Striker nodded. 'You check here and the kitchen, I'll start in the bedroom.'

Felicia agreed, and Striker headed down the next hallway. Halfway down, he reached the bathroom. Here, the smell of disinfectant and cleaners filled the air strongest. Inside, the tub and tile looked freshly cleaned.

Striker looked behind him, saw the landlord.

'This is where he did it?' he asked.

A disturbed look filled the man's face, and he reached up and removed his headset, as if out of respect for the dead.

'Yeah,' he managed.

'Shotgun?'

'Yeah.' He made a vague gesture to the face area.

'Under his chin or in his mouth?'

The man looked green. 'I'm . . . I'm really not sure. There was just so much . . . so much *red*. I kind of froze. Then I freaked out and called the police.' A heavy gust of breath escaped his lips. 'Christ.'

Striker didn't want to lose the man so he kept talking. 'Aside from the actual suicide, nothing else seemed odd or out of place? Suspicious?'

'Well . . . like what?'

'Like anything.'

A lost look filled the man's eyes. He may as well have had a vacant sign on his forehead.

'Just let me know if anything comes to mind,' Striker said, and moved on.

In the bedroom, he found the lone smoke detector the apartment owned. He took out his lighter, flicked the flint, and held the flame under the detector. Within seconds, an ear-piercing blare filled the room.

The device was legit.

Striker reached up and hit the mute button, then began scouring the room.

Like the rest of the apartment, the bedroom was messy. Worn clothes lay here and there on the old brown carpet; clean ones were piled up on the dresser. Not folded or arranged, just piled. Next to the bed were more empty beer bottles and two spiritual books:

The New Jerusalem Bible, and *The Power of the Present.*

Both books seemed incongruous with the rest of the elements.

Striker picked them up, one at a time, and flipped through the pages. They were bent and crooked in many places, as if the passages had been read over and over again. On the inside of the rear cover of *The Power of the Present* were four numbers, scrawled lazily:

1410

The numbers stuck out to Striker, but from where, he was unsure.

He took out his phone and googled the numbers. The first three hits belonged to a radio station, a restaurant, and the address for a bank on Granville Street. Striker added the word *Bible* to the search line and was redirected.

Revelations 14:10.

He read it slowly:

And the smoke from their torture will go up forever and ever, and those who worship the beast and his image will have no rest day or night . . .

He stopped reading. Felt uneasy. The passage was an odd find, and under the circumstances, it seemed fitting. He wrote the information down in his notebook, then put it away and continued searching the room.

He found nothing in the closet, nothing in the drawers, and nothing on the floor. He was about to leave the room when he took a quick glance under the bed to be sure nothing had been missed. There, he spotted a small kitchen knife with a short blade.

He shone his light on it.

The blade was dusty and covered with flecks of paint and bits of drywall. Too far to reach, so Striker stood up and grabbed hold of the bed post. With a couple of hard yanks, he edged the frame out from the wall and looked down the other side. What he found behind the bed frame and mattress was as disturbing as it was sad.

One word had been carved into the wall more than a dozen times.

Mercy.

Eighty-Six

Monster went to her.

Filled with pain and agony and grief and hurt. It was more than he could bear. When he reached her side, he crumbled. Like the walls of Jericho. And long heavy sounds of despair rumbled from his throat. He slumped against her side, his massive frame against her diminutive one.

The giant against the doll.

Like always, her power came through. She ran her fingers along his neck, and through his hair. And when she spoke, there was a soothing effect in her words. They somehow slowed his heart. Made the hurt go away.

A little.

Just a little.

But even that was something.

'You need to stop,' she said.

'I'm almost done,' he said.

'No, you need to listen to me. Before it's too late. You need to *stop*.'

'Not yet . . . not yet.'

'But . . . *why*?'

'Because,' he said. 'It must be done.'

For a long moment, neither one of them spoke. They just sat there, Monster with his head in her lap, and she slowly caressing his scalp.

It was soothing to Monster. Relaxing. Almost hypnotic. And he could almost have fallen asleep – had that one horrible thought not kept blasting through his brain in explosion after explosion.

'Violet is coming,' he finally said.

She said nothing back. She just continued to rub his scalp and stroke his hair, and calm him bit by bit.

When his breathing finally returned to normal, when his muscles no longer strained from constant contraction, and when the thick scarred fingers of his disfigured hands finally unclenched, she spoke again.

'You have me,' she said. 'You will always have me. And nothing will ever change that.'

He listened to her soft words. Absorbed them. And he could have cried.

Three weeks ago he'd had no one in this world. A creature of contempt, a monster in every sense of the word.

And then she had come to him.

Saved him.

And he was no longer completely alone in this world.

More tears fell and he let them.

'You're all I have,' he said.

And he meant it. In a world that was dark and cruel and cold, she had become his only light.

She was everything.

Eighty-Seven

Striker got Ich to sweep for electronic devices – in Terry's down-stairs suite and in Jordie's apartment. By the time the sweep was done, the results were less than helpful. No other bugs had been found. No audio devices, no cameras. In desperation, they also performed a physical search, then one of radio distortion, and finally a heat scan.

But still, nothing.

Not even a fingerprint around the base of the smoke detector mount.

Now, sitting in the passenger seat of the undercover cruiser, Striker held the cell against his ear and went over things with Ich some more. 'And what about the actual unit itself?' he asked, referring to the fake smoke detector Striker had removed from Terry's suite. 'You trace that back?'

'Stolen,' Ich replied. 'In a break and enter a few months back.'

'From where?'

'The Spy Guy.'

Were he not so dejected, Striker could have laughed. The Spy Guy was an actual surveillance store located in the downtown core. Most of what they sold there went to criminals attempting to thwart police surveillance. To hear that they had been the victims of a burglary had a dark sense of irony to it.

'Any video of that incident?' he asked.

'Unfortunately, no,' Ich said. 'It wasn't their actual shop that got burglarized, but one of their trucks during the unloading process. Probably a crime of opportunity more than anything else. But either way, there was no video of the theft.'

Striker gave Felicia a stymied look, and she got the gist of the results. He took down the file incident number for The Spy Guy break and enter, then hung up.

Felicia looked over. 'No leads, huh?'

'Zero.'

Felicia started the car, got them moving, and they headed for Vincent Calabrese's house.

For a long moment, Striker said nothing as Felicia took them deeper south into the Sunset area. Striker used the time to run the names he'd found on the Post-it note back in Terry Calvert's suite: *Jeremy Stol, Frances LaFleur,* and *Vincent Calbrese.*

Striker didn't look away from the computer. 'I've run all three names,' he finally said. 'From what I can tell, Stol left the province a decade ago and hasn't been heard of since. LaFleur committed suicide six years ago.'

Felicia clucked her tongue. 'That's three suicides now – doesn't that seem like an awfully high percentage to you?'

Striker gave her a grave look. 'Both brothers committed suicide because their father passed away? Sorry – I don't buy it. No matter how wonderful the man was. Sure, Terry and Jordie were upset about that, no doubt. Who wouldn't be? But they were stable for three days following the man's death.'

'Something else must have happened,' Felicia said.

Striker thought of the listening device he'd located. 'I don't think Terry's death was a suicide at all.' He looked down at the last name on computer, *Vincent Calbrese,* and brought up the man's known history. Immediately, three letters on the entity page caught his eye; they were linked to every file.

EDP.

An Emotionally Disturbed Person.

It meant that Vincent had been apprehended under the Mental Health Act.

Felicia stopped at a light. While waiting for it to turn green, she scanned her eyes down the page for details. 'He suffers from depression and anxiety,' she said. 'And look – he's been institutionalized a half-dozen times. Four in the last year. Looks like he's breaking down.'

Before Striker could respond, the light turned green and Felicia hit the gas. They turned the corner and immediately reached the 8600 block of Barnard Street. Felicia pulled up to a building that was dark green in colour with white picturesque windows. It looked like a remodelled cannery more than anything else, or a rebuilt warehouse.

Trendy and chic, but old.

'Vincent lives here,' she said, and rammed the vehicle into park.

Striker looked at the building. In the upper left window, standing behind the muddy pane of glass, someone was watching them.

Then the blinds came down.

It left Striker with an uneasy feeling.

'Be ready for anything,' Striker told her. 'Our guest knows we've arrived.'

Eighty-Eight

The front door registry had a listing for four separate units that were labelled from 1 through 4. Beside Unit 4 was the name *Calbrese*. Striker opened the front door of the complex and saw a stairway leading up the centre of the building to the second floor. On the right side at the top was a door with a big white 4 on it.

'Top right,' Felicia said.

'Great. There's virtually no cover. Be ready.'

She nodded her reply, and they went up the stairs.

When they reached the door to Unit 4, Striker did not knock. Instead, he put himself against the door frame and listened. Inside the suite, a TV was on. The local news. Talk of the fire down at the ports and the death of Luther Faust were the topic of the hour. After a long moment, Striker gave Felicia a nod to let her know he was ready, then he knocked.

No one answered.

He knocked again.

When no one answered a second time, Striker pounded harder.

'Vancouver Police, Vincent. We know you're home. You can either come talk to us, or we can come talk to you. Either way, we're talking.'

For a short moment, there was no response. Then the hard

metallic sound of a lock turning. The door jarred, creaked open an inch, but remained in place due to the inside door chain. Before Striker could speak, a sliver of Vincent's face appeared behind the chain. Thin. Wide-eyed. Gaunt.

'What do you want?' he demanded. 'I'm fine. I'm taking all my medications just like Dr Goren told me – I'm *not going back*.'

'Easy, easy, easy,' Striker said. 'We're not here to take you anywhere, Vincent. We're here on another matter entirely.'

'Then why? *Why?*'

'Maybe we should come inside,' Felicia suggested.

'You got a warrant? You need a warrant to come inside. You got a warrant? Let me see it!'

Striker sighed. 'All we want to know is how you're connected to Terry Calvert.'

'I— I . . . I don't know Terry. I never met the guy.'

'Strange, you seem to be on a first name basis.' When Vincent said nothing else and instead moved further back from the door, Striker added, 'Listen Vincent, we know you two knew each other. I saw his phone records. I know you called him.'

'He called me. He called *me!* I was only calling him back. It's not my fault!'

'Why was he calling you, Vincent?'

'Because he was depressed. Having . . . having problems. He wanted someone to talk to. Jesus, all I did was talk to him – there's no law against that! I was only *talking* to him!'

'But why did he call you, Vincent? I mean you specifically?'

'We knew each other. Went . . . went to the same school.'

'What school?'

He voice trembled. 'Our Lady of Mercy.'

The name of the school hit Striker like a cold wave.

Mercy.

Just like the word Jordie had carved into his wall a dozen times.

Striker looked at the terrified man hiding behind the chain and did his best to soften his tone. 'A lot of people are dying right now, Vincent. And in some horrible ways. One of the connections here is that school.'

'I— I don't know what you're talking about.'

'What happened at that school, Vincent?'

'Nothing – nothing happened – leave me alone!'

'Vincent—'

'Go away. I'm not talking to you anymore. *GO AWAY!*'

The door slammed shut, and the sounds of footsteps could be heard racing across the apartment. The television volume turned up to full.

Striker sighed. Making entry was not an option; they had no powers of arrest here under the criminal code and no legal means for an apprehension under the Mental Health Act.

Everything was S.O.L.

He turned to Felicia and saw the darkness in her eyes.

'This file is going to a very bad place,' she said.

Striker only nodded grimly. He knew that she was right.

Eighty-Nine

The Boy With The Violet Eyes sat perfectly postured on a hard wooden chair and looked at the man before him.

Vincent Calbrese was an absolute *mess*. His skin was slack and pale, and grooved with age lines that filled Violet with a stark fear. Those lines were an indicator of just how much time had passed. They were not only an image of Vincent's ageing process, but a reflection of Violet's own.

And he hated the man for it.

'I told them, I told them, I told them,' Vincent said mechanically.

The Boy With The Violet Eyes said nothing back; he just looked upon the man. At his lined face. And greying stubble. And thinning hair.

It repulsed him.

'I did what you *said!*' Vincent cried.

Violet was unmoved. But an anxious man was a weak man, so he said, 'You did good, Vincent. You did very, very good . . .'

The man finally breathed out – one giant gust of nervous air.

The Boy With The Violet Eyes stood up. Crossed the room. Stopped at the door. He paused a moment, his eyes on the knotted wood of the door, and thought things through. He did not turn when he spoke.

'The police may return,' he said.

Vincent let out an anxious whine.

'If they do, do *not* answer the door.'

'I'll tell them nothing. *Nothing!*'

'You certainly had better not.' Violet swept his head around and fixated his cold eyes on the man. 'Remember, Vincent. You don't want to make God angry.'

Ninety

They sat in the car with Striker at the wheel and Felicia googling *Our Lady of Mercy* on her iPhone. Striker didn't drive, he didn't even start the car. He just sat there in the cold air with the windows fogging up, and kept silent. He gave Felicia a few minutes to sort through the various links. When she finally made a few sounds indicating she was interested in something, he stared at her with hopeful interest.

'Anything?'

She raised an eyebrow in disappointed fashion and looked up. 'The school was located way up in Squamish,' she said.

Striker nodded. He knew the town. It was a small junction, a half-hour drive from the city if you took the Sea-to-Sky highway. The population was probably less than ten thousand people.

From what he could remember, Squamish had been founded at the turn of the century with the building of the railroad. Nowadays, the core work force belonged to the small port and lumber mill, which was really the only business left there. A lot of people lived there, but commuted into the city for work.

'School closed down ten years ago,' Felicia continued. 'It was associated to the Heavenly Mother.'

'Heavenly Mother?' Striker asked.

'Father Silas's church.'

Striker raised an eyebrow. 'Yet one more connection.' He

turned the engine over and cranked on the defrost. 'Let's go talk to Father Silas about the school. Maybe he'll have some answers on Terry and Jordie. God knows we're getting nothing else out here.'

Felicia agreed.

They swung by the Holy Cross church in Dunbar. When they found out Father Silas wasn't there, they drove down to the St Jude's church in the Southlands. It took less than ten minutes, and yet they got there with no time to spare.

As Striker pulled in front of the old brick walls of the church, Father Silas was just stepping out. He was dressed in a pair of faded blue jeans and a black mid-length coat. Beneath it, a dark grey turtleneck crested his chin. He craned his neck to look back at a pair of crows that were fighting and squawking up high in the bell tower. When he turned back down the walk, he spotted Striker and Felicia. A warm smile spread his wolf-like moustache.

'Detectives,' he greeted. 'Two visits to the church in one day? You must have done something *extremely* bad.'

Striker smiled, and they both climbed out.

Felicia asked, 'Heading out?'

Father Silas nodded. 'Back to Squamish, I'm afraid. I need to attend the Heavenly Mother.'

That got Striker's attention. 'I thought that church was closed down.'

'Technically, it is. But the building still remains. It's now used as an archive,' – a crooked smile found his lips – 'God loves paperwork.'

'Then we're lucky we caught you,' Felicia said.

'Why? What can I do for you?'

'Jordan and Terrance Calvert,' Striker said. 'Did you know them?'

A sad look took over the priest's face. 'Jordie and Terry? Oh yes. And quite well, in fact. They were such nice children. Really good kids.' His face took on a darker look. 'Their biological parents were extremely addicted people. And because of that, Terry and Jordie suffered much.'

'So you knew Jolene and Big Roy.'

'Well no, not personally. But the children were . . . well, *damaged*. Anyone with a pair of eyes could see that. Which was why it was so good to see them finally get placed, especially at their age.'

'Their age?' Striker asked.

Father Silas nodded. 'Most potential parents want infants or toddlers, not the older kids – and especially not ones with baggage.' He took a moment to remove a pair of gloves from his pocket and pulled them on as he spoke. 'I'll tell you this: the Calverts were extremely good people. Kind people. Compassionate. *Selfless*. World needs more of them.'

Striker nodded as he thought of Gregory Calvert and his sudden heart attack. Then of Mother Calvert and her sickness. The thought of such good parents leaving this world in such a bad way depressed him. It was wrong. Unjust.

'Big Roy,' Striker started. 'He had kids with several different women . . . but what about Jolene? The records on her are pretty sparse. Did she have any other kids?'

Father Silas shook his head. 'Just Jordie and Terry, thank God.'

Felicia made a face. 'Thank God?'

The priest shrugged glumly. 'At the time of their adoption, I was in charge of the Heavenly Mother. So their adoption and care was one of my duties and responsibilities. Jordie and Terry were good kids; I've already told you that. But they were terribly messed up – abused, physically and emotionally. Confused.

Mistrustful and angry and closed-off and terrified.' His eyes took on a lost look as he remembered. 'The nightmares they endured every single night were enough to keep me drained, let alone all the other issues we had with them. It was a trying time for all.'

Striker wrote some of this down in his notebook.

'What other issues?' he asked.

Father Silas spoke the words with regret. 'Terry attempted suicide, more than once. I had to have him under constant watch. It was one more reason why the Calverts were such wonderful people – they took these boys knowing full well the problems they faced . . . it's just so sad to see how it all turned out.'

Striker said nothing. But the moment was yet one more thing that drove a nail into his faith.

When the silence turned heavy, Felicia changed the subject. 'It must have been very hard on you – having all the responsibilities of being a priest and a manager.'

The change in conversation seemed to give the priest back some energy. 'Oh I wasn't their priest at the time,' he said. 'I've actually only been in the service for four years now – back then, I was simply a deacon.'

Striker found this interesting. 'Then who was the head priest in charge of you at the time?'

Father Silas looked at Striker as if he was joking. When he realized that the man truly did not know, he splayed his hands and smiled.

'Father O'Brien,' he said.

Ninety-One

It was five-thirty by the time Striker and Felicia pulled up to the small Blenz coffee shop located in Westbrook Mall. Striker hadn't planned on going all the way down to the University grounds, but one wrong turn put him on Marine Drive, and that was where they ended up.

After killing the engine, Striker looked east. Darkness had invaded the sky like a giant rolling wave, coming in suddenly. It made everything feel colder.

He swivelled the computer mount his way.

On the screen were three PRIME reports from police incidents at the Calvert family home. Two were from four years back when Mother Calvert had called 911 to report a domestic disturbance happening across the road; the last report was from an incident where their car had been broken into, almost a month later.

Striker read over all of this as Felicia tried to sort out the various paper reports they had gathered along the way, some of which were only addendums and follow-ups to the Apprehension Car files. When Striker reached the end of the page and came up with nothing new, he let out a long breath. Part anger, part exhaustion, a whole lot of frustration.

He looked to Felicia for hope.

'Anything?'

She shook her head. 'A lot of these reports are pretty bare

bones on the whole, and some of the professionals' statements are so thin, they're laughable. From what I can tell, the brothers were all taken by the Apprehension Car to the Faint Hope Foundation as a temporary measure, then transferred to Our Lady of Mercy on an interim basis until they were adopted by the Calvert family.'

When Striker made no response, she shouldered open the door. 'Dig some more,' she said. 'I'll grab us some eats.'

'Roast beef for me,' Striker said, then she was gone.

Striker read more reports and waited.

Felicia returned ten minutes later with sodas and sandwiches. After she slammed the cruiser door shut, she handed Striker a sandwich. He looked down and saw devilled egg.

'I asked for roast beef.'

He reached for the other sandwich, she yanked it away. 'Didn't have any roast beef. So leave your grubby fingers off my food. They're *both* egg.'

Striker said nothing. He just began unwrapping the cellophane. As it crinkled, a thought crossed his mind. He looked back at her oddly.

'Say that again,' he said.

'Say what?'

'What you just said about the sandwiches.'

She shrugged. 'They're both egg.'

'Exactly. You said *both*.'

She looked at him like he was nuts. 'Yes. Because they're *both* egg salad sandwiches, Jacob. I just told you. They had no roast beef.'

He threw his sandwich on the dashboard and turned in his seat to face her. 'That's not what I mean. What would you have said if there were *three* egg salad sandwiches here? Would you still have said both?'

She shrugged. 'No. I would have said they were *all* egg salad.'

'Exactly . . . *all*.'

Striker reached up to the dash and took the stack of papers he had set there. He grabbed the report Felicia had been reading and scanned through it until he found what he was looking for. 'Right here,' he said. 'On the statement made by Moses. From when he worked at the Faint Hope Foundation. Look how he's written it.'

Felicia did. She read it aloud. 'The brothers were all adopted . . .'

'Exactly. *All*. Not both.'

She put down her sandwich. 'You think there's more brothers out there?'

He raised an eyebrow. 'At least one.'

Felicia thought it over for a moment, uncertain. 'But Father Silas said there was just Jordie and Terry.'

'As far as he knew there was just Jordie and Terry – but he was only involved with the adoption at the end of the process, not in the beginning. That was all dealt with by the Ministry. By Child and Family Services.'

'Meaning Luther.' Felicia looked at the computer. 'This system only goes back nine years,' she said. 'We'll need to hit Ministry archives again.'

Striker nodded and put the car in gear.

'Next time, get roast beef,' he said, then headed for the downtown core.

Ninety-Two

Like everything else in the policing world, obtaining information from the Child and Family Services centre was a time-wasting exercise in frustration. The office headquarters had no records on the children, which Striker found unusual. When he searched back through the years, large sections were missing. Because of the length of time that had passed, many of the files had been purged.

Dejected, they returned to the car with only one other option in mind – to seek out actual records from the provincial government. Which was a depressing thought, because that was where the red tape really started.

Although the new ICS – or Integrated Children's System – was said to be exceptional, any records dating back twenty years or more fell under the ungodly mess of the MIS, or Management Information System. It was outdated, user unfriendly, and complicated with an infinite number of security levels. To add to the clusterfuck, any MIS files older than eight years were archived on fiche and lodged at IronLock.

And that was only if the files hadn't been purged from existence in the first place.

It was maddening.

Normally, the obtaining of IronLock records required a court order, or paperwork sent by way of the Freedom of Information Act.

'Warrant?' Felicia asked.

Striker sneered. 'On what grounds? Everything we got here is circumstantial.'

'FOI then?'

Striker frowned at that too. Freedom of Information requests took an average of thirty-one days. 'We need a backdoor, Feleesh.'

She looked back at him with concern. 'If we go that route, nothing we find will be admitted into evidence.'

He shrugged. 'What choice do we have? We need records belonging to Jolene Whitebear and her children. We don't have thirty-one days to waste.'

Felicia nodded slowly, then got on her cell.

It was nearing six-fifteen by the time she managed to locate one of her contacts with IronLock.

A half hour later, back at Major Crimes, the secure-line fax finally began to click and turn.

Striker and Felicia took turns pulling the papers from the fax as they came in. It was on the fourth page that they found what they were looking for – a list of entities. The first was Jolene Whitebear, mother. Then Roy Baker, father. And then came Jordan, the first born, Terrance, the second—

And there, at the bottom of the page, the final, forgotten entity. The youngest of all the children. The third born.

Henry William Whitebear.

Felicia held up the page and stared at the name, her lips forming a tight line. She swore out loud. 'Why the hell didn't we see this on the other reports?'

Striker figured it out. 'Henry was adopted,' he said, '*before* Jordan and Terry were brought into the Calvert home. So he never appeared on the Calvert reports.'

Felicia couldn't hide the urgency from her voice. 'We need to find this kid.'

'He's no kid anymore, Feleesh. He'll be a man now.' Striker gave her a hard look and spoke the words he almost regretted. 'Prepare yourself for this one – Henry William Whitebear just may be our prime suspect.'

Ninety-Three

They returned from the fax area to their work station.

'Run Henry through PRIME,' Striker said. 'See if there's any hits.'

The moment they found an empty row of cubicles, Felicia dropped down into a desk and started up one of the drones. Once she was logged on, she began searching. It didn't take long. Five minutes later, she sat back and frowned.

'This is strange. There's nothing. Not in PRIME or the jail mugshots.'

'Try the secondaries,' Striker said.

Felicia was already on it. She ran *Henry Whitebear* through all the accessible databases – LEIP, the Law Enforcement Information Portal; PIRS, the Police Information Reporting System, and even JUSTIN – the computer system used by crown counsel.

'Nada again.'

'External?' Striker asked.

Felicia opened up the extraneous search window and ran the name through the insurance and driver's licence databases.

Again, nothing.

On an outside chance, she opened up NCIC.

The National Crime Information Center was the United States' version of the CPIC database. It stored information on everything from missing persons and fugitives to stolen property and serial numbers. Most importantly to Striker, the system also maintained records of criminal history.

And in that section, they finally found what they were looking for.

'Right there!' Felicia said, her voice rising. 'Winter Harbor.'

'Winter Harbor? Where the hell is that?' Striker used his cell to google the name and found Winter Harbor to be a small fishing town, just south of Cape Breton.

'It's an assault file,' Felicia said. 'No charges were ever laid.'

Striker took down the author's name, looked up the telephone number to the Winter Harbor sheriff's station, and called. Within minutes he was redirected, and a bullish-sounding man came on the line.

'Garrison.'

Striker identified himself as a fellow police officer in Canada and explained the purpose of the call. When he was done, the sheriff let out a gruff sound. 'Yeah, I remember Whitebear. Most would, I think. Pretty hard to forget that kind of man.'

'And why is that?'

'Lotsa reasons. Big brute of a man. And he'd been burned-up pretty bad too. Half his face was scarred.'

Striker thought of the mask the man had been wearing. A disguise?

Or for protection?

The sheriff continued: 'He's in some trouble, I take it.'

'Murder – do you have a booking photo on record?'

'Must have,' the sheriff said. 'You got a police email?'

'Of course.' Striker gave the email address, then thanked the sheriff for his help.

By the time he hung up, he could feel the iPhone vibrating against his side. He grabbed the cell and read the display. When

he saw the name *Stacey Mills*, he paused. She was the Sergeant of
4/8. The Dunbar-Kitsilano-Kerrisdale region.

He picked up.

'What you got, Stacey?' he asked.

She didn't mince words. 'Prowler call on the board. Legit too.
Came in from two separate sources.'

Striker had a bad thought, and closed his eyes.

'My house?' he asked.

'Worse,' she said. 'The Calvert home.'

Ninety-Four

To Striker's dismay, the prowler call had been on the board for well over a half hour, which was unusual for any call that was considered to be in progress. When Felicia dug through the call history, she figured out how and why the error had happened.

'It was labelled wrong,' she said.

He looked it over. 'How?'

'Put on the board as a *suspicious circumstance* by one of the call takers. By the time the dispatcher had a good read, it had been well over twenty minutes. They changed it to a Priority 1, but like I said, *after* twenty minutes had passed.'

Striker said nothing. For the most, dispatchers and the call takers did a bang-up job. But in a city that fielded over four hundred thousand calls per year, screw-ups were inevitable. Given the time delay, chances were good that the suspect would be long gone now.

But Striker wanted to be sure.

'Units already search the area?' he asked.

'Yeah. Plainclothes.'

He clicked his jaw – the joint was still stiff from the blow he had taken two days earlier – and drove on. When he reached the corner of Highbury Street, he took the turn and soon spotted the Calvert home.

'Who called this in?' he asked Felicia.

She scanned the call. 'Neighbour on 35th Avenue. Her back-yard faces the backyard of the Calvert home, just across the lane.'

'Any description?'

Felicia found the remarks section. 'Here it is. Tall guy, thin, with a baseball cap. Hanging around in the backyard of the Calvert family home.'

'Tall guy, thin, baseball cap – wonderful. That rules out half the population.'

They parked the cruiser out front of the family home. The moment Striker killed the engine, his cell phone vibrated. When he looked down, he had an email message from the Winter Harbor Sheriff's Office. He opened it up. Saw a jpeg attachment. Clicked on it to open the image.

And suddenly he was staring at the face of Henry Whitebear.

Felicia looked at the image. 'Oh dear *God*.'

Striker understood her sentiments. Half of Henry Whitebear's face had been destroyed. The flesh looked rough and thick and completely disfigured. A good portion of his hair looked like it had been burned away and had never grown back, and this made his already large head appear uneven and enormous.

'Now we have a face to go on,' he said.

He forwarded her the email.

They climbed out of the car in unison. Whether it was from the chill of seeing Henry Whitebear's face or the contrast between the car's warmth and the night-time air, Striker shivered. From the front room window, between the parted sheers, a figure looked down at them. Thin, pale, ghostlike.

Mother Calvert.

Somehow the night-time darkness combined with the artificial lighting of the house made her pallor even worse. Her eye sockets and cheeks looked hollowed out. The drapes swished, she disappeared.

'I'll talk to the family,' Felicia said. 'You check with the witness.'

Striker nodded back. As much as he hated to admit it, part of him was glad to leave the discussion with Mother Calvert to Felicia. Seeing the woman so ill and frail left him with a rather despondent feeling. Reminded him of some of the horrors of his own past.

Ones better left forgotten.

He walked around the corner, one block down.

The house of the complainant was a small rancher that looked grey in the darkness but was probably white or cream coloured in daylight. Striker got Dispatch to run an IHL on the place before entering. When Sue Rhaemer responded, telling him there was no history of threats associated to the address, he knocked twice.

He was soon greeted by a small woman who identified herself as Ms Hicks. She looked to be somewhere in her mid-fifties. She wore a soft green blouse and a pair of women's dress slacks, and her make-up was done with too many shades of blue. This, combined with teeth that were so large and so white that they had to be dentures, gave her an odd appearance – like a doll some child had painted make-up onto.

Striker introduced himself, stepped inside the house.

'Thanks for calling this in,' he added.

'It's no problem at all, Officer,' she said. 'It's a good neigh-bourhood, but we still have the odd break-in around here, so I'm always vigilant.'

Striker took out his notebook. 'So this person, what did they look like?'

'Oh *tall*, he was quite tall. Wearing a baseball cap, I think. Dark in colour. It was very difficult to see out there – my porch light isn't working.'

'What made you notice him?'

She led Striker from the foyer to the kitchen window, which looked out over the lane between her house and that of the Calverts. 'I heard a noise out back. By the time I looked outside, he was already hopping the fence.'

Striker clarified. 'So he went from your backyard into the rear lane?'

'Yes. I know he was in the lane because the garage light went on. I thought that would have spooked him, made him run away. But he didn't. He just crossed the lane, ever so calmly, and then cut through the gate.'

'Into the Calverts' backyard?'

'Yes, that's correct.' She shook her head in a concerned fashion. 'I grabbed the portable phone to call it in, but by the time I got back to the window, he was gone. I hope he didn't do any damage to their place.'

Striker stood at the kitchen window, looking out over the yard. The fence was perfectly positioned for anyone doing recon of the Calvert home – close enough and unobstructed, yet providing cover. He scanned the yard for any signs of damage or evidence, found none—

And then caught sight of the camera attached to the garage.

'You have *video*.'

Ms Hicks nodded enthusiastically. 'Oh yes. I had it installed right after the break-in a year ago.' Her cheeks rouged and she smiled half-embarrassedly. 'I couldn't sleep without it.'

'I need to see that feed.'

She steered him out of the kitchen and down the hallway to a bedroom that had been converted into a small home office. It was very plain. A desk. A chair. A computer system.

The woman logged on. The security system was a Defender 1, put out by the ASTech Group. One of the better systems, by Striker's observations, and definitely one of the more pricey.

Striker took control of the mouse and scanned the timeline backwards until he saw movement on the screen. The video was grainy, but watchable. The timeline read 02:11 p.m. – a sight that made Striker pause. He checked the time of the computer clock and saw that it was now 7:11 p.m. When he checked his own watch, the time was the same – which was significant, because it meant that the computer time was correct.

He turned to the woman. 'When did you call this in?'

'Oh hours ago,' she said.

'Around quarter after two?'

She nodded. 'The moment it happened.'

Striker struggled not to curse. The call had been botched from the beginning – delayed not by a half hour, but by almost *five hours*. It was unacceptable. Somewhere up at E-Comm, someone had screwed up royally.

And they would hear about it.

He looked at the programme timeline – at the 02:11 p.m. – and realized that the suspect had been there at the exact same time that he and Felicia had been on scene speaking to Mother Calvert and her daughter. Even when they had been searching through Terry's suite.

Striker reached forward, hit the enter button, and the video played through.

There on the screen was a man. Tall, just as Ms Hicks had said – but *not* thin. Heavy. Thick. This guy must have been a hundred and fifty kilos, if not more. And he wasn't wearing a baseball cap either. This man was wearing a hoodie.

Striker looked at the lady. 'Is this the man you saw?'

The woman's face filled with confusion. 'I could have sworn he was quite a bit thinner. That man is a giant.'

Striker leaned forward towards the screen.

Even within the expansive folds of the hoodie, the enormous

size of the man's physique was easily apparent. Wide shoulders, wide hips, a barrel chest. In the feed, the man was looking at the Calvert home. Then, in one quick moment, he turned slightly and looked behind himself.

Striker hit the pause button. Then zoomed in.

As the digital image expanded, the suspect's face came into view. To Striker's relief, the image quality remained decent. Despite the overhang of his hood, the outer edges of his face were viewable, and Striker knew without a doubt that what he was staring at was a mask.

The man in the feed was their suspect.

Striker zoomed in as far as the programme would allow and focused on the mask. It was a strange-looking thing. Some kind of soft mould. A gel form, maybe rubber. And around the edges of the mask, on the left-hand side of the man's face, the outer edges of skin could be seen.

The flesh looked wrong. Rough. Distorted.

Burnt.

Striker used his cell to look at the photo that Sheriff Garrison had sent from the Winter Harbor Sheriff's Office. He stared at the broad-faced image of Henry Whitebear. Large square head. Wide-set eyes. And burns to the entire left side of the head, face, and mouth.

A jolt of adrenalin pulsated through Striker, because there was no doubt about it anymore. They had identified their suspect.

Henry William Whitebear.

Ninety-Five

Monster headed for the Southlands.

As he left the swerving lanes of Marine Drive and hiked down the steep decline of the Balaclava Bikeway, his eyes involuntarily shifted southwest. A mile or two down was the Musqueam Indian Reserve. Where Roy Baker had lived.

Big Roy.

A man Monster hardly knew – and yet a man who had surely destroyed his life and Terry's life and Jordie's life every bit as much as all the others.

Now he had paid for his sins.

Monster turned his eyes away from the reserve and focused on the bell tower of the church ahead. It was under repair, surrounded by beams and planks of scaffolding that made it look like a giant tinker toys set.

St Jude's.

Monster studied the dark red brick, the white window trim, and the stained glass images. Then he looked at the snow-covered cedars that ran alongside the promontory. And at the old wooden gazebo that was the centrepiece of the lawn. The building itself was actually quite appealing. Rustic.

Beautiful, even.

Monster was not so damaged he could not see that. And he also understood, on some deeper level, that there was true beauty within that church. The *idea* rather than the reality. In some ways this thought only increased his sadness. His sense of loss was deep. His inner desolation was everything. And he coped with it the only way he knew how.

He let the rage flow freely.

Supplies in hand – the canisters of kerosene and diesel; the flare gun; the nails and nail gun; and the photo that was now more than two decades old – he entered the church yard and headed for the front door. Of all the acts he had committed, this one would be the most horrendous. The most *sinful*.

And yet the most necessary.

The thought struck him oddly, filled him with a deep-bellied ache. And instead of pushing the feeling away, he opened himself up to it. Accepted it for what it was. Because sometimes the truth was horrible.

He opened the door and went inside.

It was time to set things right.

Ninety-Six

After burning a copy of the video evidence to disc, Striker used Ms Hicks' computer to save still images to the desktop, then he printed them up on her colour Laserjet. He made three copies and took them with him, back to the Calvert home.

Inside the living room, Felicia was still speaking with Mother Calvert and Sarah. Striker knocked and entered, wasting no time. He took out the printed picture, showed it first to Mother Calvert, and then to Sarah.

'Have you ever seen this man before?' he asked them.

For a long moment, Mother Calvert said nothing. She just stared at the photo and her face looked awfully pale and thin.

'No,' she said softly.

Sarah leaned nervously forward in her seat and raised a hand as if to touch the photo, then stopped herself. 'His face . . .'

'He's been burnt,' Striker said.

She touched her hand to her mouth. 'It must have been . . . so terribly painful.'

It was Mother Calvert who spoke next, and when she did, there was a note of caution in her tone. 'Why are we looking at this photo?' she asked.

'Because this man was in your backyard earlier today.'

'Our backyard? But . . . *why*?'

'Because he's Terry and Jordie's brother.'

'*Brother?*' Mother Calvert spoke the words with a note of disbelief – as if she thought she must have misheard Striker. Her grey face blanched to a slightly paler colour. She closed her eyes. Took in a long slow breath.

Sarah looked at her mother. 'A brother? Did you know?'

Mother Calvert opened her eyes. 'He had already been adopted by another family,' she said softly. 'They . . . they moved back East. We never heard from them again.'

Striker offered no reply; he just watched the scene unfold.

Sarah looked away from her mother. Looked all around the room, as if searching for something she could not find. When she finally spoke again, she ran all her sentences together. 'He needs help,' she said. 'He needs a family. He's Jordie and Terry's brother – he's *my* brother.'

She finally stopped, if only to take a breath.

Striker fixed the girl with a hard look. 'He's *not* your brother, Sarah. Don't ever think of him that way. He's a very dangerous man.'

Sarah said nothing back, then looked at her mother with desperate eyes. 'We need to help him, Mother. It's the Christian thing to do.'

Striker had heard enough and he intervened. He moved right up to the young girl. 'I'm ordering you to stay away from this man, Sarah.' He made sure she looked back at him and saw the seriousness of his expression. 'He's one of the most dangerous and violent predators I have ever met.'

'But—'

'Be *quiet*, Sarah!' her mother snapped. 'Return to your room.'

'But Mother—'

'*Now.*'

The young girl's hard expression crumbled and tears pooled in her eyes. She jumped up from the couch and scampered up the stairs, the frantic sounds of her feet echoing in the foyer. When the bedroom door slammed shut, Mother Calvert's eyes turned to Striker. They were hard now. Wary.

'What does he want *from us*?' she demanded. 'Why was he here?'

Striker wished he had some information to give her. 'We don't know. Maybe he was trying to contact his brothers, maybe he doesn't know they've passed on. Or maybe he does know and he wants something they had. At this point we're unsure of his motives.'

Mother Calvert offered no response, and the room turned silent.

Thoughts of Monster returning for revenge filtered through Striker's mind, and it left him cold. Could Mother Calvert be part of the man's revenge list? For adopting his brothers and not him?

He sat down on the sofa and met the woman's distant gaze.

'You have to be completely honest with me here, Mrs Calvert. You've never had contact with Henry Whitebear before? Never? Not in person, not by letter, not even a phone call?'

Mother Calvert looked away and closed her eyes. She looked ill. 'We had only heard of him. Greg asked Father O'Brien about the boy. But he'd already been placed with other parents, and like I said, they had moved back East.'

Felicia stepped forward. 'Did Jordie and Terry ever speak of him?'

Mother Calvert's eyes took on a faraway look. 'The boys never talked about the past – and we never encouraged it. It was just too painful for them. Sure, Greg and I knew that their father had *many* other children out there. But we weren't in the same financial shape as we're in now. We were having trouble getting by financially. There was nothing we could do.'

Striker offered no comment. He looked at Felicia and saw the concern in her face. 'I want this address flagged,' she said.

Striker couldn't have agreed more.

'Priority 1 the house. And make sure that CPIC adds a warning – Violent and Anti-Police.' He gave her a dark look. 'I don't want any more cops getting killed over this.'

Ninety-Seven

Deep Cove.

The Boy With The Violet Eyes was fast losing patience. He could feel it, slip-slip-slipping away from him like a fading dream. He stood on piles of broken window glass and sorted through the patient files, one by one.

He found nothing.

Frustrated, his eyes scanned the entire room – the laptop computer on the desk; the opened file cabinet in the corner; the pulled-out drawers that now lined the floor. All around the room were streams of people's personal information. The psychiatrist had been very good at amassing that. But despite all that information, there were no links to Monster.

Not a one.

And Violet screamed out loud, uncaring who heard him.

He felt his fingers curl into fists. If only the doctor was home now. Or at her office. Or at any of the places he had sought her out.

But Luna Asawa-Tan was nowhere to be found. And The Boy With The Violet Eyes was beginning to wonder if she would ever reappear. Like so many old ghosts, she too had faded from existence. Perhaps forever.

Like my youth, he thought sadly.

Like my youth.

Dejected and anxious, he left the house via the front door.
He would have to find Monster another way.

Ninety-Eight

Despite an extensive ongoing search, Henry Whitebear was nowhere to be found. They were batting zero, and the more time that passed, the more anxious Striker was getting.

He sat in the cruiser, brooding as much as investigating. While he made certain the Bolo – *Be On the Lookout* – fan-out for Henry Whitebear was properly listed on the CPIC database, Felicia read through the rest of what they had scavenged from social services, now that they had a name to go on.

Although there was nothing recent in Henry's file – everything was fifteen years old – the situation was made more clear. The order of how things had happened fell into place.

Henry had been adopted before his brothers, by a family known as the Browns. Then, when Henry was gone from the orphanage, Terry and Jordie were both adopted by the Calverts. Months later – when the adoption had failed – Henry had been returned to the school, only to find his brothers gone.

It was a sad history.

Felicia read on. Included at the end of the report was an addendum stating that, after returning Henry to the school, the Brown family had moved back to their original home in the faraway province of Prince Edward Island.

It seemed a very odd situation.

Felicia looked up at Striker. 'Conrad Brown was Henry's

adoptive father,' she said. 'At least for a little while . . . Maybe he knows where Henry's hiding.'

'Worth a shot,' Striker said. 'Got a number?'

She did. She read it out loud and Striker dialled. The number was no longer in service, but after a quick search, Info managed to locate a possible new one with a matching address in a place called Stone Park, which was just outside of Charlottetown, according to Google Maps.

Striker called the number and was connected to voicemail:
You have reached the Brown family. Please leave a message.

Striker waited for the beep, then left a message. He explained the urgency of the situation. 'Call me the moment you get this message – no matter the time.' Then he hung up. If no one got back to him by morning, he'd send a CPIC message to the Charlottetown Police Department and have them do a knock and talk.

Until then, it was a waiting game.

'What next?' Felicia asked.

Striker said nothing. It was getting late now, nearing eight-thirty, and he was tired. They'd been going at this three hard days now and had put in fourteen hours already today. He looked over at Felicia and asked, 'Who signed off on the adoption papers?'

'What do you mean?'

'For Henry. When Terry and Jordan were adopted by the Calverts, Father O'Brien signed off on it. But what about Henry?'

Felicia began rifling through the file until she found the entity list. She made a *hmm* sound and looked up at him. 'It was Father Silas.'

'Father Silas?' Striker asked. 'You sure about that?'

'Yes.' She nodded, then looked up in realization. 'Which would mean—'

'That he damn well knew there was a third brother all along.'

Felicia shook her head. 'If that's the case, then he's been lying to us all along . . . But why?'

Striker put the car in drive, U-balled on Dunbar, and headed for the Southlands area. More specifically, for St Jude's church.

'Time for confession,' he said.

Ninety-Nine

The confession booth was dark and cold, and far too small for Monster; it was all he could do to fit inside. He sat in the confessor end with the nail gun at his feet; his other supplies had already been placed behind the booth, lined up against the church wall.

His giant hands were cupped together in his lap. His head was covered by the hood of his kangaroo jacket. And his face was hidden by the mask. He looked down towards the floor for a long moment, then angled his eyes towards the wire mesh window and stared at the priest on the other side.

'Forgive me, Father, for I have sinned.'

Father Silas nodded, the general outline of his shape barely visible through the screen and dimness.

'How long has it been since your last confession?' the priest asked.

'Long, Father. Childhood, maybe.'

'I am listening, my son. Which commandment have you broken?'

'The sixth, Father.'

There was a long moment of silence in the booth. 'Thou Shall Not Kill?' the priest finally asked.

'Yes,' Monster said. 'The Sixth Commandment. Many times.'

There was another pause, followed by the weak words of an

uncomfortable man: 'I am listening, my son . . . but . . . the word *many* is a general term.'

'Five,' Monster clarified. 'In two days.'

'Recently?'

'Very. And Father? I am not yet done.'

The priest took in a deep breath and shifted on his side of the booth.

Monster could feel the rage boiling his blood and causing his hands to shake. His fingers were sweating now; he could feel them. Sweating. Trembling. Balling into humungous fists. And finally, he could take it no more. He pushed his face right up to the screen divider and lowered his voice.

'You don't even recognize me, do you?'

Father Silas made a barely audible sound. 'I . . . I . . . *Pardon*?'

Monster pulled back his hood. Peeled off his mask. Pressed his face right into the thin mesh separation of the confession booth and stared at the man on the other side. Even in the dimness, he could recognize the priest. Even after all of these years. The man's face had changed. Age had taken hold of him and hardened his once-softer features.

It reminded Monster that even Father Silas was mortal.

And Monster was about to prove that.

'Do you recognize me *now*, Father?' he asked.

The priest's eyes narrowed for a moment, and then widened. A gasp escaped his thin lips, and he recoiled from the screen. He jumped up from the seat and grabbed the exit door.

But Monster was already moving.

Nail gun in hand, he threw open his own door, blocked the path of the fleeing priest, and slammed him back inside the confession booth. Then he upended the booth, so hard that the entire church echoed with the sound of wood slamming against the tiled floor of the nave.

He wasted no time and got to work.
Nail gun and nails.
Fuel and fire.
Absolution never felt so good.

One Hundred

The moment Striker stepped out of the car onto the snowy path of the St Jude's walkway, he spotted the dark wisps of smoke seeping through the front door. 'Jesus Almighty,' he exclaimed.

Instinctively, he drew his pistol and raced up the front walkway.

Felicia ran with him.

By the time they were halfway there, loud screams came from inside the church. A man. In terror. In agony.

Howling like an injured animal.

Striker reached the front door, found it already ajar. With a quick snatch of his hand, he gripped the cold iron handle and yanked it open. As it swung outwards, it brought with it a gust of black smoke and ash. Immediately, the screams of the man inside became louder, and the crackling hiss of fire owned the air.

Far ahead, at the northeast side of the nave, the confession booth was tipped over and ablaze. Fire consumed the wooden booth, flame and smoke pluming high into the air and licking at the long sweeping frills of the church tapestries.

'Dear God,' Felicia got out. 'The whole place is gonna go up!' She raised her hand, as if to ward off the ash and smoke, and gaped at the fire.

Striker stepped into the church.

As quickly as the screams of the man inside the confession booth had started, they ceased. Leaving only the popping and crackling of the fire. In near disbelief, Striker took another step towards the flames, his eyes sweeping ahead to the crossing and apse areas, scanning for any sign of threat.

He found one.

Standing tall at the opposite end of the church in the western transept, by the foot of the stairway leading to the bell tower, was the man they had been hunting these last two days. In the black churning smoke and red light of the flames, Henry Whitebear looked every bit the devil himself.

Gigantic. Hulking.

Grotesque.

With his hood now pulled back and his mask removed, the twisted curves of his fibrous flesh and patches of burnt-away hair were visible. In one hand, the man held a steel tool of some kind – a cordless drill, perhaps, or a nail gun. In the other was a large red gas canister.

Striker raised his pistol.

'Don't move!' he ordered.

But before he could so much as place his finger on the trigger, Henry Whitebear spun away from him, faded into the smoky chasm and disappeared behind the first turn of the staircase.

'He's running!' Felicia yelled. '*He's running!*'

Striker gave no response. He was already in pursuit.

One Hundred and One

Striker raced up the stairs two at a time, keeping his SIG aimed ahead of him, trigger ready for the pull. He cut the angle of the stairs wide, making sure Henry wasn't suckering him into a trap, made the first turn, and raced on.

'Stop, Henry!' he called. 'We know who you are!'

But the man remained far ahead of him.

Striker pushed on hard. The bell tower was only three storeys high, so soon enough the man would run out of room. Still, with the place under repair, Striker worried he would escape down the scaffoldings.

Losing him again was not an option.

Striker pushed on, reached the final turn – and came to a hard stop.

Standing there in the small alcove of the bell tower was Henry Whitebear. In the limited space of the loft, the man looked like a giant. He stood tall, unyielding, like a living gargoyle stationed there to defy entrance. At his feet was the gas canister and steel tool; in his hands now was another weapon.

A pistol.

Striker reacted. He took quick aim, lined Henry up and had him locked in his iron sights. 'Don't move – not a goddam muscle.'

Henry did not move. He merely looked back at Striker with

dead eyes. Then he slowly shook his head in an odd sort of sympathetic way.

'You should never have come here,' he said.

The words made Striker uneasy. He stepped back and made sure there was distance between them; he'd fought Henry once already, had suffered at the hands of the man's immense strength, and he had no intentions of getting into another fight.

Not far behind him, Striker could hear Felicia making the final turn of the stairs.

His backup had arrived.

'Put down the gun, Henry – it's over.'

'I never wanted to hurt you,' Henry said.

'Put down the gun.'

'You should never have come.'

'Put. Down. The. *Gun*.'

'You gave me no choice.'

A bad feeling slithered into Striker's chest, and he slid his finger inside the trigger guard. He kept his eyes locked on the pistol in Henry's hand and was prepared to shoot the man if he raised it. He was just about to give the command to drop the gun one final time when an odd thought struck him.

The gun Henry was holding was not merely hanging down at his side – it was *pointed* down and forward.

Aimed at the floor.

Striker glanced down at the stairs he was standing on. Saw the wetness of the wood. Breathed in and smelled the diesel and kerosene. And then he realized.

Not a firearm – a *flare* gun.

Then Henry pulled the trigger.

One Hundred and Two

'RUN!' Striker called out.

He turned to flee back down the stairs, but was far too slow. In one brief instant, the entire loft and stairwell turned from a cloudy black to an overpowering yellow-white colour as flame from the flare streaked across the dusky space, contacted the fuel, and ignited.

Fire exploded in the narrow passage.

And Striker ran.

By the time he was a third of the way back down, the flames were at his heels. By the time he was two-thirds down, the fire was all around him, turning the staircase into a funnel of flame, eating up the wood and tapestries.

Striker caught up to Felicia. Aimed the barrel of his SIG away from her. And then drove his shoulder into the centre of her back.

He felt them connect. Hard. Heard her grunt out in pain and surprise as she rebounded off him and cannonballed out of the stairwell. She tumbled back into the transept area, where she was temporarily safe from the flames.

It was then – only after he saw that she had escaped the fiery tunnel – that Striker realized he, in fact, had not. The blaze had over-passed him now. Flames were on him. Eating up his clothes. His coat was blazing, the heat immense.

He dove forward through the air. Through the smoke and flame. And hit the hard wooden surface of the transept floor. Pain shot up his arm and shoulder.

Fire! – he was *on fire*!

A terror suffused him. Thoughts of burning to death overtook his mind. Flashes of Courtney and Felicia and a near-uncontrollable fear bombarded him. It was almost impossible not to panic.

He let go of the gun.

Tried batting out the flames.

Dropped and rolled on the ground.

But the fire was on him now. Reaching through the barrier of his clothes. Snaking up towards his face and hair. Burning him up. Eating him alive.

I'm gonna burn to death – I'm gonna BURN UP.

It was his only thought.

And then a wall of blackness hit him – thick, heavy, corded. Suddenly, he was pinned to the floor, enveloped by the wide thick sheets of one of the tapestries. And someone was on top of him. Holding him down. Pinning him there. Yelling for him to 'Stop moving, Jacob – STOP MOVING!'

A command that was impossible to obey.

It was Felicia, he realized.

Felicia.

She was smothering the flames.

One Hundred and Three

Midnight had long since come and gone by the time Striker and Felicia returned to his little home on Camosun Street. Once inside, Striker grabbed a couple of cold beers from the fridge – Miller Genuine Draft – and plunked himself down on the couch. Despite the hours that had passed since being set on fire, Striker still had the shakes. He fumbled with the twist-off, finally got the cap off.

Felicia saw his hand tremble.

'Adrenalin dump,' she said.

He just nodded. Then offered her one of the beers.

She sat back next to him on the couch and let out an onerous sound. She rested the side of her head against his shoulder. Said nothing. Rubbed the soft of her hand along his forearm.

They drank their beers in silence because exhaustion had set in. Fear too. It had been that kind of day.

'You smell like smoke,' she finally said. She squeezed his forearm, then looked up at him. 'That was close today, Jacob.'

He offered no reply. No jokes, no jests, no nothing.

Not a year ago, he'd been injured in a fire out by the projects – a second-degree burn that had healed well. But today had been different. Today he'd been covered in flame. And it had left him shaken.

Though the skin of his wrist and forearm was red and raw,

today he had managed to escape the blaze. He looked down at the bandage and knew how fortunate he had been this time. But sooner or later, his luck would run out.

It always did.

He tried not to think about it, and struggled to get the image of the flames out of his head.

It seemed impossible.

'The church repairs,' he finally said.

Felicia looked at him, lost. 'What are you talking about?'

'The scaffolding . . . that's how he escaped. He must have made the jump.'

Felicia thought back. 'That's a hell of a jump.'

'There was no other way.' Striker pinched the bridge of his nose and closed his eyes as he thought. 'Father Silas makes six deaths. Six murders in just two days . . . Henry is an effective serial killer.'

Felicia nodded.

'Don't let Laroche hear you say that. You know how he hates that word.'

Striker scoffed at the mention of the superintendent's name; he and Laroche didn't see eye-to-eye on most days, and today had been no exception. With the media now in a feeding frenzy over a homicidal pyromaniac being loose in Vancouver, the animosity between the two men had been rekindled.

'The press is sweeping in and he's losing his mind right now,' Felicia added. 'I had the pleasure of dealing with him when you were getting checked out by the doctors. He was none too happy.'

Striker didn't much care. 'The man didn't even ask how bad my burns were, much less tell us he was relieved we were okay.'

Felicia shrugged. 'He's just stressed out about the file.'

'Aren't we all.'

'Jacob—'

Striker was too tired to belabour the point. 'It doesn't matter, Feleesh. Regardless of how things look, the file *is* progressing. At least we now know who our guy is.' He took a long gulp of beer and savoured the malt sweetness. He looked to her for confirmation. 'We've done all we can do, right? Bolos are out. Borders alerted. APBs in the States. Hospitals on alert. Planes, trains and ferries all notified . . . am I missing anything here?'

'The Priority 1's on the Calvert home,' she said. 'And every diocese Father Silas was ever associated with. They're all on high alert.'

Striker nodded thoughtfully. But there was something else they were missing. He knew it.

'Luna,' he said.

'APBs and Bolos out for her too,' Felicia said. 'No hits . . . so far.'

Striker fiddled with the gauze around his forearm until Felicia grabbed his hand and told him to leave it. He stopped pulling at the bandages and fixed her with a questioning look.

'So we got it all covered?' he asked.

'As good as this nightmare can be.'

Striker nodded, but he wasn't so sure. He felt lost in the details. And he talked them out for the millionth time: 'Jazz, Jolene, Big Roy, Moses, Luther, and now Father Silas,' he said. 'Which also means the police department, the Apprehension Car, social services, the non-profits, the adoption agencies, the church and the school – I get all that.'

'*But?*' Felicia asked.

'But I'm still at a loss on the satanic stuff.'

Felicia made a nervous sound, as if she'd been thinking about this all along. 'You ever think that maybe they're one and the same?'

Striker blinked. 'How so?'

'Think about it. Henry went after Father Silas for a reason. And we've seen the altars and pentagrams firsthand. We need to ask ourselves, what kind of rituals were really going on? And *where* were they doing all this? At the church? Or the school they closed down? At Our Lady of Mercy?'

Striker listened to Felicia's theory and closed his eyes. Even the notion of it left him feeling sick. He thought of Vincent Calbrese, and just how terrified the man had been – especially after bringing up the old school. It was yet one more connection to consider. Striker tried to mentally determine what was possible as opposed to plausible, and found he couldn't do it.

Felicia looked at him tenderly. 'You're exhausted, Jacob.'

'It's just the meds.'

Felicia downed the rest of her beer. Stood up. Arched her back. 'I'm gonna shower and crash.' She gave him a long, hard look. 'You should too. You look like the walking dead.'

'Sure, sure.'

'You'll be useless tomorrow.'

'I'm coming, Feleesh. Just . . . just gimme a minute.'

She looked at him silently – the acquiescent look on her face suggesting she knew his stubbornness too well. Knew he would not come. Not until he was good and ready. So she let the conversation go and headed down the hall. She'd gone barely halfway before he called out to her.

'Feleesh.'

She turned. 'What?'

'You did good out there today. Saved my life.'

She looked back at him and smiled.

'Goodnight, Jacob,' she said.

She disappeared down the hall, and Striker was left with nothing but the cold darkness of the living room and his troubled thoughts. He refused to go to bed because he knew sleep would not come – not so long as his mind was in overdrive.

So he got up, grabbed himself two more beers, and returned to the dark confines of the den. Exhausted and depleted as he was, he was also itching to get back to the investigation. There was a madman out there, and until Henry Whitebear was caught, there could be no peace. Not for him. His sense of duty would not allow it.

This was his own demon. His own monster.

And it would never go away.

ACT THREE
Sinner and Saint

Friday

One Hundred and Four

What time Striker finally got to bed, he had no idea – two? Three? He hadn't a clue. But it was still early when he awoke.

Outside his bedroom window, the night was black and thick, and the yellow illumination of the street lamp was almost non-existent, overpowered by the heavy clumps of falling snow.

A reddish glow garnered his attention. He looked over and saw his digital alarm clock. The red numbers were flashing 00:00.

Power went out.

He considered getting out of bed, but then felt the coldness of the room and the inviting heat of Felicia's body, and decided against it. He lay there, the details of the file floating back to the surface of his mind. He went over things until the strident beeping of his cell phone interrupted him.

He frowned. Odd hour calls always worried him, so he leaned over and snatched up the iPhone on its first ring. He jammed the device to his ear.

'Striker,' he said.

'Detective Striker?' The voice was wary. 'This is Conrad Brown. I'm sorry for calling at such an early hour, but the message you left said *any* time.'

Striker sat up in the bed and the comforters fell to his waist. 'No problem at all, sir, I appreciate you returning the call. I need to know everything you can tell me about Henry Whitebear.'

The man on the line let out a regretful sound. 'This is a call I've dreaded for years. What . . . what has Henry done?'

'Have you looked at the Vancouver news lately?'

'Yes, I have. But . . . you're not suggesting the fires . . . Oh dear God.'

Striker said nothing back. He gave the man a moment of time, and Conrad Brown used it. He took a few seconds to re-gather himself, then let out a long tremulous breath before speaking.

'Henry was always prone to violence, I'm afraid. He could turn to rage in the blink of an eye, and often over nothing. Which of course was totally understandable, given all he'd been through – that boy had suffered much, I'm afraid. My heart went out to him. Abused by his parents. Abandoned and alone. Tormented at that school—'

'*Tormented?*'

'Yes. The other children were merciless towards him. Made fun of his disfigurement constantly. One of them even killed his pet. It's why Henry became so reclusive, I guess. Why he turned out the way he did. He was also in a lot of pain – have you seen his burns?'

'Yes, I have. How did he get them?'

Conrad Brown let out another heavy breath. 'There was an accident at the school. At Our Lady of Mercy. Something happened between him and the other children – either they were playing or fighting; we never did get a proper answer from any of them. Regardless, Henry ended up falling into the open face of the wood stove.'

'Hands and face?' Striker asked. 'Seems odd.'

'His deformity was one of the reasons we tried to help him,' Conrad Brown continued. 'Because we knew finding a home for him would be next to impossible. Out of all the children we saw at the orphanage, he was in need of a family the most.'

Striker cleared his throat. 'Who told you all of this?'

'The priest who ran the school.'

'Father Silas?'

'No, a man named Father O'Brien. He had a real soft spot for the boy. Was determined to get him out of there.' Brown made a helpless sound. 'My wife and I, we could feel the man's desperation. It's why we tried so hard – and believe me, we did try hard. We did our best. But Henry *scared* us, Detective. Scared the hell out of us.'

'Did he ever hurt you physically?'

'Not us, no. But he was capable of it. Capable and willing.'

'And what makes you think that?' Striker asked.

Conrad Brown cleared his throat, as if talking about this made him uncomfortable. 'When Henry got something in his mind, or when he became angry about something, he was damn near obsessive. It was almost impossible for him to remove himself from a situation. And aside from his size, he was smart as well. Extremely smart. *Cunning*.'

Striker found that last comment intriguing. 'In what way?'

'In every way. Every time things got out of control, Henry would put on the charade. He knew exactly what to say and how to act to make everyone believe he was over something. But it was all an act. His anger was always there, smouldering away below the surface. And eventually it always came out.'

'With violence?'

'Yes.'

'I never saw any reports—'

'That's because there are none. He was too smart to catch. I remember one time, when one of the neighbourhood children – Oliver; I'll never forget his name – was teasing Henry about the burns on his face. I went right over and spoke to his parents about it, and the boy was made to apologize. Henry forgave him, and acted like the two were friends again. Hell, they even played video games together for the next two hours. Everything seemed fine.'

'But it wasn't.'

'Not even close. That night Oliver's house went up in flames. An arson, no doubt. Accelerants were used. And the area of ignition? – Oliver's bedroom.'

Striker found this news unsettling.

'The family all made it out,' Brown said. 'But I'll never forget what Henry said to the boy after that. "Do you find my scars funny now?" He said it so calmly, so . . . detachedly, that it scared the living shit out of me. And that wasn't an isolated incident, Detective. If you ever crossed him, even in the slightest, watch out – because sometime, some way, something was coming back at you. *Tenfold.*'

'Sounds like he was a scary kid.'

Conrad Brown laughed for the first time, a sound that resonated with cynicism. 'You have no idea, Detective. And he got even stranger after that. Secluded himself more and more. He saw threats and insults in everything and anyone – including my two daughters.'

The moment Striker heard that, he understood why the boy had been returned to the orphanage.

'You feared for their safety?'

'I never slept a night.'

The words seemed to take something out of the man. Striker could hear it in his tone. 'When Henry was with us, I constantly feared for my girls. You want God's honest truth? – Our move back to Charlottetown wasn't to be closer to relatives, it was to get my children as far away from him as possible. That's why our number's unlisted now, and all our mail goes to a PO box. I've worried every day about him finding us again.' He took a moment to calm down, then continued. 'Before we even met Henry, he was an angry child – angry about being rejected by his father, angry about being abused by his mother, and angry about being sent to the orphanage. Father O'Brien told us much of this before we met the boy, but he seriously downplayed the danger. It didn't take us long to realize that it wasn't anger Henry felt, but *rage*.'

'You sound angry.'

'I *am* angry. Father O'Brien deceived us, and by doing that, he put my daughters at risk. It was unethical. I mean, for Christ's sake, he never even told us about the diagnosis.'

Striker felt those words like a splash of cold water. 'What diagnosis?'

Conrad Brown spoke the words as if everyone in the world knew them. 'Henry has borderline personality disorder.'

Striker said nothing back. The information wasn't shocking to him; it made perfect sense. Anyone murdering people in lakes of fire had to have something wrong with them on a much deeper level.

The more Striker thought it over, the more things fell in place.

'Tell me something,' he said. 'Who was the doctor who labelled him?'

The response was exactly as he had expected.

'Luna Asawa-Tan.'

One Hundred and Five

The moment Striker hung up the phone, he called Dispatch to see if there were any hits on Luna Asawa-Tan's name over the past eight hours. Ex-eighties rocker Sue Rhaemer was the on-shift dispatcher, snapping her gum and taking long pauses to suck back her Coca-Cola.

'Anything?' Striker asked her. 'Anyone even run her through the system once?'

The answer back was a simple, 'Naw, baby. Nuthin'.'

Striker cursed as he thought it over.

'Send a unit by her house,' he finally said.

'That's technically North Vancouver,' Sue warned. '*Federal* territory. You want us to use an RCMP officer or just send one of our own?'

'Send one of ours,' Striker said. 'But let the Feds know we'll be in their jurisdiction. Make it an unmarked car, if you can. Plainclothes, if we got one. Tell them to have a good look first, see what they find. And tell them to be on their guard – Henry Whitebear's still out there somewhere and he's as dangerous as they get.'

After a few clicks of the keyboard, Sue made the choice. 'I'll send Echo 21.'

'Thanks, Sue. Tell them to call my cell *immediately* if anything important comes up.'

'Sure thing, Strikes. Keep on rockin' in the free world.'

'I'll do my best,' he said.

And the line went dead.

Striker hung up the cell. He laid back down in the bed, tried to go back to sleep, and got a return call not ten minutes later. Jolted, he looked down at the screen and saw the number for Echo 21. He answered, listened for a long moment, then hung up the phone and sat up.

Beside him, Felicia lay awake, awaiting the inevitable. 'Well?' she asked.

'Get up,' he said. 'Bad things are happening – or maybe it's good for us. I'm not sure yet.'

She squinted up at him. 'What are you talking about?'

'Luna's house,' Striker said. 'It's been burglarized.'

One Hundred and Six

Located at the foot of Seymour Mountain and blocked off by the narrow cliff waterways of the Indian Arm fjord was the small town of Deep Cove. It was a bay town, secluded, a sleepy little hollow.

Resort-like.

The drive into the cove was a dream in the summer months and equally a nightmare on most winter days. Given the sheets of snow falling from the early morning blackness above, the drive there felt as treacherous as the file they were investigating. When Striker steered into the slow lane and hit a patch of black ice, the car shifted hard towards the inlet and Felicia made an uncomfortable sound.

'Is this really necessary?' she asked.

'We need to see Luna's place,' he said. 'Figure out what's going on.'

'Why don't we just get surveillance to grab her?'

Striker gave her a stymied look. 'They lost track of her late last night – after you'd gone to bed.'

Felicia let out a sound somewhere between frustration and resignation, then went quiet.

Striker felt the same irritation.

'We're almost there,' he said.

They exited Strathcona Road and made their way to Harris

Place. When they found the target address – a long ocean property, looking out at Boulder Island – Striker slowed down to avoid side-swiping the undercover police cruiser parked out front. It had been parked with its back end jutting out into the roadway, and was further hidden by the pressing darkness of the night.

Once stopped, Striker and Felicia climbed out. They made their way down the walkway, pushing through the growing winter wind until they reached the front door. The door was half-open already, expecting their arrival.

Standing in the den were the two plainclothes cops. Both were looking out the six-metre-high windows, marvelling at the bay beyond, where the first traces of purple sky were creeping up in the east.

Striker looked at Felicia and shook his head. 'Look at these clowns – we could sneak right up behind them and they wouldn't even know what hit them.' He cleared his throat and got their attention.

The taller of the two men, a thick guy with red hair, turned around.

'Oh hey,' he said.

Striker frowned. 'If you two are done being enamoured with the view, maybe we could get some police work done here – where was the break-in?'

'Uh, the office.' The redhead jabbed a thumb towards the hall.

'Is the rest of the house cleared?' Felicia asked.

'Yeah, of course, of course.'

'Then you two take front and rear,' Striker said. 'Guard detail. Now.'

When the two cops secured their positions, Felicia took a moment to scan the interior. She let out a whistle. 'Wow. Teak floors. Two outdoor gas ranges on the patio. Six-metre-high windows over the bay – what you think this place is worth?'

'An eternity in hell,' Striker replied.

Felicia looked around for a security system. 'You'd think the alarm would have gone off.'

'What alarm? This is Deep Cove. No one here has alarms.'

'Then how'd we find out about it?'

'This is Deep Cove,' he said again. 'Everyone knows everyone – neighbour called it in.'

He headed down the hallway.

The room where the break-in had occurred was easy to find. Broken cubes of glass littered the floor, and all the folders from the file cabinets had been removed. Their papers had obviously been rifled through, with the remainder dropped on the floor. Everywhere Striker looked he saw different diagnoses: post-traumatic stress disorder; borderline personality disorder; bipolar depressive; schizophrenia – the list went on.

Felicia saw them too.

'A disgruntled patient?' she asked.

'Maybe Henry. Who knows.'

Striker looked at the files spread out across the floor, and at the numerous papers scattered everywhere. The dates on the reports were old. Some of them over ten years.

Luna's own personal archives.

'Call in the Feds,' Striker said. 'See if they got anyone who can do some prints on this area.'

Felicia just nodded. She got on her cell, swore when she couldn't get a signal, then exited the room in search of a better area of reception. Striker heard her step through the patio doors out onto the veranda and begin speaking with one of the plain-clothes cops.

Big Red.

For a brief moment Striker debated on whether they should wait for the processing of the scene to be done, or just start searching now. The last thing he wanted to do was screw up a lead, but at the same time, the Feds usually printed during dayshift. Chances were good that no one would get here for hours.

And that was time he couldn't waste.

He made his decision.

He moved into the room. Without touching any of the discarded files, he looked down and scanned them all, looking for not only evidence but some kind of commonality.

A similar diagnosis.

Or a shared programme.

Even a therapy group.

He found none of those, and he found no other visible evidence either. And the more he analysed the scene – and saw not a single trace of print on any of the glass surfaces – the surer he was that whoever had broken in here had been wearing gloves when doing the crime.

He walked over to the desk and tried to log on to the computer. A password protection warning came up immediately, notifying him that too many failed attempts had locked the computer. It was interesting. Someone else had tried to get into the system as well, and they had failed.

With no other route of search, Striker scavenged through all the desk drawers, found nothing, then left the office.

He searched the rest of the house. Though the rancher had been constructed with a spare no-expense mentality, the place was relatively small. Less than fourteen hundred square feet, he was sure.

Taking advantage of the break-in – the crime allowed him a warrantless search for pertinent evidence – Striker took his time looking through the bedroom, performing a deep search of the closet and en-suite. But again, he found nothing of interest. Luna Asawa-Tan was obviously a minimalist. All she owned were the basic necessities of life.

Certainly no altars.

In fact, the place seemed relatively normal. Chic and luxurious, but normal.

When he left the bedroom, he walked back down the hallway towards Felicia, who had finally come back inside and gotten off the phone. She met him halfway, back at the entrance to the office. 'We're looking at a few hours for a forensic tech,' she said. 'Unless we pull in one of our own guys.'

Striker checked his watch. It was nearing seven now. 'By the time we get our own guy here, it'll make no difference. We'll get Bert and Ernie out there to guard the place and call us when the Feds are done.'

Felicia agreed with the plan. The two headed down the hall.

Striker got less than three steps when something bothered him. He turned back, reached the doorway to the office, and looked inside the room.

'What?' Felicia asked.

He said nothing and moved inside. In the centre of the room, he crouched down and examined the files once more.

'*What?*' Felicia asked again.

Striker did not touch the folders, but gestured to them. 'The names,' he said. 'Look at the names.'

Felicia did. There were many. She read a few out. 'Chambers. Epson. Rodriguez. Drummond. Arnold – there must be a hundred of them, maybe more.'

'I know. Continue.'

She gave him a look of irritation, but continued. 'Yiddow. Randorph. Jackson. Sullivan. Tanguay. Oates.' She let out a long breath. 'You can fill me in on the blanks now, Jacob. Anytime.'

He looked up at her. 'What letters are missing?'

The irritated look left her face and was replaced by one of curiosity. She scanned the papers and then said, 'There's not a single file here that starts with B.'

'Or a W,' he said.

'But why . . .' she started to say, then understood. '*Whitebear*.'

'Exactly.'

'But why the Bs too?'

'Who was Henry once adopted by?'

'Shit – the *Browns*.'

Striker nodded. 'We're not the only ones looking for Henry,' he said. 'There's someone else.'

One Hundred and Seven

Without the mask covering his scarred flesh, Monster felt incomplete and unprotected. He felt *vulnerable* – even within the safe confines of the place he had now made his home.

It was odd. He had become accustomed to the second layer of skin – to that barrier protecting him from the cruelty of the outside world. It was another shield to guard him.

Another place to hide.

Now, as the cold draught touched his face, he felt like he was back on the fishing vessels of Winter Harbor. He'd done many jobs over the years – road crew, roofer, tree-planter. All of them up North or out to sea. All of them away from the general populace. Sometimes, he found himself wishing he had never left Winter Harbor.

At moments like this.

It was a sad thought. A bad thought. And he killed it.

From the old desk in the corner of the room, he grabbed his painter's palette and knifed the red with some black and yellow to create a hot angry crimson hue. Then he turned to face the canvas. He stood there. Waited. And nothing came. No inspiration, no muse.

No matter how he tried, he could not focus.

The pain was part of that.

Following the death of Father Silas – and directly after

escaping the big detective and his partner – Monster had jumped down from the scaffolding of the bell tower into the church's rear lot. The drop had not been overly far. Just two storeys. But the ground had been hard and icy, making for a difficult landing. He had hit the ground hard, slipped, twisted, and torn something inside his ankle.

Now it throbbed, stealing from him the joy he normally got from standing and painting his scenes.

He wished he had something to kill the pain and slow the inflammation. But there was nothing left. The drugs – in fact, *all* of his medications – had run out a long time ago. It was the reason for his mental difficulties, he knew. For struggling to find focus. As much as he wanted to deny it, he was a slave to the meds.

Without them, he unravelled.

He put the brush back on the palette. Dropped everything on the floor. And sat down on the concrete. He grabbed at his temples. His brain pounded. So much that he barely recognized the ringing of . . .

His cell?

Finally, he picked up.

'Are you okay?' she asked nervously. 'I've been worried about you.'

'I'm out of medicine . . .'

'Which one?'

'All of them. My head . . . it hurts.'

'I'm coming up there.'

The line clicked off before he could respond.

For a long moment, Monster just sat there, listening to the angry screams of the wind outside and staring at the half-finished painting he had created.

The Lake of Fire.

A core part of him was desperate to finish the piece because he knew that it would be his final work. Soon there would be no more painting the Lake of Fire. Soon he would be in the Lake of Fire himself.

Monster knew that. He understood that. And he had accepted that from the start. There was a cost to what he was doing. An eternal one. Whether he lived or survived this day, one thing was undeniable: there would be a price to pay. Eventually, he would face the fires of Hell.

Just like Jordie and Terry.

One Hundred and Eight

Striker and Felicia left the wintry bay of Deep Cove and fought their way back along the icy coast roads to the city. The entire way there, Felicia scoured the numerous databases – everything from various emergency service systems to the Insurance Corporation of British Columbia. They were desperate to locate another possible address for Luna.

As a last resort, Felicia called some of the client names from the folders they had found on the floor of Luna's home office. Unfortunately, the end result was the same. Everyone they got in contact with said that Luna had seen them in their own place – just like she had told them. And the cell number Felicia got from them was the same one she already had.

It went straight to voicemail.

It left them with nothing but a waiting game, with a situation that was out of their hands, and that was never good.

When Striker turned down Smithe and eventually parked out front of the Vancouver court house, Felicia looked across the way at the Ministry office where Luther had worked.

'Why are we here?' she asked. 'You got an idea?'

Striker just shrugged. 'Desperation,' he said, then walked up the path.

Once in the office, Striker and Felicia located the vehicle sign-out log. It became clear quite quickly that the vehicles weren't assigned on an individual basis, but rather as part of an ongoing pool. A first-come, first-served basis.

Striker scanned the list for Luna's name.

She hadn't signed out a vehicle. Not yesterday and not today. All the cars were accounted for.

'S.O.L.,' Felicia said.

'Maybe, maybe not. Hold on.'

Striker read more. On the previous days of the week, Luna had signed out numerous vehicles. So Striker wrote down the ID number of each vehicle she'd used over the past two weeks and the corresponding date of sign-out.

Then they returned to the car.

Once inside, Striker got on his cell. He called up Dispatch and got Sue Rhaemer to log on to the GPS system. Then he gave her the list of vehicle ID numbers. 'I need you to print up a list of the coordinates for each of these vehicles.'

'For right now?' she asked.

'No. For every day it was signed out this last week. Every half hour.'

Sue groaned. 'Oh weak, man. This'll take an hour.'

'I need it, Sue.'

'You know you're supposed to go through management for this kind of stuff. It's an emergency-only system.'

'This *is* an emergency. A woman's life is in danger. I'll take the heat for whatever comes. I'm heading up to E-Comm now.'

Sue groaned again, but Striker ignored it. He hung up the phone and found Felicia staring at him.

'Well?' she asked.

Striker told her his plan. 'We'll cross-reference all the days and see where the woman has been. Maybe there'll be a common place somewhere.'

'Like an office?'

'That's the hope.'

'Sounds like a long shot.'

'Yeah? Well, zero plus zero still equals zero,' he said. 'We got nothing else to go on.'

He looked out the window at the heavy flakes of snow that were now sticking to the hood. Then he put the car in gear and hit the gas so hard the tyres spun.

They headed for E-Comm.

One Hundred and Nine

Over an hour later, they had obtained the list from Sue.

With the 9 a.m. sun hidden by the torrents of falling snow, Striker and Felicia sat in an On The Run parking lot with the heater cranked and the windshield wipers going full bore. They drank fresh coffee and cross-referenced Luna's GPS from the past two weeks.

The vehicles the psychiatrist had signed out had all stopped at three similar locations every day. The 2100 block of Cambie Street. The 2500 block of Main. And the 500 block of Railway Street.

Striker dismissed the first two immediately. 2100 Cambie was the police station, where social workers often stopped to speak with police officers on cases that involved mental health as well as criminal code issues. The 2500 block of Main Street was the coffee shop Bean Around the World – a known stopping ground for all emergency health professionals. The coffee there was good, the baked goods were fresh.

The one location that Striker couldn't explain was the Railway Street coordinates. He put the car in gear and began driving there. As they went, he glanced over at Felicia.

'Check the address call history,' he said. 'Might give us some clues.'

Felicia shook her head. 'Already checked. That's a big no.'

'Well Luna went here for *something*. And on too many days

for it to be a coincidence.' Striker found himself more than hoping, he found himself desperate. 'She must have a clinic down here somewhere – some place to store her files.'

'She stored them at home.'

Striker shook his head. 'No. Those were archives. Past patients. Nothing there was *current*. She has to keep her folders somewhere close to her work, and most of her work revolves around central Vancouver. She can't keep her private files at the Ministry either, due to patient confidentiality. So there has to be a place. We just need to find it.'

Five minutes later, Striker drove into the 500 block of Railway. The first thing he noticed was that they were in the hub of old offices overlooking the railroad yards – just east of the ports, where Luther had been murdered.

'It's all industrial down here,' Felicia said. 'Warehouses and office rentals.'

Striker got out and slammed the door. As he did, a small patch of sun fought through the cloud and snow.

It did little to warm his skin.

He looked around. At the east end of the block was a shipping and receiving warehouse. To the west was an old storage facility that had been renovated into condos. Sitting mid-centre was a brick building with shiny new reflective windows.

A sign on the front glass door said:

COS Co. *Space Available.*

Striker had never heard of the place. He googled it and found the website:

The Communal Office Space Company.

'Sounds like a rip-off of Costco, if you ask me,' Felicia said.

'It's temporary office space,' Striker said. 'Rentals. Day to day or month to month.' He smiled widely. 'We might just have a winning ticket here.'

They went inside.

The COS Co. foyer was a small room with a long front counter. Behind it sat a plump-looking secretary with hair so red and curly, and skin so pale and freckly, she looked like Orphan Annie had grown up and developed an eating disorder.

The receptionist looked no more than twenty years old. She was reading the morning newspaper with a coffee and a savoury scone by her side. She looked up when they entered.

'Can I help you?' she asked.

Striker nodded. But before he spoke, he noticed the chain around her neck. Silver and thin, and from it dangled a shiny star. Not like the pentagrams he had seen before in the basements of Luther and Moses, but a *six*-pointed one.

The Star of David?

Striker averted his eyes, badged the woman, and said, 'Vancouver Police – we're here looking for Luna Asawa-Tan.'

'Dr Asawa-Tan's not in right now. Would you like to leave a message for her?'

Striker looked at Felicia and the two shared a smile.

'Do you know where she is? Or when she'll be back?'

'No, I'm sorry. We just provide office space and bookings. Nothing else.'

Striker nodded. 'When was the last time you heard from Dr Asawa-Tan?'

The woman made a cautious face. 'Well, a few days ago now, I guess. Is . . . is everything alright?'

'No, it's not,' Striker said plainly. 'We fear for her safety and have reason to believe she could be in danger.'

'Where is her office?' Felicia demanded. 'We'll need to see it.'

An uncomfortable look spread across the woman's face, distorting the pattern of her freckles. 'Well, Dr Asawa-Tan rents out office 108. But it's private. She's a *psychiatrist*, you know. You'll need a warrant for that.'

'No, we won't,' Striker said. He told her his badge number, got her to write it down. 'These are exigent circumstances. I have full authority here.' He said nothing more, just walked down the hallway to the southeast corner of the building, and Felicia followed.

The layout was odd. They bypassed unused offices, then had to branch down a long corridor to a rear partition. For a moment Striker thought he must have taken the wrong route, but then he found a dark wooden door with 108 on it.

He opened it and they went inside.

The first thing that struck Striker was how ordinary the room seemed. After dealing with Luther and Moses, and their places, he had expected something more sinister in appearance back at Luna's home. When he hadn't found it there, he'd expected to find it here. But there was nothing out of the ordinary. No candles or incense or strange ceremonial knives.

Certainly no altars.

'I find it strange,' Felicia said. 'Out of all the office spaces she could have rented, she chose this one. Way back here. It's so secluded.'

Secluded.

The word bothered Striker.

He searched the office. It took no time. The filing cabinet in the corner of the room was empty. The desk was full of supplies, but devoid of anything useful. And the one treatment room that existed had nothing in it but a pair of chairs, a coffee maker, a mini fridge, and a tall bronze standing lamp.

'Not a single file,' he said curiously.

Felicia shrugged. 'Maybe she keeps her current files with her – in a dossier or something.' She looked at the computer. 'Also,

it is the digital age – maybe she does everything electronically.'
She grabbed the mouse and moved it.

Immediately a password request came up on the screen.

'Call Ich,' Striker said. 'Tell him to get his ass down here and
seize this thing. I want him to scan the hard-drive ASAP. Top
priority.'

Felicia agreed and was already dialling.

As Striker waited, he looked north. There, the entire wall was
glass, much like Luna's den back home. It overlooked the train
yards and the harbour beyond. Slightly to the east, in full view,
were the ports. It dawned on Striker that he could see the exact
place where Luther had died – where Monster had burned the
man and escaped into the inlet.

'Jesus Christ – she saw it,' he said. 'She saw the whole event.'

Still on the cell, Felicia looked over and mouthed the words,
what event?

'Luther's murder.' Striker shook his head. 'She saw it all.
Watched the whole thing go down from here. No wonder she's
so messed up.'

He turned around, and his eyes caught sight of the south wall.
On the white plaster was red calligraphic script. A saying
someone had hand-painted.

As Above, So Below.

It was an odd saying. *As in Heaven, so in Hell?* he wondered.

On the east wall was another red script:

As I Will It, So Shall It Be.

And on the west wall was another one:

Three Times Bad and Three Times Good.

Striker looked at all three of those sayings, and an odd feeling
fluttered through his guts. They were odd, no doubt. But satanic?
With hints at Hell, the first one seemed so – at first. But it was
also ambiguous. The second saying seemed more of a mantra,

the power of the mind. And the third? Well, he had no idea what it meant.

He left the office and returned to the front desk. The Orphan Annie receptionist looked up with a nervous expression but forced a smile. His eyes found the star-shaped jewellery hanging around her neck. He gestured to it.

'That necklace you're wearing,' he said. 'You mind me asking the significance?'

The woman absently reached up and grabbed the star. 'This? Well, it represents my faith. I'm Jewish.'

He nodded. 'So it is the Star of David?'

She smiled. 'Yes, that's right.'

'I'm not Jewish myself, but I was wondering: does the saying *Three Times Bad and Three Times Good* mean anything to you?'

She shook her head. 'No, I've never heard of it.'

'What about *As I Will It, So Shall It Be*?'

'No. Sorry.'

As the receptionist finished speaking, Felicia walked back out.

'Ich's on the way.' She looked at him and frowned. 'Is everything alright?'

'No, it's not,' he said. 'We need to go back to the jail.'

'The jail? Why?'

Striker felt his jaw tightening.

'I need to speak to Solomon again.'

One Hundred and Ten

The door to the jail interview room shut with an electronic clicking sound as the lock engaged. Striker purposely left the video recording equipment off. He allowed Felicia to move behind the desk first, then sat down next to her.

Across the desk sat their Satanist, Solomon Slowitzski. A day's worth of facial growth now took away from his pencil-thin goatee. His stare was flat, his eyes looking upon them with obvious disdain.

'I gave you what you wanted,' he said.

Striker nodded. 'And I didn't show up at your court hearing.'

'Then why am I looking at you?'

'I need to pull from your wisdom a little more.'

A smug look, something between a grin and a sneer, formed on the man's lips. 'So what now? You come across some pixie murders?'

Striker ignored the barb and just splayed his hands. 'Same file, Solomon. Though I've been going over what we told you earlier, and I'm starting to think we led you astray.'

The Satanist steepled his fingers together under his chin and sat back in the chair. 'How so?'

'With leading questions . . . I think I might have gotten something wrong here along the way. About the pentagrams we saw at Moses' and Luther's places.' Striker removed his notebook.

'They were pentagrams, alright. But how do we know they were indicative of *satanic* practices?'

'Was it a five-point star?' Solomon asked.

'Yes.'

'Encircled?'

'Yes.'

'And which way was the star pointed? The fifth peak?'

Striker thought of the orientation of the star. 'Downward,' he finally said.

Solomon leaned back in his chair and shrugged uncaringly. 'There's no doubt it's a satanic symbol. It's a pentagram.' He raised his voice. 'The Sigil of *Baphomet*.'

Striker said nothing for a long moment. He gave Felicia a look and she only shrugged. Something about the two scenes still bothered him though, he just couldn't figure out what. Something about the pentagrams.

And then he got it.

'Tip pointed down?' he asked again.

Solomon nodded. 'Tip down. It's a symbol. It represents what we see every day – that the material world rules over the spiritual.'

'But in relation to what?'

Solomon blinked, as if confused. 'What do you mean?'

'Tip down in relation to what?'

'Well in relation to the altar, of course.'

'But doesn't that depend on where you are?' Striker asked. 'I mean, are you standing in the circle looking at the altar – or is it the other way around? Are you standing *behind* the altar looking out at the pentagram? That changes which way the star is pointed.'

A wry grin formed on Solomon's lips, as if he knew a secret no one else in the room knew. 'You're smarter than you look, Detective . . . The altar is the base. It is always the base.'

'Which would make the star I saw point *upwards*, not down.'

Solomon's grin widened like a boy caught with his hand in the cookie jar. 'That is correct.'

'Which would mean the opposite of what you said – that the spiritual world rules the material world, not the other way around.' Striker looked at Felicia and saw the understanding forming in her eyes.

'This isn't about Satanism,' she said.

Solomon clapped his hands in a sarcastic fashion and let out a deep-bellied chuckle. 'Bravo, Detectives, Bravo. How very good for you. You finally figured it out.'

Striker wanted to hammer the man, but refrained from doing so. Instead, he continued to feed into Solomon's ego. 'I don't get it. If they're not Satanists, then what are they?'

Solomon spoke the words with revulsion. 'They're practising *Wicca*.'

The revelation stunned Striker and yet it made his heart clench. The satanic theory regarding Luther and Moses and Luna had affected so many parts of their investigation. Images of the strange rooms belonging to Luther and Moses returned to him, only now he saw them in a new light.

Solomon looked back at them with a twisted grin on his thin lips and a dark light in his eyes. He was clearly enjoying the moment, feeling smug and smart and above them all.

Striker fixed the man with a cold glare. 'You knew all along, didn't you?' he asked. 'You purposely misled us.'

Solomon's smile widened and he raised an eyebrow.

'What can I say?' he laughed. 'I'm a Satanist.'

One Hundred and Eleven

Striker and Felicia crossed Cordova Street, going from the jail to the police annexe, and took the elevator up to Major Crimes. Once back at their desks in Homicide, Striker fired up Google and the two of them began researching the religious practices of Wicca.

The first thing Striker looked up were the sayings in Luna's office. *As Above, So Below* meant quite simply: As it is in Heaven, make it here on earth. *As I Will It, So Shall It Be* was a positive mantra: you have the power to change your life and others'. And the more cryptic *Three Times Bad and Three Times Good* was a saying taken directly from the *Rede of the Wiccae*, meaning that whatever you do in life, it will come back to you threefold.

After twenty minutes, Striker sat back and rubbed his eyes.

'This explains a lot,' Felicia said. 'Why they've all been so guarded with us from the start – they don't want their religious practices to be known.'

Striker nodded. 'It also explains that photograph we found – the one of Moses and Luna having sex.' He opened up a second search window and punched in the date of the photo: December 21st, along with the word *satanic*. Within seconds, the screen was filled with numerous links to the satanic holiday Feast Day.

Felicia nodded towards the screen. 'I've seen this. It's a sexual rite – in Satan's honour.'

Striker agreed. 'But now watch this.'

He erased the word *satanic* and replaced it with the word *Wiccan*. A dozen new links appeared on the screen. He clicked the first one, and a new web page loaded. On the screen was a description of a ceremony known as the *Great Rite* – a time when monogamous couples engaged in sexual activity as a form of celebration of something called *Yule Lore*.

Felicia read through the page with great interest. 'It's done around the Winter Solstice,' she noted. 'A time when couples engage in sexual activity in celebration of fertility.' She scanned down the page. 'Says here, it's always done between monogamous couples and is supposed to be an act of life and love.'

Striker nodded. 'A far cry from Feast Day.'

After a moment, he looked away from the page, his thoughts elsewhere. His mood suddenly darkened. He exited the web browser and logged off.

Felicia saw the upset expression on his face. 'What's wrong?' she asked.

Striker turned in his chair. 'Father O'Brien knew about this all along.'

The words surprised her. 'You think?'

'Undoubtedly. It's the real reason why he had Moses removed from the Faint Hope Foundation . . . We need to talk to him about this.'

One Hundred and Twelve

A half hour later, Striker parked the cruiser out front of the Holy Cross church in Dunbar. The drive would normally have taken fifteen minutes, even in wintry conditions, but with the snow coming down in sheets, the side roads had been damn impossible to navigate.

It had taken them twice the usual time to get there.

By the time they had exited the cruiser and hurried up the front walkway, their hair and clothes were covered in snow. Felicia was in the process of stomping the clumps off her boots when Striker opened the front door and spotted Father O'Brien ambling up the nave towards them.

'Jacob,' the old priest said, his voice as warm as ever.

'Hello, Father.'

'And Detective Santos.'

Felicia smiled. 'Hello, Father.'

'What brings the two of you back to our humble abode?'

'A little bit of everything,' Striker replied, his tone not overly warm. 'There's a few unusual things I'd like to go over with you.'

'Unusual?'

Striker did not smile. 'Seems like everything in this file is interconnected in some way. I need to get a few things straight.'

Father O'Brien nodded slowly, then extended a hand to welcome them inside the nave. The three of them took a seat near the front of the church, just before the crossing. Striker was about to speak when he saw the pamphlet in the old priest's hand – the same one he'd seen back at the Calvert family home.

'Is that the pamphlet from Greg Calvert's wake?' he asked.

Father O'Brien looked down as if he only now remembered he was carrying it. 'Yes it is. I was just . . . reviewing it.'

'Reviewing it?'

Father O'Brien looked up with an expression of sadness. 'Greg was an amazing person,' he said softly. 'He made this world a better place for all of us. He was not only a member of my parish, he was a very good friend of mine as well. We used to have coffee, him and I. Quite often, in fact. I guess . . . I guess I haven't quite come to terms with losing him myself.'

'By all accounts, he was a wonderful man,' Striker said.

Father O'Brien nodded. 'And with Mother Calvert being so ill . . . well, all we can do is pray for her and Sarah.' He forced a grim smile and patted Striker on the arm. 'Never lose faith, my son. Sometimes it's all we have left.'

Striker made no reply on that matter. Instead, he said, 'The young girl, Sarah. She's barely a year older than my own daughter. What's going to happen to her if her mother doesn't make it?'

'Jacob,' Felicia said softly, as if this was none of his business.

He ignored her. 'Does she have any other family around?'

When the old priest said nothing back, Striker just shook his head. 'So she'll be all alone then.'

'You were alone, Jacob. You were only eighteen when your parents passed away. And with the love and support of the church, you grew up to be a fine man. Whatever the Lord has in store for Sarah, she will be fine. Her faith is strong.'

'Terry and Jordie had strong faiths too. Where did it get them?'

The words came out harsher than he had intended them, and the old priest's face crumbled. Striker immediately felt bad. 'I'm sorry, Father. I didn't mean—'

'It's not you, my son.' Father O'Brien looked at the pamphlet in his hand and shook his head sadly. When he looked up again, there was a sense of regret on his face. *Deep* regret. 'They came to me, you know.'

Felicia blinked. 'The boys?'

'No. Mother Calvert and Sarah. Asking me about God and suicide. About whether it was a mortal sin to kill yourself.'

'What did you tell them?' Striker asked.

The old man closed his eyes. 'Because Mother Calvert had brought Sarah, I naturally thought this conversation was intended for her.' He looked away and rubbed his brow. 'I thought she wanted me to turn Sarah away from dark thoughts. So I told them, in no uncertain terms, what I believe the Bible says about the matter.'

'And what is that?' Striker asked.

'That life is the most precious gift the Lord has given you. And to throw it away is a sinful act. And that, because of the *finality* of that act, there can be no time for repentance.' He lowered his voice and spoke slowly. 'Suicide dooms the soul to Hell.'

Striker said nothing for a moment, he just noted how frail the old priest looked. 'And you actually believe this?' he finally asked.

The old priest splayed his hands. 'I'm afraid the Bible is very clear on the matter, Jacob. It wasn't until the following day that I heard about what had happened . . . about Terry and Jordie taking their lives. And of course, by then, it was too late to take back my words . . . or at the very least, soften them.'

For a moment, the priest looked broken. And it pained Striker to continue the conversation. But there was no choice in the matter.

'I'm sorry about Greg Calvert and his two sons, Father. But that's not why we came here.'

The priest looked back as if confused.

Striker met the man's stare.

'I know what you did,' he said. 'I know about Moses.'

One Hundred and Thirteen

The Boy With The Violet Eyes stood far back in the shadows of the sacristy and watched the two detectives speaking to the old priest. A hard lump had formed in his throat, like a ball of sorrow he could not swallow. An aching hollowness ran throughout his chest, causing him to tremble and quiver and want to vomit.

Father Silas . . . *gone.*

It was impossible to accept.

Not three days ago, Violet had received the phone call from the beautiful priest. He could still hear his melodious voice: *I maybe have need of you.*

And Violet recalled the celestial feeling it had brought him. Like the life breath of God.

And now this . . .

This *Hell.*

He had heard the terrible news on the radio, early this morning, when the night was still as black as Monster's heart. He'd heard it. He'd disbelieved it. And he'd immediately braved the storm to reach St Jude's church.

Or what was left of it.

Gone . . . the thought came again, a tormenting whisper in his head.

Killed by his enemy.

By Henry Whitebear.

By Monster.

Violet's mind floated uncontrollably, back to earlier times. When they were but boys. Children. When he had first seen the selfishness and jealousy of Henry's soul . . .

Violet was eleven once more. And growing taller. Standing in the centre of the sacristy and changing into his vestment. He was there with the rest of the boys. With Henry. And Father Silas was seated just behind the group, watching them as he always did, with such devotion and care.

Violet loved the man. He always had. And he turned to smile at him.

But Father Silas did not even see him standing there – despite the fact he was tallest and the most beautiful. It was as if he had suddenly become invisible, for Father Silas looked right through him. At the newer boy now. The *younger* boy.

At Henry.

The moment sickened Violet.

He moved up to Father Silas. Blocked the view. He even reached out and touched Father Silas on the arm. When the priest did not so much as respond, he moved the soft flesh of his fingers down to the man's thigh – and then on to the other areas the priest favoured.

But still the man's eyes stayed with Henry.

'I love you, Father,' Violet said.

Desperation. Love. Fear.

And finally Father Silas turned his eyes. Looked upon him. And Violet felt his stomach fill with flutters.

'Leave,' the priest said.

'F— Father?'

'Leave. And take the other boys with you.'

Stunned, devastated, Violet did as instructed. When he had ushered almost every last boy out, Father Silas spoke once more.

'Not you, Henry,' he said.

Henry said nothing; he just walked slowly across the room towards the priest, and when he was close enough, Father Silas ran a hand through his thick brown hair. After a moment, he turned and looked at Violet.

'Close the door behind you.'

'But—'

'Close the door.'

'I . . . I love you, Father Silas. I *love* you! More than anything.' His voice dropped to a whisper. 'More than *God*.'

The priest stood slowly, his vestments crooked near his waist, and crossed the room. He walked right up to Violet. Looked him in the face.

And then closed the door.

And just like that, Violet knew that it was over. He had been replaced. And he would now be discarded. Something that was used and left to be forgotten. He was nothing now.

Nothing.

Henry had stolen Father Silas from him.

The Boy With The Violet Eyes broke from the memory like shattered glass. Something between a gasp and a cry escaped his mouth, and spittle stuck to his lips. How he wished time could have frozen before he turned eleven. How he wished he had never grown up.

He had tried. Oh, how he had tried. To stay young. To regain his innocence. To become something that one day – maybe one wonderful day – Father Silas would see and love once more.

By sleeping half his life away.

By keeping his calorie intake low and half-starving himself to death.

By injecting hormone blockers.

By taking herbal testosterone limiters.

And more. So *much* more.

But time was as cruel as it was relentless. Despite his best attempts, it had happened – he had become a man. And how he hated it. Hated what he had become.

Adulthood had cost him everything.

And now, with Father Silas gone forever, what did it matter? There was no chance for a return of love and acceptance. No hope for salvation. It was gone. And the only thing that brought him any sense of peace and escape – any alleviation from the grief and remorse – was the thought of having his retribution.

The thought of killing Monster.

Henry would die. In pain. In fear. And filled with remorse.

Violet swore it.

It was all he had left.

One Hundred and Fourteen

'I know you petitioned to have Moses Sabba removed from his position,' Striker said to Father O'Brien. 'And you succeeded in that. What I need you to tell me is *why*.'

The old priest said nothing for a moment. 'I don't see the connection—'

'It matters.'

The priest's face tightened further. 'His relationship with Luna—'

'We've heard that spiel before.' Striker turned on the bench to better meet the old man's eyes. 'You're a man of the cloth, Father, and we're sitting in the house of God – are you seriously going to sit here *and lie to me* about why you did this?'

'I'm not lying,' the priest said indignantly. Then the tight expression on his face lessened and his eyes softened. 'Listen to me, Jacob, it was very . . . *complicated.*'

'I'm a good listener.'

A look of regret crossed Father O'Brien's face, but he explained. 'The Faint Hope Foundation was supposed to be a centre for people in all kinds of need, and it was – but, primarily, it was designed to be a network for children. Before its inception, I knew Moses. I had counselled Moses. Gotten him away from a life of drugs and gangs and violence. So when he came to me with this idea, and told me that he was desperately in need of funding, I saw the good in it. And I sincerely wanted to help. I did what I could. So I began raising funds.'

'In other words, you got investors,' Felicia clarified.

'Shareholders, is more like it.' The old priest tried to explain. 'The only way to have enough capital to start up the Foundation and routinely fund it was through the community as a whole.'

Striker nodded. 'Particularly, the *Catholic* community.'

'Does that surprise you, Jacob? It was my only real power. And that's exactly what I did.' A small smile spread his lips. 'People wanted to help, Jacob. They really did. And in the beginning, it all worked beautifully. But when Moses started dispensing all that magic stuff,' – the smile on his lips vanished – 'well, I warned him several times to stop it. To cease immediately. I simply could not allow that.'

'And he refused.'

The old priest's face darkened. 'He was *insistent* about his new faith. He gave me no choice in the matter. I had to act. On behalf of our Catholic sponsors.'

'So you had him removed from his own organization.'

'It was justified. Moses may have started the Foundation, but it was anything but his own project. After all, a man may start his own church, but it is still the house of God.' Father O'Brien looked back at Striker and there was defiance in his stare. 'Moses should have put the children first – not his religion.'

'Like you were doing?'

The priest's face darkened even further. 'I have made mistakes, Jacob. I am well aware of that. To err is only human. Obviously, I want to instil the Catholic faith in these children. It is my core belief in life. I'm a man of the cloth, as you said. But this situation . . . it went well beyond my own personal preferences.'

'In what way?' Striker demanded.

'If Moses had remained on the board, doing what he was

doing, all my sponsors would have pulled out on us. And then what? Without the money, that Foundation would have had its doors closed in two months. What would have happened to all those children then?'

'Someone else might have stepped up.'

The old priest laughed sourly. 'You would like to think so, wouldn't you?' He cupped his hands and looked back at the crucifix on the wall, as if for support. When he spoke again, his voice was gentle. 'Nowadays, the needy are better supported. There are entire networks of support for charities and non-profits. But what we're speaking of did not happen today – it happened two decades ago. Back then, times were different.'

'Father—'

'Why do you think I helped your family so much after your own parents were killed?' Father O'Brien continued. 'There just wasn't the level of services back then that there are now. So with Moses and the Foundation, well I really had no choice in the matter. The children needed the money.'

'And a more appropriate religion.'

Father O'Brien said nothing. He just nodded slowly and splayed his hands in acceptance. 'I speak the truth, Jacob.'

'Well I hope it sets you free, Father. Because it sure as hell imprisoned Moses Sabba.'

The words clearly hurt the old man. 'I understand that, Jacob, and it is regrettable. Believe me, the situation saddened me – but I wasn't the one who dictated what happened. That was Moses. As much as we all like to deny it, we are each responsible for our own actions.'

Striker nodded. 'I'm glad you feel that way, Father. Because this entire nightmare that's going on can be traced directly back to Henry Whitebear, your Foundation, and the list of horrors that happened at your Catholic boarding school.'

'The school?' he asked.

'Our Lady of Mercy – which was anything but, with Father Silas acting as guardian.'

An apprehensive look flitted across the old priest's features. 'Father Silas . . .'

'Do I really need to say it?'

For a brief moment, Father O'Brien looked down and the confused expression on his face slowly mutated into one of disbelief. 'Dear God . . . Oh dear God.' He placed a hand to his chest. Over his heart. Looked shaken.

Felicia touched the old man's shoulder.

'Are you okay, Father?' she asked.

He touched his temple with a shaking hand. 'My . . . my blood pressure pills.'

Father O'Brien stood up. He turned to head down the aisle to his office, and Striker stood up to go with him.

'I'll walk you,' he offered.

But the old priest just held up a hand. 'I need . . . a moment, Jacob. For my thoughts.' He turned away and walked down the aisle, and disappeared behind his office door.

Striker stood there, staring at the empty space and feeling horrible. He had just destroyed the one man who had cared for him his entire life.

One Hundred and Fifteen

Monster found the work slow and agonizing, but brush stroke by brush stroke, his final piece was almost complete. It was odd to see this one, his latest version of the *Lake of Fire*. In it, the flames reached so high that they seemed to crest right over the top of the canvas.

Like the swelling tide of a fiery ocean.

It was hard to finish. So very hard. Because the deeper Monster got into his work, the more vicious the memories became. It was a side effect. From the agonies of the past. The haunts that would never leave him, not even in his sleep.

And because he was now out of medications.

He was slipping now. He could feel it. One moment here, one moment there. Little flashes in time.

Flash

He was back with Mother.

Hanging from the pole in the closet, the leathery smack of the belt stinging against his skin. 'Where izzit, Henry? Where dija put it this time?'

And he was crying – crying, because, like always, he had no idea what she was talking about.

Flash.

He was back with Father Silas. And the priest was touching him. In places he knew were bad. In places that made him feel nervous and sick and scared. And then Father Silas was grabbing Henry's own hand. Making him touch back.

'Look at me, Henry . . . *Look at me* . . . There, that's better . . . You want to be closer to God, don't you? You don't want to make God angry, do you, Henry?'

'No, Father.'

And then Father Silas would smile. Touch his face.

'That's my boy.'

Flash.

He was in the cellar again. And The Boy With The Violet Eyes was there. Lurking somewhere in the shadows.

'You stole him from me, Henry – you *stole* him! You ruined everything!'

Violet's screeches went through him in a way that made his teeth grind and his spine tingle.

And then there was the violence that followed. The payback for stealing away Father Silas's attention. For leaving Violet feeling *unloved* . . .

Absently, Monster reached up and touched the disfigured flesh of his face. In truth, he couldn't remember much of the incident itself. Just little bits and pieces. Most of what he recalled was a mass of churning emotions.

Pain. Anxiety. *Terror.*

Violet – taller, stronger Violet – ordering him down to the cellar. To stock the stove with new wood.

It's Father O'Brien's orders.

Even now, Monster recalled walking down those old stairs. Hearing them creak and groan, as if to warn him of what was to come. He recalled the darkness of the corridor. The black steel grate of the stove. And the molten red glow of the fire inside.

The rest eluded him. It was if his mind knew that to remember any more would break him completely.

His next real recollection was coming home from the hospital, so many months later. He could still feel his eagerness to see the other boys, for he had missed them terribly. But instead of returning to friendship and kindness, he found laughter and cruelty.

Mockery over what had happened to his face.

Violet standing there, urging them on. 'Look at him, look at his face! My God, he's not a human being at all, he's a gargoyle. A freak. He's a *monster*!'

And then all the children were chanting as one:

Monster! Monster! Monster!

And they were right.

It was what they had made him. What he had become. A self-fulfilling prophecy.

He stood there now, feeling the disfigured flesh of his face, trapped in the awful gale of cold memories. And the spell wasn't broken until the wind, blowing in through the boarded-up windows, wailed and got his attention. The heavy breeze rushed through the room. The remaining silver crosses Monster had draped off the edge of the easel fluttered in the wind, fell and landed on the floor. When he reached out to grab them they slipped through the crack in the old floorboards and disappeared from sight.

The moment hit Monster like a physical force. He stood there, looking down at the empty space and wondering. Perhaps, this was a sign. That the crosses would be of no more use to him. Because he would never catch them all.

It was an angry thought. And it made him tremble.

When the sound of an engine roared outside the front door, it mercifully broke him free of the moment. He looked away from the cracked floorboards, out between the old planks that boarded the east window. He saw the car in the driveway, and he smiled.

For she had arrived.

Numbly, he took the phone from his pocket. Dialled the number for the Holy Cross church. And waited for it to be answered.

A line clicked, and Father O'Brien came on the line.

'I have her,' Monster said.

One Hundred and Sixteen

Striker and Felicia sat on the first row of the nave and waited for Father O'Brien to return from his office. The old man seemed to be taking an unusually long time to get his medications, and Striker was beginning to worry. When Felicia touched his forearm and said, 'Maybe you should check up on him,' Striker was up in an instant and walking through the crossing.

The office door opened, and Father O'Brien stepped through.

The sight of him relieved Striker, and he let out a held breath. 'We were starting to worry about you. Did you get your pills?'

The old priest looked around for a brief moment as if lost. 'The pills. Yes. My medication.' He moved forward and sat back down on the first row of the nave – gently, as if too much of a collision might shatter his frail bones. He looked like he'd had the wind knocked out of him.

Striker sat down as well. He hated to press the issue but there was no choice. 'Father, what happened during Greg Calvert's wake?'

The old priest looked confused. 'Happened? What do you mean?'

'I think something happened,' Striker said. 'It was a pivotal moment for the boys. For Terry and Jordie. I mean, they handled their father's death well enough – until that day. Until the wake. *Something* must have happened there, to trigger their emotions.

Something other than the wake itself. Do you remember anything out of the ordinary? Anything at all?'

Father O'Brien shook his head. 'You misunderstand, Jacob . . . I wasn't there.'

Striker blinked. 'But you were listed on the wake pamphlets.'

'Yes, yes I was. You see, I was supposed to preside over the ceremony. But my own brother took ill. I had to leave for Calgary unexpectedly the night before.'

Striker thought this over and got a bad feeling. 'Then who took your place?'

Felicia knew the answer already.

'Father Silas,' she said.

The old priest nodded, almost imperceptibly, and then let out a heavy breath. He opened his mouth, stammered. 'If I had known at the time . . . about Jordie and Terry . . .'

But the words left him.

Striker sat up straight and looked glumly around the church. At the wooden podium in the crossing. At the large golden crucifix behind. And at the stained glass displaying the Virgin Mary. He closed his eyes, and for the first time in days he saw clearly.

'Father Silas's presence at the funeral was what set those boys off. It was bad enough for them to have to say goodbye to their father, but for the man presiding over the wake to be the one who molested them? – it was too much. It brought back all the memories of the past, and it sent them into a tailspin. One they never got out of.'

Father O'Brien said nothing, but his expression changed.

Striker turned his thoughts away from Jordie and Terry and back to their long-lost brother. 'The one thing I just don't understand here is *Henry*. I mean, you knew how bad his injury was, Father. And you must have known he was being ostracized by all the other children. And you were the one who signed the adoption papers for his brothers, so you knew he was without them. Why didn't you at least tell the Calverts he had been returned?'

The old man's stare was far away. 'It was a mistake not to,' he said softly. 'One of the biggest regrets of my life. But it wasn't an easy decision, Jacob.'

'Then explain it to me,' Striker said. 'Because all I see now is an abused little boy who was afraid and all alone.'

The words cut into Father O'Brien, and he spoke. 'I didn't tell the Calverts for many reasons. Henry's return wasn't immediate, it took time. And by then, the shock of the boys being separated was over. I worried about reuniting them. Jordie and Terry were finally moving forward with their lives. They were happy and healthy and doing well.'

'And Henry?' Striker asked. 'How was he doing?'

'Henry was difficult. It would not have worked. Besides, the Calverts could *not* afford to take on another child. It's just that simple. They had barely been able to take on one child when they'd adopted Jordie, but when they learnt Terry was his brother, they did everything they could to adopt him as well. But a third child? It was impossible – and you'd be wrong to think there was anything out of the ordinary with this process. It's a sad thing, I know, but siblings are broken up all the time during adoption processes. The most important thing is *placement*. It is a very difficult task. And all that aside, Jacob, I was very worried.'

'Worried? About what?'

'About Henry,' the old man said. 'About what he might do. The problems he might cause. Even before the fights with the other boys, and long before the accident which disfigured his face, there were issues with him. Serious ones. And I worried he would lead the other two down a bad path.'

'The Calverts might have been able to steer him right.'

'Or they might have done what the Browns did – broken down from the problems and just returned all three of the children. If that happened, I doubted I could find them another home again. They weren't toddlers anymore. They were grown boys.'

Striker stared back, unblinking. 'I guess we'll never know now, will we?'

The old priest's eyes narrowed at the comment, but he nodded slowly. 'Fair enough, Jacob. Fair enough. But I won't swallow *all* the blame here. A large part of the problem was with that meddling woman – Henry's psychiatrist.'

'Luna?' Felicia asked.

Father O'Brien nodded. 'She made everything so difficult. Almost impossible, really. Her intrusions and her labelling.'

'Her diagnosis,' Felicia clarified.

'Call it what it is,' Father O'Brien said. 'She gave Henry many of them – so many that the college made her recant some. Eventually she labelled the boy as having a borderline personality disorder. The moment prospective parents heard that, they walked away. No one wanted him. And he was forced to stay at the school forever.'

Felicia's face turned sad. 'With that horrible man.'

Striker had heard enough. He stood up and rubbed his face and looked all around the church as if searching for something he couldn't find. When he focused back on Father O'Brien, a glint of silver around his neck stole Striker's attention. He leaned forward and looked at the priest's neck, and was darkly intrigued by what he saw.

A silver chain.

Striker pointed to it. 'Father, does that chain have a pendant on it?'

The priest reached up and grabbed the chain, pulling it out of his Roman collar. 'This? It's a cross,' he said softly. 'It's a symbol of our church.'

Striker looked at Felicia and could see that the moment had winded her too.

'What about the school?' he asked. 'Did people wear it there too?'

Father O'Brien nodded. 'Everyone did.'

'Even the children?'

'Especially the children.'

Striker laughed softly in a humourless sort of way, because only now he could see it. He could see it all. He looked around the church, a sick feeling taking over his guts. 'This is what it all comes back to,' he said. 'This is why Henry is murdering everyone.'

Father O'Brien looked up with fear in his eyes. 'You don't seriously believe—'

'My God, Father,' Striker snapped. 'Haven't you heard a word I've said? Can't you can see the parallelism here? The years of abuse? Henry's brothers being driven to suicide? And according to you, now having to spend an eternity in Hell? Don't you see? – that's how he's killing everyone.'

'In a lake of fire,' Felicia said.

Striker nodded. 'It's *retribution*. On everyone who's been involved in this process from the beginning to the end. His mother and father for their years of abuse and neglect. Jazz for when she was working with the Apprehension Car. Luther for his role with social services. Moses for his part with the Foundation. And Father Silas for the molestations.'

Felicia agreed. 'The night Jazz went to the bus yards, she got a phone call. It must have been from Henry.'

'Luring her in.' Striker looked hard at the priest. 'Henry may already have gone after Luna as well – we can't find her anywhere – and he still may come after you.'

The notion of his own demise didn't seem to impact on the priest. He just looked down and cupped his hands. His face was a mess of lines.

Striker pulled out his cell. 'I'm putting you under protection, Father.'

'No,' the old man said softly.

'It's not open for debate.'

'I said *no*, Jacob.'

Striker dropped the cell away from his ear and looked at the man, confused. 'He's a madman, Father.'

The old priest shook his head sadly. 'If Henry comes to me, then let him come. I know the boy. I will speak with him.'

'There's no speaking to this man, Father. He's not the little boy you remember.'

'I know this, Jacob. And I understand.'

'I don't think you do.'

But Father O'Brien held up a hand and smiled sadly. 'It is you who doesn't understand, son. I will speak to Henry when and if he comes. There is no choice in the matter. It is quite simply something I *must* do . . . It is my act of contrition.'

One Hundred and Seventeen

The Boy With The Violet Eyes remained hidden in the shadows of the sacristy, watching the scene unfold before him. He couldn't hear all the words, but he got some. The big cop was frustrated and angry while the female cop looked more uncertain and concerned. Regardless of the police, one thing remained eminently clear from the situation: he had been right all along. Henry was going after everyone responsible for putting him and his brothers in that school – going after everyone who had tainted his life.

The confirmation of his theory elated Violet, for it gave him his new lead – and that was Father O'Brien. The old priest would undoubtedly be one of the targets. Perhaps even the final one. So all Violet had to do now was follow the priest wherever he went, and eventually, Monster would be there.

And then Violet could exact his revenge.

The thought was not merely pleasing, it was a relief beyond measure.

He stood there, watching until the two cops finally left. Until Father O'Brien broke down and wept like a baby in the cold dusky light of the stained glass windows. The sight of the priest's sadness filled Violet with a cruel pleasure. And he watched in blissful silence. Watched until the priest finally stopped crying, and just sat there, not moving for a long time. Staring off into the distance.

Then Father O'Brien's cell phone rang, and he answered it.

'Yes,' the old man said softly.

'Yes,' he said once more. 'I am coming.'

Expressionless, the priest hung up the phone. Grabbed a set of keys from his office. Then headed out the rear door of the church.

The Boy With The Violet Eyes followed him.

The beginning of the end was near.

One Hundred and Eighteen

Protection of Life was the foremost duty of every man and woman who wore the badge. Usually, it was a straightforward task. Where it became complicated was when the person in need of protection refused assistance.

By law, no one could consent to grievous bodily harm or death, but that didn't mean they had to accept police protection. The catch-22 made for a bad conundrum, one that was sending Striker's blood pressure to unhealthy levels.

'I'm doing it anyway,' he said.

He got on the cell, called Dispatch, and ordered a pair of unmarked cars to be parked out front and back of the church. When he hung up, Felicia was staring at him intently.

'Sounds like a protection detail to me.'

Striker didn't much care. 'It's not protection detail. It's just good old-fashioned police work. We know Henry might come after Father O'Brien, and we know that Henry is wanted. So therefore, we're not technically here *protecting* Father O'Brien, we're trying to locate Henry.'

Felicia grinned.

'Good old-fashioned police work,' she said.

Striker nodded.

Not ten minutes later, a pair of plainclothes units arrived

– one two-man team from District 4, the other borrowed from 3. They set up on the lot.

'Call me the moment anything happens,' Striker told the foursome. 'And be ready for anything – this guy's a cop-killer. Don't ever forget that.'

The moment everyone understood their role, Striker and Felicia cleared the area. They drove north on Dunbar until they reached West 34th, where Striker took a hard left.

Felicia crooked her neck to face him.

'The Calverts?'

Striker nodded. 'I thought we'd take a quick drive by the place. Make sure their protection detail is properly set up too.'

'Why not? We're already in the area.'

Felicia began flipping through the various dossiers they'd collected over the course of the file. Striker said nothing. He just drove and struggled to clear his head, but no matter how he tried, he could not. The image of Father O'Brien sitting there, looking like a broken man, returned to him over and over again.

'I hope he'll be alright,' Striker finally said.

Felicia looked over. 'You were pretty hard on him, Jacob.'

'I had to be.'

'*Had?*'

Striker glanced at her. 'I love the man. But let's be honest about it, Feleesh. He wasn't exactly straight with us from the beginning. He knew the boys had a brother and he never told us. He knew about the problems with Moses and his odd religious practices. And he also knew about Luna's diagnoses. He wasn't exactly quick to bring that up either . . . I *had* to be hard on him. To get some answers.'

She thought it over, and nodded. 'It doesn't make sense. Why would he withhold information from us?'

'I know exactly why – he's protecting his religious beliefs.

Doesn't want anything to come up that might harm the church. It's what he's built his life upon, and he can't ever separate that.' Striker shook his head. ''You know, it was things like this – like what Father Silas did – that made me leave the church in the first place. It was shit like this that killed my faith.'

'Faith in the church and faith in God are two entirely different things.'

'Yeah? Well, it's not always easy to separate the two. Not when the ones representing God are abusing children and Lord knows what else.'

'Jacob—'

He cut her off. 'Even what Father O'Brien did to Moses. It was wrong, Feleesh. He damn near destroyed another man's life because of his religious politics.'

Felicia shook her head. 'I don't entirely agree with that. Moses has to share some of the blame. He was running a foundation for children in need, and he let his arcane religious beliefs get in the way of that.' She shook her head. 'My God, you can't go around apprehending children while wearing a pentagram around your neck.'

'But a cross would be fine, right?'

Felicia looked over at Striker, licked her lips, but said nothing.

'You're exactly the same,' Striker said. Before Felicia could respond, he continued. 'That was why Luther and Luna bowed out of the Foundation right after Moses was removed. Why Luna couldn't defend herself over the allegations at the clinic. And why Luther was always keeping us at an arm's distance – because they were all *Wiccan*.'

Felicia remained sceptical. 'Is that reason enough?'

'Sure it is. Think about it. The last thing they wanted was for someone to uncover their religious beliefs – it would have destroyed their careers. Luther's job was apprehending children for the Ministry, for Christ's sake. If he'd been fired, he would have lost it all – his job, his salary, his pension. Everything.'

'They couldn't be fired over that,' Felicia said.

'Just like Moses couldn't be removed from the Foundation?'

Felicia said nothing.

'And Luna worked with troubled youths,' Striker continued. 'Kids who've been abused physically, emotionally, sexually. You think many Catholic or Christian sponsors would want her to remain as the children's psychiatrist? Don't kid yourself. *Everything* was a threat to the woman because she couldn't have her beliefs exposed. It's why she's been so evasive all along.'

'That may be true,' Felicia said. 'But they picked a religion that borders on mysticism. Altars and Great Rites and God knows what else – it's only natural to expect your average person to be suspicious of them. I sure as hell wouldn't want my kids being apprehended by them.' She fixed him with a cool stare. 'If Courtney had to be taken away when she was six years old, would you have a problem with them being the ones who did it?'

Striker turned the corner and gave her a glance. 'Hey, I'm not sitting here defending Wicca,' he replied. 'They can pick the religion of their choosing – it's their charter right. I don't care. All I'm saying is, it makes sense why they were so closed-off towards us. So secretive about everything.'

He took the final turn on Highbury Street. When he reached the end of the road and looked up at the Calvert home, the dark look on his face grew even darker.

Something was wrong.

One Hundred and Nineteen

'Where the hell are all the units?' Striker asked.

Felicia looked up from the computer and frowned. The yard was nothing but a barren landscape of snow, snow, and more falling snow. She tried to peer through the constant downpour, but still saw no one. And no police cars on the street.

'Maybe they went to the store or something.'

Striker didn't like it. He got on the cell and called up Dispatch. Sue Rhaemer answered on the third ring, sounding tired and irritable. 'What now, dude?'

'We're outside the Calvert home,' Striker said. 'There's no units here. What gives?'

'They cleared a while ago.'

'*Cleared?* Why?'

'Uh, the family's no longer there.' Sue took a moment to check the log reports, then made an *ahh* sound. 'Here it is: they went to Vancouver General. Mother's got a poison party.'

'Poison— what?'

'A chemo session.'

Striker was growing rapidly frustrated. 'Did Patrol escort her there?'

'Of course.' Sue spoke the words like she was insulted. 'What do you think I am, an idiot? God, you can be so *Milli Vanilli* sometimes.'

Striker pinched the bridge of his nose, felt the pressure going all the way into his brain. 'Just make sure you keep units on their place when they return. Anyone says otherwise, you call me – immediately.'

He hung up the phone and turned to bitch about the guard detail to Felicia, but she was on the phone. When he went to put the car in gear, Felicia reached over and touched his arm.

'Wait,' she whispered.

He looked at her curiously, but waited. As she spoke, he realized pretty quickly she was on the phone with Police Archives. She was making notes and flipping through the pages of the book they'd taken from Jordie's room.

The Power of Present.

She was now staring at the last page, where Jordie had written down four numbers: *1410*. After a long moment, Felicia let out a pleased sound. She hung up the phone and turned to face him. She tapped the book on her lap.

'These numbers look familiar to you?' she asked.

Striker nodded. 'I looked them up already. Revelations 14:10.' He pulled out his notebook and flipped back to the verse he'd written down:

> *And the smoke from their torture will go up forever and ever, and those who worship the beast and his image will have no rest day or night . . .*

He closed the book and looked back at Felicia.

'It was a good try,' she said, 'and it made perfect sense at the time, but I think you're wrong.'

'About which part?'

'The whole thing. It's not Revelations. I think we just got steered there because of the whole Satanism thing. I think the numbers are for something else.'

Striker looked back at them again. 1410. 'What are they, then?'

'A police report. I got Archives to search every year for the last thirty years. And they found a report that matches. From thirteen years ago. We need to pick it up.'

Striker's eyes narrowed. 'One of our own?'

She nodded. 'Vancouver Police. Two charges, one file.'

'On what?'

'Sexual interference and sexual exploitation.'

Striker felt excited and anxious all at once. 'Who was the victim?'

'Henry Whitebear.'

Striker had heard enough. He put the car in gear and headed for Archives.

Fifteen minutes later, Striker and Felicia sat in one of the unused interview rooms just outside of Archives. Because the report was older, long before the existence of the current PRIME system, there was no link to Henry Whitebear's computer entity. And the fact that the allegation had been deemed *Unfounded* by the investigating officer made certain that the file would forever be buried.

Striker read through the entire report, as did Felicia. It was small. A one-pager. When they were done reading, a grim feeling overtook them both. Felicia was the first to speak, and when she did, there was a sadness on her voice. 'Henry tried to tell them,' she said. 'He came forward about the abuse, and no one believed him.'

Striker said nothing, he just scanned through the facts a second time. They were basic.

Henry Whitebear, age twelve, had accused Father Silas of molesting him and his brothers. He had provided this information to Luther Faust and Moses Sabba, who were guardians of the Faint Hope Foundation. They in turn had gone to Jasmine Heer, requesting a formal investigation. She had spoken to the other children involved, but none of them admitted to such acts.

Added remarks in the conclusion text stated that Henry Whitebear was known to have made false allegations in the past, particularly against his doctor, Luna Asawa-Tan, who had deemed the accusation to be a form of *transference* by the confused boy.

The file was closed. *Unfounded.*

Felicia frowned. 'This case just gets worse and worse.'

'You have no idea,' Striker said. 'Look at the follow-up section.'

She did. One read through, and her face turned tight, her eyes sad but hard.

'They warned Father O'Brien too,' she said. 'They warned him about Father Silas . . . and still the abuse went on.'

Striker nodded gravely.

'For twenty years.'

One Hundred and Twenty

Outside the church, the snow was coming down harder, in between the waves of sleet. Striker and Felicia reached the Holy Cross, and Striker jumped out. He pressed on, separating from Felicia, who stopped with the protection detail for updates.

Striker went inside. The moment the church door slammed behind him, the soft moan of the wind was cut off, leaving nothing but a strange hollow sound inside the church.

'Father O'Brien,' he called out.

There was no response.

'Father O'Brien!'

He scanned the area of the nave and narthex, saw no one, and continued down the aisle. When he reached the crossing, he called the priest's name again, but still got no response. He took a quick look in the sacristy, and was hit by old memories of when he was a boy, dressing in his own vestments. Seeing that the room was empty, Striker headed for the pulpit. He came upon the door to Father O'Brien's office and gave it three solid raps. When no one answered, he gently turned the handle and opened the door.

'Father O'Brien?' he called.

But the room remained silent.

Striker stepped inside and closed the door behind him. An odd smell hit him. Something herbal. Maybe from the candles.

At the end of the office was a small foyer and a rear door leading to the back parking lot. It was slightly ajar – as if someone had left in a hurry. At first Striker wondered if someone had taken the old man by force, but then he caught sight of the coat rack. Father O'Brien's heavy coat and scarf were also gone.

Hardly things of importance to a kidnapper.

Everything suggested that the man had left of his own accord. As Striker assessed everything, he soon realized that the old priest must have exited through the rear of his office the moment he and Felicia had left through the front door. Because mere minutes after that, the plainclothes protection had set up on both sides of the church.

Striker opened the exit door and looked out into the rear parking lot. Large wet flakes of heavy snow came down from a darkening sky. An undercover police cruiser was parked in the laneway out back. But nothing else.

Certainly no Ministry cars.

It was odd.

Striker slammed the door shut and cut back through the office. Halfway there, he stopped and looked down at the priest's desk. The phone's message light was blinking. Striker didn't know the password, so he scrolled through the list of received calls.

Only one call was listed.

He dialled the number, and it rang and rang and rang but was never picked up. No voicemail either. He hung up and wrote the number down in his notebook, then spotted a leather dossier beside the desk. He opened it. Inside was a single envelope. From a Cardinal Fairweather.

From Rome.

The letter had been sent FedEx with signed delivery to Father Shea O'Brien, and him alone. Across the top of the page were three words:

Personal and Confidential.

Striker opened the envelope and read through the letter. What he saw was a string of carefully worded sentences, many of which were as vague as they were concerning. The subject was about a *terribly unfortunate incident* with concerns about how it might be *incorrectly viewed in the public's eyes* and how this in turn could lead to an *irreparable loss of faith*. The summary statement was blunt: 'This is a matter best suited for internal discipline.'

Striker scowled. The letter was obviously regarding Father Silas and the abuse that had occurred at the school. He skimmed for a date and found one at the top-right corner of the page. November 14th.

Over two weeks ago.

Striker thought about Father O'Brien and felt lost in the situation.

Was Father O'Brien aware and in denial? Covering for the church? Even involved? Or was he the good and caring man Striker had always believed him to be? The fact that he no longer knew the answer told Striker how dark and forlorn this investigation had become.

No one could be trusted.

One Hundred and Twenty-One

The moment Striker returned to the car, he took out his phone and called Father O'Brien's cell number. The phone rang several times, but went unanswered. Striker wondered whether the man was purposely avoiding him, or if something bad had happened.

He called up Dispatch and told Sue Rhaemer to broadcast Father O'Brien as a missing person and a person in danger. The broadcast was to go to all four districts of the city, including the City-Wide Enforcement Team, and it was to include the vehicle and licence plate number – a 2010 black Lincoln MKS with a bumper sticker than read: *Headed the wrong way? God allows U-Turns.* CPIC messages were also sent to the federal police on the North Shore.

When all was done, Sue let out a weary breath on the phone – as if she had just been forced to run a marathon and not make a string of calls. 'You're a slave-driver, dude.'

Striker wasn't done. 'I also got a number I want you to run. I found this on Father O'Brien's call log.' He gave her the number.

Sue took less than five minutes. 'Nothing's coming up. It's gotta be de-listed or a pre-pay cell.'

Striker cursed. He thanked Sue, then hung up. He turned to Felicia with the number. 'It's up to you now. See if one of your contacts at the phone company can find us something. Otherwise, we're shit outta luck.'

Felicia took the number from him and began calling her contacts. It didn't help that it was now after five, past quitting time, and on a day when most people had stayed home from work in the first place, due to the whiteout conditions.

The first four calls were a bust, but the fifth one managed to not only identify the phone as a pre-pay cell – a Nova 16 – but came up with the date and place of purchase. She pulled the cell away from her ear and spoke:

'Bought three weeks ago.'

'From where?'

She smiled. 'Where was Henry charged with assault?'

'Winter Harbor.'

'Bingo. In a 7-Eleven.'

Striker felt a faint hope. 'Can we trace the number? See where he's at now?'

Felicia nodded. 'Already working on it.' She stayed on the phone for the better part of ten minutes as they tried to triangulate the cell towers and find the last known area of signal. When she finally hung up, her face was a mixture of excitement and relief.

'Well?' he asked.

'The triangulation pinpoints to Squamish. But exactly where, we still don't know.' She hazarded a guess. 'The church Father Silas closed down?'

'Or the school.'

'Our Lady of Mercy?' She shook her head. 'It's been closed down for years.'

'Closed down, yes. But *demolished?*'

When Felicia didn't have a response for that, Striker put the car in gear and hit the gas. Whiteout or not, it was time for a road trip.

They were going to Squamish.

One Hundred and Twenty-Two

By the time they got across the Burrard Street Bridge and entered the city core, Felicia had managed to bring up a Google image of the town of Squamish on the laptop. What she saw piqued her hopes and filled her with worry too.

Even though Our Lady of Mercy had been closed down years ago, images on Google Earth suggested that the building had never been demolished.

Only condemned by the city.

'He could be living there,' she said.

Suddenly, everything seemed very plausible. Striker thought this over and recalled the last two times he and Henry Whitebear had tangled. The man had the strength of a bear and was prepared to die.

The odds were against them.

'Maybe you should get the Feds on the phone,' he told Felicia. 'If Henry's hiding out in that school, then we're gonna need help with containment. And maybe even more help taking him down. Who knows what kind of traps he's got set for us.' He made a fist with his hand and felt the gauze stretch against his burnt forearm. 'Last thing I feel like is getting stuck in a fire again.'

Felicia couldn't have agreed more. As Striker drove them along the Stanley Park connector, the old iron pillars of Lion's

Gate Bridge came into view, its enormous structure barely visible in the snowy downpour.

They were leaving the city of Vancouver now.

Entering the North Shore.

Felicia got on her cell and tried to contact the Squamish division of the Royal Canadian Mounted Police. It wasn't easy. They were crossing the black frothy waters of the windswept Burrard Inlet by the time she managed to locate the person in charge – a corporal by the name of Travis White, who sounded young enough to be a college sophomore and who was clearly inexperienced, unsure of how to deal with an interdepartmental issue.

She was on the phone for a good half hour.

Striker could sense Felicia's frustration with the call. As he turned onto the Trans-Canada Connector and headed west, he whispered, 'Just tell them it's *our* file. All we're asking for is backup.'

She shooed him away with a flick of her hand and slowly but surely got everything organized. When she hung up, she brushed a few strands of dark brown hair out of her eyes, tucking the longer pieces behind her ear. 'It's a really small detachment,' she said. 'Only has seven cops, one of whom is on leave, and one who's away on a course.'

'Leaving us with five.'

'They only have three cops on duty right now. Corporal White's trying to call out the other two.'

Striker shook his head. 'We should have brought our own units.' He cursed himself for not thinking farther ahead. 'We should have brought one of the dogs.'

'We still can,' Felicia said.

Striker mulled the idea over as he shifted into the slow lane. The town of Squamish was less than ten minutes away now. Calling in units from the city would require ten minutes to get approval, another ten for them to organize, and another forty to drive up. He tried not to grind his teeth. Integrating departments on the fly always led to problems. But an extra hour of waiting was time they couldn't afford.

Not with Father O'Brien in possible danger.

'We'll stick with the Feds,' Striker said.

He only hoped it wouldn't come back to haunt them.

One Hundred and Twenty-Three

Our Lady of Mercy was located on a barely visible side extension that branched off of Old Dyke Road. From what Striker understood, the dyke had been built years ago to separate the town from the Squamish River, which had always been prone to overflowing in heavy run-off years.

Striker studied the map.

The long driveway into the school snaked off the main road, ran through a thicket of trees, and eventually evened out onto a small circular patch of land. This promontory looked out over the Squamish River.

It would be best to go in on foot.

Covertly.

Striker went over their current position on Old Dyke Road and didn't like it. If they drove any farther off the road, they risked getting stuck in the heavy snow banks. But if they remained on the road shoulder, in the darkness of the evening and the downpour of falling snow, it wouldn't be long before another vehicle ploughed into the back of them.

He looked ahead and spotted the driveway. It had almost disappeared under the snow-covered canopy of the cedar trees. 'That's it right there.' He glanced down the main drag behind them, then ahead once more.

He saw no lights, only blackness.

'Well, where the hell are the Feds?' he asked.

'I'll check it out.'

Felicia got on her cell and called the corporal back. She'd barely said ten words to the man when she placed her palm against her forehead and cursed under her breath. 'Well tell them we're here *now*, and we need backup.' She listened some more, then said, 'As soon as possible.'

She hung up.

'What's the problem?' Striker asked.

'Six-car pile-up on the Sea-to-Sky,' she said. 'Fatalities.'

Striker just nodded. A major accident like that in a whiteout like this was a nightmare. It meant one thing for him and Felicia.

They were on their own.

'The corporal's got some units coming from North Van,' she said.

'That's a half-hour drive. In good weather.'

'They left twenty minutes ago, Jacob. We really should wait.'

Striker shouldered open his door.

'Where you going?' Felicia demanded.

'To do some quick recon.'

'I'll cover you.'

'Absolutely not – we can't risk missing those units. Wait here, but whatever you do, do *not* use the emergency lights or the siren. If Henry is here, I don't want him alerted to our presence.'

Felicia gave him one of her *I'm not an idiot* looks.

'I'm not sure about this,' she added.

'I'll be ten minutes.'

He closed the door before she could debate the issue further.

With the snow blustering in the thickening darkness, Striker hiked down the road. The drive was difficult to spot, blanketed in a cover of fresh snow, and the angle of road was sharper than expected. It seemed to almost circle back on itself.

By the time Striker reached the end, where the drive flattened out, he came across a small oval recess. There, two cars were parked. The sight of them caused his heart to flutter.

Both were black Lincoln Sedans. MKT models – the same cars he had seen parked at the Holy Cross church.

He approached the first vehicle and saw that the rear window had been smashed. Darkness made the glass shards difficult to see. He leaned down and peered inside. Even without the light, it was apparent that the dash had been broken. Wires hung down below the steering column.

The car had been hotwired. Stolen.

But by whom?

Striker bypassed the first vehicle and zeroed in on the next. It was parked directly in front. And when Striker neared it, he saw that all its windows were intact. He looked down at the bumper and saw a sticker. In the darkness, it was unreadable. So he took out his flashlight and shone it on the bumper.

Headed the wrong way? God allows U-Turns.

It was Father O'Brien's car.

'Jesus Almighty,' Striker whispered.

He made his way around the vehicle. On the passenger seat was a file with a yellow sticky note attached. He grabbed the door handle, tried it, and the door clicked open. He leaned inside, used his flashlight to illuminate the paper, and examined what he found.

On the yellow sticky note was black writing.

For Homicide Detective Jacob Striker.
Vancouver Police Department.

Striker quickly flipped open the folder and scanned the first page. Then the next. And then the next. What he was looking at was a well-documented investigation into Father Daragh Silas. And from the looks of things, it had been going on for quite some time.

Father O'Brien had been doing his own investigation.

The discovery should have filled Striker with a sense of relief, but it did not. For where now was the man?

Striker snapped the folder shut, closed the car door, and quickly scanned the area. Everything was black and bleak, and the winds were howling like a wounded beast. When he saw no sign of Father O'Brien – saw no sign of anything – he began running across the oval area.

Within ten steps, he caught his first glimpse of the school. The moment surprised him. The darkness had hid the building well, and suddenly it was right there upon him.

Closer than he had thought.

The facility was large and old, with deteriorated retaining walls that appeared to run all around the lot. Snow and vines covered the crumbling brick, and wooden planks covered most of the windows. No light seeped out from behind those planks, only a darkness that seemed as deep and cold as the night above.

Striker went to turn on his flashlight for a better look, then hesitated. He didn't want to alert Henry he was coming, but he also couldn't be fumbling around in the dark. After a moment's debate, he made the decision.

He turned the light on.

Shone it down the side of the building.

From this angle, Striker could see the school in full view. It was longer and larger than he had expected. Up ahead was a rectangular off-branch, which looked like a place for housing – a dormitory for the boys – and extending in behind the two structures, peaking higher than both buildings, was a large steeple.

A school church.

Striker considered going in the other way. But on the other side of the school was the bluff. And judging by the way the land was shaped, it appeared as if a section of the earth had caved in some years ago and fallen into the river below.

It was a dangerous way to go, especially in snow and darkness.

As Striker turned away from the bluff, the beam of his light caught a third set of tyre tracks in the snow – shallow and almost completely refilled with fresh snow. They led past the crumbling retaining walls out back.

He knelt down, examined them.

The tyre span suggested a bigger vehicle than the Lincolns out front. Probably a van or a truck. And within the walkway ahead, he saw two pairs of footprints. One set large – Monster.

And one set small.

Father O'Brien.

Immediately, Striker started for the front of the old school, dialling Felicia as he went. By the time he was halfway there, he realized the effect the storm was having on the telecommunication lines – the signal would not go through.

He tried twice more, then gave up, and the horribleness of the situation fell upon him. There was no time to go back for Felicia, no time to wait for support.

Not now.

Not with Father O'Brien somewhere inside.

Striker lowered his hand, made sure his pistol was snug in its holster.

He would have to face Henry alone.

One Hundred and Twenty-Four

Striker approached the front of the school.

Two large doors, old and wooden, led the way in. And when Striker gently pushed them open for a peek inside, he found that the hinges on the left door had long since seized.

It would not even budge.

He pushed the right one, and a loud creak resonated in the chamber ahead – a warning to all that he was coming.

Keeping behind the cover of the door frame, he reached down. Felt the rubberized base of his SIG Sauer. And drew the gun.

Then he looked inside.

All along the wall, the window panes had been broken and covered with plywood. Being night-time, with the snow coming down, they were all but useless.

Darkness owned the room, giving Striker no option but to use the flashlight. He turned it on, and the interior was illuminated in a pale bone-white.

He scanned the way ahead.

The room was long and narrow and screamed of disuse. Shards of broken glass littered the floor. Here and there, wooden floorboards had been torn up in places, exposing the crawlspace below. Where the floor was not torn up, mainly in the centre of the room, a handful of children's desks were lined in rows. Most of the desktops were long since broken and the steel legs were reddened with rust. The empty seats gave the room a haunted feel, as did the series of old coat hooks that held no coats, and the cubby holes which were all empty.

The place looked *pillaged*.

Damn near destroyed.

But that was not what stole Striker's attention. What completely occupied his focus were the paintings that lined the walls. Piece after piece of graphic, horrible images.

People writhing, screaming, *burning in flames*.

It was art as he had never seen it. A fearsome sight. And it made Striker tighten his grip on the gun. For what kind of person would paint this depiction, time after time after time? Part of him wanted to retreat to a place of cover and wait for backup.

But the thought of Father O'Brien kept driving him forward.

He moved ahead through another doorway and found himself in a small den. Immediately he was hit with the smell of old wood and dampness. And the moment the door closed behind him, the darkness deepened, despite his flashlight.

Just ahead was an old steel drum, loaded with burnt wood and garbage. The fire had gone out, but was still smouldering. The smell of ash and burnt wood was strong in the air.

Striker moved closer to it for a better look. At the base of the drum was an old pet cage, made from wire and plastic. When Striker shone his flashlight on it, he saw the remains of a dead rodent. Burned beyond recognition.

'Jesus,' he muttered.

He could not keep the word in.

Behind the drum and cage was the one item that dominated the room more than any other. And the moment Striker spotted it, his eyes locked on and did not divert. It was an *artist's easel*, covered by a sheet.

It appeared to be holding a covered canvas.

Striker took a long look at it, then wondered if it was some kind of trap. He scanned the room, searching every shadow and recess with his flashlight – the broken floorboards that opened to the crawlspace; the missing ceiling tiles; and the doorway ahead that must have led to the dormitory and church.

All of it appeared to be empty.

Finally, Striker reached up and grabbed the sheet. He pulled it off the easel and gaped at the painting beneath. Filled with crimson and gold and deepest black, the painting was as beautiful as it was creepy. It was a depiction of Hell, and in it there were three little boys, screaming in the flames. The faces had been painted well, with precision and clarity. And despite the younger appearance, there was no doubt in Striker's mind who the children were.

Jordie and Terry and Henry.

Burning for eternity in the Lake of Fire.

One Hundred and Twenty-Five

The painting of the three brothers was as mesmerizing as it was sad and disturbing – three small boys surrounded by flames. Knowing the history of what had happened here, Striker found the moment horrifying. But there was no time for reminiscing about the atrocities of the past.

He forced his eyes away from it, and moved on.

The next room was a short pre-chamber. To the left of the chamber was a boys' dormitory, while straight ahead was a long corridor that led to the church. Both areas were shrouded in a dusty darkness that was permeated only by the thin beam of his flashlight.

The dormitory was closer, so Striker went there first.

When he crested the doorway and looked inside, Striker saw the remains of old beds. They were barebones now. No mattresses or pillows and quilts. Just rusted wire and spring. They looked so small, lined up against the walls. And it hammered home the fact that these had been children living here.

Kids like Terry and Jordie.

Kids like Henry.

Striker killed the thought and kept moving through the dorm. The green-blue paint had long since flaked off the walls, and here and there, the plaster was crumbling. On the south wall was some children's writing.

Billy loves Jenny, written inside a big heart shape.

Striker moved past it all until he reached the boys' washroom. There were only three stalls, and a small communal shower at the opposite end. Seeing no one here, Striker returned to the pre-chamber area and made his way towards the last room.

The church.

He found the door already ajar. It made him pause for an instant, and he listened. All he heard were the angry cries of the storm outside, muted slightly by the planks which were hammered across the broken windows. From above came the creaking and groaning of a roof under too much weight of snow.

But there was nothing else.

Just a heavy foreboding silence.

Striker reached out for the door. Pushed it open. And was immediately hit by a smell so powerful, it made his eyes water. The stink was diesel fuel.

Henry was here.

One Hundred and Twenty-Six

The stink of the fuel set Striker's heart into overdrive, and he tightened his grip on the pistol. At first glance the room looked like an auditorium, but there was an eerie orange flickering glow to it.

Candles?

He saw no immediate threat, but remained on high alert.

Striker scanned the layout of the room. He realized it must have been created for multiple purposes – a place of worship, a drama room for plays and presentations, and a gymnasium for the boys to play in.

Coming off the north and south side walls were a series of old wooden bleachers. And there, at the east end of the room, was a large elevated stage, flanked by a pair of thick sweeping burgundy curtains. It was where the light was coming from – an area illuminated by a series of freshly lit candelabras.

Instinctively, Striker took a half-step forward.

On the right side of the elevated stage stood a tall podium, dark brown with a white cross on the face – a pulpit from which the lecturers of the school had undoubtedly preached their gospel to the children. Also on the stage, far left, was an old upright piano. And high above was a row of spotlights, none of which appeared to work anymore.

Striker looked at all of this – and then found his attention stolen by centre stage. There, in the middle of everything, was Father Shea O'Brien. The old priest was hunched over, on his knees. A patch of duct tape covered his mouth and his hands were bound behind his back.

He looked like a sacrificial lamb.

'What the—,' Striker said softly.

He took a few steps into the room and spotted another figure moving across the stage. From the left side. The person he saw shocked him, and he stopped with a jolt.

'*Sarah?*' Striker asked.

It was all he could do to get the word out.

The young girl's eyes were large and wide. Even in the candlelit dimness of the gymnasium, the pale colour of her skin and lost expression on her face were easily readable.

'Please,' she begged. 'Don't kill him – it's not his fault.'

Striker took another step forward. 'I don't want to kill anyone, Sarah.'

And then, all at once, Striker realized that her eyes were not on him, but over his shoulder. She was talking to someone else.

Someone *behind him*.

Drawing his pistol, Striker spun around and came face to face with the man he had been chasing for four days.

Towering above him was Henry Whitebear.

'You shouldn't have come,' he said.

One Hundred and Twenty-Seven

It happened so fast. In an instant.

Seeing Sarah Calvert there had already thrown Striker off balance. Changed the entire situation. Striker took a reflexive step backward, raised his SIG—

And was levelled by a punch from Henry Whitebear.

The man's gigantic fist seemed to come out of nowhere, travelling through the darkness and colliding with the side of Striker's skull in a lazy, roundabout hook. The impact was severe. Striker's head snapped. He spun leftward and backward. Reeled in the darkness.

And Henry was still coming.

Striker hit the ground hard. Rolled with the momentum. He scrambled back to one knee and raised the gun. But as he took aim, Henry was there once more. In the weak orange glow of the candelabra, he looked like a giant – a hulking, unstoppable force.

Striker pulled the trigger. The gun kicked. And an explosion filled the room.

It did nothing.

Henry hit him hard. Drove him backwards once more.

Striker was propelled through the darkness – the air exploding from his lungs and his ribs cracking from the collision. He flew uncontrollably, suspended in the blackness, and when he landed with Henry on top of him, he was overcome by a strange cold wet sensation.

A pool of liquid suffused him – thick, grimy, greasy.

Diesel.

Striker swept his arms out to the side. Realized he had landed in some kind of a hollow in the middle of the gym floor. A man-made pool.

A *lake.*

Striker coughed out a mouthful of fuel. The liquid was in his eyes, in his hair, turning his mouth rancid and burning his lungs. Almost vomiting, gasping for air, he fought against Henry's weight and went to raise the pistol one more time—

And realized it was gone.

Sent flying into the darkness.

'Shouldn't have come!' Henry said again, and there was anger there.

Striker tried to push the man away, but it was futile. Henry was massive – an anchor weighing him down. And so Striker did the only thing he could do. He stopped trying to escape and went on the offensive. He grabbed the back of Henry's head. Pulled the man towards him. And drove his elbow forward with as much strength as he had left in his body.

A bone-snapping crunch filled the room, and for a moment, Striker felt a sense of victory.

It was short-lived. Even as he felt the reverberations from the impact running up his arm to his shoulder, Henry remained on top of him, looking down on him with an expression of annoyance.

Striker tried to hit him again.

This time the giant blocked it. He reached out, grabbed hold of Striker's coat, and yanked him from the pool of fuel. One moment, Striker was floating through the air, the next he slammed down hard against the floor. Like a discarded rag doll. The back of his head snapped hard against the old wood.

And the world spun.

Darkened.

And still, Henry was there. Slamming his big fists down on top of him. His giant blocky hands pounding Striker into unconsciousness.

In desperation, Striker raised his arms. Tried to ward off the blows. But it was a battle he was fast losing. When Henry wrapped his right hand around Striker's throat, the oxygen left him too. His throat cracked, his air passage narrowed, and the world began to fade.

He was going out.

It was over.

And Striker did the only thing left he could do. He reached out blindly. Towards Henry's face. And raked his nails down the man's eyes.

A horrific scream filled the room, and for the first time, Henry flailed backwards.

Coughing, desperate for air, Striker rolled away. He crawled across the floor, his soaked clothes slick against the wooden floorboards. Somewhere in the darkness was his gun. He searched frantically for it. But it was nowhere to be found. And Henry was coming for him again.

Striker looked back. Saw the man's damaged face.

His rage-filled expression.

His vacuous stare.

'Stay back!' Striker ordered. 'Stay the fuck back—'

A shrill cry pierced the darkness – feminine, pained, *terrified*.

'Help me, Henry! – *HELP ME!*'

And Striker recognized the voice.

Sarah.

Henry spun away from Striker as if he no longer existed and turned to face the stage. There, standing overtop of both Father O'Brien and Sarah Calvert was a man – the same man Striker had seen at the ports the night Luther died.

Tall, thin, and – even in the candlelight – eerily pale.

His face was twisted into an ugly sneer. A long knife was gripped in his hand. And he had Sarah Calvert on her knees – her head pulled back and the soft flesh of her throat exposed for all to see.

'Welcome home, Henry,' he said.

One Hundred and Twenty-Eight

For a brief moment, Monster froze.

The sight of Violet standing there did something to him. Sent a chill running through his body – one every bit as cold as the man's eyes. In a rush of memories, he was suddenly a child again. Helpless. Back then. And he remembered it all.

The fiery coals.

His flesh burning.

And the other children taunting him.

Monster! Monster! Monster!

He absently reached up. Felt his scarred face. And then his eyes fell to the girl on the stage. To Sarah.

The one person who had been kind to him. Who had treated him like a human being. Who had never seen him as the monster he had become.

The one person who had sought him out and found him and *saved* him.

Sarah.

Monster looked up at the girl. Her young face was so pale. And it was filled with fear and a horrified understanding. Tears made her mascara run down her face in blackish trails, and her mouth fell partly open – as if she wanted to cry out for help but couldn't find the words.

Monster took a step towards the girl, towards the stage, and

Violet grabbed her. He dug his fingers into her long blonde strands of hair and yanked her head backward – so hard that he lifted her off her knees.

She let out a cry, and Henry stopped immediately.

'Let her go, Violet. She's done nothing.'

'Everyone's done *something*, Henry.'

'Violet—'

'Come one step closer and I'll slice her neck open.'

Monster stopped moving.

The Boy With The Violet Eyes only let out a strange hyena laugh. He grabbed the same tape used to bind Father O'Brien and now bound Sarah's hands behind her back. Then, with the girl subdued, he yanked her head back even further and gently slid the edge of the blade up under her chin – all the while making sure Monster was witnessing every joyous second of it.

'Welcome to my life, Monster,' he said. 'Welcome to Hell.'

One Hundred and Twenty-Nine

The moment felt surreal in the candlelit ambience of the auditorium.

Striker heard the two men talking, their back and forth threats sounding distant and detached. Patches of darkness still clouded his mind, made everything vague – as if black silk hung in the forefront of his mind.

He struggled to roll over. Felt his diesel-soaked clothes stick to the floor. Felt blood run from his nose and mouth and cheek. His head felt wrongly attached to his neck. Henry had broken something inside of him.

He could feel it. Things didn't work right.

Ignoring the pain and fighting through his semi-conscious state, Striker swept his fingers along the floor. Searching, searching, searching for the SIG.

On the stage, the tension was growing.

'You took everything from me!' the thin man raged. 'Everything!'

Henry did not move. He just stood there, statuesque, looking back.

'I'm not afraid of you, Violet,' he said. 'Not anymore.'

Violet let out a high-pitched laugh. 'Now you're brave? *Now?* And why is that, Henry? Because you burned a few people?' Violet pointed the knife at Henry and smiled cruelly. 'Take a look in the mirror – I know a few things about that myself.'

'And I will kill you for it.'

Violet laughed again. Heavily. Bemusedly. Then the laughter left him and he gave Sarah's hair another hard tug until she cried out. There was only hatred in his eyes, and determination on his face. 'Then come get me, thief. Come get me – and I'll show you what real fear is.'

Striker let the two men talk.

The longer the angry conversation went on, the better his chances of saving Sarah and Father O'Brien.

He crawled through the darkness, in behind Henry, near the makeshift pool of fuel. Through the dusky candlelight, he finally spotted the black outline of his SIG. He extended his arm, felt his entire body shake from the effort, and then touched the rubberized grip of the gun.

In one fluid motion, he snatched up the pistol. Struggled to one knee. And turned to face the stage.

There, the conflict had reached its zenith.

He was almost out of time.

One Hundred and Thirty

Up on stage, Violet forced Sarah's head backward so hard the angle seemed unnatural. He made her look up at him. Face him.

To look upon him with her eyes.

'Such a foolish girl,' he said. 'You were helping him all along, weren't you? Trying to turn him away from the darkness.' He smiled condescendingly. 'You actually thought you could save him, didn't you?'

The young girl looked back at him with fear – and yet also defiance.

'I *did* save him.'

The smug look on Violet's face mutated into a menacing grin. He twisted her hair to make her cry out once more, then – keeping one eye trained on Monster – he leaned down closer into her face.

'You're a fool,' he said. 'You couldn't save your father. You couldn't save Jordie. And you couldn't save Terry. You can't even save your dying mother. So why would you think you could save *him?*'

'Because,' – she looked right into his eyes – 'he's my brother.'

Whether it was because she had the audacity to talk back to him, or whether it was because he hated her answer, Violet was unsure. But the result was the same. He drove his knee into Sarah's back, heard her cry out, felt her shudder. Her pain gave him great pleasure because he knew everything he did to her hurt Monster even more. She was a *vice* to him.

The only thing left in this world that he still cared for.

To Violet's left, also kneeling in submission, was Father O'Brien. The old man's brow was wrinkled and sweating, and he was making harsh wheezing noises through his nostrils.

Breathing was getting increasingly difficult for the old priest.

Violet glanced at the man. In the dim glow of the candles, Father O'Brien looked small and frail and old. So terribly, terribly *old*.

The sight of it repulsed and angered Violet. So he took the hilt of his knife and drove it into the priest's temple. Father O'Brien made a muffled sound, then went limp and collapsed to the floor, his body slapping against the stage.

The violence startled the young girl kneeling before Violet, and Sarah let out a cry.

Violet barely noticed. He was growing tired of this game. Anything shiny eventually lost its lustre. And that had happened here.

The end had come.

And it was as if Monster could sense it, for he started coming towards the stage.

'Let her go, Violet,' he said softly. 'Let her go and you can have me.'

The words were spoken submissively, in a pleading tone, filled with emotion – fear, uncertainty, desperation. The sound of them filled Violet with a disturbed form of sadistic pleasure. And yet it also angered him beyond control.

He tightened his grip on the knife. Shook.

'I can have you, can I?' he asked. 'As if you'll *let* me.'

'Violet—'

'When we were children, you took Father Silas from me,

Henry. Like a dirty beggar. Like a *thief*.' His voice trembled with rage. 'And it still wasn't enough for you, was it? No. You had to go after him again. To kill any chance I had left of salvation. And you did it. You killed him. You killed everything I ever *loved!*'

Monster said nothing, he just moved slowly closer to the stage. Violet broke down. Sobbed.

'You *ruined* everything. You *destroyed* everything. Everything you touched – everything you so much as looked at.' His eyes narrowed into angry slits. 'But I'll tell you a little secret, Monster. I got even with you. I took something from you too.' A cruel smile parted his lips. 'I took Terry.'

Monster's entire posture changed. *Tightened.*

'What – did you really think that he took his own life?' Violet laughed. 'Did you think the Calvert bitch just happened to find the needle laying there beside him? That Terry injected himself with that much heroin? No, that was me.'

Monster felt his throat tighten.

'Terry never did anything—' he started.

But Violet cut him off. 'Terry was *weak*,' he sneered. 'The little prick was coming forward. He was going to tell everyone about Father Silas. He was going to expose him. So I took action first.' Violet spoke the words tauntingly, smugly, even gleefully. 'I held your brother down, Monster. I stuck him with the needle. And I injected as much poison into his veins as they would take. And just so you know, he died with nothing but sadness and guilt and grief inside his heart.'

Monster began to tremble all over, his fists tightening.

'I would have killed Jordie too,' Violet continued. 'But the coward did himself in before I could get to him. No matter – he'll burn in Hell forever to pay for that sin.'

Monster took another step forward. He could not stop himself.

'I will kill you, Violet,' he said.

But The Boy With The Violet Eyes just kept smiling.

'Maybe so,' he said. 'But I have one final task to complete before you do.' He held up the knife as if it were a prop in his maniacal show, then spoke loudly – as if he were speaking to an audience filling the gym. 'Behold, Destroyer, I give back to you what you once gave to me – a lifetime of emptiness and grief and sorrow and despair. A lifetime of *hopelessness*.'

Violet yanked back Sarah's head.

Exposed the soft flesh of her throat.

And placed the blade against her skin.

One Hundred and Thirty-One

Striker held his breath.

With Violet directly behind Sarah, she was in the line of fire. There was almost nothing to shoot at.

No target. Only a hope and a prayer.

And for Striker, time slowed down.

He saw the blade press into Sarah's throat. Saw Henry Whitebear sprinting up onto the stage. And he knew without question that Henry would never save the girl in time.

In one fluid motion, Striker raised the gun.

Lined up his sights.

And pulled the trigger.

The gun kicked in his hands, and the white-hot flash of exploding gunpowder bleached out the candlelight. Reverberations echoed in the auditorium like thunder.

The bullet found its target – a near-perfect hit, taking Violet in the left shoulder. The impact jolted the man. Spun him to the left and dropped him backwards. He stumbled, yanking Sarah with him.

The young girl was screaming.

Frantic.

Clawing the ground to get away from him.

And injured or not, Violet's determination was strong. He raised the knife once more and reached for her again.

One Hundred and Thirty-Two

Monster reached the stage.

The first thing he saw was Violet. Going after Sarah once more.

But he would not get her. Not this time.

Henry lunged between the two, separating Sarah from Violet with his own body. In one quick motion, he pushed the girl aside – pushed her with all his might – and sent her tumbling across the stage. She slammed into the podium. Hit the candelabra. And knocked it into the drapes.

The old material combusted in a flash of yellow-white.

Monster was unaware of this. For the moment, his only thought was of Sarah. Keeping her away from Violet. Getting her to safety. No matter the cost.

Then he felt the coldness in his belly.

Sharp, stinging, *cold*.

He looked down. Saw the red meaty tear through his shirt. Saw the bulge of intestines poking through. And then he saw the blade – as it thrust into him two more times. Into his stomach. Then the blade angled upward. Cut high.

Up to his chest bone.

Instinctively, Henry reached out and grabbed hold of Violet. Pulled his enemy near. And held him close enough that the knife would no longer move.

But it was too late. He knew it, he could feel it. A weakness invaded his legs. His strength flowed out of him as quickly as the blood. And soon his knees buckled. He was falling, falling, falling—

And he took Violet with him.

They stumbled backward, then hit the ground hard, almost falling directly on top of Sarah, who now lay semi-conscious on the right side of the stage.

Violet struggled to free the knife. With one slow swat, Henry sent the blade spiralling out of Violet's hands and spinning across the stage. It clattered against the wooden planks – a soft scuffling sound.

And suddenly Violet was laughing. Deeply and excitedly. So loud he could be heard above the crackling of the fire that now had raced up the curtain and was spreading across the stage drapery.

'You're dying, Monster,' he said. 'You're *dying*.' The smile on his face warped like melting plastic. 'But before you do, I want you to know one thing – after you die, so will she. *Slowly and painfully*.'

Henry said nothing back. He just held on to Violet with all the strength he had left, not allowing him to escape. A coldness was invading his core. A darkness too. He was fading.

There was only one way to save Sarah now.

Henry closed his eyes. Breathed in the fumes of diesel and kerosene that covered his body. And then looked over at the fiery curtain.

Instantly, the plastic smirk on Violet's face vanished, and was replaced by an expression of absolute terror.

'No!' he cried out. '*NO!*'

Henry offered no reply. He just tightened his left arm around Violet's waist so that the man could not escape. Then he extended his right hand.

And reached out towards the flames.

One Hundred and Thirty-Three

Striker would never forget the ungodly screams that Violet released. They were high-pitched inhuman wails, and they turned into one long blood-curdling shriek when the flames exploded up and down their fuel-soaked bodies.

Almost within reaching distance was Sarah, desperately struggling to right herself. And next to her, still unconscious on the floor, lay Father O'Brien.

The flames were perilously close.

Striker struggled to his feet. Almost toppled back over. But managed to place one hand against the wall.

The room kept shifting around him. The ground, too.

Everywhere he looked, plumes of churning black smoke and white-yellow flame now roared. The entire stage curtain had burned away and fiery pieces of the ceiling were falling down onto the stage. The walls were also ablaze, turning the entire auditorium into a fiery tomb.

Get them out . . .

It was all Striker could think.

Get them out.

He struggled across the room. Climbed up the bleachers. Then moved onto the stage. He used every last bit of strength he had left to pull Sarah and Father O'Brien away from the angry flames. He dragged them down the stage steps, to the main floor of the auditorium. Once there, he used his police knife to cut the tape from their wrists, then tore off his own diesel-soaked shirt and coat.

Hot. The room was so terribly *hot.*

Everywhere he looked, there was fire and smoke and flame:

On the stage.

Creeping up the walls.

Flowing like a liquid across the ceiling.

It was a living beast now, consuming the way ahead and barring the way back. Striker scanned the room for another door, even a window – but he could see none. Only churning black smoke and crackling flame.

They were out of time.

Out of space.

Trapped.

And for the first time in his career, Striker found himself wondering, *is this it? Is this the end?* Because there was absolutely nowhere to go.

And then he heard it – the sound of hope.

'Jacob!' the scream came. 'JACOB, ARE YOU IN THERE!'

Felicia.

'In here!' he screamed. 'There's nowhere to go! We're *trapped!*'

At the west end of the room, a loud sound came. Of glass breaking and wood groaning. It came several times.

Suddenly there was a blast of artificial light, and all the smoke flowed in that direction. Striker realized that entry had been made – that the planks and boards had been removed from one of the windows. And within the glaring ambience of a spotlight, Felicia was suddenly there, plunging through the smoke and ash.

She reached them, grabbed one side of Father O'Brien, and together with Sarah they started dragging the old priest towards the west wall. Once there, Striker pushed Sarah through the window first, then he guided the groggy priest behind her.

Moments later, when Striker stepped down on the snowy ground of the yard, the cold night-time air blew into his face and a sense of relief flooded him like never before. He had escaped death. And just barely.

'Are you okay?' Felicia asked. 'Jacob, are you okay?'

He looked back at her and tried to speak, but couldn't find the words. The roaring glow of the fire burned brightly behind Felicia, giving her the appearance that she was standing in the centre of a fiery halo. And to Striker, it couldn't have been a more appropriate sight.

She'd been his guardian angel tonight.

One with a forty cal.

One Hundred and Thirty-Four

The sun didn't come up the following day until 7:40 a.m. With the storm all but ended, snow had stopped falling from the sky and the churning coal clouds that had covered the city like a sheet of steel wool had dissipated into nothingness. As a result, the entire horizon was a sort of deep bruised purple.

It matched Striker's face.

He returned to the crime scene with Felicia. She was driving today, and she steered them down the narrow pathway onto the old school's grounds. When the ground levelled out, she cast him a glance, then stopped the car. 'I can do this alone, you know.'

'Just drive, Feleesh.'

'All I'm saying is you could really use some rest.'

'I'm fine.'

'You're not *fine*. You've got one hairline fracture in your jaw and another in your eye socket – you're just damn lucky you didn't need screws or a plate.'

'I'm just damn lucky it was *you* who saved me.'

She gave him a queer look. 'What's that supposed to mean?'

'I was worried it was gonna be Mr July.'

She laughed softly, then leaned over and gave him a long slow kiss. It was as surprising to him as it was gentle and tender, wet and soft.

It was a nice contrast to everything else that had gone on last night.

After their visit with the doctors at Squamish General and after writing up the mandatory reports, they'd gotten barely two hours of sleep. To save time, they'd remained in Squamish overnight, using the RCMP police bunks to sleep in. The cots lacked any lumbur support, and now Striker's back was throbbing almost as much as his face.

'Let's go, Feleesh,' he finally said.

Mercifully, she listened to him.

They pulled onto the oval parking lot that was still covered with snow. Straight ahead was Our Lady of Mercy – or what was left of it. The fire had eaten through everything, devoured the school like a ravenous beast. Until there was little left but the concrete foundations and a blackened frame that still steamed in some areas.

Still parked on scene was the last of the three fire trucks, two RCMP patrol cars, and four white vans – one was an RCMP forensic team, one belonged to Katarina Kesla, one was the coroner, and one was the body removal team.

The men were carrying out the first white bag now. Judging by the weight of the remains and the fact that it took three men to carry the load, Striker believed the burnt body to be that of Henry Whitebear – or whatever was left of the man.

Despite all the horrible things the man had done, a sense of melancholy filled Striker. So much violence had been perpetrated over the last week, but where had it all really started? With Henry? With Violet? With Father Silas? Or maybe even as far back as Jolene Whitebear and Roy Baker?

There didn't really seem to be an answer.

The car came to a jerky stop with the snow crunching beneath the tyres. Striker shouldered open the door and stepped out.

Grey tendrils of smoke seeped from the structure like something trying to escape the school, and hovered in the air above it like a shroud. Striker's only regret was that the *entire* school hadn't burned to the ground. With all the evil that had been born within those walls, it seemed the only fitting end.

He trudged through the snow. Found the fire investigator around back, and spent a good twenty minutes going over notes and timetables. It would be hours still before Katarina Kesla was done. And when Striker spoke to the police forensics teams, the technicians told him they would be days longer.

Once discussions were done, Striker returned to the front of the school to find Felicia. They still had to return to HQ and write up the full report. Because of the fatalities, Laroche wanted it done ASAP. And as much as Striker often disliked the man, he understood the need.

The quicker the report was done, the quicker they could put this nightmare behind them.

Of course, before they could put pen to paper, there was still the issue of interviewing Father O'Brien. And Sarah Calvert. And Luna Asawa-Tan.

A hundred questions still remained.

Most of them depressing as hell.

Striker found Felicia speaking with the coroner. He stopped a few steps away and gave her the time she required to finish her conversation. When she was done, she came up to his side and touched his elbow.

'How you doing there, Balboa?'

He started to say his usual *I'm fine*, but the words never came. He was too busy staring at the smoking remains of the school. The gnarled beams of the blackened frame extended into the sky like a series of long fingers, trying to claw back anything that escaped – as if the school was still holding on to the dark times of the past.

Striker thought of all that had happened within those walls so long ago. And then of the previous night. He could still see The Boy With The Violet Eyes holding Sarah up on stage, using her as a shield, with the sharp blade of the knife pressed into her throat.

'It was unbelievable that I got the shot away,' he finally said. 'That I actually hit my target, much less where.'

Felicia rubbed his arm and smiled at him. 'You saved her life, Jacob.'

He let out a long breath and gently rubbed his hand along his jaw. It hurt so much, even to speak.

'It was such an odd moment,' he explained. 'Despite being concussed and the room being dark and having only a second to make the decision, I knew – I just *knew* – that the bullet would find Violet. It was almost like someone was telling me to take the shot. Like my hand was being guided. It was . . . *indescribable*.'

'A miracle?' she asked.

Striker smiled weakly. 'Well we *were* in a church. I mean, if not there, then where?'

The words made Felicia smile and a relieved look took over her face. 'Did it bring you back to the House of God?' she asked him.

Striker just smiled at her.

'Let's just say it opened the door.'

EPILOGUE

One

With Henry and Violet now dead, the real work of the investigation began. Interviews needed to be done. Evidence seized. Statements obtained. Reports written. And the entire package put together and forwarded to Crown and Striker's police superiors.

The hardest part – at least from an emotional standpoint – was Sarah. With Striker's jaw making it difficult for him to talk, he had deferred the interrogation to Felicia and had just stood by as witness to the event.

It pained him to put the young girl through it – and Mother Calvert too, in her dire medical condition – but there was no choice in the matter. Questions needed to be asked, and all of them hard ones:

Had Sarah been a part of the murders?

Had she purposely obstructed the investigation?

Or had she merely tried to save her long-lost brother?

There were so many questions that remained unanswered on that part, and it soon appeared that they would remain so – at least until the trial. Because the more detailed the questions got, the less Sarah said in her responses. The girl looked more than evasive, she looked detached.

Like something had gone wrong inside her brain.

Striker was concerned for her.

A half hour into the questioning, Mother Calvert – sick and frail from her latest round of chemo – put an end to it anyway.

'I think it's time we spoke with a lawyer,' she said softly.

Felicia nodded her understanding and looked back at Striker. To hear those words were beyond disheartening, they felt like a stab in the heart. Lawyering up didn't make Sarah Calvert guilty of being an accessory to the crime, but it sure as hell didn't make her look innocent.

The moment left Striker with a lost and empty feeling, and he felt terrible for her mother. Was this how Mother Calvert's life would end? Having lost her husband and two sons, and her daughter awaiting trial as an accessory to murder?

Striker hoped not. He *prayed* not. But he had little faith in the matter.

The world felt terribly dim.

Two

On one of the few positive notes, Luna Asawa-Tan was found unharmed. Overcome with grief for Luther and succumbing to the stress of the ongoing murders being committed, the psychiatrist had made the rash decision to leave the city of Vancouver and flee to the Okanagan.

On Saturday morning, RCMP officers found her halfway across the province in the small city of Kelowna. She was staying with an old friend, one from her college years, and upon being identified by the officer had resumed her hostile and uncooperative ways. She wanted no part of the investigation and even less to do with Striker.

It was expected.

Regardless of her wishes, Striker called her. Several times. Leaving message after message, explaining everything that had happened in her absence. But the calls had never been returned. As a last resort – and hoping to jar her – Striker left a message saying he knew about the 'Wiccan element' to all that had happened.

But still nothing.

'We'll never get that interview with her,' Striker said.

Felicia tended to agree. 'Not unless we can find the grounds to bring her in on a custodial.'

'Fat chance of that. You watch – she'll never return.'

'You think?'

'Luther's dead. Moses is gone. Her career is in tatters – what's here to bring her back?'

Felicia's only response was to frown.

With the clock ticking well into the late afternoon, Striker had little hope of achieving much else. The smell of the burnt coffee was getting to him, as were the flickering fluorescent lights of the office. With the threat of violence now ended, and the paperwork done, he could finally relax. And the moment he did, an overwhelming sense of exhaustion hit him.

Felicia sensed it, for she felt it herself. She forced a weak smile. 'So? What do you think there, Mr November? Should we head home?'

Striker gave her an equally tired smile. 'Nothing could sound better,' he said. 'But we have one final stop first.'

'You sure?' she said.

He nodded, almost unwillingly.

'It's not a choice.'

Three

It was nearing five o'clock when they drove into the heart of Dunbar.

High above, the last traces of daylight were fading as the night encroached. In the far-off distance, the first spherical traces of the moon could be seen, rising up on the earth.

Felicia pulled out front of the Holy Cross church and killed the engine.

'You sure you want to do this?' Felicia asked.

Striker looked at the white walls of the quaint little church and felt separated from it now. Like it was no longer a part of him. 'Like I said before, it's not a matter of choice.'

He started to climb out. When Felicia opened her door as well, he grabbed her arm and shook his head.

'I need to do this, Feleesh. Alone.'

She said nothing, just nodded her understanding and closed the door. Then Striker went inside the church.

He found Father O'Brien in the nave. Cold winter light from outside gleamed through the stained glass depiction of the Mother Mary and coloured the old man's face a yellowish hue. He was busy, head down, polishing the wood of the podium – with a large purple welt on the side of his temple from where Violet had struck him.

He did not react until Striker spoke.

'Father O'Brien,' he said.

The old priest looked up, and his face appeared startled – not so much by the sudden appearance of Striker, but by the amount of damage on Striker's face. 'Dear Lord, my son,' he said. 'I didn't realize how badly you were injured.'

Striker couldn't have cared less about the flesh and bone; they were scars that would heal.

Unlike some others.

'I'll make us some tea,' the old priest offered.

Striker shook his head. 'Not necessary, Father.'

In Striker's hand was the file folder seized from Father O'Brien's Lincoln – the notes made on Father Silas's investigation.

'I made copies for you,' Striker said. 'And I wanted to drop them off personally.'

Father O'Brien didn't react right away. His eyes fell to the file folder and remained there, staring with uncertainty. It was the proper response to the information inside – information that was a ticking time bomb.

Once again, the church – on direct orders from Rome – had purposely shielded the actions of another paedophile in their ranks, and in the process, Father Silas had gone on to abuse even more boys. Clearly nothing had been learnt from the tragedies of the past. And the failure to do so was more than negligent, it was unforgivable.

Father O'Brien grimaced. 'I left that folder for you, Jacob, because I thought I was going to die.'

'Yes.'

'If that had been the case, someone would have needed to follow this up.' Father O'Brien moved forward and gently touched Striker's arm. 'But I survived, Jacob – thanks to you. So I can continue my own investigation into this matter.'

Striker nodded. 'Of course you can. That being said, the police have a responsibility here as well.' He held out the file for the old man.

When Father O'Brien made no move to accept the folder, Striker stepped ahead and placed it in the old man's hands. 'Do with it what you will, Father. But there's something you should know. I've forwarded the entire file to our Sex Crimes Unit, and there's a very good chance they'll be proceeding with charges. I would bet on it.'

The old man's face took on a lost look. 'But how . . . what kind of—'

'Failure to Protect,' Striker said. 'Against the church as an organization. And it's going to get ugly.'

The old priest looked down at the folder in his hand for a long moment. When he looked up again, there was a pleading look in his eyes. 'Father Silas is gone now,' he said softly. 'No more evil can come from him.'

'What is your point, Father?'

The old priest shrugged helplessly. 'What good will come of this?' He reached out and gently grabbed Striker's wrist once more. 'Is there nothing you can do, son? I mean, what will this do to the Salvation Society? Think of the children.'

Striker pulled his hand away. 'I *am* thinking of the children.'

'No good can come from this.'

Striker couldn't believe what he was hearing. 'Have you learnt nothing, Father?'

When the old priest offered no reply, Striker just shook his head in disappointment. 'What was that saying you told me once? The road to hell is paved with good intentions?'

'Jacob—'

'Goodbye, Father.'

Striker turned around and walked out the front door of the

Holy Cross. His heart was heavy, and the moment filled him with nothing but sadness and despair because the end had come.

He would never return there again.

Four

The moment with Father O'Brien nearly killed Striker.

He left the church, told Felicia they were done for the day – hell, for the week – and they headed home. Too late to cook, they stopped by Kentucky Fried Chicken and picked up a bucket of extra crispy with some slaw and fries. Even a few Cokes, because last Striker had heard, Courtney was staying home for the night and Tate was coming over.

Once inside, Courtney and Tate took the bags of grub and started laying everything out on the table. Felicia went to the cupboard and grabbed some plates and forks and knives. Striker went to the fridge and pulled out a few bottles of MGD. As he popped off the cap to one of them, Tate looked over at him and stared at the damage his face had taken.

'Keep looking and yours will match,' Striker warned.

The young man looked away, and Striker grinned.

'Kidding, Tate.'

Courtney handed Striker a plate. 'Dig in, Dad.'

But Striker put the plate down on the table and said, 'You first, Pumpkin.'

When Courtney and Tate began filling their plates with chicken and fries, Striker took his beer and headed for the front porch. The week had been long and trying, and the moment with Father O'Brien defeating.

He needed a little time. To rest. To think.

To *heal*.

Felicia saw him heading for the door. 'Hey, where you going?' she asked.

'I just . . . got to find something,' he said.

He exited through the front door before she could ask what.

The moment Striker closed the door behind him, the harsh cold wind of winter touched his face. And it felt surprisingly good. It was jolting. Refreshing. Cleansing.

He stood on the porch for a long moment, staring at the park and field across the street, then at the night above. It was so dark, the heavens looked like black ink, except where the twinkling of stars dotted the skies. To the east, one of the stars was bigger than the others, and far brighter.

Venus.

Not a star. A planet.

Striker stared at it numbly as he sipped his beer, and slowly, a parallelism dawned on him.

Venus.

The morning star.

Morningstar.

It reminded him of Luther and Moses and Luna. And the thought was troubling. They'd gone through so much – lost so much – to protect their religious beliefs. And as much as he didn't share those views, he respected their right to them and was equally impressed by their determination and perseverance.

The fullness of their belief made him realize how empty his own faith had become. And that left him feeling hollow and depleted. More than anything, he wished for something to believe in. Something to make him feel whole again and complete.

He scanned the entire skyline, looking for something, looking for anything.

A sign, perhaps.

For something to believe in.

And then, behind him, there was laughter.

Striker turned and looked through the front room window. He watched Felicia as she stood in front of the fireplace, telling a story of some kind to Courtney and Tate. The two youths were nestled up to one another on the couch, their arms touching, their fingers interlocked.

And then it hit him. The signs were right there in front of him, and they had been all along. He'd just been looking in the wrong direction.

A moment later, the front door opened up and Felicia stuck her head outside. She saw him standing there, leaning on the front porch railing, and she fixed him with a dubious stare.

'What are you looking for, Jacob?' she asked.

Striker said nothing at first. He just put his beer down on the porch railing. Wrapped his arms around Felicia's waist. And gave her a soft, slow kiss.

'It's okay,' he said. 'I think I finally found it.'

Acknowledgements

Too many people assisted in the making of this novel to ever thank them all. But this book would simply not have been possible without the following people and their support:

- Joe Cummings, AKA 'Sloppy Joe' (reason for nickname never to be revealed publicly). He was the critical eye during the development stages; and
- Kirk Longstaffe, who is so amazing at catching details that he's one step away from being Rain Man.

I'd be remiss if I didn't thank the following people:

- My awesome team of Mike Loeppky, George Specht, and Nathan Gock, and Julie Birch who not only covered my files, but proved that good friends do indeed fall from the frozen tree of concentrate;
- Ray Gardner, for his investigative suggestions, thick skin at my humour, and for making Mondays worthwhile;
- Shawn Shipper, for taking my on-call shifts, his intolerable puns, and for giving me the gluten-free guide to the galaxy, whether I wanted it or not; and

- Stephen Thacker, for having my back during those inevitable times when publication dates and projects collided.

From Simon and Schuster, I must thank:

- Emma Lowth, my editor, who began the editorial process;
- Jo Dickinson, the publishing director of fiction, who came in at the eleventh hour and was superb in every way;
- Carla Josephson, the fiction editorial assistant, who was always a rock of stabilization for me during the end of this nerve-racking process;
- Keshini Naidoo, the copyeditor, for her thoroughness and attention to detail;
- Paul Gooney, jacket designer, for being so patient with my requests and delivering such gripping cover art;
- Amy Jacobson, Anneliese Grosfeld, Alison Clarke, and Felicia Quon for being my Canadian connections;
- And, of course, Publishing Director Suzanne Baboneau, who took a chance on me and was there from the beginning.

From the Darley Anderson Agency, AKA the Dream Factory, I must thank:

- Clare Wallace, Mary Darby, and Rosanna Bellingham for their patience with my questions and their tireless efforts behind the scene;
- Darley, for his ongoing guidance;
- And, of course, my dream agent, Camilla Wray – the first professional to ever show faith in me as a writer. Some things will never be forgotten, and this is one of them. You're the best, Camilla!

Last but not least, on a personal level, I must thank my daily support team:

- My mother, for her unyielding support, and her perpetual enthusiasm that never fades (even during those times when I wish it would);
- My wife, Lani, who is a full-time wife, full-time mom, full-time goddess, and works wonders with coconut oil. She also acts as the first reader on all my novels and has saved me from humiliation on more than one occasion;
- And finally, a very special thanks to Stormy Girl and Hockey Star, for their patience and understanding during those long weeks when Daddy's time is rare.

For anyone else I might have missed, apologies all around.

Batons and bullets,

Sean